JORUNN'S SAGA

A Journey of the Spirit

JORUNN'S SAGA

A Journey of the Spirit

Kimberly Nygaard

RTP
RESEARCH TRIANGLE PUBLISHING, INC.

Research Triangle Publishing, Inc.
PO Box 1130
Fuquay-Varina, NC 27526

ISBN 1-884570-93-3

Cover Design by Kathy Holbrook

Library of Congress Catalog Card Number: 98-68451

Printed in the United States of America
10 9 8 7 6 5 4 3 2 1

JORUNN'S SAGA

One

TEMPTATION

❧ That early morn on Valgaard began as every other. There was no air of expectation, no hint of change imminent. In the courtyard a young woman stood pegging sheets to a line stretched between two frame outbuildings. Her face was smooth; her countenance bore no evidence of concealed longing.

There were many small outbuildings clustered in the yard, separate from the large white farmhouse, yet enclosed within a fence linking them to one another. Each spare structure served a different purpose. In the one nearest the girl a black pot boiled with water and lye soap and the bed linen she had yet to rinse and hang. Steam rose from the linen as she stretched it tight, smoothing it with chafed hands. Her movements were deft of long practice, carefully measured. They bore no testimony to impatience lurking beneath a calm exterior.

Across the yard, close to an open shed, her father swung an ax with easy precision, his fluid movements giving lie to his age. The kindling beside him mounted swiftly to a large pile.

When the last sheet had been hung the girl bent to retrieve the basket, hoisting it against one hip, her slim figure as sinewy as the old man's. She crossed to the white house, turning her face toward the morning sun stealing over the mountain that bordered the farm to the east. Basking in the muted glory of pale yellow rays, she paused for a moment, squinting against the light and staring toward the ring of mist that encircled the mountaintop. The snow was melting from the craggy sides of the cliff, teasing promise of an early spring after a harsh winter. Soon she would be on her way up the mountain, to the cabin where she stayed each summer. In the mild months, from May until first frost, the girl would live there alone, tending the sheep, letting them graze themselves fat and content.

A movement in the shadows midway on the mountain caught her attention. Tensing, she lifted her hand to shield her eyes from bright sunshine, straining to recognize the figure. No one was expected. At this distance it was impossible to determine if the man making his sure way down the rocky mountainside was known to her, or a stranger.

"Someone's coming!" She called an alert to her father before hurrying toward the farmhouse. Inside, she stood by the kitchen window to observe unseen the approach of the man.

As the figure neared the bottom of the slope he stepped from its shadow and into the full morning light. From her view at the window the girl discerned the man to be Erland Halvorsson. Their neighbor to the east, his land started at the base of the mountain, just on the other side. She recognized him easily. She had studied him before, from a vantage point high above, when she was in the summer cabin, or on the hillside where the sheep grazed. From there she would watch him work, tending his animals, mending the fences that connected his buildings.

The farm Erland Halvorsson had inherited was much like their own. It was many acres, but in reality only some small patches suitable for cultivation. This land was tucked between mountains carved by glaciers long ago, much of it covered by vast, dense pine forests so dark that even on a summer midday she dared not wander far into the wood.

At times, when the flock she was tending had neared the mountain base, Erland Halvorsson had come to help her herd them back up, away from crops planted at the border of the two farms. He was aloof, and seldom spoke except to give instruction. When she thanked him he only touched his brow and nodded before retreating to his own place.

Through the kitchen window she watched as he approached her father. She moved quickly to the front door, which stood open to light and air. In stealth she positioned herself directly behind the door, in its shadow, so she might listen to the errand which brought her neighbor this March morning.

"*God dag*, Sigurd Johannesson." Erland Halvorsson bowed slightly in the direction of the older man. In hurried afterthought he removed his hat and stood worrying it, bending and distorting the brim as he stared unseeing at his wide, callused hands.

Sigurd Johannesson paused in his labor, inclining his head slightly in the direction of the young man, a silent invitation for him to relay the reason for his errand.

"I come to ask for your girl, Jorunn Sigurdsdatter, in marriage." He said it in a rush, all in one breath, exhaled in anxiety and relief. For an instant his face grew lighter, and Jorunn, from her hidden position in the shadow of the door, thought he looked handsome. Her face flushed hot; her fingertips were cold as she pressed them to bright cheeks. Her heart hammered with such intensity she thought it might burst. She pressed both hands to her breast in a vain attempt to still the calamity there.

The older man set down the ax and straightened to study his neighbor. His face was grave. Erland Halvorsson shifted uneasily. "You may be thinkin' she could do better. My farm's poor, buildings need mendin'. With Pa passed on, and my brother traveled to Christiania, I can't tend everything. Should've taken a wife sooner, but there's never time, not enough hours in the day. Now I got to make time. I need sons to help till the earth, hold the forest in check. It's closin' in from the west. Can't afford to lose ground."

The sense of urgency in the young man's voice was thick, almost tangible. For a moment Jorunn forgot that her own fate was irrevocably tied to the decision her father would make in regard to Erland Halvorsson's proposal. In the shadows she felt something stir within her at this man's determination.

After a long pause Sigurd answered. "I hear that brother of yours is hangin' out with the likes of Ole Gabriel Ueland, and that rabble-rouser, Marcus Thrane. Agitators, the lot 'em. Call themselves 'intellectual liberals', I hear. Seems to me that's a contradiction."

Erland Halvorsson's jaw squared, yet his voice was steady when he spoke. "He's a man who stands up for what he believes in. Nothin' wrong in that."

"*Ja, vel*, suppose not. Truth is, the apple didn't fall far from the tree. I remember your pa marchin' toward Christiania

with that gang o' cotters a ways back. Let's see, must've been
'bout 1820. You was born two seasons later."

"It was 1818," the young man corrected. "They marched
in '18, and my brother was born in '20. I was born in '22, same
as your girl, Gerd."

There was a pause, then the old man grunted in affirma-
tion. "That sounds 'bout right," he conceded. "Never could
understand it, a man like your pa, who owned his farm free
and clear, gettin' mixed up with a bunch of farmhands. No
more'n squatters they were, and him wantin' to give 'em a say
in how to run the country. Why, your pa and me, we've been
freeholders all our lives; our people have called their land their
own since our ancestors gave up raidin' to settle and staked a
claim. Vikings, they were. Great men, and far-sighted enough
to know land was what was worth havin'. All the plunder they
got, silver and gold and the like, gone now. But the land they
staked has kept their people for a thousand years. Land's the
only thing that lasts. Don't hold with politics and government
myself, can't understand why your pa and that brother o' yours
got mixed up in it. Egil Halvorsson should've stayed home
and tended his land, kept his birthright."

The old man fell silent, lost in contemplation. Erland
shifted uncomfortably, unwilling to provoke the old man by
further defense of his brother. In attempt to bring Sigurd
Johannesson back to the discussion at hand he cleared his
throat and said, "You're right 'bout that, my land's what keeps
me goin'. But I can't keep it up alone. I need sons, and for
that I need a wife. I figure your girl needs a husband, a place
of her own. I was thinkin' maybe we could make a go of it
together."

"She's the last of my five girls. She's got no dowry," Sigurd
Johannesson answered at length.

Erland looked around the yard, at the tidy cluster of outbuildings, the fences, the main house. All in good repair, everything in good order. "She's got what I need," he answered.
Then he paused, searching for the right words. "There's one
thing. Like I said, it's sons I need. I got to know she can bear
children."

Sigurd Johannesson straightened in surprise, his face suddenly guarded. "Her mother won't allow it. She's God-fearin',
and won't hold with what the church condemns."

"I'm God-fearin' too, as good a man as most," Erland defended. "But I'm not a rich man. I can't afford to practice the

teachin' of a church with no regard for practical matters. If the bride I take can't bear, my land will lie fallow. I'll be swallowed by the forest, lose my fields. Nature's a powerful force; a man alone can't fight her."

He paused, shifting uncomfortably. "Besides, seems to me the priest reads the Bible and gets from it what he wants to hear. He preaches chastity, but I read the Scripture, too. Ecclesiastes preaches two are better than one, promises they'll have good reward for their labor. He said, 'If they fall, the one will lift up his fellow: but woe to him that is alone when he falleth; for he hath not another to help him up. If two lie together, then they have heat, but how can one be warm alone?'" The young man's voice trailed away, his face flushed with embarrassment in sudden awareness of the words he spoke. Then his features hardened in resolve.

"I got to insist on a betrothal period. When your daughter's carryin', we'll get married quick. I'll pay penance to the church, fix things with the Lord before the babe's born."

The old man studied the younger, his expression inscrutable. The practice of which Erland Halvorsson spoke was not uncommon. A farmer spent his able years wresting his living from the land, and when his body was too worn with time and work to continue, he must have a son to care for him and his place. Without, old age and growing infirmity allowed nature to gradually reclaim the land. The good years of a man's life would be spent in wasted endeavor, the end of it finished in decline and deprivation. Each passing spring, as the forest encroached insidiously, there would be less land to cultivate, every fall a harvest more meager. Without a son a farmer endured a life of hardship for nothing.

Out of this reality it had become customary for young, able farmers to choose their wives with great care. A young woman fortunate enough to have many brothers was likely to have several offers of marriage. No dowry was required; it was assumed she carried within her the gift of many sons. Other young women married, but it was usual they bring gifts of a more tangible nature. Livestock, a parcel of land, a sum of money that would allow improvements in an existing homestead, or the purchase of a new one; all these things were acceptable. In lieu of these a young woman might bring into marriage proof she could ensure her future, as well as that of her intended, with new life already begun. In poor farming communities dowries were scarce; it had become usual for young women to prove themselves before the marriage. It was not uncommon that beneath the heavy wool of her wedding dress a bride felt a flutter, the quickening of new life, on her wedding day. The practice evolved of practical considerations; it was deemed a necessity by many. Yet the church condemned this; it was lectured by priests in every rural pulpit that such life, conceived in sin, was the devil's own making. Repentance was crucial, restitution required. This was deemed fair by most, and after the birth of a healthy child a farmer would pay his penance gladly, considering it a small price to pay for the rich blessing of a child. If the child was a son the penance seemed small, and was often increased, assuming more the nature of a gift than the punishment intended.

Sigurd Johannesson studied the young man before him, his face inscrutable. After a long while he replied: "You're a sensible man, if not righteous. Your people been my neighbors for a lot o' years. I wager you'd be a good man for my Jorunn, but it's not for me to decide. I got to speak with her mother. A woman bears a child, it falls to her to rear it. My wife makes the decisions regarding our daughters. I best speak with Jorunn, too. She's got a strong will for a girl of twenty. I'd be doin' you a disfavor if I promised her in marriage against her wishes."

Erland smiled and the tension was broken. "I heard she's willful. Still, I figure I need a determined wife. Way I see it, determination and a strong will go hand in hand."

The old man nodded, no further exchange required between men spare of word. Erland turned to retrace his steps up the mountainside.

In the shadows where Jorunn stood watching, long-awaited opportunity presented itself. Scarce hope surged and she rushed to the center courtyard to seize chance, make it her own. Without pause Jorunn reached out to wrest her destiny from the hands of fate. "Erland Halvorsson, wait!"

He turned back. With a glance toward her father Jorunn crossed the courtyard and stood to face Erland. "I accept your proposal, and pledge myself to you. In two months time I take the sheep to the mountain for summer grazing. You come to me at the cabin. In the fall, when the harvest is in, if I'm with child, we'll wed. If not, I'll release you from obligation."

Erland stared at the woman in front of him. Her flaxen hair fell in a thick braid to far below her waist. Her almond eyes glinted bright in the sunshine, her face was fair. A flush stole upward from the neck of his coarsely woven shirt, turning his color high.

"That's all right, then," he answered.

With an awkward bow he turned from her and began his ascent of the mountain. His feet were sure in their placement, finding an easy way. In the courtyard Jorunn watched until he disappeared into the mist quickly disintegrating at the top. From behind her she heard her father's voice.

"You're a determined girl, Jorunn, and headstrong, sure enough, but I've never known you to be rash. Pray to God when autumn comes you're bearin', or you'll be ruined."

Turning slowly to face her father Jorunn replied, "Ruined? A person with nothing doesn't fear ruin, and I've got nothing." Her voice was strong with conviction, even her agitation did not mar its fluid lilt. Her words were clear, her speech strangely compelling. "If I stay here my life will be barely tolerable. For as long as you live I'll be your daughter, the last of five girls, my mother's bitter disappointment. Your last hope gone."

Her father opened his mouth to protest, but she silenced him with a quick gesture, a touch to his lips.

"There's no need denying what we both know is true. With my birth your chance of a son was taken from you. According to Mother, even in her womb I was stubborn and obstinate; my strident nature was the cause of her terrible suffering in birthing me. There's no doubt in her mind the havoc I wreaked on her body left her barren."

Sigurd Johannesson was silent. It was useless to refuse the truth Jorunn spoke regarding her mother's convictions. He was by nature a pragmatic man; from him his daughter had this trait. In silence they agreed and she continued.

"With no dowry I never expected to marry. That was my fate, no purpose served by complaining. I tried to be grateful for your generosity. In spite of everything you would have me here. Mother wants me gone, sent to a life in the service of her God. If I'm not wed soon, to a man of flesh and blood, then I'll have to resign myself to a spiritual union of her choosing. But I never heard the call," she said, unconscious of a wistful note that crept into her lovely voice. "Seems even Christ won't have me for his bride." She smiled to pass the remark as jest, yet the words were sharp with bitterness; they erased the forlorn expression that flitted across her fine, even features.

"Mother would send me to the church so I could spend the rest of my days atoning for the sin of my birth," Jorunn ground out. Her face was suddenly closed, her full mouth set in a grim line. "If it would right the grievance I've done you, Pappa, I'd go gladly, and let her Lord put up with me. But I haven't got the calling, and I'm afraid Christ would consider my trespass in his house even greater sin than the injustice caused by my birth, and punish us all. Mother's vengeful God... I won't risk causing His wrath to be visited on you."

Jorunn stopped, arrested by a look that crossed her father's countenance. He grimaced, as if in pain. His eyes reflected torment; his lips twisted in a smile that lent no glint to his blue gaze. "You forget, girl, it's the sin of the father what's visited on the child. The load of guilt you carry on your shoulders isn't yours to bear," he rasped, his voice suddenly gruff.

Jorunn waited, stunned to silence. It was new to her, and foreign, this idea that her father might harbor guilt for a sin. Her vision of him was pure, and perfect. She stood still, breathless, waiting for his explanation, yet suddenly apprehensive.

He turned from her abruptly, without further word, and she knew he would not share with her his sin. The breath she held escaped in a hiss of relief. In that moment Jorunn had sensed a revelation that would forever shift her perspective, and was inexplicably fearful. She would not know his secret. She was resigned to the truth she had learned at her mother's knee, that she alone was responsible for her fate in life. Her mother's instruction on that point was clear. Only God knew why her situation was as it was, and only He could lead her forth from it. If Jorunn would place her faith in Him and follow without question, then God would show her the way He had chosen for her. Yet His choices for her thus far had done little to inspire her faith; trust in her mother's vague, vengeful God eluded Jorunn. Recognizing her faithlessness, she added it to the list of sins for which she must atone. When she was forced to kneel beside her mother for long hours praying it seemed to Jorunn her sins whirled about her in an evil circle, no beginning and no end. Nowhere within that ring did she fathom redemption. Her prayers inspired no hope.

Astrid Asbjornsdatter came from the creamery bearing two heavy wooden buckets frothing with milk. Her quick eyes spotted the movement of Erland Halvorsson midway on the mountain.

"Am I no longer mistress of this place: Why was I not called to make welcome a visitor?" she demanded. Her blue eyes were sharp as they raked her daughter's countenance. Astrid's face was long and thin, creased with age. Once, Sigurd Johannesson reflected, his bride had been beautiful. He had been the envy of every man in the valley of Dal, and even beyond it. But his wife's beliefs were strong, and the effort of keeping her convictions and holding others to them had worn her, made her old before her time. He shifted his look instead to the countenance of their daughter and searched it for a memory of the woman he had made mistress here on Valgaard.

"He wouldn't stay. Our neighbor's business was with me," Sigurd spoke.

Astrid's eyes narrowed, the blue irises visible only as chips of ice. "What business has he with you?" she demanded.

Sigurd hesitated, stunned for an instant by the sheer force of his wife's voice as it resonated across the courtyard. Years of marriage had not lessened the awe his wife's voice inspired; the power of it compelled an answer. Long ago the sound of her soft lilt had been as sweet as music, the enchantment of it irresistible. Even now, the melody gone, her scant conversation commanded his attention, yet he would not reply. It was not a woman's place to pry into her husband's affairs. He would share with Astrid the purpose of Erland Halvorsson's visit when he deemed it suitable. He would not be prodded, like a dumb beast. His face hardened, the lines suddenly deeper, the angles sharper. Without reply he turned his back to his wife, and lifting his ax, returned to his labour.

Behind him he heard his daughter's voice ring out, clear and melodic, full of conviction, tinged with rebellion. "Erland Halvorsson will have me to be his wife."

Sigurd swung around, in his surprise letting the ax fall. His eyes were riveted to his daughter. Tall, like him, she stood aloof, looking down at her mother. He was amazed to find her suddenly a commanding presence.

Astrid's jaw sagged, her mouth dropping open in surprise. She recovered quickly, pressing her lips together in their customary line. A stain of color flushed upward from the collar of her brown dress. "I do not believe it! You have no dowry, nothing to make you attractive. If it is true he would have you then he is a fool," she declared, her voice resonant with contempt. "Surely even you would not have a fool for a husband? In any case, you are promised to another."

Jorunn felt a flash of anger, white and hot. "I never promised myself to your Lord, and if you and your priest have entered into an alliance on my behalf, then it's an unholy one. And you're wrong about my attractiveness. I possess the one thing most valuable to a man, the ability to bear a child. Like any man, Erland Halvorsson needs a son," Jorunn spat out contemptuously. She watched the color in her mother's cheeks drain away and was satisfied her words had hit their mark. Anger carried her along, banishing trepidation. "I'll give him a son, and in return he'll make me mistress of his place, Stridheim. When I have Stridheim I'll have no use for your God. The land will nurture me, and all mine; we'll live off its bounty. Your God has never been gracious in His offering to me; I could hardly do worse on my own. I won't pledge my life to serve Him, or be thankful for His meager blessings."

Astrid stared at her daughter, her face pale with shock. "You forget yourself, girl, and God's message. 'Honor thy father and thy mother: that thy days may be long upon the land which the lord thy God giveth thee'," she exhorted, yet more from habit than with any remaining conviction. Her voice rose vibrant and clear, more inspiring than the message it carried. "And He said, 'Children, obey your parents in the Lord, for this is right,' Astrid continued to admonish, but the look in her daughter's eyes told her more clearly than words that the gospel fell on deaf ears. Scripture so often uttered it had become a litany to them both, devoid of true meaning now. Astrid spoke distractedly, her mind busy framing the rest of her message to her daughter, thinking there was something frightening and unfamiliar in her demeanor. The child—no, woman, for that was what she had become, was openly irreverent.

Inspiration came to Astrid, and she lifted her prominent chin to speak forcefully: "'And the Lord said unto Moses, I have seen this people, and, behold, it is a stiffnecked people.' Be warned, Jorunn, you are indeed stiff-necked, and do not bend to the will of God. In His word to Moses the consequences are clear: 'Now therefore let me alone, that my wrath may wax hot against them, and that I may consume them.'" Astrid's chin quivered in indignation as she spoke.

Jorunn listened impassively, impressed by the clear resonance of her mother's voice, yet unmoved by her message. New hope for her future buoyed her, made her careless, prompting her to argue, "Yes, Mother. But the Lord listened to Moses and 'repents of the evil which he thought to do unto his people'."

Jorunn's face was bright with the elation of her new circumstances, her voice lilting with mischief as she goaded her mother. Astrid stared at her daughter, her outrage tinged with disbelief. For a moment she faltered, sensing her tenuous hold over this child was severed. Unexpected trepidation niggled; she struggled to tighten her grasp of the situation and this brazen young woman, lest she slip from her altogether. But she could think of nothing that would bind the girl to her, and in desperation she threatened: "'Cast out the scorner, and contention shall go out; yea, strife and reproach shall cease!'"

She spoke vehemently, yet Jorunn sensed, and Astrid knew, that she would not be cast out. Astrid had not the strength to sever the flesh of her own flesh from her being. In defeat, she turned and stumbled toward the house, sloshing the milk as she went. She disappeared into the darkness within, but her voice was clearly audible. "In the name of Our Lord, Jesus Christ, 'Father, forgive them; for they know not what they do.'"

Much later, Astrid's prayers for her daughter's forgiveness were done, yet the rest of the day she remained on her knees in front of the alter Sigurd Johannesson had fashioned from fine hard wood for his wife. "'Blessed are the poor in spirit: for theirs is the kingdom of heaven,'" she prayed. "'Blessed are they that mourn: for they shall be comforted. Blessed are the meek, for they shall inherit the earth.'"

Jorunn entered the dim hallway and crossed to the kitchen, heavily laden with baskets of clean linen. As she set irons in the fire she felt her mother's eyes on her and dared to meet her gaze. Defiantly, for she would have her share of the earth now, while she lived, and she let her mother see her determination.

Astrid's lips pressed into a grim line and she continued, with great fervor, "'Blessed are they which do hunger and thirst after righteousness; for they shall be filled. Blessed are the merciful: for they shall obtain mercy.'"

Jorunn smiled a small smile, and knew her mother watched. While she ironed, from the corner of her eye, she saw her mother clutch the silver cross draped around her neck, and heard her pray louder, "'Blessed are the pure in heart, for they shall see God. Blessed are the peacemakers: for they shall be called the children of God.'"

Astrid's voice soared, its beauty restored as she prayed, transported by the word of her God. "'Blessed are they which are persecuted for righteousness' sake: for theirs is the kingdom of heaven. Blessed are ye, when men shall revile you, and persecute you, and shall say all manner of evil against you falsely, for my sake. Rejoice, and be exceeding glad: for great is your reward in heaven....'"

Jorunn studied the creases of care that lined her mother's face and reflected that her mother did not look glad, not at all; her mouth thinned determination. All that day, while she and her father tended the house, the yard, the animals, her resolve to do this thing strengthened.

Two

AWAKENING

Jorunn stood on the mountainside and watched his ascent. Though he was unusually tall, his movements were easy, his body lean and supple. His brown hair shone with sparks of red lit by the rays of the summer sun. As the distance between them narrowed she noted his beard was neatly trimmed. His coarse shirt and trousers were faded, worn, but not soiled. He came close and she turned her head, averting her gaze.

The sun was hot on her bare head. The cool breeze that ruffled the grass around her was welcome, yet she felt a shiver ripple through her. Beside her a lamb bleated and she bent to stroke its coarse coat, letting the motion calm her. In the moments before his approach she resigned herself to this course of her own choosing.

When his shadow fell across her she raised her face and let him see her determination. His eyes probed hers for a long moment before he bent on one knee and stroked the woolly creature.

"You're sure," he said.

She rose and looked down at his farm. "It calls to me, your place," she said simply. "It's beckoned me since I first climbed the mountain and looked down on the fields of Stridheim."

He moved to stand beside her. To the northwest acres of dense pine forests stretched as far as they could see. To the south a village lay tucked in the valley called Dal. Directly in front of them lay the yard of Stridheim, a cluster of small structures within the confines of a raw wood fence, nestled between patches of green and gold.

The fields of Stridheim were growing ripe beneath the summer sun. The fertile black earth would yield a fall harvest that promised to be abundant. Surveying his place Erland Halvorsson felt a stirring inside. "A call as old as the land itself," he replied, his voice gruff with pride. "We're not the first to hear it. 'Stridheim'—the home of discord. The place takes its name from battles fought more'n a thousand years ago by men willin' to die to heed the call, claim this land as their own."

She looked at him, unspoken question in her eyes.

"Once in a while their weapons show up in the furrows during spring plowin'. I figure those, and the earth their bodies were returned to, are the only testimony they ever lived."

She looked him full in the face and knew she understood these men. In him she heard an echo of herself. She savored his closeness, reveled in his proximity and the clean scent of him. The heartbeat of the land, the pulse of nature, throbbed in her veins. Desire rose within her in an intoxicating rush.

He watched her face, unguarded and easily deciphered. His eyes widened in surprise, then quickly narrowed in response. He leaned to press his lips to hers, then pulled her closer. She let her body brush against his, awkward in that first touch. His hands stroked her back tentatively, exploring the curves of her. She lifted her arms to slide around his neck and pull him closer still, let her softness melt against the hard planes of his body. She pulled at the laces of his shirt with fingers that trembled and were clumsy.

When she pressed her palms to the expanse of his bare chest she felt a rumble begin deep inside him and escape as a moan. Her knees went weak at the sound. She sank into the thick, fragrant carpet of grass and summer flowers, pulling him with her. The earth beneath them was her cushion, the sky above stretched in an infinite blanket of blue. She closed her eyes, surrendering without fear or hesitation to forces greater even than her own will.

Three

FAITH

✤ The summer of 1848 was long and fine in southern Norway, with sufficient rain for good grazing and a plentiful harvest. When the first frost came to Dal the farmers who worked the land there had reason to celebrate, for the plenitude with which God had blessed them that season would ensure safe passage through the winter. There would be ample food, and the forest, which in summer was constant threat to cultivated land, in winter was a blessing, providing fuel for heat, and shelter from icy winds sweeping across the land from the North Sea. Throughout <u>Hedmark county</u> there was a tide of optimism that carried Jorunn Sigurdsdatter and Erland Halvorsson along as the banns were read and their wedding celebrated.

At the feast Jorunn sat proud and erect, her newly woven scarf tied neatly over her pale hair. Fresh color suffused her cheeks as she secretly stroked the faint swell of her stomach beneath the heavy wool of her dress. The high embroidered bodice and heavy stuff from which it was made would conceal the reason for her flush for a good while to come, but the air of pride and certainty she wore like a new cloak cried aloud her success. She carried within her the life that would be the beginning of a new existence for herself. From this day forward she would be Mistress of Stridheim. This day she linked her fate irrevocably to the land, beginning her travel through life on a course of her own choosing.

Beside her Erland sat tall and proud. His face was settled in lines of assurance as he lifted his stein and cried "*Skaal!*" in answer to speeches of congratulations and good will their neighbors showered over them. His broad shoulders were set firm in determination, pride obvious in his every gesture.

Throughout Hedmark County that fall men and women recalled the union of Jorunn Sigurdsdatter and Erland Halvorsson with great enjoyment. During the long winter the memories of the feast were bright spots in the darkness and loneliness inherent to the season. And in the spring there would be glad tidings from Stridheim. Of that each wife from the surrounding farms in the county was sure. In Jorunn's bearing there had been the certainty of accomplishment a woman carries when she is with child.

In April, as the snow melted and the River Glomma ran high, word went round that the midwife had safely delivered Jorunn Sigurdsdatter of a son. There was rejoicing in Dal. The promise of spring fused in the minds of the people living there with the birth of Harald Erlandsson, and in the warm, heavy days of the summer that followed each wife called in turn at Stridheim with gifts of lambs wool and sheepskin and potions distilled from nature to keep the child safe in the months to come. Jorunn's mornings were spent tending the house and yard, her afternoons whiled away in the company of her neighbors. It was new to her, this social aspect of life. By nature reserved, Jorunn had often been overlooked in a family of five daughters. Marie Sigurdsdatter, the eldest of the flock, was talkative and vivacious, and naturally the focus of attention while she lived at home. She made a good match and moved far north, to a city called Trondheim, and focus had fallen on the second of Sigurd Johannesson's daughters, Ruth. She was shy, and lacking in charm, but Ruth was beautiful, and in the wake of Marie's ceaseless chatter it had been refreshing to focus on Ruth's inner calm and beauty. The suitors who came asking for Ruth's hand were a different sort, and Sigurd Johannesson relaxed and seemed happy in their company. Then the match was made and Ruth was gone, sooner than anticipated, and it was Gerd's turn. Named for his mother, Sigurd at times remarked the girl resembled her as well. Stocky, dark when the other girls were fair, her looks were unremarkable, her manner uninviting. The dowry Sigurd offered for Gerd was by far the largest of all his daughters'; its size left Jorunn without. Yet Gerd made a fine match and was wed to a farmer in Gudbrandsdalen, a cousin to Ruth's hus-

band. Jorunn resigned herself to her situation and bore Gerd
no ill will. Relief to be rid Gerd's oppressive company mitigated the resentment Jorunn might have harbored.

Sigurd's fourth daughter, called Sylvie after Astrid's
mother, had only a nominal dowry. Three goats and a cow
were all she could offer, but she was treasured since childhood
by a boy from the valley. Thor Simonsson, second son of Simon
Gustafsson, was a farmer in a situation similar to that of Sigurd
Johannesson. Poor, yet the boy would have married Sylvie had
she been penniless. Their union followed so quickly on the
heels of Gerd's that people would have whispered of it had it
not been understood that they had waited only out of deference to Gerd. With Gerd's position secure the banns were
read at once and Sylvie Sigurdsdatter donned the bridal crown
and led the procession to Dal Church only two months later.
Observing her sister's radiant gaze, Jorunn had reflected that
of all her sisters, only Sylvie did she envy. It was obvious Sylvie
and Thor were exceedingly happy in the company of one another. The looks they exchanged held for long seconds more
than was necessary; the casual touch permissible to man and
wife became something fascinating when between them. It
caught Jorunn's attention and held it, this passion they shared.
It stirred in her a longing that was new. Then Thor and Sylvie
traveled south of Christiania, to Drammen, to farm the homestead of Simon Gustafsson's bachelor brother, and outside their
presence Jorunn forgot the quick, lightening tension watching them awakened in her.

Until of late.

Before their wedding Jorunn had approached Erland three
times, each time she, of necessity, being the initiator. She alone
understood the mysteries of her body; it was left to her to steer
them on the course best suited to achieving their goal. Then
she was with child, and they remained chaste until the priest
blessed their union. In the first days of marriage it fell to Erland
to entice Jorunn, for at first she felt no inclination toward re-
suming the relationship they had begun on the thick carpet of
summer's green grass. So long ago, the act was a vague memory
to her now. She was replete in pregnancy, and felt no longing
for the physical act they had completed. A farmer's daughter
and pragmatic by nature, Jorunn assumed what they had done
was to procreate. With that aim accomplished she was at first
puzzled by Erland's advances. Yet he was patient, guiding her
gently. Their wedding night he lay beside her, stroking her

hair, touching her cheek, at length letting his hand drift lower, beneath fresh new linen, to caress her breast. He watched her face intently, as if searching for something, though what she could not fathom. She lay passive, her wide blue eyes studying the features of the man she now called husband. He was handsome, there was no doubt. Thick brown hair waved back from a wide forehead; his nose was thin at the bridge and very straight. His mouth was full and generous, tasting sweet, like the wine she sipped at communion. He kissed her, moving his mouth over hers slowly, with infinite care. Then he lifted his head to study her again and she lowered her lids to cover her eyes. She was suddenly reminded of the stirring she had experienced when watching Thor and Sylvie together. When Erland kissed her sensation streaked like lightening from her mouth to her breasts, then spread as molten lava through her stomach, to her groin. Inexplicably shy, she suspected Erland could see the emotion in her eyes and covered them, but he kissed her once again, undeterred. For a long while he held his mouth to hers, gently probing, until she forgot his lips and began to focus on the longing that was building within her. It grew greater, all-consuming, until she related with startling clarity this new longing to the act they had performed in conceiving the child she carried. Without hesitation she pulled Erland over her, frantic in her search for completion. When he covered her body with his, this time it was she who cried out. His breathing was carefully controlled until she relaxed beneath him, sated and sleepy. Only then did he increase his measured tempo and press inside her, moaning softly, his body relaxing afterward to cover her gently.

Each night they spent locked in embrace, each day was a dance in continuation of the intimacy they shared. When Erland passed in the yard tension snaked between them, the longing they shared as easily conjured in the bright light of midday as in the pale twilight of summer's night. Jorunn's step was light as she went about her work, the tedium of chores alleviated by the idea that she accomplished each task as Mistress of Stridheim. This place was hers now, shared with Erland as they shared every other thing. It bound them inextricably, part of her, just as it was a part of him. They moved to an inner rhythm they both sensed, in tune with the land. In time, her body grew ripe and heavy, and she delivered the son they longed for. Not merely an embodiment of their hopes and dreams, Harald Erlandsson was tangible evidence of their feeling for one another. When Jorunn nursed him she looked into his tiny face and saw mirrored utter perfection. In his features she and Erland melded and became greater than either of them alone. She had thought it impossible to feel anything deeper than that she felt for Erland, yet each time she lifted Harald from his cradle and held him close, breathing in his warm scent, a miraculous thing happened. Her heart opened, expanding to love the little person more than she had imagined possible. It was beyond her experience of this world, unearthly. 'Such gladness must be a gift from God,' she reasoned silently. Slowly she relented in her distrust of her mother's Lord and began to believe that He granted not only suffering and strife, but happiness beyond measure. Her confidence in Him was gradually restored, until one day she lay Harald in his cradle after nursing him and fell on her knees beside her child to pray aloud, for the first time of her own free will, "Thanks be to you, God, for the bounty of thy blessings."

From that day forward she prayed, morning and evening; giving thanks, asking for His guidance, one day even coming to the conclusion that her earlier life had been the trial to be borne in order for her to deserve this she now enjoyed. It frustrated her, though, that God had never seen fit to give her hint of the happiness He held in store for her. She ventured to think it would have made the first part of her life bearable. 'It's not ours to question why,' she reminded herself, and crossed herself quickly, suddenly fearful she would prove unworthy. The idea that any of this might be taken from her was more than she could bear, and she never let the thought surface. Yet it lay there coiled, a hissing serpent in the back of her mind.

Jorunn found herself so blessed, so rich in love, that it spilled over onto everyone around her and made forgiveness for the past an easy thing. Her happiness expanded even to include her mother, and Jorunn called at Valgaard often. Twice weekly she strapped Harald to her and climbed the mountain, to descend on the other side giddy with the pleasure of light and fresh air and the feel of Harald's warm body close to where her heart beat hard beneath her ribs. Astrid greeted them with outstretched arms and smiles that transformed her wrinkled face to one Jorunn hardly recognized. To Sigurd

Johannesson it was as if his Astrid had been resurrected from the shallow grave in which she had lain. Watching her with their daughter's son he felt tender, and occasionally reached out a weathered and callused hand to touch her arm, or brush her cheek.

Harald was the center of their existence; with his tiny person he bound their lives together. He lay in the crook of arms that passed him from one to the other and wove a magic spell with his wide smile and gentle gurgling. Even when his lids drifted downward to hide his round blue eyes in sleep, his charm was irresistible. Astrid spent long hours rocking her daughter's son, drinking in the sight of him, letting his sweetness fill her and smooth away the rough edges time had worn.

Summer drew to a close and the harvest was upon them. The autumn days were markedly shorter and time became a precious commodity on both Valgaard and Stridheim. Jorunn's visits were less frequent. Astrid Asbjornsdatter and Sigurd Johannesson worked frantically, alone now, and growing slower with age, to bring in their harvest. When they finished their larders were reasonably replenished, and they sat back, weary from their labor but satisfied there would be enough to tide them through winter. Coldness encroached upon Hedmark, and people withdrew into the protection of their homes, the comfort of roaring fires.

Jorunn missed her visits at Valgaard, yet had no time to spare. She spent her days in vain attempt to make livable the house at Stridheim. It was old, built when one large room was deemed sufficient for both eating and sleeping. The outer walls were fashioned of round timbers tarred black, with no inner walls to decorate, and no layer of insulation to protect from wind that seeped through. All day, and most of the night, a fire blazed in the hearth to ward off the chill. Gusts of wind swirled around the mountain and met the forest to the west, circulating down an insufficient chimney, causing great puffs of black smoke to pour into the room. The linens Jorunn had brought with her to marriage were soon stained gray from soot, the smell of smoke lingered in spite of constant washing. Yet the fire was a necessity. Without it the room turned bitter cold within few hours, and the babe was no longer thriving. A cough racked his tiny body when the smoke filled the room. He grew hot and feverish often. She dared not let the room grow cold lest he be chilled. Of late he nursed poorly, without enthusiasm, and she could feel her milk dwindling. No longer did it pour from her body in a stream at his first cry. She spent long hours close to the roaring fire, with Harald at her breast, but he often dozed. The wives who had come to visit of late had remarked that the babe was less fat than usual in an infant of nine months. Each of them recommended she stroke his cheek to awaken him. If he slept on, she should take his cheek carefully between thumb and forefinger and press gently, causing enough discomfort for the child to stir and suckle again, they advised. Many recommended some essential ingredient to be added or withheld from Jorunn's diet in order to make her milk more nourishing, more palatable. In confusion and growing alarm Jorunn took careful note of the advice of every woman who had raised even one child to adulthood. To no avail. Harald grew weaker, slept more, fretted constantly when he was awake.

In the first days of Harald's discontent Jorunn had carried him tirelessly, soothing him, searching his soft pink gums for concrete reason for his discomfort. Then the first fever had come, and she sent Erland in frantic errand to fetch her mother from over the mountain. Astrid Asbjornsdatter arrived, her calming presence soothing Jorunn's frayed nerves. After three days of careful ministrations little Harald's fever had broken. On the fourth day Astrid took her leave, still worried for the health of her precious grandson, yet convinced the crisis had passed. She paused for a moment to take stock of the home in which her daughter lived. She said nothing, but her forehead creased in concern. Jorunn watched her mother's expression and was aware that comparison of this house to the one in which she had been raised made this one look poor. Her cheeks burned in shame. Her worry over Harald and fatigue from the strain of tending him made her quick to anger. Old wounds were torn open by the look on her mother's face. To Jorunn's mind it was a continuation of the censure she had endured since her birth. Those years on Valgaard when Jorunn had accepted her lot in life and tempered her resentment with resignation were finished now that she wagered her future on Stridheim, yet they remained an open sore. Twenty years of injury could not be healed in a matter of months. Furious, she made up her mind she would no longer endure her mother's slights. Jorunn watched her departure from the courtyard, vowing not to call Astrid to her again. Not until Erland found time and wherewithal for the improvements he planned for this house. Not until she could forget the sting of pride her mother evoked with a glance around the simple room.

Harald's fever returned, and would ebb and surge almost daily. Each time his temperature climbed Jorunn's anxiety rose with it. In Erland's eyes she saw her own fear mirrored. She came to dread his arrival home each afternoon.

In this time of year there was little to occupy a farmer. When winter settled over Dal Erland spent his days indoors making plans, drawing columns of figures, talking to Jorunn of what spring and summer would bring for them by way of improvements to the house and farm. He whittled as they talked, fashioning from pieces of fine hard wood a bed for Harald. It would be richly carved, with dragons and sea snakes and creatures from the sagas Erland remembered from his own childhood. When Harald was weaned and moved from their bed to make way for the next child, his own would be ready for him. "Fine enough for a Viking prince," Erland joked, as he carefully carved the precious wood.

Jorunn had knitted and baked, washed and cooked, to the accompaniment of Erland's deep voice weaving dreams for them both in words softened by the drawling vowels of the valley. He was not an educated man; Jorunn knew her mother found his language simple, yet she grew to cherish his softly slurred bass as he propped Harald on his knee and boomed children's rhymes to the accompaniment of the child's cries of delight. *"Gull-gutten min,"* he whispered hoarsely in the babe's tiny ear, tickling him with this winter's beard, insinuating a callused finger under Harald's fat chins to stroke him gently. When Harald had taken ill, Erland had paced and fretted over the child until she had finally driven him out, crying, "Can't you find something to occupy your time? I swear I'll go mad if you don't quit worrying me!"

Stunned into silence, Erland studied her flushed countenance. Convinced she spoke the truth, he left for the rest of that day. Since then he rose to leave in the gray light of early morn, often returning after twilight had given way to utter darkness. Jorunn did not ask where he spent his days. She wondered, in the hours she spent rocking and tending Harald, yet she could not find words to beg forgiveness, to let him know it was worry and grief over Harald that drove her to say such things. Since then their evenings were quiet. The only sounds were necessary ones, and Harald's whimpers. Since then he did not turn to her in their bed, but fell asleep at once with his back turned. Since then her heart had frozen beneath her breast.

Spring came. The thaw brought rivulets of water down the mountain, washing the stones clean and bright in the sunlight. Forsythia bloomed clear yellow in the farmyard, and the fields were sprinkled green as new life unfolded against black earth. Erland ventured out to prepare for planting, while Jorunn tended Harald and prayed for his discomfort to ease. But his breathing grew more labored with each day. Nights seemed endless. Jorunn paced with the child from one side to the other of the square one-room dwelling. For as long as she walked Harald dozed, but when she rested he woke, coughing and choking, gasping for air as his tiny face creased in terror, turning red, purple, then blue. The remedies the wives brought proved useless, so Jorunn paced, until Erland woke in the early hours before dawn and relieved her of the burden that had grown distressingly light. Their fat, fair infant was diminished to a pale shadow.

In May, Harald drew his last breath, a sigh of relief. He turned from Jorunn's breast, his spirit carried away on a crisp wind.

Four

REVIVAL

The cherry trees in the valley blossomed in early June, but the beauty of slender branches festooned in white was lost to Jorunn. Her every day was dark, the bright sunshine blotted by grief and loss. The day they buried Harald she and Erland stood in the churchyard surrounded by neighbors and family mourning, yet this day one month later she could not remember a single face from that time. She remembered voices. Echoes of, "He's in God's hands now, returned to his creator," reverberated in her mind. Righteous words, meant to comfort, yet they awoke in her an anger which simmered slowly. Unbidden, Scripture she had not known she carried within her came to mind. 'A people that provoketh me to anger continually to my face, which say, come not near to me; for I am holier than thou. These are a smoke in my nose, a fire that burneth all day.' The vengeful words of a wrathful God. They were a whisper in her mind, a breeze that fanned the flames of her indignation.

'He was mine, given life through my body. He wasn't Yours to take!' she railed silently. Her fury at God's injustice spread, obliterating her pain. From across the gaping wound in the earth where Harald lay she saw her mother watch and understood she knew. Jorunn felt Astrid's eyes probe into her soul in a continuation of her mother's quest for the inner workings of her mind, laying bare her guilt. Jorunn had remained true to her vow; Astrid had not been summoned to Stridheim again. Even as Harald lay wasting away, too ill to cry or fret, Jorunn's pride had rendered her mute, unable to cry for help. It lodged, a hard stone, in her throat. She felt it still, torturous pride, its jagged edges tormenting her. She watched Astrid's nostril's flare, saw her spine stiffen and her head rear. She sensed her disapproval and condemnation. Her mother wore the pious expression of the righteous. It stated quite clearly that Harald's death was a punishment. Conceived in sin, he must atone with his young life. Jorunn and Erland paid now their true penance, Astrid's countenance spoke.

Jorunn's anger welled to drown her pain, to spill over onto everyone and everything around her. She fixed her gaze on the stone Erland had painstakingly carved.

Harald Erlandsson
April 15, 1849—May 5, 1850

She committed to memory each detail of the smooth stone, its rough edges, the bittersweet stab of love and longing the sight of it evoked. She turned and walked away from the church and yard without a backward glance, carrying with her these images, knowing she would not return. These memories of her son must last a lifetime.

At Stridheim her anger cooled and Jorunn let the swells of grief overtake her. She mourned alone, aloof and unreachable. Even Erland's pain could not touch her.

Their days passed in an endless rhythm of chores, some less necessary than others, but all having the virtue of distraction. Never had the yard at Stridheim been in such perfect repair. In between planting Erland mended fences and painted, replaced the smokehouse roof, and cleared a new expanse of land at the edge of the yard, overlooking the valley below.

Jorunn washed and mended the many linens that had accumulated during the last months, when nursing Harald had occupied her every moment. She baked and stored layer after layer of flat bread, enough for this next winter and the next, taking from ample supplies, reaping the plenitude from that which Erland had sown one year previously.

The pain grew unbearable when she recalled the joy with which they had harvested. They had reveled in the idea that there would be plenty on Stridheim in the coming years, regardless of wind and weather. The excess repulsed her now, for only the two of them. Like old people hoarding, the hams in the smokehouse would hang until tainted before they could be eaten. She thought with disgust of the potatoes carefully mounded in the cellar bins. Last year's harvest not half-eaten, yet the new crop would soon be ready. Neither she nor Erland had possessed an appetite this winter. There had been no time to cook the stews she had envisioned when the harvest was upon them last year.

Bitter thoughts assailed her each waking moment, and Jorunn rushed in busy errand to escape. She made cheeses, sour cream, and butter from milk the cow supplied in excess. All carefully stored, none of it tempting.

Erland was seldom home. He disappeared each early morn, to tend the farm, without explanation of errands that kept him away all day, occasionally two and three days running. When he was gone she ached with loneliness. When he returned the pain in his eyes served to intensify her own. When their eyes met the grief they shared burned hot between them, searing her soul. She turned away. But not before she saw him retreat, and she knew he shared her revulsion of them. Harald had been the bridge they crossed to one another. Without him a gulf yawned wide.

A child. The thought came to her unbidden one morning as she crouched milking. Another child would let them start anew, give them hope, reason for being. Yet the mere idea of another infant to care for caused her anguish, and fear. Strong and healthy at birth, Harald had wasted away in the dark and smoky house. Her best effort had not been enough.

From the stall where she crouched she heard the sound of a wagon making its heavy, creaking ascent to the yard. Finishing up hurriedly she carried the bucket to the house and returned to greet the caller. Erland had risen before dawn and disappeared wordlessly on errand, while she lay feigning sleep in the darkness of their bed.

Stepping from the house into the bright sun she squinted, lifting her hand to shield her eyes.

"Good day, Ellefsson, and Solveig," she called as the wagon rolled to a stop in the yard. She had not encountered her neighbors from a distance to the northwest for some time, and was surprised at their calling this morning. Their wagon was heavy with a load of fine, dry timber.

Solveig swung quickly down and came to Jorunn. Her husband shook the reins and continued to where Erland had cleared the new field.

"It's good of you to call, Solveig. Come in, please. I'll boil coffee," Jorunn began uncertainly. Solveig Amundsdatter was renown in the valley for her unfailing good humor, and Jorunn knew most of the wives looked forward to her visits, enjoyed her chatter. Yet Jorunn found the woman's barrage of gossip and idle talk overwhelming, like a stiff wind on a fall day. In the best of times Solveig's ceaseless conversation whirled around in Jorunn's head and left her dazed. Now, still mired down in mourning Harald, the mere thought of enduring a morning of the other woman's company sapped the strength she hoarded miserably to carry her through each day. She watched in puzzled dismay as Ellefsson stopped the team and began unloading his wagon.

Solveig studied Jorunn, her broad face careful, her blue eyes cautious. Her smile was guarded, stiff and unlike her. Solveig's manner alerted Jorunn that this was no ordinary visit.

"We come to help with the raisin'," Solveig explained, her voice artificially light, her expression cautious. "The rest are comin' soon, but I told Ellefsson I wanted to be first," she continued. "To warn you, like. Halvorsson wants it to be a surprise, but men folk don't know. They don't know women don't always like surprises."

"Solveig, what are you saying? You ramble. What surprise is Erland planning?" Jorunn was suddenly impatient with trying to decipher the message in the worried blue eyes pressed into Solveig's soft face.

"A new house. We come for the raisin'." The anxiety in Solveig's countenance was lessened by the excitement of the words as she spoke them. Not often in the valley was there occasion for a house to be raised. Usually it was an event planned for years, looked forward to by everyone as a time to work and feast together.

"All winter he planned it," she continued. "I says to Gunnar this morning, 'We'll get there early, the two of us, like as to prepare her for it.'"

She paused, doubt clouding her fair, rosy face. "I did right?"

Jorunn's mind whirled. 'All winter he'd planned it....' She remembered the figures, the calculations, the long absences. Turning to the freshly cleared patch of land at the edge of the yard, she understood at last.

In answer Jorunn reaching out hesitantly to touch Solveig's rough, chafed hand. Through the fog of her own confusion she recognized the other woman's kindness and realized she had underestimated Solveig. This woman understood her well enough to know that an event of such magnitude was something Jorunn would prefer to influence.

"It weren't nothin'," the other woman answered, her pink face flushing bright red. With a hurried glance to the south she said, "We'd best hurry, the others'll be here soon."

All morning wagons loaded with timber and supplies came creaking into the yard. From the cellar Jorunn collected potatoes and put them to boil in a black kettle, then slathered them in sour cream. Together with the other women she sliced thick hams from the smokehouse and placed piles of crisp bread on long tables hastily fashioned from planks that would later be used to finish the house. It was the first time since Harald's death Jorunn had occasion to visit with the wives from the valley. Those who had called in the weeks just after she had buried her son had found Jorunn unwelcoming and aloof, isolated in her sorrow. The word had gone quickly round that Jorunn Sigurdsdatter was of the sort who grieved best in solitude, and by unspoken agreement they had left her to do just that, waiting for some sign from Stridheim that the mistress there once again welcomed company. To most of the women her reaction did not seem unusual. There was hardly a wife in Dal who had not buried a child; it fell naturally to many of them to endure life's hardships alone. Few had the innate resilience of Solveig Amundsdatter, most were worn to stoic acceptance. Their faces bore the lines and creases of their care. Others, like Jorunn, gave testimony through their manner to the harsh reality of life as a farmer's wife in this cold and unrelenting place. They lived each day in resignation, took pride in self-sufficiency. They shouldered their burdens alone, and spent the time they shared with others in optimistic small talk. It was conversation of this sort that passed between the women as they worked. All of them shared in some small way the good fortune that was Jorunn Sigurdsdatter's this day. The memory of it would carry them through meager times, until another occasion for vicarious enjoyment happened along.

Across the yard the men worked steadily. A foundation was built of gray stone culled from a pile Erland had stacked when clearing the land. At noon the men broke for food, for rest, eating heartily from the wealth of Jorunn's stores and drinking deeply from the beer she had brewed at Yule.

"What's the news from Christiania, Halvorsson?" Ivar Gunnarsson called in good-natured taunt. Gunnarsson's farm was small, a parcel divided from his father's place in order that his second son might have his own bit of land. "Has that brother of yours got a place for the likes of us in King Oscar's cabinet yet?"

Egil grinned, taking in stride the jesting remarks of the man, his friend since childhood. "Don't know. I got plenty to do just keepin' my place runnin'. I leave politics and government to Egil."

"Good on Egil Halvorsson, I say," Dag Ottarsrud called out. A young man, his beard not yet full enough to hide the flush from the beer that mottled his smooth cheeks; yet he was sincere, and Erland regarded him with interest.

"I say all good men should unite behind Ueland and Thrane. It's right what they say, all men should have the vote. Swedes have no cause to influence our government," young Ottarsrud insisted.

"True enough," Gunnarsson returned. "Fool Swedes can't even run their own land, they should leave off tellin' us what to do with ours. But Marcus Thrane's a rash one, spent too much time with the Frenchies and turned socialist. I wouldn't like to trust my future to his hands."

"Better that than the damned Swedes!" came a cry from the end of the table. Grunts of general agreement went round. Erland rose quickly, intent on ending the conversation lest the men forget their errand and spend the rest of the day drinking, and discussing politics. Political reform interested him only to the extent it affected his farm. Long ago he had surrendered to his love of the land and left to his brother the fight to give farmers a voice in government. By mutual agreement they protected their birthright in each their own way. Erland turned his attention now to the new house he planned, preparing for the future of Stridheim in a manner more tangible, a way he understood.

Throughout the afternoon the men worked with renewed vigor, and by nightfall a wooden frame towered above the other buildings on Stridheim. When darkness chased away twilight the sounds of hammers and saws fell silent. Erland Halvorsson took his place at the end of the long table and raised his stein in salute: "In the words of the Preacher: 'There is nothing better for a man than that he should eat and drink, and that he should make his soul enjoy good in his labor.'" Cries of "*Skaal!*" rang out the length of the table, echoing off the mountains to the east and west. The feast began.

A great kettle of rich stew had bubbled over a fire in the courtyard all afternoon. Warm loaves from the stone oven were broken in the light of a clear summer moon. They ate well and drank deeply, making toasts to the health and happiness to be found within the four new walls erected that day. Cheers rang out loud and often in the still night. When darkness deepened the first took their leave, seeking rest before the return in the morn, when work would continue.

The last wagon drove from the courtyard and Jorunn slipped away. Erland found her at the edge of the yard. She stood gazing at the timber frame that loomed pale against the night sky. Behind her she heard gravel in the yard crunch beneath his boots as he approached. He stood close, the feel of him warm in the chill air. He lifted the heavy golden braid from her shoulder and let it slide across the calluses ridging his palms. "You're pleased?"

After a pause she answered truthfully, "I'm surprised."

"That's how I planned it," he answered. Jorunn could hear the smile that framed his words. "And you're pleased?"

The quiet of the night deepened as Jorunn chose her words carefully. "I'm pleased."

He dropped her braid to let it hang heavy down her back and slid an arm around her shoulders, pulling her to him. Turning, she lifted her face to his smile, his kiss. He pulled her closer still, pressing her body to the length of him, until she softened and returned his embrace. A tide of longing swirled around Jorunn. Before she let herself be swept away she placed both hands against Erland's chest and pushed him away.

"Erland, from now on I want to know. No more surprises."

His features, soft with desire, hardened in resolve. "It's a man's lot, decisions like this. You tend the house and yard, I'll see to the rest. It's best that way."

Anger sparked and flared within Jorunn. She found the line that separated a wife from her husband's affairs preposterous. It seemed to her the decisions that fell under her jurisdiction were trivial in comparison to that which Erland considered his. She railed silently against the customary division of a woman's realm from that of a man. This new house was to be her domain. When finished it would fall to her to run it, yet from Erland's perspective it was unseemly she should have a voice in its planning. She silently resolved to end to this unfair delegation of influence.

Erland studied his wife's face carefully, watching a tableau of expressions flit across her countenance, until it settled into lines all too familiar. Her lips were pressed into a thin line, her brow knit in concentration. He was vaguely uneasy, yet with his arm firmly encircling her waist he led her across the yard, into the dark warmth of the house. Jorunn walked with him, pacing her gait to his. Erland stood watching in the dim light as she undressed, waiting, until she slipped her shift over her head and turned to him. He reached out with eager arms, but she pushed him away. In his face she saw surprise, uncertainty. She stretched out one slim arm, let one slender hand carefully pluck at the laces of his shirt. It opened beneath her touch. She glided forward and slid both arms around him to lift it over his head.

He reached for her greedily and she stepped away. When his arms fell to his sides she advanced again, this time gently untying his britches, her fingers nimbly freeing him of the last of his clothes. When he stood naked before her she took one measured step backward. In the darkness they stood, her appraising, and him searching, until at last she moved close, pulling both his arms about her. Pushing him gently toward the bed until he lay back, she covered his body with hers and kissed him, opening herself slowly, rising on her knees to encompass him completely. Above him, supporting her slight weight on both arms, she looked down where he lay, his eyes clouded in passion. She whispered triumphantly, "It's best this way."

His answer was a low moan of pleasure.

Five

REBIRTH

❧Just after the slaughter, during the brewing of Yuletide beer,
Jorunn's suspicions were confirmed. Since the housewarming
at Stridheim she had waited anxiously each month for a sign
that new life would soon stir within her, but each morning she
woke with hearty appetite and not a trace of the sickness that
had plagued her that first summer when she carried Harald.

With the harvest upon them there had been little time for
pensive thoughts; the days passed quickly. Then the leaves
dropped, leaving the courtyard blanched gray under a weaker
sun. Jorunn grew anxious.

She counted the months since she'd last held Harald in
her arms, wincing with the ache of emptiness. 'So long, it's
been so long,' she murmured to herself as she stirred the brew.
She lifted the ladle to her lips to taste the beer, then shuddered. It was bitter. Staring with disbelief at the foaming con-
coction, she slammed the lid on the barrel in disgust. Barely a
fortnight until the feast at Yule, and the beer was soured. Despair rose like bile in her throat and hot tears burned her eyes.
She turned and fled the house, rushing into the cold air outside, letting it clear her head and calm her spirit.

Sinking onto the bench Erland had built along the porch
railing she leaned her head against the rough timber of the
house and closed her eyes. Her head swam and she opened
her lids in alarm, drawing in deep gulps of the fresh cold air,

fighting to hold focus on the well in the center courtyard. Her sight cleared, and she relaxed. In the next instant a wave of sickness washed over her, sweeping her away on a dizzy tide. As she fought to maintain control, joy rushed up to war with the nausea. Pressing both hands to her flat stomach she smiled broadly, knowing suddenly that the beer was fine. The beer at her wedding feast had tasted bitter as well, and for the same reason. She was with child.

She rushed inside to fetch her cloak and scarf. Dressing hastily she hurried toward the wood that bordered the yard. Erland had left early that morning to fell timber. This winter, as last, he passed time clearing the forest. Not in order to procure land for cultivation, but for the value of the timber itself. In his quest to finance a new home and repairs to his farm Erland had stumbled upon a source of extra income. As a farmer, the creeping forest covering much of his land had been a constant threat to his livelihood. Erland had discovered the trees were worth gold and silver when floated down river and milled to timber. The dry winter months, before the snow fell too deep, he spent sawing and logging. When spring came he planned to have sufficient funds to buy modern machinery for planting and harvesting. Together with his neighbor, Gunnar Ellefsson, he worked tirelessly, spurred on by the vision of acres of crops, green and glorious beneath a ripe summer sun. Jorunn had watched the shadows in the depths of his dark blue eyes slowly give way to fragile hope.

In the first weeks after Harald's death Jorunn had been almost unaware of Erland's suffering. It was later, after the fog of her own grief had begun to lift, that she realized Erland's mourning was complicated by something else. In moments he was unaware she searched his countenance for some clue. It was a subject still so raw they never gave voice to their thoughts. Erland's formerly expressive face was now habitually guarded. The summer had passed them by, both of them numb to the seasonal beauty of Stridheim. Then it was fall, and almost against her will Jorunn's body began its customary response to the heavy smell of wheat and oat and ripe, red apples ready to be harvested. She had found herself watching Erland as he moved through the fields, his blue and white striped shirt open at the neck to reveal smooth skin beneath the course fabric. Deep in her groin she felt a tightening, and knew her cheeks flushed as red as the apples in her basket. She chose one carefully, dark red and smooth to her palm, and carried it to him. He stopped his work and turned to her where she stood waist-high in the waving wheat. Extending her hand she offered him the fruit, raising her eyes to let him read hers. Then she turned to leave, feeling his stare hot on her back. That night they joined their bodies to the sound of rain pelting the roof of their new house. After, he lay beside her and pulled her close, her head nestled in the crook of his arm, her golden hair splayed over the pillow beneath them.

"A good house," he said, listening to the drops of water beat down overhead. "Fine home for a family. A child would be safe in this house." He was quiet for a long moment, then he sighed. "I ought to thought of it before."

It was then she understood the look in his eyes. Guilt, an echo of her own. Too painful to recognize before, now it shamed her. All those months she wallowed in self-pity without a thought for Erland, doing nothing to lighten the burden of his grief. She realized that as great as her own pain had been, Erland's had likely been worse. She knew he felt things more acutely than she. She loved him, but his passion for her took her breath away. Remorse welled within her and she turned in his arms to hold him, to cover his mouth with hers and blot out his pain. That night they found deliverance from sorrow in each others arms.

The memory of that night sped her along as Jorunn hurried down the forest path intent on her errand to share her news with Erland. She rushed to him, knowing his boundless joy would intensify even her own great gladness. Following the sound of the water she turned toward the River Glomma, knowing the men would be working near the source of transport for the logs. The rush of water grew steadily louder, until she came to a clearing. A few hundred yards away Erland and Ellefsson crouched sawing, pulling to and from, intent on their task, unaware of her presence. Suddenly wary, she stopped, half-hidden by the tree she leaned against. She felt the bark, rough against her open palm, as she hesitated, her reluctance stemming from the dread of Ellefsson's gaze upon her. Of necessity she encountered the man more often of late, since he and Erland had agreed to work as a team. Yet she sensed that on Erland's side it was an uneasy partnership, and she shared his unspoken sentiments with regard to their neighbor. Ellefsson's dark eyes were sunken beneath a heavy brow, in a face sharp with too many angles. When his gaze rested on her she felt her skin burn under the intensity of it. Never by

deed had he given her cause for distrust, yet his person inspired in her that, and more. Fear slithered and coiled in the
pit of her stomach in his proximity. She stood in silence to
watch them work and wait for the courage to approach.

While she watched Erland paused in his labor. With a word
to Ellefsson he stood to stretch and walked toward the rushing
water that ran high in the banks. He turned back and spied
her at once. The bright woolen scarf covering her fair hair
glowed richly against the dark wood. He came to her, concern
evident in his countenance.

She met him in the clearing, suddenly happy again at the
sight of him. She smiled, calling, "Not to worry, everything's fine!"

Catching her hands in his own rough ones he pulled her
to him, for the moment unaware and uncaring of Ellefsson's
presence. "What brings you? If you're well, it's got to be loneliness, the want of a man, you brazen wench," he teased.

"If you insult me I won't share with you my news," she
replied. Feigning affront, she snatched both hands away and
turned to leave. She felt him approach from behind, sensed
his arms would wrap around her in restraint, even before she
felt the warmth of him. She stopped and turned to him, lost
for an instant in the white mist of his breath as she tilted her
face to his and whispered, "The beer tastes bitter."

The mist cleared between them and she saw puzzlement
in his clear blue eyes, watched his smooth brow furrow in confusion, until he understood. With a whoop he tightened both
arms around her and lifted, swinging around in delight.

"When?" he demanded. "When will he be born?"

"I don't know, I couldn't guess. If you wouldn't carry on
so, it would be easier to calculate," she teased. "The way things
are I can't be sure."

"You got to go to the doctor this time," he said suddenly,
concern etched in the furrow between his blond brows. "Tomorrow I'll drive you to the village. Doc Tveter will know when
the babe will come. He'll tend to you at the birth. This time
will be different."

Seeing the pain in his face Jorunn felt a stab of fear. She
quelled it quickly, saying, "There's no cause for that, Erland.
Harald's birth was easy, and when the time for this one comes,
I'll know. We have to be patient, that's all."

Suddenly her fear loomed larger, darker. In desperation
she said, "We have to trust in God, only He can make things
different this time."

Erland's open face and clear brow hardened in resolution. "I won't hold with a God who took from me what's more dear than my own life and left me with no reason," Erland ground out.

The bitter anger in his voice stunned Jorunn. She stepped back. "Don't say such things, Erland." In her fright and confusion she fumbled, "We can't know, or be sure...." She said no more, but he read the fear in her face accurately.

"Look at you, Jorunn! You cower, scared to death of this God you worship! Is it the fear of God that's inspired your faith in Him? What's happened to you, woman? Are you like your mother: 'Holier than thou' and so scared of life you don't dare live it? You gonna hide behind church walls and pray for His protection, like she does? The woman bowed her head in shame at our wedding. She wouldn't tend you in the birthin' of our son, she was so afraid of her God. I watched her at Harald's funeral; what she had on her mind was written plain on her face. 'It's a punishment,' she was thinkin'. That's what her religion is about."

Squaring his broad shoulders he stood straight, towering over Jorunn. At one with nature, he seemed greater by association with the land he was a part of.

"I'll have nothin' to do with her God, Jorunn. I won't worship Him out of fear, I sure don't trust Him. If He visited a judgment on us through the death of our boy, then I'll worship no god at all before I'll hold with such a vengeful one."

Stunned, Jorunn stepped back, then further away. She felt the rough bark of a tree square between her shoulder blades and stopped, mesmerized by the passion she saw reflected in the still features of this man, stirred by the raw anger he revealed. Her heart hammered in her chest. Not in fear, she discerned, but in excitement. She was reminded that Erland's passionate nature could plunge him to great depths as well as the heights his mood often scaled. The bond between them pulled her with him. She turned in confusion and retraced her steps through the forest.

*ჯ *ჯ *ჯ

Summer came, and the crops grew as Erland had envisioned. Great expanses of green and gold promised rich bounty during the harvest, Stridheim was ripe and prosperous. At the same time her mistress grew heavy with child, and it was during the hectic time, when every pair of hands must work together to gather in the crops, that Jorunn's labor began.

That early morn had been chill, the promise of frost soon to come evident in the air. Erland had risen before dawn and driven the team to the fields, leaving Jorunn to lie alone in the dark, aching under her burden. Rolling onto her side, she pushed herself upright with both arms and struggled to her feet. Her movements were clumsy. She was swollen, her back ached with an intensity previously unknown to her. She hobbled through the courtyard to the outhouse, intent on her morning's errand, clutching a shawl about her to fend off the morning air. With the other hand she pressed firmly against the small of her back in attempt to ward off the pain situated there.

Halfway across the yard the pain radiated from her back, down her thighs, to spread as a dull ache through her body. The ferocity of her discomfort was so great the air was squeezed from her, leaving her gasping.

'It's the child,' she realized, 'I'd best send for the midwife.' No sooner had she formulated the thought than another pain ripped through her body. Strong enough to make coherent thought impossible, it swept her along on a tide of misery.

When the pain receded she was alarmed. She had not expected her time to come with such quick intensity. With Harald, labor had been slow and progressive, the first half spent in frantic late preparation for the babe. She had assumed this time would be easier still. She had formulated no plan for summoning help, except that Erland would be sent on errand when he returned from the field, either at noon, or in early twilight.

Another pain gripped her, and she fell over from the force of it. The gravel in the yard pierced the flesh of her palms and knees, but she was unaware. When it receded she sat back on her haunches and stared with dismay at the flecks of blood on her hands. Rational thought returned and she realized she must use the small increments of time between pains to accomplish necessary errand.

She rose and made her way to the outhouse, managing the door before another pain was upon her. After her stop there she returned to the house, pausing twice along the way to grasp a pole, then the handle on an outbuilding, to give her support as another wave of labor washed over her. She thought to boil water and make ready the linen, yet when another pain came she realized that was beyond her. Falling upon the bed she lay there until it abated, concluding that when Erland came he must see to the necessities before riding out for attendance.

An expanse of time passed. How long she could not be sure, but the pains were too many to count. When her head cleared she could only attempt to mark the passage of time by the shadows that fell through the window of her bedroom.

When the branches of the birch tree cast short dark fingers of shadow across the blanket she judged time to be near eleven. Soon midday, and Erland would come home. Desperation stalked her as another pain came, crushing in its intensity. The fear she might not be able to wait for help assailed her, but she pushed it away, into the dark corner of her mind where panic lurked.

The sound of the scraping of Erland's boots penetrated the fog of misery she lay suffocating in. She called to him, one great cry full terror. In the next moment he leaned over her, his face creased in concern.

"How long? How long you been like this?" he demanded, his voice loud, breaking for lack of control.

She opened her lips to answer, yet only a cry escaped. Speech was beyond her. She shook her head to signify that she did not know, before another pain was upon her, tearing her apart from inside. She abandoned conscious thought, letting herself slide into the darkness that had threatened to overtake her for so long. At times she was vaguely aware of sound, a scream that came from somewhere far away, a place far removed from where she lay tortured.

Quickly Erland crossed to the kitchen where fire still smoldered in the stove. Casting more wood upon the embers, he grabbed the kettle and a large pot, then raced to the yard where he filled them from the well.

Back inside he set them to boil while he searched the linen chest for something suitable to swaddle the child. Jorunn's screams from the bedroom turned to a long keening wail and he snatched linen from the top of the chest and ran back to her. A pool of blood stained the front of her nightdress, spreading insidious red. Her face was swollen, contorted almost unrecognizable, her pale hair turned dark gold and matted with sweat. Drawing a deep breath he leaned over her and raised the night dress. Voluntarily she lifted her knees. At the center of her bulged the head of the child.

Jorunn opened her eyes and stared into Erland's. Lifting her shoulders off the bed, she pushed. A great guttural moan escaped her and the face of the child appeared, contorted and smeared with blood. He reached between her legs to take the infant in his hands, easing it from her body.

Jorunn collapsed against the pillow, gasping for air. A tiny mewl came from the foot of the bed, and gathering the remnants of her strength she lifted her head again. Erland held the babe, unspeakably fragile, in his broad hands. Her blood was smeared across the front of him as he clutched the bundle to his chest, his face transformed, all the hard edges softened. He spoke, in a voice strangled with emotion, "My daughter."

Jorunn lay back against the pillow in exhaustion and let swift sleep swallow her, the image of shiny rivulets coursing down his brown cheeks etched against the blackness behind her lids.

Six

JUDGEMENT

❧ The next day Erland rose at dawn, as was necessary during harvest, yet lingered until early morn, unwilling to leave.

"Go, we're fine. Strong and healthy, the both of us," Jorunn urged from where she lay pillowed against clean white linen.

Erland turned from the window where he stood anxiously watching for sign of Astrid's approach. His work beckoned, yet he would not leave until he was certain both of them were delivered into safe keeping.

The sound of boots scraping heralded Astrid's arrival. The front door opened and as she paused to hang the heavy cloak she wore she called in her clear voice, resonant with ebullience, "I have come, Jorunn. To care for you, and to see my daughter's daughter."

As she spoke she came to the doorway, her face happy. When she saw Erland her countenance dimmed, then darkened with displeasure.

"I assumed you would be in the fields by now," she said without hesitation.

Jorunn watched in dismay as Erland replied, "I'm leavin'," before walking past her mother without pausing.

Lying in shocked silence, she heard the front door slam, startling her to her senses. "Mother, what's the matter? I've never seen either of you behave so badly, and on such a happy occasion, too," she cried reproachfully.

Astrid crossed to the bed where Jorunn lay cradling the infant. She bent to lift the babe carefully into her arms, answering, "It is indeed a joyful occasion. Yet the happiness of it is marred by rumors that waft in the valley below. I would not like to distress you at this time, but there is something you must know. I will not share a roof with a man who professes himself to be heathen."

"You mean Erland? Don't talk foolish, Mother! I've never known a better man. What lie gives you cause to call my husband heathen?" The dismay in Jorunn's voice gave way to anger. She felt her face grow hot, her color rise.

"It is no lie, for I asked him of the matter myself last eve when he came over the mountain to call me to your lying in. I asked if there was truth to the story circulating in the dale that he refuses to worship our God in heaven. He replied, 'I won't ask favors, or put my life in the hands of a god who can be as cruel as the one you worship.'"

Suddenly Jorunn remembered the conversation in the wood the day she had discovered she was with child. In her mind's eye she saw clearly Erland's fierce expression as he decried God's goodness and refused his mercy. Behind Erland, in her memory, was a shadow. Gunnar Ellefsson had stood leaning on his ax, listening to the exchange.

"Mother, you have to know, you've got to understand the depth of Erland's pain at God's taking of Harald. He doesn't mean what he says. He's just talking, denying events, not God. Give him time and he'll return to God's flock."

"He shall have all the time he needs, and if it is not enough he shall spend eternity in damnation! He shall burn in the fires of hell, but I'll not burn with him for association with a heretic. I shall tend you and the babe, but I'll not rest under the roof of a Godless man." Astrid's clear voice vibrated with conviction.

Jorunn sat up straighter, anger and revulsion clear in her face. "What language you use, Mother! You're condemning my husband with far less forgiveness than Jesus showed his crucifiers. Apostle Paul promised that the doers of the law should be justified. It seems you forget that righteousness isn't measured by hearing the law, or loudly professing to believe in it, but by following the law, and acting accordingly. No one can say Erland violates Christ's law by his actions. But you, Mother, if you're to walk in the path of the righteous, then you'd best instill in yourself the goodness God grants His children. Erland sees God as vengeful, is in pain at the idea he's being punished in spite of the penance he paid. It's your Christian duty to show him the kindness and mercy God grants His followers. It's through this Erland will be saved."

An ugly flush stained Astrid's pale face. "There is no forgiveness for a penance which is not a true one," Astrid replied, drawing herself to her full height. "And you are in no position to preach to me, you who remain in God's grace only by the skin of your teeth," she spat out contemptuously. In the angles of her thin face Jorunn saw the unpleasantly pious expression to which Erland had referred that day in the wood. In her heart she felt unease. Something close to dislike formed in her mind. She struggled to quell the thought before it was fully formed, striving for patience and clinging to composure with every ounce of her strength.

"Erland is as good and kind a man as God ever created,' she insisted, her voice thin under the strain of keeping her temper. "In his ways he keeps the teachings of the disciples. He holds the commandments easily, because his soul is pure and clean. If his words give lie to the beliefs his ways reflect, then it ought to be simple enough to let the words fall on deaf ears and appreciate the man as he is, since a better example of Christian values doesn't exist."

"I do not agree, Jorunn, and it pains me to hear my daughter speak such," Astrid continued in rebuttal, raising her voice over the cries of the infant she held too tightly. "If, indeed, you see this man no more clearly, then I have failed in my duty as a mother to you. I fear your soul, and the one of this babe, are in peril in this house. Consorting with heathens and heretics will bring you no closer to the gates of heaven."

Holding out her arms for the wailing child Jorunn nestled it at her breast, her color high, her anger barely in check.

"There's one truth in what you say," she said finally. Lifting her head to face her mother fully, their eyes locked and she bit out, "You have failed me."

The color drained from Astrid's face, leaving it sallow and old. Jorunn watched as the passage of time was visited upon her mother. The folds of her skin sagged, aging her in that moment. Astrid turned and left the room without a word. There was the rustle of woolens as she retrieved her cloak, the sound of a door closing. Jorunn held the child more firmly to her breast and struggled with animosity that overwhelmed her. The pain of her mother's rejection she smothered in the flame of old anger easily rekindled.

'It's like Erland says,' she concluded. 'Such a God and His followers are a fearful thing. Better to be led by the still, small voice of conscience than be ruled by fear and dread caused by the teachings of religion.'

She lay the sleeping infant beside her and struggled from the bed. She did not feel the necessity of lying in. There was much to be done. She dressed slowly and began a new day, her face set in lines of determination.

Seven

ILLATION

❧ Astrid Asbjornsdatter left the house of her daughter with her spine straight, head held high. Her strides were even, measured, taking her quickly to the grove of apple trees that clustered at the base of the mountain. In the shelter of limbs heavy with ripe fruit she relaxed her desperate grip on composure. Her thin shoulders slumped forward, her head dropped to her chest in a low keening wail.

This was her punishment. She had thought God, in His graciousness, would spare her daughters, for He had promised that the fear of the wicked would come upon him, but the desire of the righteous would be granted, and in every aspect of life Astrid strove to be righteous, to keep the covenant. Yet today, she thought in anguish, her fears were confirmed. The shell of her righteousness could not erase that which had gone before. The smell of rotting apples that littered the ground rose up, calling to her mind original sin, reminding her that the wages of sin were, indeed, death. Her heart withered in her breast and she mourned the death of part of her. Her daughter, her last child, who must bear the burden of guilt for the sins of her forebears.

The girl bore the mark of the devil. Spreading insidious black above her right breast, just as it had on the three sons Astrid had borne Sigurd; all of whom, mercifully, had been stillborn. God had not granted them souls; their lives were over before they had begun. They had been spared the inevi-

table torment of their situation. When Astrid had been delivered of her last child and seen the mark, she had refused the
child. She had lain in bed listening to the wails of the tiny
creature, turning away when Sigurd would press the babe on
her. She had not expected her to live, had waited for the forces
that kept her alive to cease and release the babe's body so she
might be laid to rest. But this child would not die, suffering
through three days of Sigurd's fumbling care; in the end Astrid
hadn't the strength to follow through her conviction to let the
child waste away. Sigurd had not understood, and she would
not share with him the secret of her guilt. He imagined the
child like himself. But he had never known Astrid's own
mother, Sylvie Helfridsdatter. Jorunn's broad brow and wide
eyes were like those of the woman Astrid's father, Asbjorn
Olavsson, had sketched on small scraps, on the back of old
sermons already delivered. Jorunn's heavy hair waved from
her face, dipping to form a small peak in the middle of her
forehead, just as Sylvie's had. Her mouth formed a soft bow;
her chin dimpled in the same way. Yet it was the mark Jorunn
bore above her right breast that made Astrid certain Sylvie's
sins were revisited upon her child. In every sketch Astrid's
father had penciled of Sylvie he had drawn gently sloping shoulders above the swell of a soft bosom, the beauty of which was
marred by a mark he drew in angry strokes with jagged edges.
It was small, almost unnoticeable in some of the sketches. In
those Asbjorn Olavsson had drawn in Astrid's early childhood
it had been so tiny she had thought it a smudge, but as years
passed and her father drew this woman, his wife, the mark grew
to an ugly black cancer he carved out of her mother's breast
with the tip of his pencil. Astrid watched him surreptitiously
while he made long black slashes that soon obliterated the face
he drew, and she wondered about her mother, the woman who
had died in birthing her. Her questions were rebuffed when
she dared ask of her, but in time Astrid came to understand
her mother's death was punishment for a wicked nature. In
time, Astrid came to understand that Sylvie Helfridsdatter was
no ordinary woman.

"She was the offspring of a crone who lived in the wood
and spawned the child alone, perhaps with the devil's own
seed," her father told Astrid on the eighth anniversary of her
birth, for then he judged her to be of an age to understand
the dire circumstances in which she lived. "She used her wiles,
the devil's gifts, to try to take from God that which was His,"

he explained, "for I had already heard the call from God, and was intent on joining the church. In my early ministry, in the Year of Our Lord 1774, I went to the wood to bring the witch, Helfrid, and her daughter, Sylvie, salvation. They conspired to steal my soul from God," he intoned, his rich baritone swelling with the awfulness of such a thing, "and for a while, I succumbed."

God had blessed Asbjorn Olavsson with a beautiful voice, supple and smooth, powerful enough to inspire his followers to belief in the unfathomable. Asbjorn recognized the gift as invaluable to his calling, over time honing his diction to perfection to make the most of God's generous grant. He used his voice with the skill and precision of an artist, was capable of painting in the imagination of his congregation both the glory of heaven and the horrors of hell. In relating the story of Astrid's mother, Asbjorn effortlessly conjured dark images the little girl would carry with her the rest of her life.

"I drifted in sin and wantonness, seduced by the devil's own child," he said, in such a way that Astrid experienced physically the revulsion that filled his words. "I could have withstood the temptations of an ordinary woman," he insisted, strong in his conviction, the light of defiance flickering in his gray eyes; yet the look faded quickly. After a silence he continued in his usual liquid baritone, softened with time. "She was my Jezebel, as lovely as the rose of Sharon, as fair as the lilies of the valley."

Drifting in memory he wandered through the past, forgetting in his reverie the little girl at his feet. His captive audience, she listened as he replayed his life, his voice painting images in great sweeping strokes on the clean white canvas of the child's mind.

"She lay in wait for me in the cool green depths of the forest, like a wood nymph, and as alluring. I would happen upon her and she would laugh at my surprise, come close and beckon me to her soft embrace. Yet even in the face of her wiles I was strong. I turned away, invoking the name of the Lord against sin. 'Lead me not unto temptation, deliver me from evil,' I prayed, and He gave me strength to leave her there, with the sun dappling her white-gold hair and flushed face. But on Midsummer's Eve, on the day of St. Hans feast, when the spirits are restless and the devil is strong, she caused my fall from grace. I passed through the wood, wary she lay in wait, steeling myself to withstand her temptation, and I heard a round, a sigh carried on the wind. Beckoning me... an irresistible call. I found her floating in the dark depths of the river, the white skin of her neck glistening above the surface, the pale flesh of her breasts floating just below. The wanton rose from the water slowly, mesmerizing me with her unnatural beauty. She was guided only by the pleasures of the flesh; she wove a spell about me, seducing me with sensual experiences beyond the scope of my imagination. She led me to a thick carpet of green and lay down, pulling me to her with deceptively slim arms. Delicate, yet entwining like ivy to hold me prisoner in her world of sin. I was bewitched, captive in her spell."

Astrid sat riveted, hardly daring to breathe, fearful of these words she did not fully understand, yet fascinated. It was the first time in her young life her father had lifted the curtain that veiled the past. She waited, breathless, for further glimpse of her mother.

Her father's face brightened with the holy light that shone from within him when he delivered sermons, dispelling the cloud of memory on which he floated. "Glory be to God, He saved me from that sin!" he cried out suddenly, his voice ringing with conviction. "He showed me a new way; I heard a new calling. He made it clear I should abandon priesthood to take the devil's daughter for Him. As I walked the wood He spoke to my heart and gave me a message to bring to His people. Like the Apostle Paul, I was struck down. The scales fell from my eyes, and I could see clearly. I understood Paul's message was to be mine: 'So labouring ye ought to support the weak, and to remember the words of the Lord Jesus, how He said, It is more blessed to give than to receive.' In the valley, and across most of the land, I had seen for myself how those who were blessed with bountiful harvest each summer hoarded their stores, even unto their ruin, while others starved beside them. I understood my calling was to remind His people that faith, if it hath not works, is dead. That in their faith and good works lay salvation.

"The still, small voice of God instructed me to wed Sylvie. I was to be her salvation, she my first convert. I went to her at once, rejoicing in the news I brought, and she listened and was touched by His message. We were wed, repenting our sins, and began the life God intended."

The light inside him faded, he was quiet a long while before he continued. Beside him the little girl waited, wrestling to make sense of the story, to commit it to memory so she might study his words later and decipher their meaning.

"It seemed all was forgiven and right with Our Lord. We traveled through the fall and winter, bringing His message to many so remote from church and priest that they worshipped no god, some even carrying on with pagan practices related to the old gods. We brought them salvation; I knew He was pleased. Then Sylvie grew heavy with child, and all that spring we sheltered at the farm of a Godless man who refused our message. I believed Our Father had visited Sylvie's infirmity upon her so we might tarry in the farmer's presence and convert him, for he was a kind man, and grew fond of Sylvie. Yet the spring passed, and he refused God's word. In the early summer Sylvie began her labor to deliver the babe."

Her father fell quiet again, for so long Astrid wondered in her child's mind if the story was finished. She was far away in thought, sorting all her father said, when he called her attention back .

"In birthing you God chose to mete out his punishment for Sylvie's sins," he said quietly, sorrow stealing the light behind his gray eyes. His voice was flat, its usual resonance stilled by grief. "She suffered three days before He released her. Yet He saved you, Our Gracious God, and gave you to me to guard and keep holy. The Godless farmer's punishment came in those three days as well, for I watched him suffer and sweat from the agony of Sylvie's cries. I was lost in prayer, cloaked in God's comfort through the ordeal. The old man refused the solace of prayer I offered and suffered alone. When we buried Sylvie and I left her there, I understood it was God's way of reminding the farmer of his punishment for refusing Him. I traveled on with you, as I still do. It falls to us to carry on His work now. Yet you must understand it is only through His grace you survived. You owe Him your life. Do you understand?" her father asked, his voice suddenly harsh, devoid of the mesmerizing grace which had held her spellbound. His expression was fierce, so altered he seemed a stranger, and Astrid was afraid. She could only nod, her throat too close to speak, yet her father was satisfied with her mute acceptance of God's will. He sent her away saying, "You are a good girl, Astrid, one of God's chosen. Go now, and contemplate the good fortune He has bestowed upon you, while I finish this sermon."

His voice was gentle and low again, and Astrid hurried away relieved, yet quivering inside, still puzzling over his words.

Words she pieced together over time, until she came to an understanding of that which had gone before, and what she must do to atone for the sin which begot her. When she learned that God was a jealous God, visiting the iniquity of the fathers upon the children, she understood she must wrest her salvation from the grip of the devil's handmaiden, her own mother. Her fate depended on it.

Astrid lived each day according to God's mandate. She disciplined her willful and stubborn nature into subjugation. Though it cost her great anguish to follow where He led, she walked in the path of the righteous. No matter how great the price, it was small in view of the redemption she bought.

She had felt no calling to the land, would not be a farmer's wife; yet when the man she took for her wedded husband bid her accept this life, she obeyed him. She had vowed before God she would. When God reclaimed her three stillborn sons she accepted His will. For her redemption, and the sake of her daughters, she did not question Him. 'Faith is the substance of things hoped for, the evidence of things not seen,' she reminded herself, and trusted Him, believed in Him with all her heart. She kept the faith.

When Jorunn was born with the mark of the devil and against her expectations was spared, Astrid had fallen on her knees and prayed for the way to Jorunn's salvation. Mystified at the magnitude of God's mercy, she searched endlessly for the meaning of it, and His will. This ambiguous God, who vowed to visit the sins of the father upon the child, had granted her the chance of redemption for her daughter. Yet in the end her best effort was not enough. Jorunn rejected God, as He must have known she would. There was no salvation for her.

Astrid straightened from where she leaned against the gnarled trunk of an apple tree and lifted her face to her Father in silent acceptance of His will. A multitude of ripe apples clustered in the midst of lush green leaves; in them she saw the trespass for which all mothers must atone. Resignation fell, a heavy blow that bowed her shoulders. She walked from the grove with a broken gait, climbed the mountain stooping beneath the weight she bore. She would not risk her own salvation by association with a heretic. It was too dear, bought at too great a price. It was everything to her.

Eight

PERSECUTION

❧ In the valley it was said that Jorunn had become unstable and reclusive after the birth. She had delivered the child unattended, it was rumored, and no one knew for certain if the child was right. It was witless, some asserted, yet others maintained that the child was eerily bright, and of uncommon beauty.

In the following years Stridheim prospered in an incredible manner. It was whispered that Erland Halvorsson had become heretic and was reaping an unholy reward for a pact made with darker forces.

The child was a changeling, a witch, the older children told the younger; they ran away with shrieks and laughter when the little girl came close in the meadows where they played. She stood, a lone figure almost hidden in the tall grain, with hair that shimmered pale gold, and wide eyes the color of the summer sky.

"Such perfection is surely unnatural," it was remarked when the wives caught sight of the girl. It was said she often played alone in the dark forest where no other child dared venture. It had been widely spoken that Jorunn Sigurdsdatter had had no lying in or churching after the birth. No God-fearing woman would dare be about after the birth of a child until both she and her babe had been cleansed of sin and accepted into God's fold. Yet Jorunn Sigurdsdatter had been seen in the village only five days after the birth of Valdis Erlandsdatter, and now, five years hence there had been no churching, no christening.

"An unholy name," it was asserted by one of the wives, who declared it originated from Valkyrie, the heathen goddess of Odin who chose which warriors should be slain and escorted to Valhalla. "A wise woman would keep her sons far from the grasp of such a girl child," another remarked, and nods circled the group round.

There had been no other surviving children born to Jorunn Sigurdsdatter and Erland Halvorsson. Twice Jorunn had conceived, and both times the infant had been born too early to survive. When Erland laid to rest the third of his sons he vowed there would be no more. Jorunn's grief was great each time she delivered the small, half-formed bundles. She halted broken and defeated for months afterward. Never again would he burden her such, Erland promised after the last time, and in her despair she replied, "I think it's best we quit trying."

She did not believe it was a punishment. Yet in the early morning hours when she awoke to the sound of the cattle or sheep she lay in the darkness and wished she could pray.

'To believe in some greater force would be a comfort,' she reflected. To realize there was nothing to be relied upon except one's own strength was a heavy burden to shoulder. She faced it resolutely and went forward.

She took comfort in noting that God's followers seemed poor things, their behavior often reflecting an intolerance and suspicion abhorrent to her. She determined that at Stridheim there would be no religion, only honor and truth. Valdis would be raised to believe in these. She felt it her calling, made it her occupation.

Valdis was her reward. An easy child, she spent her days playing in the yard or the fields surrounding it. She trailed after Jorunn at times, curious and eager for instruction in the many tasks that filled her mother's day. When there was time Jorunn included her daughter in her work, letting the little girl draw ineffectually on the cow's teat, watching her delight when a small stream of milk dribbled into the bucket. Then the cow would shift impatiently and Jorunn would send Valdis away. "Run along now, and play in the meadow. Fashion a wreath for me from the dandelions growing there," she would instruct, her affection for the child obliterated by the sense of urgency that always accompanied Jorunn.

The little girl would scamper away, to later reappear, eager to knead the loaves Jorunn baked. But time was scarce. It was virtually impossible for Jorunn to accomplish all the tasks necessary in one short day, and she would send the child away. "The wreath is beautiful, *jenta mi.* Leave it there, on the table. I'll wear it for you later. Now I have to hurry. It's soon dinner, and if we're to eat bread this better be finished quickly."

Valdis wanted to stay. She longed to bake her own small loaf, as she sometimes was allowed. But more than that she wanted to be a good girl, to please her mother. She wandered away, to circle the yard and search her mind for an idea with which to entertain herself. It was the way she spent most days.

Each night, as Jorunn tucked her daughter beneath crisp white linen, she would reflect on how good and perfect the child was. Aloud she would say, "You're the best little girl in the whole world, *skatten min,*" and Valdis would squirm with pleasure. She would drift into sleep in a hazy glow of satisfaction that she had pleased her mother.

If an image could reflect reality, then Valdis embodied goodness and beauty. Her hair was like spun gold. Her blue eyes were clear and set wide apart in her round face. Her cheeks were soft and ripely full, her mouth generous. Once, when they walked together after their child in the wake of a fine summer rain, Erland pointed to a rainbow that shimmered in the distance. "She's like that," he said.

"*Det er sant,*" Jorunn agreed. "Bright, a mirage of lovely colors melded together to one perfect image. But always distant. The inner workings of Valdis' mind are as elusive as the gold at the end of the rainbow."

He looked at Jorunn, his surprise obvious. Yet he did not deny there was truth in her observation.

"She's everything to us, Erland, but we can't be everything to her," Jorunn said gravely one afternoon during Valdis' eighth summer. "She needs the company of other children, one day she'll want a husband and family of her own. These things we can't give her."

"I can't abide the idea she'll pay a price for our ways," Erland said gravely, "but I can't see life any different."

Jorunn frowned as they followed Valdis through the summer field. "There's time, she's young yet. We'll find a way."

In the dry months of that winter Erland carried his saw into the forest for the first time in many years. For a long while warm summers and sufficient rainfall had made prosperity an easy thing, there had been no cause to fell timber. When he returned that first afternoon Jorunn met him in the yard, lifted her face for his ready kiss, and asked with a smile,

"What nymph calls you to the forest? The larders are full, the buildings in good shape. What causes you to turn to logging again?"

Linking an arm around her shoulders Erland walked with her toward the house. "It's a man's business, *kona mi*, not a woman's concern," he teased.

At the porch she stopped and pulled away, seizing the broom that leaned in the corner and turning to face him. "Tell me, or suffer the consequences," she laughed, shaking the broom at him.

"Have mercy," he pleaded. "I'll tell you everything if you'll let me be." He hung his head in mock dejection. "I'm a poor excuse for a man. Good thing we're shunned by folks for miles around, so my shame's a secret."

Laughing softly she leaned the broom in the corner and sat on the porch bench, gesturing for him to sit beside her. He pulled her close and they sat to watch the early winter moon rising over the treetops, bathing the yard in pale light. As the night deepened, so did his mood. The lighthearted banter of moments before darkened into despair.

"Valdis has to go away, to my brother and his wife in Christiania," Erland said, his voice quiet in the evening. "I got to get money for her passage, and keep."

In the dim light shock registered clearly in Jorunn's face. "What are you saying? Have you lost your wits? How can you suggest we send our child away?" she demanded. "You love her more than life itself, of that I'm certain. What possible reason could you have for sending her away?"

"If I didn't love her so much I couldn't do it," he answered, his voice grating and raw with pain. "Knowin' she'll have a better life away from me is all's keepin' me goin'. Woman, listen to me. We got no choice, we made up our minds to live the way we saw fit, not thinkin' about what was goin' to happen a ways down the road. If there's one thing I've learned about life, there's always a price to be paid for just livin'. Time's come for us to pay up."

He took her hand and squeezed it, the calluses on his palm pressing into her flesh. "She's got no friends. Your people don't claim her. The only family she'll ever have is us; one day we'll be gone and she'll be alone. I can't do that to her."

Jorunn was quiet, silenced by the ache in her heart at knowing he spoke the truth. He continued in a quiet voice.

"My brother's got no children, only a heap of money. He married the only daughter of a rich man, but she can't bear. She's ailin', and he writes she'd be glad of the company of our girl. They'll care for her like their own, Jorunn. She'll go to a fine school, meet with folks her own age. One day she'll be wed and have a family. That's what I want for Valdis. Here she'll be...."

"Don't say it!" Jorunn cried in interruption. "I can't bear to hear the words." She dropped her face into her hands. At last she lifted her head and pleaded, "Not now, she doesn't have to go now. She's only eight; a few more years can't matter."

He brushed her damp cheek with a callused hand. "Not yet, then. In a year. I got to have money for her keep, and a dowry. That's what I'm workin' for."

Jorunn nodded. The quiet of the night at Stridheim was unrelieved, enveloping her, suffocating her. She thought of Valdis, consumed by the solitude of life here. "We have to do this. We've chosen our way, we have to find one for our daughter," she said in resignation, her voice heavy with despair.

In February the weather turned mild and Erland began to anticipate the thaw. He hoped to begin early transport of the logs he had felled. When the ice broke on Glomma he would send the wood toward Fredrikstad, he planned, and with this aim in mind he began to walk the forest, crossing from his land to Ellefsson's, where there were men in steady employ logging and transporting his neighbor's timber.

A short distance down river he encountered the first group of loggers, but his inquiries regarding transport of his timber fell on deaf ears. None of the men would speak with him. Later, in other groups, some turned their back to him when he approached. "Workin' for Ellefsson," was the standard reply as Erland approached. Others merely refused to answer his queries.

After two days of tramping up and down the banks of the Glomma, Erland Halvorsson hitched his wagon and rode northwest, through the forest, toward Ellefsson's place. As he passed deeper into his neighbor's property he came upon great areas of cleared land. It was apparent Gunnar Ellefsson had prioritized timber to farming these past years. Erland Halvorsson was a farmer in his soul, to the very depths of him. For him it was unthinkable to let the land lie fallow year after year while plundering the forest instead, yet it was obvious, as he rode into the courtyard of Ellefsson, this was his chosen course.

Situated at the center of the yard was a fine new house, one Erland did not know had been raised. Climbing from the wagon he approached the door. As he neared it was opened; Ellefsson stepped out.

He stared at Erland without greeting; the look of him told Erland he was unwelcome. He realized his day's errand would be wasted.

"I come to ask if you'd hire out some o' your loggers. Some got nothin' to do, I need transport for my timber."

Ellefsson appeared to weigh the request. Then his face hardened and he replied, "*Nei*, I won't do it. They're my men, they work for me. Anyways, like as not none of 'em would work for you. Heretics ain't likely to prosper from the sweat o' my men's brows."

Color suffused Erland's face, anger coursed in his veins. Ellefsson back away, fumbling for the door behind him. It appeared Halvorsson was beyond control. Then Erland turned and leapt back onto the wagon. From his position high above Ellefsson he looked down. "I know full well folks think I'm heretic. And I know where the lie started. It's a curiosity, and somethin' I think about. I figure any man as God-fearin' as you profess to be got to know that to break one of the Lord's commandments is to wind up in the fires of hell, but in bearin' false witness against your neighbor, that's just what you've done. I know the price I'm supposed to have sold my soul for. I wonder, what did you get for yours?"

He cracked the reins and rode out of the cobbled yard, the horse's hooves heavy on the stones.

Erland's anger and frustration stayed with him all that day, and the next, as he returned to his forest to inspect the piles of timber that lay waiting for transport. In the afternoon he crossed from the wood to the banks of the river and stood staring at the ice covering the water rushing below. Feverishly he searched for a way. He must somehow find the money to send Valdis to a new life. He paced up and down the bank, his mind exploring new channels. As twilight began to thicken the air the thought occurred that across the river there lay a farm belonging to Magna Gustavsson, a man reputed to be fair, and generous. His farm sloped away from the valley, few people in Dal knew him well. In Erland's ventures downriver he had noticed old clearings from earlier logging on the man's property. This man might know of a logging crew that would help him float his timber to the mill.

Looking heavenward Erland judged there to be at least an hour of daylight remaining. Loathe to return home and waste yet another day he determined to cross the river and search from one of the old clearings for a path leading to Magna Gustavsson's yard.

The river spanned less than one hundred yards at the point where he stood. So early in the season he judged it to be frozen fairly solid. He searched until he found a large stone and with both hands he lifted, heaving it onto the ice. It landed with a satisfying thud. Erland stepped onto the ice to cross.

Midway he heard a creak and his heart raced. 'Air pocket,' he thought, dropping flat and spread-eagled to more evenly distribute his weight. He could feel the ice beneath him rise and fall with sickening clarity. He carefully shifted his weight to his knees in order to crawl to the other side. A few more yards, and he dared breathe easier. The bank loomed ever closer. At the forest edge an owl hooted and his heart stood still. The ice creaked, then gave way with a thunderous groan.

The water was icy for only an instant. Blackness enveloped him in the next heartbeat. The water beneath the ice was running swift and clear, carrying him away.

Nine

CRUCIBLE

❧ In the logging camps the spring of 1860 the tale of Erland Halvorsson was often repeated. As a warning, sometimes, but the men who worked the river were of the sort who found such a story entertaining as well.

It was early in April that one of them came through the forest, following the path from the clearing where Erland's timber still lay, to the yard at Stridheim. Standing just inside the fence he looked about appraisingly. Erland Halvorsson was obviously a man of means. It puzzled him that a prosperous farmer would try to float timber, but he was not a thinking man. He dismissed the idea and set about his errand.

He crossed the yard and entered the barn, taking stock of the size of the farm and a quick guess at the number of livestock kept. His mouth twisted in a grin as he realized there was even more wealth here than he had first supposed.

A noise startled him and he moved quickly into shadow. From the bright light outside a woman stepped into the darkness of the barn. A scarf covered her head, but from the fleeting glimpse he judged her to be fair of face. The situation became more appealing with each passing moment.

The woman walked toward the nearest stall, opened the door and led a cow to the space near where the man stood. Placing a pail of food in front of the animal, she pulled a stool from the corner and crouched beneath the cow to milk. He watched her slender figure from the shadows. In his groin he felt a stirring. He decided he would approach her sooner, rather than later.

Stepping from the shadow to stand a few feet behind her he cleared his throat and said, "G'day, ma'am. I'd like a word with you 'bout that timber you got layin' in the forest."

Jorunn started, squeezing the cow's teat unmercifully, causing the animal to kick in retribution. The pail overturned, the milk running over her boot, trickling warm and sticky through the laces.

Rising quickly and turning in irritation she demanded, "What are you doing on my property? How dare you follow me in here without making your presence known? Get off my land! That timber isn't for sale, like I've told you all before. Now get off!" Her blue eyes blazed and the scarf slipped off the back of her head. As he watched her the stirring he felt turned painfully hard. Her anger was palpable from where she stood before him.

He smiled, his teeth showing yellow in his shaggy beard. He stepped closer saying, "What'll you do with a load o' timber and no husband to log it or float it? Seems to me you need a man 'round the place. Why don't we go inside and talk it over?" His lips stretched wider; his dark eyes glittered in the dim light of the barn.

Jorunn pulled herself to her full height, unwilling to take the step back she longed for in order to put more space between them. "There's nothing to discuss. I've no wish to have you here. I asked you to leave." She lifted her chin as she spoke, staring straight into his dark eyes. Something flickered in their depths and she caught her breath. Evil sparked there, pure and undiluted. In a split second she knew to be afraid.

Whirling she reached out blindly in search of a weapon. Her hands fumbled with the handles of farm implements she encountered leaning against the rough timber wall. Grasping one at random she swung around unseeing, every atom of her strength concentrated in her swing.

With the agility of a cat the man ducked and came back up laughing as she staggered and fell from the momentum of her swing. She scrambled backward in the soft dirt and hay, retreating under his steady approach. She felt the wall behind her and knew she was trapped. She drew breath in ragged gasps, transfixed in horror as he stood above her fumbling with the laces of his britches.

The leather gave way beneath his clumsy fingers and he fell on top of her. His wet mouth sought hers and she turned her face away, feeling his hot tongue squirm against her cheek. Her slight frame was no match for the strength in his wiry limbs. He pinned her easily beneath the weight of him, dragging up her heavy skirt, tearing at the fabric of her drawers.

Suddenly the mist before her eyes cleared and she focused on the tools stacked carelessly beside her in the corner where she lay. She saw the shears, the metal shining dully in the dim light. Without thought she lifted both arms above her head and stretched, grasping the round wooden handles in both palms.

Between her legs the man paused, sensing the change in her position. He lifted himself off her upper body, supporting his weight on his forearms, looking up just as the shears came slicing downward. Jorunn scarcely felt resistance, and marveled at how easily they pierced his neck. He fell heavily upon her, the handles twisting in her grasp.

In horror she fought to remove the weight of him. She heard screams, and realized they were her own. With every ounce of strength she possessed she pushed at his body until at last she was free. She rolled over, dragging herself up against the wall. 'Such a lot of blood,' she wondered dazedly as she looked down at the front of her dress where dirt and hay matted in a vile paste.

"*Mamma, Mamma!* Did you cry out?" Valdis called from the house where she was put to work knitting. The alarm in her child's voice settled an icy calm over Jorunn.

"All's well, Valdis," she called out quickly, stepping back into the darkness of the barn. "The cow has kicked and spilled the milk, that's all," she lied, her voice cool and smooth. "Return to the knitting or we'll both go naked this winter," she finished, one part of her mind marveling at her own calm as she stood staring into the open eyes of the man she had murdered. A great well of his blood seeped around the shears where they punctured his throat and pooled beneath him, almost black in the soil.

Instinct gave her clear instruction. She must hide this man, and well, until she could devise a plan. Grabbing both booted feet she attempted to drag him, grunting under the weight of him. She would not come far in this manner. Dropping his legs she turned her back and lifted his feet again, tucking them beneath her arms and pulling with all her might. At the second stall she was winded, shaking from shock and exertion.

Opening the door to the stall she dragged him inside. From the corner she fetched a pitchfork and tossed mounds of hay over his body. As he disappeared beneath the yellow mound, fury at what he had done overwhelmed her. In a last surge of energy she lifted the fork and plunged it through the straw, feeling it strike the body below.

Returning to the barn door she looked out at the well in the center of the yard. She dared not go there. Looking around she thought of the water trough that ran along the side of the barn, filled to the brim from showers this past week. Untying the laces at her bodice she stripped away the cloth that was already drying stiff. She raised her arms to peel away her blood-soaked shift, then quickly removed her boots and stockings. She made her stealthy way around the building to the trough. She lay down in it slowly, bracing herself against the cold water. An icy calm gripped her. She lay there for as long as she dared, her arms crossed over her bare breasts, her hair floating around her, staring up at the clean blue sky. She wondered if Erland floated somewhere now, or lay on Glomma's rocky bed, his body and mind as cold and dead as hers.

❧ ❧ ❧

That night she waited until the moon rose to give her light before she left the house and made her stealthy way to the barn. She opened the door carefully, its creak loud in the still night. The animals stirred, and she cringed at their noises of protest. She stayed still for some time. There was no sound or movement from the house. Valdis slept the deep and untroubled sleep of innocence.

In the barn she approached the stall where the man lay and made quick work of what she knew must be accomplished. With bare hands she raked the straw away until she came to his body, cold and stiff already. Tying a rope about his waist, she tossed one end over the rafter and attached it to Blakken, the horse that made half of Erland's team.

"Pull," she commanded in a low voice, leading Blakken at his head. He did his job well. The body of her attacker rose eerily from the hay and hung suspended in the air while she maneuvered the cart into the stall and positioned it beneath him. Returning to where Blakken stood obediently holding his load she looked back at the corpse hanging illuminated in the clear moonlight, searching for remorse, even revulsion.

She felt nothing. Since Erland's death she was frozen in time, as removed from life and living as Erland, as remote as Valdis. The days passed in a chill fog, each one filled with duties practical in nature. This night's work struck her as only another necessity.

With a quick movement she pulled on the knot attached to Blakken's harness and watched the body fall with a thud onto the cart below.

They drove into the wood, she and her willing accomplice, Blakken. Into blackness, where the trees overhead shut out the moonlight and the horse found his way only by habit and smell. She let him have his rein, her trust in him implicit.

When he nosed his way into the clearing the white light of the moon seemed as bright as a midday. She maneuvered the cart toward the river and dumped the body without hesitation, watching as the silent stream swallowed her victim with scarcely a ripple. She returned home with nothing more than a pleasant feeling of satisfaction at a task well completed.

The next days she spent thinking carefully, assiduously, over the story she would tell if someone came looking. There was not a trace left after the man, of that she was certain. She might simply deny he had been there at all. Yet she occupied her mind weaving tales to be told in the eventuality someone came looking for him. Some of her stories were amusing, and made her grin. At times she caught Valdis watching her curiously, and she would hastily rearrange her features into customary repose. Since Erland's death the child was even more introspective and withdrawn than usual, and Jorunn sensed she need not fear her curiosity. If Valdis noticed anything untoward it would remain locked inside her self-contained daughter.

A full two months passed before Jorunn heard the sound of a rider on the road leading to Stridheim. She stood in the kitchen kneading bread in a great wooden trowel, watching through the window the antics of a gray squirrel in the elm tree that stretched it's long limbs protectively over the yard. That day, for the first time since she'd been brought news of Erland, a feeling of peace was within her.

When the faint sound of hooves in the distance carried through the open window she felt the hair on her arms rise and a chill descend upon her in spite of the fire in the oven and the heat of summer midday. She paused in her labor, then continued resolutely. As the sounds of approach grew

nearer the chill spread, numbing her. She stopped her kneading, her icy fingers refusing to continue their ministrations to
the dough. On shaking legs she crossed to the sitting room
window which afforded her a view of the meadow below the
house. In the distance she could see Valdis' fair hair shimmer
in the bright sunlight. The child sat weaving a wreath of summer flowers, bright yellow and blue.

The sound of a horse whinnying in the courtyard caused
her heart to knock hard against her ribs. She grasped the window sill and held fast. The creak of leather heralded the dis-
mount of the rider, yet the quick rap on the door that followed
startled her such that she cried out softly. Taking deep, gulp-
ing breaths to steady herself she crossed to answer, rehearsing
once again the story she had perfected. In her distress the
stories merged and she could make sense of none of them.
She turned back one last time, toward the window, for a final
look at Valdis. Another rap, this time more insistent, and she
knew this could not be postponed.

Squaring her shoulders she crossed the room with even
strides. Grasping the handle and pressing the release she
swung the door back and stood straight to face her accuser.

The sun was high overhead and shone down on the man
who stood there, transforming from russet to blond the hair
that waved away from a smooth clear brow. Blue eyes were set
wide in a broad face, his nose was straight and fine. A thick
beard covered the angles of his jaw and partially concealed
the fullness of his mouth, but staring full into his face Jorunn
knew exactly how he looked without it. In her mind she had
traced those lips with a gentle finger a thousand times these
past weeks. The same lips she had kissed in her dreams this
very night.

The impossibility of the situation overwhelmed her and
she feared she must be mad. Blackness hovered above. Looking upward she went readily to meet it, content to be released
from consciousness and the enormity of her predicament.

Ten

TRIBULATION

✤ Erland. These many months she had lain awake nights
envisioning him lost, frozen, lying along the banks of Glomma
or deep in the icy waters. His body had not been recovered,
an impossibility before the thaw, and unlikely after. The idea
that he had had no burial tormented her every day since
his death. Yet this very day he had appeared to stand on the
threshold.

"I am aggrieved at the distress I've caused you. It was never
my intent. Upon receiving your letter I rode out straight away,
with no thought to write first."

The voice, that same deep timbre, yet the words were
wrong. Not the softly slurred vowels of the valley, but the clean,
crisp sounds of the city. A familiar rhythm, her mother's pre-
cise speech. This man hailed from Christiania.

Jorunn shook her head and answered, "It's not your fault.
It's your resemblance to your brother that unnerved me.
Erland never said." She was strangely disoriented, suspended
somewhere between the past and this new reality, as if she balanced on a precipice. Desperately Jorunn struggled to find
solid ground, and all the while his voice continued to wreak
havoc with her senses.

"We thought nothing of it, the two of us," he said. Others
remarked upon it, yet we were so different by nature that we
were usually unaware that our physical resemblance was so
striking."

This man across from her looked so uncannily like her Erland. Her heart ached all the while her eyes feasted on his countenance.

"I didn't think you would come. I wrote that there can be no burial. We haven't...."

Jorunn's voice broke. She looked down at where her hands rested on the table, and was surprised when Egil Halvorsson reached across and covered them with his own. It was a hand very like Erland's, broad over the palm, strong fingers, yet soft where Erland's had been callused.

"I know this is difficult. It is why I have come. While we cannot lay Erland's body to rest, we must put his affairs in order. Have you thought what you will do now? Will you return to your family?"

Jorunn started in surprise. She thought briefly, without regret, of the breach which loomed wide between her and her family. She had neither seen nor spoken with her people since Valdis' birth eight years ago, yet her world, while Erland lived, had been complete. For twelve years they had shared one life, exploring avenues of marriage she had not dreamed existed when they first entered their union. He had become the other half of her, making her whole for the first time. Since his death she grieved, not only for loss of Erland, but for the death of part of herself. She was cleaved asunder. Each day she woke and plunged into her duties as Mistress of Stridheim in desperate attempt to cling to life. Every task comforted her in some small measure. The solid security of the land beneath her boots as she crossed the fields and meadows grounded her. She clung to this place, her place now. Stridheim was all that was left of the life she had made for herself, for Erland's death seemed to have severed the slender thread that connected her to Valdis. The child was locked away behind an exquisite facade, unapproachable, unreachable. Jorunn floundered, alone. Fear assailed her and she beat it back into the dark corner of her mind to which she banished such things and held tenaciously to the only thing she had left.

"I'll surely not return to Valgaard. This is my home now, and has been these past twelve years. I belong here, on Stridheim. I'm staying here."

After a silence Egil Halvorsson spoke. "And do what? You have no sons, no man to run this farm. Already it is June and there are no crops planted."

Jorunn stared at him, watching as he chose each word with measured precision. So like Erland, yet different in his core, she sensed.

"Not this year, but our stores are plentiful. There's enough to feed the livestock through the winter. Next year I'll plant."

"That is a task too great for a woman. The acres Erland has cultivated are many, far greater than when I left. The farm appears too great for even one man to tend. Is there someone who works the land with my brother."

"There's no one," she answered. "The prosperity and growth of Stridheim are the result of Erland's labor alone. He was a good man, and industrious. 'A farmer in his blood and bones,' he used to say. And he was as ambitious for Stridheim as you've been for yourself," she finished, lifting her head proudly.

Egil frowned. "You imply I have not cared for Stridheim. It is true I left to make my way in the capitol; it is right that my calling at that time was another one. Erland was always intended to have this farm; it was only by accident of birth I stood in line to inherit. We knew Erland loved the land and could make it prosper far greater than I could. I left of my own accord, yet I left because it was the right thing for Stridheim, and Erland, too. My course was to meet the future head-on, to carve a place for my fellowman in the future of Norway. Farmers like my brother, and my childhood friends, need a voice in governing our land. They must be allowed to exercise their right to protect their farms, their interests. I went to the city to campaign for my own cause, it is true; I would protect Stridheim. Yet in truth my brother and I shared the same cause—to keep our place strong. We merely went about accomplishing our goal in different ways."

Jorunn listened carefully as he spoke. She was uneasy, sensing there was a purpose in this man's visit that he had not spoken.

"Then you did an honorable thing, the right thing for everyone," she replied. "As you can see, Stridheim has flourished, and I've been by Erland's side all the while. I'll continue to run the farm just as Erland has. I'll hire a man to help. Maybe two...." At the look of him she faltered.

"There will be no need for you to concern yourself with the running of Stridheim," he interrupted. "It is my duty to take over the farm. I am already planning for it." His face hardened, the resemblance to Erland dimming.

"But you're busy with your affairs in Christiania!" Jorunn cried incredulously. "Not only are you active in politics, but Erland said you own a large mercantile, and that one day you'll take over your father-in-law's business affairs. You don't need Stridheim; you have no time for it." Concern etched lines in her face. Then she added simply, "It's all I have."

"Surely that is untrue. You have your family. I am certain they will be relieved to have you home, safe with them once again. I will, of course, give you ample compensation for the improvements you have shared the burden of making here. The yard is finer than I ever imagined, this house is solid and good. You have been a good mistress to Stridheim. You shall not go unrewarded for the care you have taken."

Angry spots of color rose to Jorunn's face and her voice shook as she spoke, "There's no cause for you to reward me for the labor I've invested in my own place. I won't be leaving it."

"You have no choice. It is mine by right. The shift in ownership from myself to Erland was never official. If Erland had a son to inherit, the situation might appear different, but a girl-child has no claim to this land. I will settle a sum for her, but I will not pass to her my birthright. When she marries this farm would fall from my family, and the land that was my father's, and his father's before him, for a thousand years, would be lost. It is my duty to return to steward this land."

"Don't you consider Valdis family? She's your brother's flesh and blood. She meant more to him than his own life. Do you mean to say she's of lesser regard than a male child would have been?" Jorunn cried. "You profess to be liberal in your way of thinking, to fight for the interest of your fellow-man. What, then, of women? Does your idea of egalitarian society encompass only your brethren? Have you no sense of duty to the rest of us?"

Then she lashed out, "In any case, you've no son either, and according to Erland no prospect of one, with that ailing wife. Valdis is all you have, and she's mine!"

Her chest heaving, anger causing her blood to rush in her ears, she stared at him, this man who threatened her very existence. She saw him pale and felt triumph.

At last he answered, "You are wrong. I still have hope."

She rose and crossed to the door, holding it wide. "Then *I* hope you have some measure of comfort from it, because it's all you'll ever have of this place. Take it and leave. I won't have you in my home."

She was shaking with anger, but stood firm, resolute. He passed her, turning in the courtyard to say, "I leave for now, but make no mistake, I shall return. I am of this land and it calls me back. It is mine, and I shall reclaim it. You must use these next days to accustom yourself to the idea, and make plans for yourself and your daughter. In a fortnight I return. We shall reach an agreement at that time."

The echo of the door slamming reverberated around the yard, and she had the satisfaction of seeing the horse rear as he mounted and steadied the animal with some difficulty.

Eleven

INSPIRATION

✤ The next fourteen days Jorunn spent every waking moment searching for some solution to her situation, and at night she dreamt. Of Erland, that he was alive and back with her, or that he lay frozen and lost to her under the waters of Glomma. She dreamt of rolling acres of grain on the hills of Stridheim, or of black earth sodden and left to lie fallow. She dreamt of Valdis, beautiful and perfect, or Valdis lost to her as she searched in vain to find her. All the while precious time elapsed, and she was no closer to finding her way from the predicament.

'A son,' she sighed. 'If only one of our sons had lived, surely Egil wouldn't have thought to reclaim the land.'

At the thought guilt rose up and warred with her desperation. Every day of her life she pined for the sons she had buried. Valdis was her mainstay, yet even as an infant, more so as a child, she was inexplicably removed from Jorunn. When Erland lived Jorunn maintained a connection with her daughter through him. He had seemed to possess an instinctive understanding of their beautiful, aloof child. Jorunn often experienced the sensation of reaching out greedily for something Valdis did not understand and was incapable of returning. The child remained distant in spite of Jorunn's hungry advances. She had, at length, learned to accept her daughter as such, but silently, in her hidden heart, she carried a yearning for a son who would quench the fires of longing, douse the embers still glowing in the wake of Harald's death.

When her anger faded she came to terms with the idea that Egil could, in fact, reclaim the land as his own. By law she was due recompense, but cultivated land was passed from father to first son. She was in every way at the mercy of Egil Halvorsson.

Yet he struck her as a fair man. His decision to reclaim the land was not unreasonable, merely unexpected. Erland had described his brother as ambitious, called to politics and government, employed in trade. According to Erland, Egil's career had been successful even beyond his expectations, and in marriage, too, he had been ambitious. His own fortune secure, one day he would inherit the fortune due his wife. He would be a wealthy man. Knowing this Jorunn had assumed Egil Halvorsson would have no interest in Stridheim. She had not suspected he would feel a call to the land. She had not supposed he would assume it his duty to return.

It was in this miscalculation her peril lay. She had made no plan for the eventuality she might be sent from Stridheim. Her family were as strangers to her. Together with the rest of the inhabitants of Dal they shunned her. In part because of her association with Erland, who had been considered heretic, but also because she flaunted the code which ruled their society. She had not crossed the threshold of a church since the day she quarreled with her mother. The hypocrisy and unchristian attitudes Astrid had displayed had so infuriated her she'd vowed never to associate with such pious fools again. If she worshipped at all it had been in the forest and fields. When she walked there she sensed a presence near, and was at peace, at one with nature and the forces that ruled her existence on Stridheim. In the breeze she had long ago heard the still, small voice of God; she imagined that even now, if she had been of a mind to, she might hear it again. Never had she longed for the company of others, nor did she desire it now. Yet if she must leave Stridheim there was no choice for her except to appeal to her mother for forgiveness.

The strength to do this was beyond her. All her life Jorunn had felt equal to any challenge, yet this one thing she knew she could not accomplish on her own. For the first time in years she wished she could pray. She left the house and crossed the yard, climbed the mountain that separated her father's land from her own. From the top of the mountain she looked down on Valgaard. The fields were planted and spread in a neat patchwork below. The yard was neat and in good repair.

She readied for her descent. She turned to look back one last time at Stridheim. Her land lay spread before her, acres of rich earth, deep forests of pine. She studied the yard and buildings from her vantage high above and felt pride buoy her. She was mistress of this place. In twelve years she had stamped Stridheim indelibly with her mark; in turn it had become part of the weave of her. The spirit of this land intertwined with her very soul and was inextricable. In this she found the strength to go forward, to do what must be done.

The breeze that had cooled her during her climb blew stronger now, gusting and swirling, tugging at her skirt. Suddenly a passage long forgotten sprang to mind. 'He said, Go forth, and stand upon the mount before the Lord. And behold, the Lord passed by, and a great and strong wind rent the mountains, and brake in pieces the rocks before the Lord; but the Lord was not in the wind: And after the wind an earthquake: but the Lord was not in the earthquake: And after the earthquake a fire; but the Lord was not in the fire: And after the fire a still small voice.'

In the wake of the memory she heard the words, 'A son.' They echoed in her mind, whirling around her consciousness. She stood quite still, listened until she understood their meaning.

She lifted her face heavenward, to the sun, blinded by its white glare. In that moment of blindness she found enlightenment. A son would be the salvation of her. Erland's son she could never bear, but Egil was of the same flesh and blood. A son by him would secure her future. In a flash of clarity she knew what must be done.

Turning, she retraced her steps down the mountain toward Stridheim. Her land, her farm, her home; its call to her was undeniable.

Twelve

HEARKENING

At the end of the fourteen days Egil returned. Jorunn was in the kitchen when the sound of his horse stepping on gravel alerted her to his arrival. Hastily she ladled juices over the leg of lamb and returned it to the oven. The potatoes were bubbling, turning light brown. The bread she had baked that morning cooled near the window.

Hurrying to the bedroom she removed the scarf that covered her fair hair and lifted her hands to smooth it from her face. Staring into the glass that hung on one wall she noted that her cheeks were flushed from the heat of the oven. Her eyes shone with new purpose, their color heightened by the blue of her dress. Quickly she removed her apron. When the rap she expected reverberated through the hall she drew a deep breath and sailed toward the door with confidence born of knowing that at least in her appearance he would find nothing objectionable.

Pulling open the door she said, "Egil, so good to see you. Come in, won't you? We've been waiting." Her voice was warm and resonant, she consciously mimicked the formal manners her mother had insisted she and her sisters practice in the vague hope they should achieve a better station in life than farmer's wife.

Surprise registered clearly on his face as he entered the hall. Jorunn held out her hands for his hat, while she called upstairs, "Valdis, come down at once! Your Uncle Egil is here. You must make him welcome."

Together they stood in the hall, looking upward to watch Valdis' hesitant descent. Always shy, since Erland's death the girl had withdrawn and was reluctant to make an appearance, yet Jorunn had insisted, and was glad now she had. Daring to glance at his face Jorunn relished the shock she saw register there. Even the close proximity of daily living did not dull the effect of Valdis' beauty. Seen for the first time it was breathtaking.

Valdis stopped in front of her uncle to curtsy, her eyes trained shyly to the floor. Her hair slipped over her shoulders, shimmering white and gold in the light from small windows that framed the door.

Egil turned to Jorunn in silent astonishment, and she bit her lower lip to hide her smile of satisfaction. Valdis' role in Jorunn's play was to unsettle this man; she had done her part well.

"Come and rest, you must be thirsty after your ride. Valdis, bring your uncle a stein of beer from the keg lying cool at the base of the cellar steps," she directed, and turned to lead him to the sitting room. She noted that his eyes followed Valdis as she disappeared through the kitchen door.

"She's beautiful," he stated flatly. "Erland never said. I had no idea. I realized he judged the company of local youth to be unacceptable, but I did not think why. It is now clear."

"It's not her beauty that sets her apart, I think, but her mind," Jorunn replied coolly, keeping her voice carefully clear and melodious. "Erland thought it his duty to educate her himself. She's clever, as he was."

Egil nodded, "We shall certainly see to her education. There are fine schools for young ladies in Christiania. I shall make it my business to secure for her a place at one of them. And she shall have an ample dowry. Although in her case she would likely make a fine match even without it."

Jorunn gestured for Egil to be seated in the chair that had been his brother's, while she rested on the sofa placed opposite. Looking down at her hands, her gaze hidden, she replied softly, "I'm sure you'll be generous. I've never doubted that."

There was a pause. Egil shifted uncomfortably. "I realize I handled our first meeting badly," he began. "I must have appeared uncharitable. It was never my intention to turn you and your daughter from Stridheim without first making your position secure another place."

Looking him full in the face Jorunn replied honestly, "I sensed you were a fair man. On reflection I understand your position. Let's go forward from this point rather than look back at what can't be changed."

Egil nodded, his relief obvious.

Valdis returned with a brimming stein, and the rest of the afternoon was passed in conversation and enjoyment of the meal Jorunn had so carefully prepared. It was late when Egil finally broached the subject of the business which brought him.

"I understand you have no wish to return to your family. Yet it would not be appropriate for you to stay here. I must live here for the months of planting, and during the harvest, at the very least. My suggestion is that you find a suitable house in the village, and I shall arrange for its purchase."

Jorunn lowered her glance to the cloth covering the table, pretending to study the weave closely. "How generous of you," she murmured, keeping her voice purposefully gentle.

"I shall provide for you an allowance as well, or if you prefer, a lump sum to be settled at once. If you do not feel comfortable managing the sum you might find the allowance preferable."

Two spots of color appeared high on each cheekbone in Jorunn's face. She burned with anger, but bit her lip and deferred from comment.

"In regard to the child, from talking with her I realize you do not overestimate her intelligence. She is clever. And she is of a sweet disposition, as Erland wrote when he asked if she might come to stay as companion to my wife. I feel certain Berit would benefit greatly from the company of Valdis. I suggest the child come to live with us now. We shall treat her as our own daughter. She shall have the best of everything we can offer."

Jorunn lifted her eyes, reigning in her temper with great difficulty, and said as calmly as possible, "I know your offer is made in kindness, and surely, in a year or two, Valdis must come to you, like her father planned. But I can't be without her now. She has to stay with me a while longer."

Egil paused, appearing to weigh the subject carefully. "I do not think that wise. The child needs to continue her education, and you will be busy beginning a new life. You are young yet, and will undoubtedly find happiness again with another man. It will be best if you are independent."

The anger Jorunn had barely contained flared and she retorted, "I have no interest in another husband, not now, not ever." With difficulty she controlled the urge to tell this man to mind his own affairs. If she was to secure her future with him she would have to remain on the best of terms with him, at least for a while to come.

"Perhaps not," he apologized. "No insult was intended. I only meant to say that you are young, and attractive." He fumbled for words, obviously disconcerted. "I am sure there will be many offers made to you in the future. I would not think ill of you if you chose not to spend the rest of your days pining for my brother."

Even in her anger she registered satisfaction. He had noticed her, of that she was certain. The way to her future might not be so difficult as she first imagined.

Turning her mind to her aim, she smoothed her face and kept her voice glossy. "There's one matter of business which I think needs your immediate attention," she began. "In the forest, near the banks of Glomma, there's a load of timber already felled and ready to be transported to the mill. There've been some inquiries, one from my neighbor Gunnar Ellefsson, but I don't trust him and wouldn't give him an answer. I was hoping you might stay with us a while and see to that, and a few other things. Is your wife anxious for your return?" she asked, lifting one brow in question, studying his reaction carefully.

Clearing his throat he answered, "No, she will be well looked after in my absence. As you know, she is not well. She spends time resting, and is engaged in church service. I shall not be missed."

Jorunn smiled warmly and said, "You'll stay with us, then. We have plenty of room, and it will be more convenient for you to be near."

After only a moment's hesitation he replied, "In that case I accept. I would like to see Stridheim in closer detail. The place is so changed I hardly recognized it. You must show me everything."

"My pleasure," she said, her voice silky with satisfaction. "The evening's mild; the light's good. As you say, Stridheim has grown and expanded. It'll take time for you to cover everything. You'll have to stay with us a week, at least. Maybe longer. There's a lot to be accomplished, things a woman can't do alone."

In the courtyard she slipped her arm through his and led him down the path toward the river.

ℰ   ℰ   ℰ

In those first days of Egil's stay Jorunn was surprised to find that in the five months since Erland's death the buildings had begun to fall into a state of disrepair. Without constant vigilance Stridheim would deteriorate quickly. For the first time she felt responsibility for the place rest heavy on her shoulders.

"Don't think about that now," she muttered to herself as she crouched under the cow milking. The bucket was soon full, and she rose to remove it. Frothy white bubbles sloshed over the side as she lifted it and replaced it with another. Streams of milk splashing against the tin were accompanied by the rhythm of sounds Egil made as he lifted great forkfuls of hay. She watched him covertly. His movements were mesmerizing. With his back to her she could easily imagine him to be Erland. The same lithe figure, a similar bearing. At first the resemblance had caused her pain, but of late she felt a fascination in it. Often she felt her eyes drawn to where he worked, distracted from her own tasks and the singleness of purpose with which she planned.

She squeezed her eyes shut and focused on what must be done. Before the time elapsed when the farm was brought to order and Egil took his leave she must be with child. Seduction was a sport at which Jorunn possessed no skills, never having need for them earlier. Instinct would carry her far, she assumed, yet with such an unresponsive target her plan was proving difficult. Eight days had passed and Egil showed no signs of being aware of her in any other way than his brother's widow.

Each day they worked closely, in accord, sharing the burden of reinstating order at Stridheim. Each evening they dined together, sharing food and the pleasurable feeling of accomplishment. They were united in a common goal, and an easy camaraderie was born between them. Yet each time Jorunn passed him in the narrow hall, letting her body brush close to his, Egil moved away unaware. In the barn the air was close and warm. Heavy, ripe with the smell of rich earth and hay. It was a midsummer scent that never failed to put Jorunn of a mind of sensual pleasures, and Erland, too, had seemed to feel the connection. Yet Egil worked beside her completely unaware. 'Maybe he has no love of the land,' she mused, 'and is too removed to feel its pulse.' Yet in the time he had been here she felt convinced that Egil worked the land with the same passion Erland had. After twenty years away his movements were not as sure, his body unused to physical labor, but in only a short while he found an easy rhythm born of his earlier years on the farm. His hands still wore the ragged bandages he fastened around them each morn, his palms still bled and wept with the ravages of unaccustomed labor, yet it was evident he enjoyed his days on Stridheim. He wore an air of contentment he had lacked upon his arrival.

The second pail was brimming and Jorunn rose to stretch her long limbs, easing her back. She picked up both buckets and turned toward the creamery house, then reminded herself of her purpose. Setting them beside her she called, "Egil, these buckets need to go to the creamery. Would you carry them for me?"

She placed one hand flat against the small of her back to demonstrate a weakness there, and stood waiting while he approached. She did not move from her position between the buckets, forcing him to bend near to retrieve them. As he came close her heart beat faster with anticipation, her nerves alert for some sign that he was aware of her. Yet he bent and fetched the pails appearing in no way affected by her presence. She stood in the wake of him, perturbed by his disregard, annoyed that the smell of him caused such a tumult of her senses. She followed after him belatedly, struggling with frustration, reminding herself once again that she must not forget her purpose.

When a fortnight had passed she became aware Egil's time on Stridheim was drawing to a close. The buildings were in good repair, the yard readied for winter. The harvest was upon the rest of the valley. At Stridheim there would be no reaping this year. With no master to plant, the earth had lain fallow. Next year would be different. Egil had tilled the weed that had sprouted and the earth lay heavy and ripe, waiting for seed to be planted in the spring. An air of expectancy hung over the land at Stridheim. It was to this Jorunn attributed her own tumultuous feelings as time for Egil's departure drew near.

"Before you go, could you inspect the roof of the smokehouse?" she invented. "I'm afraid the provisions there might be spoiled by leakage when the rains come."

"Tomorrow, then," Egil replied.

It was early still, and she did not think him tired. She suspected he was loathe to leave, as she was to see him go. Not

for want of her company, she judged, but rather for the pleasure of being at Stridheim. She knew now she had misjudged
Egil and his reasons for coming back to reclaim the farm. The
calling he felt was real. He was content here.

'I'm content here, too' she reminded herself, lest she be
distracted. 'This is my home, the rhythm of this place is in my
marrow as well. I won't leave. I can't.'

In a moment of panic she realized that unless her aim was
complete when Egil rode away from the farm she would have
no choice. He would send her away, pawn her off with gold
crowns as a substitute for her land. He assumed she could buy
a new life, one removed from this place. In his arrogance he
disregarded her feeling for Stridheim and would have it only
for himself. 'He won't,' she reminded herself, steeling the
determination that had waned. 'Tonight I'll have Egil
Halvorsson, and in the spring I'll bear his son. I've got to.'

The rest of the afternoon she spent in concentrated cal-
culation. When supper was through it was usual that Valdis
cleared the dishes and washed them while Jorunn and Egil
wandered Stridheim, taking stock of their accomplishments.
Egil often gave voice to the plans he had for the farm. He was
ambitious; of that Jorunn was already aware. He saw possibilities for Stridheim far beyond those Erland had.

"The timber here is as gold," he explained to her. "With
the rebuilding of the city after the great fire in '58, and the
growth of new industry in paper manufacturing, the demand
for wood has never been greater. I plan to clear more of the
forest, plant new crops. There is a hardier strain of wheat I
have heard mentioned, I should like to try that in a year. And
I judge it would be wise to increase the livestock herd. Import
wheat from Russia and America is sold more cheaply than we
can produce it. Our growing season is too short, so in that
market Stridheim cannot be competitive. The land could be
used more effectively for grazing."

"But already we produce more milk and cream than we have
need of," Jorunn protested. "I have more butter and cheese
stored than we can use. Why increase our cattle herd when we
already have too many head to feed from our grain supply?"

"I intend to produce dairy goods for sale. With more land
cultivated we can be very nearly self-sufficient in grain production; in the event we need extra I shall buy cheap import. This
is the future of agriculture, Jorunn. Small farms for self-sup-
ply are not efficient; they will not survive the revolution in in-

dustry taking place now. New machines can do the work of ten men; a tractor does the work of a good team in half the time and needs no fodder, little care. I plan to invest in such machinery, and make other improvements to Stridheim. I intend to run the place as rationally as I manage my mercantile."

While he talked Jorunn planned, hardly listening, unwilling to let herself be distracted. When they came to the river she stood silent, staring at the flow of water, fairly still on this quiet harvest evening. Unbidden there sprang to her mind a passage long forgotten. 'And he showed me a pure river of water of life, clear as crystal,' she suddenly remembered, 'and in the midst of it was the tree of life which bare twelve manner of fruits, and yielded her fruit each month.'

Her brow furrowed in confusion, sensing enormity in the message she imagined she heard in the twilight. The sun was sinking low, lending a pale blush to the blue heavens above them.

"Something troubles you?" Egil asked, looking at her questioningly.

She hesitated for a moment, trying to sort in her mind the jumble of her thoughts, yet the sense of them eluded her. "It's nothing," she answered finally.

They stood together, watching the river's ceaseless flow, until he broke the silence with a sigh. "I know you are pained at leaving Stridheim. I would that it could be otherwise, but there is no other way. You shall have a house in the village, near enough to visit when you will. You shall always be welcome here. You are the only mistress Stridheim knows."

The ache Jorunn felt at Egil giving voice to the thoughts which tormented her was a terrible thing, yet in that searing pain came her deliverance. In an instant her way was clear; she set her mind to accomplish this thing which must be done.

"I need some time alone. Leave me, please. I'll come in a while."

"The light is fading. I do not like to leave you on this side of the wood alone."

She felt her lips twist in a smile as she replied darkly, "This forest holds no terrors for me. I've faced all my terrors, and conquered them." A sound escaped her, a laugh that held no humor, and he stared at her intently in the hazy twilight.

"I shall leave you then, but do not linger long," he cautioned.

She watched as he turned and retraced the way down the path. Before the forest swallowed him she called, "If I don't come back you must promise to come rescue me!" Her laughter rang out, forced to her own ears, yet reassuring enough, for Egil replied with a grin, "*Selvfølgelig*. Ever at your service, Madame."

She watched him go, then turned to wait. Darkness fell, and in those moments after the sun's rays gave way and the moon's light took hold Jorunn considered the fate of the two men whose bodies had been swallowed by Glomma. To her surprise she could not recall the face of the man whose life she had taken that day not so long ago. Erland's face sprang to mind instantly, etched in her memory with startling clarity. For a moment she felt him close. Then the sensation faded and she was alone. The black waters rushed on regardless, a heedless source of transport from this life to the next.

A silver orb rose, full and perfect, against the velvet sky, and in the reflection of white rivulets she saw rebirth there as well. Like life, flowing on until eternity. She rose and unlaced the bodice of her dress, letting it fall at her feet. Slipping her shift over her head she let it lay, luminous white against the bark of a fallen tree. She approached the river and stood staring at the lacy currents, waiting for a sound, a signal that the time was right.

The time that elapsed was a journey for her. When she heard the snap of twigs behind her she had arrived at some place far removed from where she had begun this venture. Listening to his approach she moved forward to the water and stepped into it, let its silky coolness swirl about her ankles. Behind her she judged him to have entered the clearing. Then there was only the sound of water. She knew he stood watching. She walked from the shallows and let the water swallow her. She lay back in it, feeling her hair float, staring up at the crystal moon, watching the rise and fall of her breasts above the water as she breathed.

She turned, resolutely, toward the bank and walked toward the shallows. Her body shone pale, glistened wetly. She saw him clearly, watching her. She stopped only yards away. Lifting her arms she beckoned and he came to her without hesitation. In a single movement he shed his shirt, tossing it to lay beside her shift. When he unlaced his britches and stood before her she did not wait for him. Reaching out she slid both arms around his shoulders to pull him close, covering his mouth with hers.

The heat emanating from his body warmed her and she clung to him, pressing her flesh to his the length of her, feeling the hardness of him against her softness. She let herself melt against him, reveling in the tide of desire that washed over her. Strong arms lifted her and she wrapped her legs around his waist as he walked into the water, holding her fast. When he entered her she relaxed and let herself float as he moved with the same fluid grace of the river. She was swept along in a liquid tide until she could bear the pleasure no longer and cried out in the night, feeling him tense and spill inside her.

He cradled her to him while the river swirled past. Then she released him and he led her back to the shallows, where their clothes lay abandoned on the bank. He bent to retrieve his shirt.

"Egil, don't go," she spoke simply, her voice stark in the night.

Turning back he looked her full in the face, his voice harsh as he answered, "I must. I have no choice. Berit...."

"Quiet," she commanded, reaching out one hand to cover his mouth. She would have no thought of any person who stood between them. She would only have him.

His lips moved against her fingers, she felt his tongue touch her flesh and she shivered. When he reached for her she surrendered, no thought for the future, none for the past. She melded her person to his in utter abandonment for this moment, no more.

❧ ❧ ❧

The creaking sounds of leather and the crunch of gravel under the hooves of Egil's horse relayed the message of his departure. Jorunn stretched out an arm and reached for him in the bed beside her, but found the sheet cold. Struggling awake, she sat up to find the day not yet dawned. Darkness obscured the far corners of the bedroom, the only light the pale blush of early morn that filtered through the small paned window.

He would not stay. She had known that. She had taken that into careful consideration when she planned his seduction. Yet now she was filled with longing at his leaving. Lying back against the pillow she pondered the change in her own attitude. Her feelings had altered, yet she dared not examine the reason for it.

In exasperation she rose and dressed hurriedly. There was much to be done; she was called to her duties as Mistress of Stridheim. Those alone would remind her of the true reason for her actions.

Thirteen

HERITAGE

🏵 Sigurd Johannesson left the yard at Valgaard and turned east, toward the mountain. The sun had topped the crest, pale yellow against a bright blue sky, its weak rays barely touching the frost that laced the purple heather. Nine years had passed since Sigurd had last climbed the mountain; the incline was sharper than he remembered. He climbed easily enough, of old habit finding his footing with little trouble, though his body was worn, and the creak of his knees, the burning in his lungs, served to remind him of passing time.

Pausing midway to rest his aching muscles, he turned back to his place and surveyed the land. The harvest was safely in; grain fields lay covered in pale stubble, vegetable patches were turned to black furrows ready for spring planting. The season had been good and their stores would see them through the winter. Yet with each passing year the surplus was less; he knew sometime in the future there would be a summer when drought, or too much rain, too little sun, or pestilence, would destroy his crops and they would have little saved to see them through lean times.

'Nothin' to be done about it,' he reasoned. 'Gonna happen sooner or later, no use worryin'. Still, it's a shame when it comes to this.'

His musing was without real regret. He had known for many years his life would end this way, was resigned to it. Yet looking out over the fields he was gripped by uncharacteristic nostalgia. He remembered the place as it had been in his father's time, when he was a child. In his earliest memories there had been nothing planted below the rise that stretched before the yard, but his father had held a grander vision of the place and had eventually wrested viable land from the rocky, unyielding earth. Far west there had been dense pine forests where he and his brother, Henrik, trapped small game. Later they helped their father clear the land, cultivate acres of grain. The yield from their harvest that year had been sufficient to allow for a new house to replace the dark, simple dwelling that had stood on Valgaard since Sigurd's great-grandfather's time.

In March the next year, just after the thaw, a new house was raised. He remembered his father carving the cornerstone of the foundation; with his index finger he had traced the numbers 1789 while the stone was still warm from the chisel. Johannes Henriksson's happiest days. Sigurd realized that had been the pinnacle of his father's life, the feast to celebrate the new house Johannes Henriksson's finest hour. In his mind's eye Sigurd saw him standing to raise his cup in a toast, could see even now the way his father's fair hair glittered pale gold in the late summer light, gilding him, the image of a man who brought to mind the old gods. Fine features, broad shoulders, grace that should have been foreign to such a rugged man. Wives watched Johannes Henriksson with eyes too bright and flushed cheeks, maidens studied him surreptitiously, fluttering nervously when his glance chanced on one of them.

His father had been aware of his effect on others, Sigurd knew; he had understood even then that Johannes Henriksson used his charm to further his own ends. An ambitious man, with cunning and hard work he had established himself as a farmer of means. Johannes Henriksson had chosen his wife carefully. Gerd Ulfsdatter was the only daughter of a wealthy landowner, with a sizable dowry to compensate for her plainness, and dour manner. The prospect of financial gain had attracted many suitors, yet for a long while Sigurd had wanted to believe his father had been different. When he was a little boy he had nestled in the warm softness of his mother's lap and listened to the story of how it all began for her and his father. Sigurd had sensed the depth of her emotion, watched as the light of her love transformed her plain face. He had thought her beautiful, and had told her as much.

"It's what's inside what counts, *gutten min*," she had replied with a gentle smile, sudden sadness in her brown eyes. He watched the light die and saw her as others might. Short and stout, broad from her wide forehead to her thick ankles, dark hair plaited and pinned above a round face. "Folks never understood 'bout Pappa and me," she had said. "From the minute our eyes met we knew we were right for each other, that's all."

In retrospect Sigurd supposed that to be true, though not in the way he had imagined as a child. His mother brought into marriage money, and livestock that enabled his ambitious father to build his place into one of the finest farms in the county. And for a while, at least, his father might have loved his mother. He knew she had felt it so.

"He gave me you and your brother," she had told him, her face aglow with the light of her love. "More than I ever thought I'd have, worth more than gold and silver."

Sigurd realized that given her fine mind and canny understanding of people his mother had understood none of her suitors courted her in affection. She had not waited in the hope that one would; she had waited for the man she could love. Beneath her ample bosom had beat a romantic heart; she had treasured the idea that in the arms of the right man the shell of her plainness would cease to matter.

For this dream his mother had traded the ease and comfort of her father's house for the simple, hard work of a farmer's wife. The hours she spent washing, cooking, spinning, knitting were passed in happy anticipation of the evening, when his father returned. He wanted to believe that in those years his father overlooked his mother's plain facade and saw instead the soul that burned for him, let the flame of her love kindle his affection. Sigurd thought he must have admired her determination; she had worked tirelessly to improve Valgaard. The place grew and prospered. The livestock Gerd brought to marriage proliferated, the new fields Johannes cleared and planted each spring increased their harvest each fall. His mother birthed Henrik in '79, and he had been born in '80. Johannes Henriksson had been successful even beyond his own high expectations.

Looking back, Sigurd thought it was then the fire of his father's ambition waned, and in its place the restlessness took root. There was an energy that pulsed through the man, a strange excitement that kept him on razor's edge. Like a current dammed to restrict its flow, there was the sense that he was filled to the brim and must have release. He began disappearing without explanation. There was pattern to it, an ebb and flow. For a while Johannes Henriksson kept his exploits far from home, far enough away that no gossip should sully his reputation in Hedmark County. It was during the harvest, when he could not be spared on Valgaard, that the heavy scent of ripe wheat, the pulse of the land, pushed him to the edge. He let desire take him into the dark wood, in search of release.

In stealth Sigurd had followed him, deep into the forest where the trees were so dense they shut out the silver sphere of the harvest moon. His father had moved swiftly in the darkness, on a path well-traveled. When he came to a clearing and stepped into white light, Sigurd understood at last the way they had taken. He recognized the place his father had searched out with familiar ease; he remembered how fear and dread had knotted in the pit of his stomach. He stood very still at the forest edge and watched his father make his steady way to the shelter where the witch lived. The woman emerged from her crude dwelling, her white hair loose, her pale, perfect features ghostly in the silver light; she walked straight into his father's embrace.

A perfect union, he had sensed. Later, when the whispers in the village grew louder, he heard his father had been under the spell of the witch, Helfrid, since he was sixteen. Johannes Henriksson's wandering on the dark side had been common knowledge then; some even said he had sired the child the witch had borne that April. Others insisted that was an impossibility for mortal man, that the child was the spawn of the devil. It was an old argument, but one revived that summer of Sigurd's eleventh year, when a young priest managed to wrest the witch's daughter from Satan's grasp and bring her to God. Her salvation caused those who believed the girl to be half-mortal to reiterate their arguments. All agreed it was unlikely the devil would surrender one of his own so easily.

In the swirl of darkness, adultery, treachery, Sigurd had watched his mother suffer and grown to hate his father. Ambitious, greedy, selfish. The man was despicable to inflict such pain on them all. Sigurd wished him dead, and his wish was granted. In November his father fell ill, burning with a fever that lasted ten days before it finally killed him.

Sigurd had watched his mother tend his father for the last time. She washed him tenderly, smoothing the cloth over his long limbs, laying each arm gently to rest by his side. She bathed his flat stomach with small circular motions, moved upward to scrub his chest, sunken already. Pale white skin stretched taught over the outline of his ribs, the dark blemish on his right breast seeming larger, somehow, in death. His mother had paused in her ministrations to let the cloth lay, white against the blackness of it, for a long moment. Then her soft round shoulders had slumped forward in defeat and she had sobbed, "Damn you, Johannes! How many bastards wear your mark?"

Forgotten in the shadows of the room, Sigurd remembered lifting his hand to the mark concealed beneath his own shirt and feeling the shame of it burn through.

In all these years he could not forget. He turned from Valgaard and continued to climb, determined to erase the guilt he harbored.

♣ ♣ ♣

In the wake of Egil's departure the last weeks of fall passed quickly on Stridheim. There was no crop to harvest from the fields, yet the black earth yielded ample quantities of nature's own bounty. Jorunn and Valdis collected blueberries from the forest and made pots of jam to be eaten with pancakes and winter gruel. The red and black currant bushes that grew alongside the creamery hung heavy with fruit, one whole week passed in picking those. The next week they spent pressing the berries, then boiling the juice to reduce the volume. Jorunn taught Valdis to sweeten the concentrate with honey and store it for later use. Then it was apple season, with the prospect of fresh cider and apple cakes and smooth apple butter. Jorunn left the yard and made her way to the cluster of fruit trees that grew just beyond, at the foot of the mountain. The sun was bright, but the wind was chill already, diminishing the little warmth its rays offered. Jorunn carried two baskets, one stacked within the other, locking them loosely between arm and hip.

"Valdis, *kom barnet mitt!* The apples are ripe, and ready to fall," she called to the girl who played close by. Valdis came obediently to where her mother stood beneath the tree and began to collect the fruit that had fallen recently, inspecting each apple carefully before placing it in the smaller basket.

"*Mamma,* look," she said, pointing with an outstretched arm toward the mountain. Sigurd Johannesson descended the steep slope with a steady gait, his long legs moving easily in spite of rocky terrain. Jorunn paused in her work. After a moment's hesitation she instructed, "Stay, Valdis, and bid your mother's father good day."

The child stood quietly by her mother's side, her blue eyes huge in her pale face. Jorunn knew Valdis had no recollection of her grandfather. Sigurd remained loyal to his wife and had not crossed the mountain that separated them since Valdis' birth. He approached quickly, then stood wordless before them. His gaze shifted between Jorunn and the child, blue eyes too bright as he considered them. He looked at the basket, his eyes narrowed in concentration. He reached up one long arm and pulled a heavily laden bough to within Jorunn's reach.

"Folks in Dal say your husband's brother is here," he began at last, his tone searching.

"He was," Jorunn replied shortly. She turned her back and worked methodically to fill her basket, grateful for the excuse to hide her face, which bore a telltale flush. "He's gone back to Christiania, to his wife and business there."

"I'm relieved," her father said.

At the implication Jorunn's flush deepened to the same dark red as the apples in her basket. For the first time since she had conceived her plan guilt snaked its way forward in her conscience. Resolutely she ignored it, sent it slithering back to the deep recesses of her mind.

"He came to claim Stridheim?" her father asked, all hesitation gone. She felt his eyes probing, searching. Jorunn dared not lift her gaze to meet his, fearing her eyes were mirrors of her guilt. She merely nodded, continuing to pluck apples, place them in her basket.

"What'll you do now?" he probed. "You can't stay here. This place belongs by right to another man."

Emotion warred within Jorunn, anger exploding to drown out all other consideration. "This place is mine, no one's going to take it from me!" she snapped.

Her father paused. He let go the bough he held and it sprang up and away, far from Jorunn's reach. Extending one arm he tucked a finger beneath her chin and lifted her eyes to meet his, letting her feel the full impact of his stare. "You got to come home. Your mother's agreeable, it's what's right."

Jorunn laughed, yet there was no mirth in the harsh sound that grated from her constricted throat. "It's so simple for her. Right or wrong, black or white. The rules she lives by are the rules of a simple mind, one with no questions. I can't pretend to understand her, I surely can't share her roof."

There was a pause while her father searched for words. At length he replied, "It might fall easier for you to understand your mother if you knew the truth." His voice was strangely brittle, it caught her attention and held it. Jorunn watched his eyes and saw mirrored a war waged within.

"Her life seems easy to you, her choices simple. But the life she's livin' wasn't the one she chose. It was forced on her. I did that to her, and I hold myself responsible for the woman she's become. If you got to judge one of us, then judge me."

Jorunn shook her head in confusion, her look one of mute appeal.

"Your mother's a good woman, Jorunn. Too good for the likes of me. I come from a bad lot, and it's true that blood will tell. Ambition and greed were my father's legacy, passed on to me, together with his mark."

Sigurd lifted his hand to touch his chest, and Jorunn envisioned the dark blemish on his right breast. The thought of the mark she bore sprang to mind. She pressed her hand to it unconsciously, as if to conceal it. "*Far,* there's no truth in that," she insisted. "My father's father was a good man, a hard worker who changed Valgaard from a potato patch and a dirt-floor cabin to the farm it is today. You've told me the story many times...."

"I told what I wanted you to believe, no more," he interrupted. "You got to know the rest, so hear me out, girl. The Lord said, 'I the Lord thy God am a jealous God, visiting the iniquity of the fathers upon the children into the third and fourth generation.' Hard words, and God keeps His word. You're my girl, Jorunn, the child I love best. You're like me. Ambitious, determined to have your own place and make it great. Selfish, you'll keep what's not yours, thinkin' it'll make you happy. That's a sin, girl. The Good Lord said, 'Thou shalt not covet thy neighbor's house, nor anything that is thy neighbor's.'"

"*Hysj,* I won't listen to you!" Jorunn cried, two spots of color high on each cheekbone. Her blue eyes sparked with anger. "This place is mine! With the sweat of my brow and the blood of my body I've made it mine, and no one will take it from me, do you hear?" Then the anger in her voice faded, making her last words a plea: "This place is as much a part of me as Valgaard is of you, can't you understand?"

Sigurd looked at his daughter's face, heard the desperation in her voice, and recognized himself. "I know better'n
you can imagine what you're feelin' now, girl; of all my sins my
greatest was envy. 'Wrath is cruel, and anger is outrageous;
but who is able to stand before envy?' the scripture asks. I'm
not man enough, life's taught me that. I fell hard, traded my
soul for a piece of land and a vision of greatness. I stole my
brother's birthright, killed him in my anger and envy, and I'll
burn in hell for it. But before I go I got to try to save you."

Jorunn watched her father, fear and confusion mingling.
"*Far*, there's no truth to that," she refuted, yet to even her own
ears her voice sounded high and unsure. "Uncle Henrik died
in the epidemic of 1808. I've heard the story, from many
people...."

The steadiness of her father's gaze silenced her. "Half a
story is as good as a lie, *jenta mi*, I got to tell you the rest.
Valgaard belonged to Henrik, my father's first son. All my life
I knew that's the way things were, but I coveted my brother's
birthright, envied him in every little thing. Often enough I
whiled time away thinkin' about life; the way it was, the way it
could be if there was no Henrik."

The old man fell silent, dropped his head in shame. The
look of him caused the consternation in Jorunn's eyes to turn
to fear, shadows of her own past rising up to haunt her. "Don't
tell me any more, *Far*," she urged quickly. "Take your secrets
to the grave with you, they're a burden I won't bear."

"Don't you see, you got no choice, girl. These are the sins
of your father. Your only hope's the truth, in it He promised
salvation. And I got to find redemption. I don't want to die
the way I've lived. I want to save you from the mistakes I've
made."

The pain in her father's voice, the flicker of hope in his
eyes, kept her silent. In resignation she tucked her skirt beneath her and sank to the ground. Sigurd moved to sit beside
her on a flat stone, reaching for the child and pulling her onto
his lap, finding strength to begin in the comfort of holding
the girl close.

"Our father died when we were still boys. Henrik was barely
thirteen, but from that day he took over the farm and kept the
place goin'. He was like our mother; strong as an ox, solid as
a rock. Could do the work of two grown men, and seven days
a week that's what he did. I helped out, but it was Henrik that
was master; he carried the responsibility for Valgaard on his

shoulders. He got us through. By the time I was twenty I was a man and ought to have been out makin' my own way, but I loved the place like it was part of me, and Henrik knew it. He wouldn't ask me to go. Then our mother died, and it was just the two of us, both of us knowin' Henrik should take a wife, have sons to take over after him. But then there'd have been no room for me on the place, and he didn't like to do what he knew he had to. I just held on, hopin' he never would.

"Our mother had been dead five years, and we were figured for old bachelors before he told me he'd made up his mind to marry. For the sake of the place. He had to have a son if Valgaard was goin' to keep on after we were gone."

Sigurd fell silent for a moment, then he ground out, "I knew it was right, but my envy turned me rotten, and I hated my brother then. I listened, coiled like a viper near his heart. He told me he'd found his bride, a girl I'd heard of. Folks said she was beautiful, and good to the core. Her father was a preacher man who came bearin' a new message in the valley. The Acts of the Apostles was the word he preached: 'I have shewed you all things, how so labouring ye ought to support the weak and to remember the words of the Lord Jesus; how he said, It is more blessed to give than receive.' Paul's words. Easy enough said, hard to inspire folks to act on. Hard times had taught folks better than any preacher that to have anythin' in a rough spot you had to hoard durin' plenty. But the preacher man believed in what he said, and practiced it too. He and his daughter drove from place to place collectin' anythin' folks would spare and givin' it to those who'd hit hard times. Angels on earth, some said. I made up my mind to go see for myself, wanted to see this slip of a girl my brother would marry. She'd be the end of me, I knew. I had to see her for myself."

Her father fell silent for a while, searching for words. Jorunn watched him, holding her child on his lap easily, and remembered sitting where Valdis perched. Safe, secure. A sudden longing for that time surged, and she struggled to quell it, to hear her father's words when he spoke again. "I'd never felt a call to Him, never worshipped, 'cept as how I did in the fields, or on the mountain lookin' out over His creation. But I knew the preacher talked down by the river on the Sabbath, so I left Henrik in the fields and went to find her. I found the congregation in the shade of old trees on the banks of River Glomma, listenin' to him preach. But I wasn't listenin'. I couldn't think of anything 'cept the vision I'd seen of an angel standing in the middle of the crowd. The sun shinin' through the trees on white-blond hair she still wore down. The most beautiful woman I'd ever seen. Henrik judged her to be too young for weddin', didn't plan to speak to her father until her sixteenth birthday, but I knew just lookin' at her she was a woman already. And I made up my mind to have her."

Suddenly it occurred to Jorunn that this girl her father spoke of was her own mother. She had a vision of how the girl must have looked; much as Valdis did now, Jorunn supposed. The child was possessed of an unearthly beauty, many would say angelic. Then she thought of Astrid as she had been when Jorunn had last seen her; withered, harsh lines etched to deep furrows that erased the beauty that had once been. Jorunn shivered, a cold wind brushing her cheek. She turned her mind resolutely from sudden presentiment and listened again to her father's tale.

"I had nothin' to offer. Henrik had Valgaard; the idea he'd have her as well burned me up inside. I made up my mind to do whatever it took to have her, and to hell with him. He could take the place and rot with it; I'd have the girl and the satisfaction of knowin' he wanted her. I joined her father's flock, so I could be near her, find a way to have her.

"The rest of that summer, and into the fall, I followed Reverend Olavsson, and by the feast at Yule, Christmas as they called it, I was the most trusted member of his congregation. Like my father I could hold folks attention; when I talked people listened. Olavsson noticed, figured I could help him carry the message. He worked out a plan where I'd go in a new direction and spread the word, the two of us able to reach more people separate than together, and I agreed. I said I'd go in the spring, but I didn't want to go alone. I asked for his daughter to be my wife and helpmate, and the Reverend Olavsson gave her to me in marriage the last Sabbath in March, four days before her sixteenth birthday."

Jorunn saw the light in her father's blue eyes. They shone with pride, and remembered love. But the look was fleeting, and he sobered quickly.

"Everyone rejoiced that day. The congregation saw a holy union, one that would further the works of God. I finally had somethin' my brother wanted, and a callin' I imagined would see me through the loss of Valgaard. I hurried back to the place, took my bride to meet my brother, who had spent most of the last year gettin' Valgaard fixed up so he would have more than just himself to offer the girl he planned to marry. He didn't figure that was enough. Raised a new house for her, a fine timber house, with his bride in mind...."

Sigurd faltered, the shame of his memories causing an ugly red flush to stain his weathered cheeks. "When I brought my bride home to the house my brother had built for her, Henrik said nothin'. He hadn't suspected. A farmer in his blood and bones, he never observed the Sabbath; he wouldn't take a day free from his toil of the earth. He worshipped on the land, where he found God. He'd heard no rumor of my treachery; it must have come as a terrible shock, but he kept his own counsel. In three days time we left to start our ministry, and durin' those three days he never asked. He never said a word."

Sigurd stopped his story and dropped his head in defeat. "Henrik died the next winter. I never talked to him again."

Her father's pain was more than Jorunn could bear. She felt his shame, his loathing for himself, and was suddenly, unexpectedly, protective. "You had nothing to do with his death, *Far*. It was influenza...." she protested.

"The blow I dealt crippled him, made him weak," Sigurd replied levelly. "Henrik died alone, cheated and betrayed by the brother he loved."

Jorunn was silent, shaken by her father's revelations, yet in the very core of her being understanding him. Reason reasserted itself and she asked, "Is this the sin you imagine I'll be punished for? Then be easy. I don't believe your sin was so grave. What's more, I don't believe in your God," she said, and her voice rang out with true conviction.

"*Ja vel*, but you're still young," he said, reaching out to gently stroke her cheek. "And you're my daughter. My likeness, my sins are visited on you. Now I know we walk by faith, not by sight, but then I didn't believe either. My faith was pretend, a means to my end. As soon as Henrik died I left my ministry and came home to Valgaard. The land, my place at last. That was my callin'. I forced your mother to come with me. She had another callin', had heard the voice of the Lord. I cheated her."

Jorunn looked at where her child nestled in the crook of her father's arm, saw the fragile innocence of her daughter, and was overcome with sadness at the thought of its inevitable loss.

"Oh *Pappa*," Jorunn cried softly. Things suddenly clear, their illumination so bright after years of darkness that Jorunn squeezed her eyes shut to block out the painful light.

"You had to know, *jenta mi*. The Scripture says, 'Ye shall know the truth, and the truth shall make you free.'"

She lifted her face and looked into her father's eyes. "Truth is surely salvation, but for me it comes too late," she confessed. She pressed a hand to her still flat abdomen, let him read her secret in her eyes, then she averted her gaze, unable to endure the pain she saw distort his fine, even features. "Don't look at me like that, *Pappa*, I have a plan..." she began, then faltered, her voice breaking. She sensed his defeat, watched his body sag with it. His lifeblood ebbed through the wound she inflicted. The light of hope and determination in his eyes was snuffed; they were faded and aged. "You don't understand," she protested, her voice forlorn.

"*Ja*, I do. You're my daughter, flesh of my flesh, and after my heart," he said in despair. "A pair of foolish sinners; we haven't kept the commandment of the Lord. Scripture says, 'The Lord seeks a man after his own heart, and that man's kingdom will last forever.' We're not after His heart, *min datter*."

His voice broke, and Jorunn looked away from his watery gaze, unable to face his grief. He mourned the inevitable loss of Valgaard. His place, the land of his people for over a thousand years. His life's work would come to nothing. After his death the black earth of Valgaard would lie fallow because he had no son to entrust with his land. Nature would reclaim the fields, time would obliterate even the memory of the place called Valgaard, and its people.

Slowly he put the child from him and stood to leave. Jorunn watched him climb the mountain. His shoulders sloped, his step was unsure. He was grown old.

Fourteen

SACRIFICE

❧ Winter of 1860 came to Hedmark early, and with a vengeance. The harvest was barely in when snow fell deep; by the feast at Yule the farms lying in the upper regions were closed to access. At Stridheim the road snowed under in early December, and Jorunn settled in with Valdis to wait for the melt in the spring.

Their stores were plentiful, with ample wood for heat. There was no cause for concern. Jorunn had lived at the base of the mountain for long enough to accept in resignation the inevitability of being snowed in for a season; this year it came as more of a blessing than an annoyance. Each morn she rose fighting waves of sickness; all day the ache in her breasts reminded her she bore new life in her womb.

After her father's visit Jorunn resigned herself to her course. The specter of him as he had been that day reoccurred occasionally; a man broken, the futility of life apparent in his faded gaze. She averted her thoughts and concentrated on her plans for the future. She was at peace with herself and the way she had chosen, yet she knew how others would see it. In the valley they would whisper of the child who had been conceived only months after Erland's death. The people she had once called her own would cringe in shame at this new life she bore. The day of reckoning would come eventually, resolutely. She was glad of opportunity to hold public censure at bay. She would remain safe in the womb of Stridheim and nurture the life that grew within her. In the spring Egil would return for the planting as promised. When her time came she would send him on errand for the midwife.

It was Valdis, who occasionally stared at her mother's ever-expanding girth with wide blue eyes, that concerned her. For herself she had no dread of the talk that would arise from her condition. But Valdis' innocence was a precious thing and she longed to preserve it. She thought of the many ways in which a person so sheltered could be injured and cringed in fear for her daughter. She resolved to do anything within her power to protect her. The only solution to present itself was the obvious. In spring, when Egil came, Valdis must be dispatched at once to Berit. Entrusted to her care she would be safe from the pious whispers that would rise from the indignant and righteous in the valley. The very idea of sending Valdis away was painful and she shied from it, yet she knew this to be the only course. In the months from Yule to March she became resigned to it.

It was a winter in which time hung suspended. The days were milky-white, with fresh snow falling in lazy patterns to cover the already thick blanket which lay in insulation about them. Sound was muted, as were the hard edges of reality. Jorunn lived with Valdis wrapped in a cloak of contentment and well-being, her only forays into the world outside being to gather wood for the fire, or food from the outbuildings. Further afield she had neither need nor desire to wander.

Time gradually heeded nature's call and spring came. When the snow melted it flooded the yard and ran down to Glomma, swelling her banks to almost overflowing. The black earth in the fields of Stridheim appeared at last, but lay soggy for the duration of March. By mid-April Jorunn knew her time drew near and felt the first fingers of apprehension come stealing over her. If Egil postponed his arrival too long she risked being alone when the child came. The skin over her stomach was stretched taut, almost to bursting, it seemed. Daily the life within her grew more apparent. Arms and legs assailed her from inside when the child turned in its narrow confinement. She sensed it would not be content there long.

The last week of the month she stood in the courtyard when she heard sounds of approach. She suffered spasms in her lower back and even the short journey from the outhouse and home again was a trial. She was leaning against the wall of the well, waiting for her discomfort to abate, when she heard the whinny of a horse and knew Egil had returned at last.

She turned, eager for the first sight of him as he topped the hill. He rode straight and proud, his horse a fine one. She felt a flutter beneath her heart and blamed it on the babe. Unable to steel her countenance she felt a flush rise and a smile break through her reserve.

Once in the yard he reigned in his horse and dismounted, his eyes sweeping the place. When he saw her his face grew slack with surprise. Even from a distance she registered his shock, and her own elation died. She had almost forgotten he was unaware. His obvious horror at the sight of her swollen belly was the first tangent of reality to pierce the wall of seclusion and privacy at Stridheim in these many months. In his eyes she saw what the rest of the world would see. For the first time since conceiving this child she was afraid.

He dropped the reins carelessly and came to her. Staring at her in disbelief, comprehension dawning slowly, he said at last, "The situation is unthinkable. What in the name of God will happen now?"

Feeling the wound of his words she drew herself to her full height, raised her chin, and replied, "A child will be born, that must be obvious even to you."

"That is not what I meant, as you well know," he snapped back, offended at her tone. "I mean that your predicament is unbearable. What will you do?"

Anger flared and she flashed back, "My predicament is absolutely bearable. I've borne this child so far, and I'll give it birth. But you seem to have overlooked the fact that while I'm the one who has shouldered the responsibility, I wasn't alone in conceiving it. An equal share of that responsibility rests with you. Will you abdicate that by sending me away from here even though I carry your child?"

"My child," he echoed, paling visibly. The enormity of the situation rushed over him and he kneeled suddenly on the gravel, dropping his head to his hands. Pity smote her, washing her anger away. Looking down at his bowed head tenderness overwhelmed other emotion.

"The babe is ours together, conceived on the night of the harvest moon," she said softly.

He raised his face and she saw clearly his guilt. Searching his countenance she found none of her joy mirrored there. Whatever hope she harbored was dashed.

Her face was firm, her tone resolute as she said, "Whatever regrets we may have the reality of the situation must be dealt with. I can't move into the village with a child who'll be called bastard by everyone living there."

Rising, he put his arms around her in the first gesture of tenderness he had shown since his arrival. She drew in the scent of him greedily, comforted by the warmth of his embrace, the strength in his arms. She dropped her forehead to his shoulder and rested there, giving in to weakness she despised.

Stroking her back gently he murmured, "Come, you must rest. It cannot be easy for you to stand here."

She let him lead her to the porch bench and he helped her sit there. "Have you thought what you would do? Have you a plan?" he asked at length.

She dropped her gaze an instant to hide the triumph in her eyes. "It's obvious; there's only one choice. I have to stay at Stridheim. People won't talk any more if I stay here with you than they will if I move to town with the child. And it won't bother me, whatever they say. I don't care what they say about me. My only concern is for Valdis."

"She must be protected, of course," he answered. Stroking her hand where it lay on her swollen stomach he added, "I know it pains you, but you must send her away now, at once. I shall write Berit she is coming. I must ride to the village this afternoon to arrange her passage."

Regret at the loss of Valdis dimmed her satisfaction at a plan so carefully executed now coming to such satisfactory completion. Yet her way was chosen. She accepted the sacrifice and continued. "It's the only way, but I'll miss her terribly."

He made no answer and his quiet unnerved her. When she dared, she raised her glance to his. What she saw there evoked the smallest measure of guilt. His blue eyes brimmed with remorse. "I am unspeakably sorry for the injury I have caused you," he said simply.

"It's no injury," she answered truthfully. "I have the pleasure of feeling life stir inside me. The situation is difficult, but we'll find a way."

Rising resolutely he said, "With that aim in mind I must ride to the village. Explain to Valdis her passage, and bid her pack her things. I shall arrange that she leave in the morn."

A cloud of doubt passed over Jorunn's face and she amended, "In two days time, Egil. That will be soon enough."

Unwilling to distress her further he nodded, and crossed the yard to mount his horse. As he rode away she watched him with a small smile. Everything would be as she had planned. Her smile dimmed at the thought of sending Valdis away. 'Losing Valdis is inevitable,' she reasoned. 'She was never really mine. A child is only borrowed. I can't lose Stridheim as well.'

❧ ❧ ❧

A carriage collected Valdis in the gray light of early dawn two days after. Jorunn stood with Egil in the courtyard, lifting her arm in a gesture of farewell. She fought sudden panic. In an instant she was aware that with the removal of Valdis' physical presence her bond to the child was severed. There was so little between them that without the proximity of daily living she feared her child would be forever lost to her.

She stood long moments after the carriage disappeared over the rise, staring after it. Suddenly her blue eyes swam with tears. A careful hand stroked her back, the warmth of it mitigating the coldness that held her in a viselike grip.

"She shall be well cared for," Egil reassured her. "Berit has looked ahead to her coming with happy anticipation. She will be glad the child comes earlier than expected."

Jorunn nodded, her face hardening in resolve. "It has to be this way," she answered before turning to cross to the well. Lifting the bucket she let it fall into the depths and began to crank. An echo of the searing pain in her heart tore through her womb; she welcomed the physical suffering that blotted out the calamity of her thoughts.

Fifteen

THE LAMB

Valdis sat alone in the carriage and fought back tears that burned behind her eyes. For a while she was able to postpone them, staring unblinkingly through the tiny window at the figure of her mother waving her farewell. But when they descended the hill and her mother disappeared from view, the pain and confusion of these past few days welled up to choke her, blinding her with a rush of tears. She understood little of all that had transpired. Until the death of her father not so long ago she had lived in a world changed only by the seasons. Safe, secure in the knowledge of what each day would hold. She had assumed things would always happen in the same way. Life was constant, predictable. In June there were ripe strawberries to be savored with fresh cream; then bright, tart raspberries glazed in honey from the hollow tree her father plundered each July. In August a lid of heat would settle over the valley, making her father lazy, causing her mother to slow the quick pace she usually kept. Those days were spent languidly savoring the pleasures Stridheim had to offer. A plunge into the icy waters of the River Glomma, a picnic on its shady bank. Afternoon naps on a soft woolen blanket her mother spread for her beneath the leafy green canopy of the oak tree in the yard. When the wind grew sharp and August drew to a close there were the frantic days of the harvest. Her father would suddenly come alive, refreshed after weeks spent in idle relaxation. Her mother, by then, was heavy and languid, as if she, too, was ripe for the harvest, and when it began the scent of freshly mown hay and threshed wheat wafted and swirled around Stridheim, sweeping them along on a dizzying tide. Valdis went unnoticed in this heady whirl, alone in the midst of two people complete in one another. She recognized early that she was different to her parents. She did not hear the natural rhythm to which they responded, her heart did not beat in time to the symphony that was Stridheim. Yet she had lived there all her life and the rhythms were so familiar to her that she felt at one with them. It was the only life she knew.

After the fall harvest life took on a new pace. Slower, and in years when the harvest was good there was an air of satisfaction about her parents. They were replete. Valdis felt safe then, and secure. And she enjoyed the excitement and anticipation that brewed within her as the days became sharp and wet. Heavy, dark skies and razor's edge air meant that snow would soon blanket the yard and fields. One morning she would wake to a fairy-tale world of white; on that morning, when the snow was soft and new, her father would shake her gently and she would open her eyes to find him smiling, his teeth very white against the beard he wore in winter. From behind his back he would produce with a flourish a pair of new skis freshly carved from the finest cured wood. Waxed with tallow, perfect for the fluffy new snow. And when she asked, "*Men Pappa*, wherever did you find such a treasure?" he would laugh aloud his huge laugh and reply, "The elves brought them last night, *lille venn*."

She laughed with him and pretended she believed in the elves. Even though she sometimes crept from her warm bed in the early evening and sat on the top stair to watch her parents as they whiled away the last hours of the day by the fire. From her vantage point high above she spied on her mother, who sat spinning or knitting, and her father, who whittled away the wood to fashion for her the fine new skis he insisted the little people of the forest brought.

She had never told him she knew; she was glad, now, that she had not. He would have been disappointed.

When the thaw came her mother's pace became frantic. There was much to be done, and sometimes by then food was scarce. There was porridge for breakfast and the evening meal for as long as the honey and fine oat lasted, with a small bit of cured meat for her, and Pappa, too. When the smokehouse neared empty Mamma insisted she had no taste for the pork or venison left there, giving it to them. Valdis ate the thin slice of meat to make her mother happy, yet in truth she found that she, too, had no taste for the food when there was not enough.

When the porridge was done they made do with coarse gruel. Until the new potatoes were ready, and then there was a spring feast of lamb and potatoes swimming in cream and butter, and Valdis ate until the ache in her belly forced her to stop. Her mother would lecture her on greed, but Pappa always silenced Mamma with one of the looks they sometimes passed between them, out of Valdis' reach. It stopped Mamma's lecture, but did nothing to ease the ache in her stomach, and each year she vowed never to eat so much again.

Then it was time for sowing, and Valdis trailed behind her father, watching his broad shoulders and long legs as he stepped off the distance across the furrows. She was lonely then, the only time of the year when she noticed a longing for the company of the children who played games of tag and leap frog in the market square, or in the lower fields. She didn't like the other children, though, and the twinge of loneliness she sometimes suffered was never enough to tempt her to wander near them. They were cruel children. In the past they had shouted at her, taunting her with words she did not understand, but caused her to tremble with fear and sting with pain. So she avoided them, in spite of her loneliness. When her father looked at her closely in the spring he would stop his work and come to her, abandoning duty to chase after her until she fell gasping with pleasure in the new grass. He would roll her and tickle her until she could no longer breathe, but then he must return to his task while she lay flat on her back to stare into the pale blue spring sky and watch fluffy white patches of cloud skirt past.

Time with her mother was more limited, more dear. Her mother was always rushing from one task to another, her slim figure in constant motion. Valdis often played close to where her mother worked, glad to be near her, but she learned early never to interrupt. When her mother worked her face was smooth in concentration, her mouth a straight flat line. But if Valdis disturbed her, worry knitted her brows and the corners of her mouth pulled down in displeasure. Valdis was ashamed, knowing she was naughty, and responsible for delaying her mother's endless succession of chores. She felt mean and selfish, being such a bad girl. She tried hard to be a good girl and entertain herself during the day, leaving her mother free to finish her day's work. Then, at night, her mother would linger with her at bedtime, reading aloud from a book of stories about trolls and goats and witches. And when the story was over and the candle snuffed her mother would kiss her with soft lips and whisper, "*God natt, lille venn,* and sleep well. The best little girl in the whole world...."

Valdis would drift away into sleep, wrapped in clean white linen and a warm hazy glow induced by her mother's voice.

Valdis worked all day at being good. She was patient, did not complain or wheedle, never cried. She did her lessons with painstaking care each day and finished her chores long before nightfall each evening. Yet in spite of her goodness her mother was sending her away. Away from Stridheim, and the only life she knew. Away from the place where her memories of her father were close. She knew he was gone forever; her mother had explained that, yet Valdis sometimes entertained herself with the fancy that he might return. If he was not drowned, only lost in the river current, he would return and find her gone. Now she feared he would never find her, for she was being sent to her Aunt Berit in Christiania. A woman she did not know, in a place she could not imagine. Neither her mother or father had ever been so far away from the valley, so there had never been stories of the place. Uncle Egil called it a city, full of people and tall houses. He promised to join her there, soon, and that made her glad, because he reminded her of her own dear Pappa. Yet in truth he was a stranger to her and she had no wish to live with him and his wife.

She had thought about this all day and most of every night since her mother first told her she must go, but she had yet to find the reason for being sent away. She supposed it had something to do with Pappa's death. Her mother had been strange since her father had gone away. Far away and lost in thought most of the time, but holding her too hard, smothering her, at others. Sometimes Valdis woke in the middle of the night to find her mother tucked into her narrow bed beside her, but in the morning she was gone again, distant, causing Valdis to wonder if she had only dreamt of her mother curled around her in sleep.

She supposed she simply had not been good enough. She had somehow annoyed her mother to such a degree that she could no longer bear having her.

There was no point in wondering now. She was already in the carriage, her things packed and sent with her to Christiania. Uncle Egil explained that she must be patient, for it would be one whole day's journey before she reached his home. Her Aunt Berit was waiting for her. Uncle Egil promised that her Aunt Berit was glad to have her come.

Valdis leaned against the leather cushion and waited. An endless blur of green leaves and white bark passed outside the carriage as they drove miles through thick forests of birch and pine. At midday the driver stopped beside water that glistened bright blue under a strong sun and handed her down from the carriage. She brought with her the basket she carried and ate bread and brown cheese while sitting on a flat gray stone. The air was crisp and cool. At first she thought the lake beautiful, but soon she forgot to notice. She sat with the bread forgotten on her lap and thought of ways to be good, better. She would not offend Aunt Berit and risk being sent away from there as well.

Sixteen

JUST REWARD

✷ I'll collect the water. You must rest," Egil said as he followed Jorunn across the yard. In the two days since the girl
had left Jorunn stayed in constant motion, her pace frenzied.
Egil recognized that she carried on to distract her thoughts
and fought the urge to restrain her physically. He was fright-
ened for her, and for the child she carried. His child. It was
still unreal to him. In spite of the circumstances he felt his
heart lift and stifled the urge to cry aloud his joy at the idea.
He had given up all hope of being blessed with a child, fear
that this unexpected gift might be snatched from him rendered
him speechless.

"I can't rest. There's work to be done," Jorunn replied as
she cranked the well wheel in agitated circles. She waited for
the spasm she knew would sear through her and welcomed it;
the punishment of her body in some way brought relief from
the agony of mental torment she endured since Valdis had
gone. Suddenly she cried out, cringing under the force of the
pain. This was different, starting not beneath her breast to
radiate across her womb, but ripping across her lower back
with enough force to take her breath away. When it abated
she became aware of a warm rush of slippery fluid between her
thighs, and fear quelled the anguish of Valdis' loss. She would
not risk losing this child as well.

Egil took careful hold of her and pulled her toward the
house, his heart pounding so hard he heard the beat of it in

his head. Jorunn read the fear in his face and spoke in a voice to calm him.

"It's time. Ride for the midwife," she instructed. "She lives in the village, near the blacksmith."

Helping her over the threshold he replied, "I'll have no midwife attend my child's birth. I shall ride for the physician at once. You must lie in wait, yet I do not like to leave you alone. Shall I call your mother to you?"

"No!" she cried in alarm, then gasped as another pain took her breath away. "I won't have her in my house!"

Surprise registered clearly in Egil's face, then gave way to alarm as Jorunn doubled over and groaned aloud.

"Hurry, there isn't much time," she told him. He turned and ran from the house without further urging, mounting his horse and riding at breakneck speed down the hill to the village below.

There was much speculation in the village the rest of that week as to the errand which brought Egil Halvorsson to the physician that day. It was said that the unholy child, Valdis, had left Stridheim only a few days earlier. Doctor Tveter rode out with Halvorsson, and from the light in his windows was judged not to have returned until long past supper, giving rise to whispers of terrible illness, even contagious disease at the farm of Jorunn Sigurdsdatter. All week the wives wondered aloud to one another, until Sunday, when Egil Halvorsson returned. This time he had hitched the team to a wagon and he drove through town with Jorunn Sigurdsdatter by his side. She sat proud, her bearing erect. His face was grave as he drove resolutely through the village, folk pausing in their conversations as they passed along the street.

In front of the church he reined in the team and climbed down to tie the horses. Returning to Jorunn he lifted his arms to her and she gave him the bundle she carried. In the stillness the sound of an infant's cry rang out. The wives turned each to another of one accord, shock evident in the faces of some, surprise worn in the expressions of others. A few exchanged knowing glances and sly smiles. The door of the church closed with a thud that resounded in the square. Conversation resumed at once, the high pitch of it discernible even through the solid walls of the church.

Jorunn turned to Egil, her face proud, her tone haughty. "What did I tell you? Far better to stay at Stridheim and let them wonder. Why should I provide grist for the mill of their gossip? Did you intend to humiliate me and bring shame on your son?"

He faced her, his voice hard in resolve. "You know that is not the case. It is best to face them at once. Time will not dim their memories or soften their attitude. 'Let he that is without sin amongst us cast the first stone.' Our errand is necessity. You must be forgiven and accepted back into God's grace. Our son must be offered to him and accepted into his fold...."

"I won't ask for forgiveness for something I don't consider sinful," she interrupted in anger, the color in her cheeks burning high.

"Then I shall ask for you. The mother of my son must live under God's protection."

Giving her the babe he took her arm and marched firmly toward the alter. The priest entered from the left chamber and Egil turned to him saying, "This our son. I come to pay penance, for he is born out of wedlock. We beg forgiveness and pray that our actions would not invoke the wrath of God upon our child. I ask you to intervene with Our Father and deliver our child into His care."

Nodding gravely the priest answered simply, "It shall be done. What shall the child be called?"

With a glance at Jorunn's stony face Egil replied, "Halvor, son of Egil."

Seventeen

TRESPASS

✤⁊ When the spring planting started Jorunn was surprised to discover that Egil had hired two men to help him.

"You must see to the old house, make it livable," he instructed. "The men I have hired will stay there. I intend to turn my attention to the wood. I've an eye toward expanding the timber felling Erland began."

Jorunn sat with Halvor at her breast, watching as his blue eyes disappeared behind heavy lids. He dozed, replete, yet she was loathe to put him from her. 'Eleven years since I held Harald in my arms,' she reflected, but the shaft of pain she always suffered at the thought was less than usual. Through the years she had carried the image of her first born in her mind's eye; she carried the void of his loss in her heart. Yet this child, her son, had miraculously begun to heal the wound of her grief. She cradled him closer, looked up at Egil and focused with effort on necessary task. "When will they come?"

"They arrive in the morn. It should be done today," he answered. Watching her he ventured, "Will you have help? There is plenty to occupy your time in caring for the child. I could arrange for a girl to come each day to help you in the yard."

Smiling up at him she replied, "I'm not that lazy yet. I'm Mistress of Stridheim, I'll care for the house and yard here."

She stood and carried the babe to the cradle Erland had carved long ago. She tucked him carefully beneath the blankets and turned to lace her bodice. She knew Egil's eyes were on her, felt warmth spread through her under his scrutiny. She lifted her gaze to his and saw the desire apparent there. She stared at him candidly, dropping her fingers from her laces, in open invitation.

Turning abruptly he strode to the door. Pausing in the hall, he did not turn to face her as he said, "It is wrong. I have prayed for forgiveness, and I will not willingly commit the sin of adultery again."

The door closed behind him and she was left to stand alone, her color high in indignation, while she listened to the crunch of gravel beneath his retreating boots.

❧ ❧ ❧

The planting was soon underway, leaving Egil free to venture into the wood to survey the land there. On the second day he left just after daybreak, returning in only a few hours.

"Jorunn!" he called as he rode from the wood into the yard. She left the bread she kneaded, surprised to hear him return so soon.

In the yard he swung down from his horse as she approached. "Jorunn, how far had Erland come in his venture with the timber? I believed from our earlier conversations that he had barely begun, and had felled only that which lay in proximity to the river."

Wringing the flour from her hands she answered, "That's right. He made up his mind to take only what was easily accessible since he was going to take so little."

"Then someone has crossed onto my land and stolen from it. Much further into the wood, a good distance from Glomma, there has been cleared a great deal of timber," he said angrily.

"Gunnar Ellefsson," she countered after a moment's pause. "It has to be."

With an abrupt nod Egil said, "I believe it to be so. Much of his land has been cleared, with no sign of replanting from what I could discern from our border."

Without another word he mounted and rode away, back through the wood, in the direction of Ellefsson's place. Jorunn felt a chill, and shivered. Glancing up at the sky she watched a thick wall of cloud move slowly to obliterate the sun. The smell of rain was heavy in the air. She hurried to collect the linen she had strung to dry earlier in the day. From the look of the heavens it would likely pour. She regretted that Egil had ridden out on such an afternoon. He would surely be soaked before his return.

The rain began in the late afternoon, soft and fine. In the gray mist the two men returned from the new fields Egil had set them to clearing, and Jorunn busied herself with ladling stew. By easy habit she sliced thick slabs of bread and served them, but her own supper went untouched.

When evening fell the sounds of the rain grew loud as it pelted the roof. The sky was black; she grew anxious for Egil's return. As if sensing her unease Halvor was restless, unwilling to doze at her breast. She fussed with him, glad of the preoccupation. By the time Egil finally returned the weather had grown so violent that it drowned out the sound of him in the yard. He opened the door and it blew from him, slamming against the wall of the house, causing her to cry out in fright. The look on his face was fierce.

"What's the matter? What's made you so angry?"

"It is worse than I first thought."

"What's worse?" she cried in alarm. "Why are you so late? What kept you so long at Ellefsson's?"

Peeling off his drenched clothing he turned to hang it on wooden pegs beside the door. When he came to his underwear he stopped and looked at her, silently bidding her turn away. She stared back, uncomprehending, intent only on discovering what had so infuriated him.

With a sound of irritation he pushed past her and climbed the stairs to the room where he spent his nights. She followed, undeterred in her pursuit of an explanation. In his room he stripped off his wet underwear and quickly pulled on new. From behind him he heard Jorunn's voice demand, "Tell me now before I go mad wondering! What's happened to make you so angry?"

Startled, he turned to find her standing close to him in the small room under the eaves.

"*Herregud*, woman! Give a man some peace, would you?" He cried, his fury spilling over onto her.

"I won't!" she retorted. "Not until you tell me what's going on."

"Gunnar Ellefsson has been clearing my timber. He has virtually raped his own land. For at least ten years he has cleared his forest without the slightest effort to replant. When his own wood started to dwindle he crossed the border and took from mine. For two seasons he has cleared my land. He farms no longer, he merely takes from the land, putting nothing back."

The anger Egil vented spilled over and she let herself be riled. "Did you talk to him? Have you tracked him down and hanged him like the thief he his?" she demanded indignantly.

Surprise at her words penetrated the fog of his anger and he stared at her a long moment before answering. "I am not a lawless man. I have spoken to him, surely. I found him at the river, sending a load of what is probably my timber downstream. I confronted him, but he denied any knowledge of the trespass, of course. He implied that if any border had been crossed it was without his knowledge, that the men who work for him had done so in ignorance."

"Could that be the case? Do you think that's what happened?"

"*Nei,* I do not. They take their orders from him. In any case, his demeanor warned me that he is not trustworthy."

"Erland never liked the man, I know that much. They worked side by side, but there was never any camaraderie between them."

She sank down on the bed, her face creased in concern. "What should we do?"

"I have made it clear he must control his men and that no further trespass will be tolerated. Ellefsson was insolent in reply, saying it was I who trespassed, and bid me leave his land!"

Jorunn saw his anger flare again and felt her own ire rise to match. "You have to go to the courts, seek recompense for what he's taken!" she insisted. "It's only fair he repay what he's stolen."

"I have considered it, yet the judge will not come for months. By then I must be in Christiania. When the Storting meets I should be in attendance. There has been great unrest in the party of late. The Swedes still refuse Norwegians the right to choose our own head of state, and many are promoting more forceful expression of our discontent. The idea of a united Scandinavia is waning in popularity; the majority of Liberals want the union with Sweden dissolved. They want independence now, at any cost. I had hoped after Thrane and his supporters were imprisoned for rioting the radicals would understand the folly of rash action, but it would seem there is always a new agitator within our ranks."

"I don't care what that fool Thrane gets up to. Last I heard he was on a boat to America, and I say good riddance! All I care is that you stop Ellefsson from stealing from Stridheim.

Herregud, Egil! You call yourself master of this place, it's time you start putting Stridheim before all other consideration! Let Ueland and Sverdrup take care of politics and government. Your place is here, protecting Stridheim!"

"Jorunn, we discussed this before. If farmers are not allowed to represent their own interests in government, no one else will. Even men like Sverdrup fight first and foremost for their own causes. He is of liberal inclination, and an advocate of the common man, but not of small farmers in particular. It is my duty as Master of Stridheim to protect my land from taxation, and my crops from cheap imports from other countries. These things have a great impact on Stridheim, they change a way life that has existed here for hundreds of years. Already imported wheat has influenced me toward dairy farming. We need greater yields, and to consider production for sale. Only those farms that expand and change to accommodate modern agricultural standards are going to survive increased trade and the industrial revolution. Farmers who cling to the old ways, who produce only enough to survive from season to season, are going to fail. It's uneconomical. There is no place for them in the future. Modern agriculture is based on rationalism and efficiency."

It was an argument he had voice many times, and against her will Jorunn recognized the truth in his words. She thought briefly of her father, and Valgaard, yet the idea of how this would affect Stridheim drowned all other consideration. If Egil must see to the future of agriculture, it fell to her to protect her land. And in the case against Ellefsson she could see no viable way of doing that.

"I understand you must go," she conceded. "Yet the courts offer no recourse for me, a woman without right even to my own place," she flashed, her voice thick with anger and resentment.

"It is for this, too, the Liberal Party fights," Egil soothed. "To make suffrage universal, for both men and women. But you must be patient; these things take time and diligence. Stay here and run this place for now; I'll see to the rest. We must overlook that which Ellefsson has taken thus far and content ourselves with having stopped his progress. I made it clear to him I shall guard my land carefully in the future."

"Surely he won't dare cross the border again," Jorunn asserted. But her voice lacked conviction, to even her own ears. Gunnar Ellefsson had never inspired her trust, she felt no real surprise at his sly trespass and thievery. She deemed him capable of such and much worse. Yet she had thought him to possess greater wit. His brazen denial of the act was open insult to Egil, who was not a man to tolerate impudence. Canny instinct warned her Gunnar Ellefsson's foolish bravado would carry him further down his ill-chosen path. A sense of foreboding settled over her, plaguing her throughout that warm, heavy summer.

The days passed quickly, spent in busy preparation for a harvest that would be unparalleled in plenitude. Egil left the hired men to tend the fields and busied himself arranging for sale of the excess crop. Jorunn was occupied running the house and yard, and caring for Halvor. Their babe grew round and fat, thriving as none of her other children had. He was strong and happy, content to spend his time eating and sleeping and watching his mother at work, his round blue eyes traveling after her as she moved.

As summer waned and the air grew chill Jorunn prepared for the harvest. She ventured into the wood, gathering blueberries which grew in abundance that year. From the yard she collected gooseberries and currants from which she made jams and pressed juice. The bounty she reaped on Stridheim that year was overwhelming. When the harvest was over she was ripe and replete, filled to the overflowing with satisfaction.

Egil took his leave one early morn when frost lay thick on the black earth of the fields surrounding them.

"We'll miss you," she ventured, hugging Halvor close.

He stretched out one hand to touch the babe's round cheek and replied, "No more than I shall miss the two of you. If you should need anything you must send word."

Jorunn smiled at the concern in his voice. "What could we need? I never dreamt of having so much. You go, tend your affairs in Christiania, so you can return in the spring with a clear conscience."

His face darkened and she regretted at once her choice of words. She pressed her fingertips to his lips and said, "Don't think about it. You've no call for an uneasy conscience. We've atoned for what you believe to be our sin. Since then you've done nothing to make you uneasy," she said. "Go now, to Berit, and to Valdis. Take care of them as you've cared for us." She kept her voice strong, her face smooth as she called to him in farewell. She watched as he rode away. Only when he disappeared from view did she press Halvor close and give way to the longing she had suppressed all summer.

Eighteen

RETRIBUTION

  Winter that year was dry and cold. Day after day the sun rose in a clear blue sky with no cloud to mar it. Pale yellow rays shone down to light each day brilliantly, reflecting off the slight scattering of snow that covered the land. Jorunn ventured out often, with Halvor bundled and strapped to her back. Almost daily the two of them went on long forays, crisscrossing fields frozen hard beneath her boots. Jorunn spoke to her son of the land, of Stridheim. Of his people and hers, and how lives had intertwined and given rise to him. "*Skatten min,* my treasure," she whispered to him, nuzzling her warm nose to his tiny cold one. He laughed in unadulterated joy, a sound clear and pure in the winter air. Never had she imagined life could be so good.

    Once that winter she caught sight of her mother. Jorunn and Halvor were crossing the field below the house, on a path that intersected the road to Dal. The wind was brisk, and came swirling down the mountain to buffet them from all sides. Halvor's small hands were cold on her cheeks as she carried him, but when he leaned close to her his breath was sweet and warm. Topping a small rise, Jorunn spied her mother coming up from the village. A lone figure dressed in heavy woolens of gray and brown, the wind whipped at her clothing. She walked with her shoulders bent against it. To Jorunn's mind she looked fragile, beaten down by forces greater than herself.

At the place where the road forked she watched Astrid stop and look toward Stridheim before turning down the path to her own place. From her vantage point on the hill Jorunn imagined she could see Astrid's face clearly, and longed to call to her. 'Mother!' She could almost hear herself cry the word aloud.

As if sensing her presence Astrid stopped and turned back. Jorunn stood poised on the hill, feeling across the way her mother's stare. She raised one arm in salute and waited.

For a moment she thought Astrid would come to her. She imagined she saw in her posture the tendency to move in her direction. Something light welled up inside her, hope she had not realized she harbored.

Astrid turned to walk the road home alone, giving no signal she had seen her daughter.

❧ ❧ ❧

When March drew to a close the fields in Hedmark County lay bare. The freeze that year was deep, there being no snow to insulate the earth. Jorunn woke each day in a frigid room watching her breath make white puffs in the air. She despaired of the bitter cold, felt a great longing for spring. For longer, warmer days, for budding forsythia. She longed for the time of year that would call Egil to back to Stridheim.

He came on a windy day late in March. Jorunn and Halvor had been on an excursion, this day walking eastward with their faces to the sun all morning, pausing to share lunch when the rays struck from directly above. Sitting on a bare stone they shared thick slices of bread and brown goat cheese she carried with them, then crossed the field to the river to drink icy water. Glomma ran remarkably low for the time of year. Little snow had fallen; even when the thaw came the banks would not swell much above their present level. Jorunn studied the water level with a furrowed brow, before turning toward the sun and following it westward, home.

She topped the rise to the yard with cheeks bright from the wind and the exertion of carrying Halvor. He had grown sturdy in his first year. "Soon you'll be walking, *gutten min*, and it's a good thing, too. You're too heavy to carry," she told him over her shoulder. He laughed out loud, uncomprehending, yet always happy to hear his mother's voice. His disposition was easy, laughter coming to him as naturally as breathing.

It was then she noticed Egil's horse tethered outside the barn. A surge of pure joy coursed through her and she rushed to the house heedless of Halvor bouncing on her back.

Egil stepped from the barn and met her in the yard. "You are glad of my return," he said with a smile to match her own. "And I am happy to be here. Everything is well?"

"Yes, we're both fine. We didn't expected you so soon. The freeze is deep, there's no hope of planting yet. I planned to send word when the time neared."

He plucked the babe from where he was tucked behind Jorunn and held him close. Halvor frowned, his lower lip drooping in discontent at the stranger who robbed him of his mother's presence. Before the wail Jorunn knew was imminent could surface she stretched out her arms to retrieve the child, but Egil refused.

"He must resign himself to me," he said over Halvor's cries of protest. "I am his father." With that he tossed the child high, transforming Halvor's wails to shrieks of joy. Jorunn watched as the two made new acquaintance. A warmth spread through her, erasing the last vestige of winter's chill.

The next morning Jorunn heard Egil ride into the wood just after daybreak. She lay suspended between slumber and full conscious and relished the idea that he was returned to her. He still kept to his room upstairs, yet it was comfort simply to have him near. All that day she went about her work with a light heart, her spirits lifted by news of Valdis. Egil related that the girl was happy and content; he and Berit considered her a blessing in their household. When evening came Jorunn opened the door to Egil with a smile.

He brushed past her, his face dark in anger.

"What's the matter?" she asked in alarm. "What's happened to make you so angry?"

"He has continued unabated in his thievery," Egil ground out, his voice harsh and bitter. "All winter he has worked, unhampered by snow, to clear great areas of my forest. For this he shall pay. I ride out early in the morning to collect a magistrate and witnesses. In the fall, when the courts convene, I shall seek recompense."

Jorunn felt her own anger begin a slow burn. "Gunnar Ellefsson," she said. "He's a liar and a thief. He has to pay, Egil," she said, clutching his arm in her distress. Egil looked into her face, saw the light of passion burning in her eyes. For a moment he was taken aback at the intensity he saw reflected there.

"This is nothing for you to be concerned with," he soothed. "The law provides recourse, and Gunnar Ellefsson shall be held accountable. You must trust in that and tend to the child, see to the yard. The rest is my responsibility."

Jorunn turned away, irked at the tone he used. She crossed to the kitchen to finish the meal she was preparing. Frustration gnawed at her. She felt sick with desire for quick retribution. With difficulty she controlled herself and picked up the carving knife to slice the joint. The blade flashed in the candlelight and something flickered deep inside her. Something that drowned the sickness she felt. She felt a tiny frisson of fear and drew a deep breath. It was as Egil had said. Far better for her to tend the house and yard while he sorted out this matter with Gunnar Ellefsson.

Spring and summer in the valley stretched on as dry as the winter had been. Those who planted waited in vain for rain that would cause their seed to spire, while on Stridheim Egil planted only minimal crops, concentrating instead on the felling of timber. When fall came the harvest was meager in Hedmark. There was an atmosphere of frustration pent up during the hot dry months, of desperation at the thought of a winter that would be hard. The cold and darkness of the coming months would be felt more keenly by people weighted by hunger and anxiety.

In late October a judge convened in the district; Egil Halvorsson was bid call witnesses against his neighbor, Gunnar Ellefsson. In the weeks before the case was to be presented Egil was moody and anxious. His presence, usually a blessing to Jorunn, became oppressive. She longed to have the affair done with so she and Halvor might resume their life alone. In idle moments she reflected that for a long while her greatest desire had been that Egil share her life on Stridheim. In her mind she supposed this would make her complete. In her heart she longed for him; with her body she craved him. Now she resigned herself to life alone with a feeling akin to relief. If she struggled at all with the disillusionment Egil's presence these past months had visited upon her it was quickly tempered by the thought that this enlightenment was a gift. Never again would she pine for the comfort of his presence during chill autumn evenings or twilight winter days. Never again would she allow herself to lie awake through warm summer nights and ache for the want of him. She came to realize she had strayed from the one simple truth she had always known:

that Stridheim offered her all she would ever need. Her place, her land. If life never offered her greater wisdom this would be enough.

On the afternoon of the third day of the hearing Egil swept into the hall heady with victory. Jorunn sat weaving in the sitting room. Rushing to her he lifted her in his arms, swinging her about in abandon.

"I am vindicated! The case was speedily assessed. The judge resolved that Gunnar Ellefsson is guilty of trespass and thievery. He has been ordered to pay recompense. Let's celebrate! Tonight we shall drive into Hamar and dine at the inn. It has been a long and confining season. I have need of a respite from this place."

Jorunn pulled away, the happiness in her face dimming. "We can't. There's the child to consider. We can't take him with us, and there's no one to care for him in my absence."

'And I don't dare appear in public with you, even farther afield than in Dal,' she thought. The fear that someone by word or deed would humiliate them was too great. Only on Stridheim was she free of the judgment of the righteous who would condemn her. Here she was at peace with her life. It was here she would stay.

The light in Egil's face faded. She watched him pull away, knew he felt trapped. It was not a life he could share with her. She felt a pain in her breast. In that moment hope died.

Early next morn Egil rode out in return to Christiania. As usual, she watched him go with regret. For the first time it was shadowed with relief.

✤ ✤ ✤

Two days later she ventured into the forest with Halvor strapped to her back. He was a sturdy walker now, yet she felt restless, impatient to distance herself from the yard for a few hours. Since Egil's departure she was stalked by discontent. She blamed him for contaminating the peace she had always enjoyed within the confines of the fences surrounding Stridheim.

She walked steadily for an hour, lifting her skirt to cross fallen limbs, shifting the weight of Halvor to make her breathing easier. She tired, and sensed a restlessness in the child. She lifted him from his perch and let him wander, following him at his pace, letting her thoughts drift. She watched her son roam the wood, dreaming ahead to the day when he would be master here. His right uncontested, she felt sure. After so many years she felt certain Berit would not bear a child for Egil. One day Stridheim would belong to Halvor.

It would be a great place. Already it was emerging as one of the finest farms in the county; with her dedication and Egil's vision she had no doubt time would serve this place well. When the time came she would see to it that Egil acquired her father's land, bordering to the west. Her sisters lived comfortably in other places, and would have no call to return. And Gunnar Ellefsson would soon be finished on his place, of that Egil had seemed convinced. It had been ascertained at the hearing that he had no money to pay recompense. That which he earned, he spent. He cleared his forest without replenishing it; he let his farmland lie fallow. Soon he would be forced from it and Egil would be well-positioned to acquire the land as part of his compensation. She smiled at the thought, carried away by visions of the future, when Stridheim would stretch far greater than current borders.

Behind her she heard a noise and turned toward it. 'An animal,' she mused, her thoughts recalled to the present. She made up her mind to turn back, retrace their way home.

Halvor was tired from his adventures, his hands full of the treasures he had collected. A stone, a large piece of bark, three red leaves, he clutched. His face was stained blue from late berries he had discovered. She lifted him to her back and turned toward home.

She had not walked far before she became aware she was unsure of her path. In her daydream she had meandered, not tracking her way. She stopped to take her bearings. Once again she heard a noise, a limb cracking. She turned one full circle, her eyes searching, yet she registered nothing. A tendril of fear rose like smoke inside her. She turned in the direction she judged correct and walked quickly.

When next she stopped to listen she was rewarded by the sound of running water. She was nearing Glomma. From there it would be simple to walk upstream until she came to Stridheim. She turned straight toward the water and saw for the first time proof she was being followed. Extending from behind the trunk of a massive pine she could clearly distinguish the outline of a broad shoulder, see the line of an arm pressed into the bark. Her heart pounding, her breathing labored, she walked as quickly as she dared.

She came to a clearing and saw the river glisten in front of her. With relief she turned upstream and walked toward her own farm, realizing she had somehow crossed the border to Ellefsson's land.

At the thought of him the devil appeared. He stepped from behind a tree, directly in front of her. She cried out at the suddenness of his appearance.

He threw back his head and laughed, the sound of it echoing eerily in the forest. She studied his face warily. His beard was unkempt, his eyes bloodshot. The still air carried the scent of him toward her. Sweat, stale beer. She stepped back in revulsion.

She watched his eyes narrow, saw that he enjoyed her reaction. He stepped toward her and she moved sideways to pass.

"Don't you got the courtesy to greet a neighbor when passin'?" he asked, his voice gravelly, his arm reaching out swiftly to take hers. The pressure from his fingers was biting, but she steeled herself not to wince.

"Take your hand off me," she demanded coolly, staring straight ahead, refusing to look his way.

"I wouldn't a' thought you'd be so high and mighty," he said with a smile. "Your husband wasn't even cold in the water when you crawled into bed with his brother."

She turned to him, fury lighting her face, pulling her arm from his grasp. "Keep away from me, do you hear? You've no cause for satisfaction. You're publicly branded a liar and a thief. Do you think anyone in the valley holds you in higher regard?"

His eyes narrowed. Beneath his thin beard she saw his face flush mottled red. "Egil Halvorsson'll pay for that, and so will his whore," he spat out.

With a long look at him she raised her head high, squared her shoulders and turned to leave. After a moment she heard him follow. She halted, and without turning said, "Stay away from me or you'll be the one to pay."

Her voice was soft, yet distinct, the threat weighted by the careful precision of her words. When she resumed walking her footfalls were alone, but she felt the burn of his gaze at her back. Her spine stiff, her jaw clenched, she made her way to the yard, gripped by a sense of forboding. She busied herself with tending the animals and readying the yard for nightfall, taking comfort in the sense of normalcy these tasks restored to her. She shared a bowl of porridge with Halvor, stirring into it an extra measure of butter and honey for comfort, and lingered over tucking him into his cradle. She rocked him gently from side to side, humming softly, watching as his heavy lids obscured bright blue eyes when he drifted into slumber. The utter contentment he embodied tempted her to lift him carefully from his warm cocoon of sheepskin and lay him gently in her bed. Quickly she checked the bolt on the door, hurrying lest the peace she borrowed from Halvor's innocence fade and make way for the fear that plagued her. She extinguished every candle and made her way to bed through the dark hall. The room was flooded with moonlight. She slipped gently into bed and curled her body around the child. She slept to the gentle rhythm of his soft breathing, savoring the warmth of it against her throat.

❧ ❧ ❧

Jorunn awoke in the middle of the dark night to the sound of livestock bleating in panic. The calamity outside set her heart racing as she threw back the blanket and ran to the window. The yard lay in utter darkness. The clouds shifted, revealing a full moon. In the silver light she strained to spot the reason for the alarm. She noticed the barn door, half of it gaping open.

She grabbed her dress from the peg where it hung and pulled it hastily over her head, not bothering to lace the bodice. With a quick glance at the bed where Halvor lay sleeping she left the room for the hall, where she stepped into her boots and pulled open the heavy front door.

In the courtyard the cold night air hit her full force, clearing her head. She was suddenly aware she was unarmed, and hesitated at the thought of investigating further. It was then she caught the first faint whiff of smoke in the frigid air. At the same time she saw yellow light through the open door of the barn and without further thought she raced across the yard and entered.

The sound of the animals was deafening. The rear of the barn was already a wall of flame, fire consuming in a heartbeat the stacks of dry hay piled there. She ran down the line of stalls and lifted the wooden latches, throwing the doors wide. The animals ran in panic, butting against her, pushing at her from all sides. The smoke was gathering in a thick black ceiling; the air was stifling. In utter hopelessness she retreated, then paused to look around in disbelief. There was nothing to be done. Her eyes streaming, she turned toward the door. She spotted him then, his face yellow and orange in the light of the flames. His eyes glittered black. He threw back his head and laughed at the look of horror on her face.

"I said he'd pay, and now he has," Gunnar Ellefsson called over the hiss and crackle of the fire. Jorunn watched him in a daze. He was transformed into something evil beyond her comprehension by the forces that raged around them. She could feel his excitement, palpable in the hot air. He fed on the flames, gathered an unholy strength from them.

"He's paid, but you owe me as well, whore," he hissed, approaching with bold steps from the corner where he lurked. In a split second her mind cleared and she turned to flee.

She was almost at the door when he caught her. Her head jerked backward and she cried out in pain as he grabbed a fistful of the hair that trailed behind her and held her fast. He pulled her to him, his arm snaking around her, one hand embedded in her hair, the other hot and rough as he squeezed her breast, the sour smell of his breath on her cheek hotter still. His tongue slithered out and curled wetly in her ear. Panic and horror overcame her and she cried aloud, a bloodcurdling scream that drowned the noise of his breath and the roar of the fire. He tensed; she felt him stiffen against her back, heard his groan of pleasure. There was a sound, a great rumble, and the earth beneath her trembled. He relaxed his hold and turned toward the wall of flame. She bolted. In four steps she was through the door and plunged into the cold black night. Reaching for the door she slammed it shut and dropped the wooden latch into place. Sparks of fire rained down in the yard as the roof at the rear of the barn began to collapse. She heard Gunnar Ellefsson cry out, saw the door reverberate under the power of his blows.

"Open the door, whore! Let me out and I'll give you what I owe you," he cried, his voice cracking in his dementia.

Suddenly the shaking in her body stilled. She took one step forward on steady legs to call through the door, lest he not hear. "Burn in hell, Ellefsson! Burn in hell!"

An icy calm gripped Jorunn, so cold that even Ellefsson's screams of rage and agony did not pierce its shell. Long after his cries crescendoed and died, while the tongues of flame licked greedily from one building to the next, she stood watching as sparks rained down, spreading the fire from one parched roof to the next. It was almost dawn when the first flames neared the house, and she returned to dress Halvor and herself. She carried him to the yard and stood watching until the roof of the house took fire. All hope gone, she strapped her son to her back and turned toward the mountain, climbing it with resolution born of despair. Halvor seemed suddenly a heavy burden to bear. Without Stridheim her whole existence shifted and his significance in her life was changed. She climbed steadily, stumbling under the weight of the child. He screamed in protest as she lurched forward to catch herself as they fell, grazing her palms against the jagged edges of the rocky mountain. In irritation she hushed him, her voice harsh in the raw morning air. The child's cries stopped abruptly, as if he was buffeted into silence by the unusual blunt edge to his mother's voice. She rose wearily and continued to climb, steeling herself against the pain as the leather straps that harnessed Halvor to her back cut into the soft flesh covering her ribcage when she gasped for air.

At the top of the mountain she paused, but did not look back at Stridheim. Below, her world lay in ruin. She could not bear the sight of the destruction. She closed her eyes and pictured instead the way it had looked just this morning. A cold breeze brushed her cheek and in it she sensed the still, small voice that had been silent so long. In her memory there was the echo of Scripture long forgotten. 'Go forth, and stand upon the mount before the Lord. And, behold, the Lord passed by, and a great strong wind rent the mountains, and brake in pieces the rocks before the Lord; but the Lord was not in the wind, and the Lord was not in the earthquake, and after the earthquake a fire, but the Lord was not in the fire, and after the fire a still and small voice.'

She opened her eyes and stared wildly around, sensing Him close. "Speak to me, then!" she cried aloud, her voice full of pain and desperation. The jagged edges of her cry struck the mountain far away, on the other side of Valgaard, and came back to reverberate in her ears. She listened for the voice, but the echo of her anguish was all she heard. She clenched her fists and ground her teeth to silence a scream that welled in her throat, but could not strangle it. The sound ripped from her, carrying on and on; when it stopped and the echo faded only the cry of the babe strapped to her back cut the still morning air. Empty inside now her fury was spent, she resolutely began her descent, ignoring the wails of her child.

The clear gray light of early morn was all around her as she approached the door to her father's house. He answered her knock, then stepped back to allow her entrance.

"I've nowhere else to go," she said.

"Flames lit the sky in the east when we woke," her father answered. "There's nothin' left?"

Jorunn shook her head. From the kitchen her mother appeared and stood in stony profile.

"Tell the woman she may not stop here. I'll give no shelter to the heretic."

"I'm your daughter, Mother!" Jorunn cried, her voice breaking. "Will you turn your back on me in deference to your God? Does He truly require that of you?"

Astrid turned to face her then, and Jorunn saw her mother's pale blue eyes blaze with righteous indignation. The woman's clear, resonant voice shook with emotion as she preached, "'For a fire is kindled in mine anger, and shall burn unto the lowest hell, and shall consume the earth with her increase, and set on fire the foundations of the mountains. I will heap mischiefs upon them; I will spend mine arrows upon them.'"

Just as suddenly the fire kindled behind those pale irises was extinguished; Astrid turned away from Jorunn.

"Our daughter is dead," she said coldly. "Bid this woman take her leave, Sigurd," she instructed before she turned her back and retreated into the kitchen.

Jorunn turned to face her father, lifting her gaze to his. In those eyes she saw mirrored her own strength and determination, yet in the face of her mother's glacial resolve he was helpless.

"Am I dead to you as well, Father? You hold her God in no higher esteem than you hold your child, twenty years of care taught me that. Does your regard for her make this sacrifice of your flesh and blood necessary?"

Her father was silent a long moment, weighing his words carefully. "It's your mother's house. The burden of childbearin' fell to her, the rearin' of 'em was her lot in life. She never questioned my judgment in that which falls to a man, and is his measure. I give her the same respect." He hesitated, then added, "And the Holy Scripture's clear: 'Every kingdom divided against itself is brought to desolation; and every city or house divided against itself shall not stand.'"

Sigurd Johannesson opened the door of his home and Jorunn passed through it, stinging with his rejection, angered by his hypocrisy. Turning to him she said scathingly, "This house has been divided since its beginning, and religion was the root of the chasm. Yet it seems I am to be the scapegoat. Will you rest easy, Father, imagining with my deliverance comes your absolution?" Jorunn lips twisted into a bitter smile, one brow arched in an attitude of skepticism. She turned resolutely and left the courtyard without a backward glance.

On the road to Dal she heard a rider approach from the rear. He passed, dismounted, then turned to hand her the reins to the horse he rode.

"For the child," he said. "My daughter's son."

After a long pause she echoed, "For the child, then." She mounted and rode in the only direction she could think.

Nineteen

EXILE

⁂ She awoke slowly, disoriented and confused. Above her rich tapestry hung in a solid canopy. The sheet that covered her was of fine linen; unconsciously her fingers traced the initials embroidered on it. She pulled herself up in the soft bed and looked around. Heavy drapes were pulled at the window, only a sliver of light filtered through.

"You wake at last."

A voice from the corner startled her and she clutched the sheet to her breast.

Egil rose from the chair where he sat and crossed to the bed. "Forgive me. I did not mean to startle you. Shall I send for the physician again?"

She shook her head. Then she asked, "Halvor, where is he?" She remembered for an instant her confused resentment of the child, then dismissed the thought as images of Egil's vision of a new Stridheim crowded her mind. While she had lain drifting between blissful unawareness and reality that occasionally impinged upon the soft gray cloud of unconscious where she sought refuge, Egil had come to her. She remembered his touch, the warmth of his hand when he held her icy fingers. He had spoken to her of the future, woven dreams for them both of a new Stridheim. Soon her place would be restored, and she would return to it with her son. Her world shifted again and fell into focus.

"Be easy," he soothed. "The child is with Valdis. She cares for him in the afternoons when she is through with school. Berit has engaged a girl to care for him in the mornings."

"No, I'll care for him myself, like I always have."

Egil rested on the bed beside her. "You have not been well. The physician insists you must rest, regain your strength."

Quite unexpectedly, she was overwhelmed with memories. "Stridheim!" she cried out. Tears welled in her eyes, coursed down her cheeks in weak streams.

"You are exhausted," he said, rising. "You must rest."

Suddenly despair engulfed her, obliterating the vague images Egil had conjured while she drifted. "It's gone. Everything was lost," she cried, sinking against the pillow and sobbing. Her body was ravaged, her soul seared and desolate, just as her land lay now.

Egil returned and leaned over her, taking both her shoulders squarely in his broad hands. "Stridheim is there, can never be obliterated. The buildings were lost, yet the land remains. It is all that matters. I shall rebuild the yard, make it better than before. Already I have hired an architect to plan for it. Stridheim shall boast a modern yard, the best in all of Hedmark County. I travel with the architect to survey the area as soon as possible. I waited only to speak with you."

"How long....?" she began.

"A few days, not yet a week. You have been ill, worn out from your rigors. If you can bear to speak of it, I must know what happened."

Sitting up, drawing her strength, she began, "It was Ellefsson."

"I suspected as much, damn him!" Egil burst out. "He's not fit to hang, I should kill him myself!" he cried, fury making him shake.

In the depths of the great bed Jorunn was quiet. Misinterpreting her silence Egil turned to her and begged, "Forgive me. I should not upset you. I did not mean that; I spoke rashly, in anger. I'll approach the magistrate and bid him bring Ellefsson to justice. I ride out this very day."

He moved to leave and Jorunn said quietly, "It's too late."

He crossed to the window and pulled back the heavy drapes, letting light flood the dim room. "It is not late, it is midday. You have lost track of time...." His voice faded away as he faced her. In her countenance he saw something that alerted him.

"Too late for what?" he asked softly, warily.

His eyes probed hers, delving into her soul. For a moment she cowered, then her strength surged. She raised her chin and said, "Justice has already been served with regard to Gunnar Ellefsson." She paused, then finished simply, "He's dead."

Something in her attitude held Egil captive. He studied her carefully, looking for clues to the person this woman was. Her face closed, hardened, and he knew it was useless.

"What are you trying to tell me? How did he die?" Egil asked her, his voice cautious.

"He burned to death in the barn that night. He died of his own hand," she asserted, her voice strong, denying him to refute it.

He stared at her for a long while, then moved away, his eyes trained on her as he backed toward the door. "Is there more I should know before I ride out?" he asked her carefully.

Her mouth thinned, the angles of her face hard in the morning light. "Nothing. Now go. Do what has to be done so I can return to my home."

Egil turned to go, but stopped at the door. With his back toward her he said, "Jorunn, my wife believes Halvor to be my brother's son. A few months difference in age is not apparent to her; she has no experience of children." He paused, but there was no reply from Jorunn. "I would not deny my son, yet in present circumstances I saw no other way," he finished, his voice strained. He left the room, closing the door quietly behind him.

Jorunn was relieved he did not turn back, would not have him see the flush that stained her pale cheeks. "We all do what we must," she said aloud in his defense, in her defense. Irritated at the shame that stirred in her conscience, she rose and crossed to the window. Pushing aside the lace that obscured her view she stared at the busy street below. Women in bright coats and frivolous bonnets strolled by; men in tall black hats paused to greet one another. Occasionally a carriage passed.

Beyond the cobbled street there was a park. Paths were neatly laid out, bordered by shrubs devoid of greenery. Poplins raised stark limbs toward a bleak gray sky.

Behind her Jorunn heard a soft rap at the door. She turned as it opened and a woman stepped in. She was diminutive in stature; hardly taller than a child, Jorunn reflected as she took stock of her. Black hair was drawn severely back from a small, pointed face. Straight dark brows framed onyx eyes that tilted over high cheekbones. Unlike anyone Jorunn had ever known. She knew at once this was Berit.

"You are up? You must be recovering," she said, her voice as cool and smooth as the waters of Glomma on a still day.

Jorunn nodded. "Halvor? Where is he?"

Berit crossed to the window and looked out. "There," she said pointing toward the park. "That is Valdis, in the dark blue coat and bonnet. Halvor sits in the carriage."

"I didn't recognize her," Jorunn breathed. In the distance she could see a graceful figure in skirts so wide the rest of her slender form seemed insubstantial. She pushed a carriage, large wheels spinning round. Halvor was hidden from view by the hood of the shiny perambulator; it was Valdis Jorunn trained her eyes greedily upon.

"She's grown," Jorunn remarked, unaware of how forlorn her voice was.

Berit nodded. "She has her height from you, I think. And the look of her as well. She is beautiful." That smooth voice was suddenly distorted by a sharp edge.

Jorunn turned to the other woman warily, but Berit's face was smooth. Her eagerness to hear more of her child drowned every other consideration. "Tell me all about her," Jorunn pleaded. "I've missed her."

"I shall, but you must first return to bed. The physician instructs you must rest until you regain your strength."

"It's not necessary," Jorunn protested, yet she let Berit lead her back to the great bed and settle her there. Berit drew a chair from the corner and sat opposite her.

"Valdis has had an easy adjustment. She attends Ole Hartvig Nissen's School for Girls, and enjoys her time there. She is hungry for knowledge, and a quick learner," Berit began. A shadow crossed her face. "There is only one area in which her education seems to have been neglected. The child has no religious background."

Jorunn felt herself rile. "No, she hasn't," she answered shortly.

A flush stained Berit's pale skin. "I see. Well, the omission has been amended. She worships at the cathedral with us each Sunday, and most afternoons she spends with me, occupying herself with errands of Christian mercy," she said, a hint of piety in her cool manner.

Jorunn made no reply. After a moment Berit rose to go, saying, "I think you must be tired. It is better we continue our conversation another time." At the door she turned to say: "Egil had some things from the mercantile sent for you. There are dresses, and a coat, in the wardrobe. In the chest you will find the rest of what you require. If the fit is not good enough I shall send for my dressmaker. I expect you will join us for dinner when you feel able. Until then, there is a cord by your bed that you should use to call for help."

Without waiting for a reply she left the room, closing the door firmly behind her. Jorunn lay stinging with the criticism she inferred from Berit's comment on Valdis' lack of religion. She flung back the cover and stood, spurred to action by her irritation, feeling stronger now. She crossed to the wardrobe, her bare feet sinking into the carpet that covered the wood floor.

A flame blazed on the hearth of a fireplace situated at the far end of the room. In front of it was a generous tub perched on molded feet. Jorunn imagined the luxury of sinking into warm water in front of the fire. Returning to the bed she lifted the heavy braided cord and pulled hesitantly. Almost at once there was a rap at the door and a girl appeared. Older than Valdis, Jorunn judged, slender in a black dress, a crisp white apron knotted about her waist. "You rang, ma'am?" she asked.

"I'd like to bathe, please," she replied, feeling a flush begin at the neckline of the gown she wore. She lifted one hand and nervously fingered the tiny pleats and delicate embroidery covering her breasts. The girl seemed not to notice. With a curtsy she disappeared, closing the door softly behind her. Jorunn heaved a sigh of relief at having crossed that hurdle and went to inspect the contents of the wardrobe while she waited for water to be drawn and heated.

The doors gave way easily when she pulled on the intricate handles. Inside were several dresses, all of rich heavy fabric, in muted colors. 'The colors of Stridheim,' she thought with a stab of longing, fingering velvet the shade of Glomma's waters on an overcast day. There was wool the color of wheat when the harvest was near, and a heavy brocade that brought to her mind the memory of heather that grew on the mountain to the west. Grief for the home she had lost overwhelmed her and she dropped her head in defeat.

A noise behind her alerted her the water was arrived. Hastily she withdrew a dress from the collection at random. 'The

color of red currents ripe in the yard,' she mused, feeling the
smooth velvet caress her hand as she laid it gently across the bed.

"There's no need, ma'am," a voice behind her said.
Startled, Jorunn turned to find the young girl she had spoken
to earlier. "My name's Birgitte, ma'am, and I'll look after you."

Jorunn stood uncertainly while the girl bustled about the
room, supervising the water as it was poured into the tub, opening the chest of drawers and extracting innumerable items
which she lay carefully on the bed, beside the dress.

When the tub was full, steam drifting in lazy waves above
it, the young man who had borne the water disappeared with a
bow in her direction and Jorunn was left alone with Birgitte.
The girl picked up a sheet of linen and held it before the tub;
Jorunn understood that she waited for her to disrobe.

"I'll manage alone now, Birgitte. Thank you," she said,
feeling a hot flush creep up her neck to suffuse her face.

Birgitte hesitated, then dropped her arms and folded the
towel carefully before laying it across a chair she pulled near
the tub. "As you wish, ma'am," she said, her eyes trained on
the pattern of the carpet beneath her boots. "Ring when you're
ready to dress." She curtsied again and left the room. Jorunn
exhaled, relieved to be alone at last. She crossed to the door
and quickly turned the key in the latch before returning to
the tub to sink into the warm water, letting it soothe away the
tension that lay in bands about her body. For a long while she
floated, her mind drifting in lazy circles, circumventing the
events of these last days. The crackling of the fire startled her
once or twice, images of that last night on Stridheim still vivid,
yet it seemed the sleep she had drifted in and out of these past
days had dulled them. It was bearable now, the idea the house
and yard were gone. Egil would rebuild them, make Stridheim
better than before. The thought caused her to smile. Hope
surged, and she sat up, rejuvenated. She stood in the water
and let it run in warm rivulets down her body, reaching for the
linen. Wrapping herself in it, she crossed to the bed and ap-
plied her newfound energy toward deciphering the underwear
that lay spread before her. Delicate fabrics, some beautifully
embroidered. She fingered them gently, before lifting a shift
and letting it fall over her, caressing her body. The corset that
lay there mystified her at first, on closer examination she realized help in dressing would be a necessity. Sighing, she crossed
to the rope and rang, then went to unlock the door and wait
for Birgitte. 'It'll take time to get used to new ways,' she reflected. When the door opened she stepped quickly behind it

to conceal herself, hoping fervently Egil would waste no time in rebuilding Stridheim so she might return to life as she knew it.

*ჯ *ჯ *ჯ

The eve Jorunn had first ridden in approach of Egil's residence she had been so worn with fatigue she hardly registered the grandeur of the house. Chiseled from fine gray stone, golden light spilling from tall windows had beckoned her. Clutching Halvor, she had dismounted the horse and stumbled up stone steps to rap wearily on the great double doors.

A girl opened and Jorunn stood on the threshold dazzled by bright light radiating from a chandelier suspended high above. Marble floors reflected yellow rays from innumerable candles burning in double sconces that hung on every wall of the vast hall. At the far end of the marble expanse a stairwell spiraled upward; ornately carved balusters framed steps carpeted in thick red wool.

Jorunn had waited, overwhelmed by the immensity of it all, until Egil appeared and bid her come in. He stretched out his arms to relieve her of the burden of the child she carried, and she relinquished Halvor to him.

She recalled mumbling garbled explanation to his worried questions, before he silenced her and bid her follow him. Up those graceful stairs, to a corridor that stretched on endlessly. She passed countless doors as they traversed the length of the hallway, her boots sinking into a fine, rich runner of patterned wool. At last he stopped; turning a crystal knob he opened a heavy door to admit her to a room that lay blanketed in darkness. The girl who followed them moved quickly, efficiently, to light many candles, illuminating treasures unlike any Jorunn had imagined. Finely carved furniture appeared, bathed in the soft light. Thick velvet draped the windows, heavy fabrics in intricate patterns covered surfaces of gleaming dark wood. At the far end of the room the girl tended a fireplace and there sprang to life a blaze of color and warmth. The flames danced, throwing light and shadow against walls the color of pale, newly churned butter. The room enveloped Jorunn, its beauty soothing her ravaged spirit. She let Egil lead her to the great canopied bed and sat docile while the girl bent before her and removed her boots and stockings. She was hardly aware when Egil left with Halvor, registering only dimly the laughter of the small boy, who seemed happy to encounter a familiar face. She had let the girl put her to sleep in

the great bed, had drifted away while tracing with her fingertips the smooth embroidery on fine linen she lay wrapped in.
    This evening, on her first emergence from the cocoon in
which she had lain, she explored the vast rooms on the first
floor, in search of the dining room. Each seemed immense.
One was decorated predominantly in green, the color of pine
trees in the forest of Stridheim. From floor to soaring ceiling
there were shelves laden with books bound in heavy leather,
gold script glittering softly in the light of the fire that burned
there. Another room shimmered cerulean blue, drapes of silk
framing the windows, accents of silver on every table; chairs
and sofas covered in pale damask invited her to sit and bask in
the muted glory. In the great marble hall a clock chimed seven,
reminding her there was no time to dawdle. She must postpone her discovery of this strange and wonderful place until
later, for the girl, Birgitte, had said that dinner was served
promptly on the hour.
    Jorunn located the dining room at length and entered to
find herself alone. Quickly she assessed her surroundings.
High ceilings loomed above, framed in scrolled plaster molding, crowned in the center with a medallion from which hung
a chandelier. Candles and prisms reflected rainbows of light;
walls painted rich red wrapped around her. The table stretched
the length of the room, massive, glittering darkly in the light from
candles in slender silver candelabra. She took quick note of the
array of dishes and silver on the table before she was distracted.
Berit entered the room, with Valdis trailing close behind.
    "I am pleased you could join us," Berit said, her delicate
features shifting into a smile. "I hope you are feeling well
enough?" The smile that touched her lips never reached her
eyes. They were dark, shuttered, an opaque curtain that allowed no glimpse into her inner thoughts.
    "I'm restored to my usual good health, thank you," Jorunn
replied, her attention distracted, for Valdis stood beside Berit,
tall and slender, her beauty breathtaking. Holding both arms
open Jorunn exhaled, "*Min datter*, it's been so long. You've
been sorely missed on Stridheim."
    Valdis came to her, allowing her embrace. Jorunn hun-
gered for the feel of her child, yet she sensed a new reticence,
something cooler even than the reserve that had always typi-
fied Valdis. 'It's to be expected,' she reasoned, stifling disappointment. 'The girl's been away for over two years. In a few
days we will be used to one another again.'

She watched with hungry eyes as Valdis moved to take her place beside Berit at the long table. She saw Valdis cast a nervous glance in Berit's direction, then drop her gaze to her lap. She was aware the girl was keenly alert to Berit's actions. Jorunn sat down gingerly opposite them, arranging the voluminous folds of skirts much fuller than she was accustomed, awkward in the petticoat of hoops Birgitte had insisted she wear. She turned her attention to Berit, who spoke to her.

"The gown fits you well. Egil has judged your size almost perfectly, I venture." She lifted her spoon, her eyes trained to the bowl a servant placed before her. Jorunn studied her countenance carefully, sensing another meaning, but if something different was implied it was not evident in Berit's expression.

"I'm grateful he was so thoughtful. Everything at Stridheim was lost," Jorunn replied cautiously.

"Yes, Egil is thoughtful," Berit agreed, glancing at Jorunn before returning her attention to the soup. "He has always been so, since I first knew him, which has been a very long time."

Jorunn shifted uncomfortably, suffering the pinch of stays in her corset and longing for deliverance from this place and its strange ways.

"Passionate, as well," Berit continued. "The things he cares about affect him deeply." She paused, gauging the effect of her words. Jorunn struggled to hide her discomfiture, searching in vain for a way out of the maze of Berit's conversation. No avenue presented itself, and Berit continued, her voice suddenly artificially light.

"We first met when he was a student at The Royal Frederick's University."

Black eyes met blue and Jorunn imagined Berit's chin lifted almost imperceptibly, her attitude one of challenge. Then Berit's heavy lids dropped to curtain that dark gaze, and she continued her story.

"He was such an intense young man, full of dreams for a liberal Norway. He came to the capitol determined he should give farmers a voice in government. Like so many of his fellow students at university he was inspired by Ole Gabriel Ueland. They envisioned a modern, independent Norway, in which political power would rest with the common man, and local self-government would play a greater role in shaping the country. Egil fairly burned with idealism in those days. His passion for his cause, I confess, touched me in a way I had never previously imagined."

Berit paused, the short silence full of innuendo. Jorunn shifted uncomfortably and glanced at Valdis. Berit saw the look and smiled, the corners of her mouth lifting slightly, her lips parting to reveal small, even teeth, white and sharp. Her dark eyes glittered, and quite unexpectedly Jorunn felt her throat constrict, heard her own breath catch. At the sound Berit's smile grew wider. "In a very innocent way, naturally. I was only a girl, but I knew. I made up my mind as I watched him pass on the street outside the parlor window that I would marry him one day. He passed this house each day. The university is situated on the corner, only two blocks away. My mother insisted I practice the piano every morning. I was not particularly gifted, and my attention wandered. I confess I committed as much of my attention toward studying passersby through the window as I did to my sheets of music." She smiled, a twist of her mouth that did nothing to relieve the intensity of her expression.

From the kitchen door a girl appeared and quietly collected the bowls. Jorunn rested her spoon on the plate exactly as Berit had. Berit did not look at the girl, yet Jorunn sensed nothing escaped the notice of those quick dark eyes. Berit sat erect, her posture perfect, her attitude one of utter control.

"You mention your mother," Jorunn ventured. "Does she live here as well?" she asked, with a glance about her. She found it impossible to register that a place so great housed only three people. There were the servants, of course. Jorunn ventured no guess as to how many people that comprised. It seemed at every turn she was confronted by another girl dressed in black wool, a white apron knotted at her waist, a starched white scarf covering her hair.

"My mother passed away when I was eighteen," Berit replied, adjusting the napkin on her lap. She waited as the girl placed before them plates carefully arranged with fine roast beef and vegetables. "Shortly after I became engaged to Egil she fell ill, and died quite suddenly.'

"I'm sorry," Jorunn said, feeling her cheeks grow warm. "I had no idea. Your father is in good health?"

"Yes, although he chooses not to live here any longer. He moved residence to an apartment in a new building erected after the fire. He appreciates modern comforts, and likes to be near his work. It is only a short walk from the Stock Exchange, on Voll Street. It is convenient for him, and a relief for Egil and myself to have more time alone," she finished, her attention on the bread she buttered carefully. Her voice was cool and smooth, but her words hung between the two women, heavy with implication.

"I don't intend to intrude any longer than necessary," Jorunn replied, her tone frosty. "As soon as Stridheim is livable I'll return. I long for it."

Berit lifted her gaze to Jorunn, her expression a studied mirror of concern. "I beg your pardon, Jorunn, it was not my intention to make you unwelcome. As my husband's sister-in-law you shall have a home here for as long as you like. I am only sorry I did not have the pleasure of knowing your husband, Egil's brother, while he lived. Yet you are family, and should consider our home your own." She lifted her napkin from her lap, patted her lips. Jorunn studied her carefully, imagining she covered a smile of satisfaction behind the linen.

Beside Berit, Valdis picked daintily at her food. The child was changed, Jorunn admitted to herself. Her movements were still graceful, her features as delicate, yet there was a new air, an attitude she had not worn before.

"Are you enjoying school, Valdis?" Jorunn questioned.

"Very much," she replied.

"Have you any friends?"

"A few," Valdis answered. "I do not spend my afternoons frivolously, as some of the girls would. I accompany Aunt Berit on her visits to the sick and poor. It is my duty as one of God's children to care for his others, those who are less fortunate. His message is clear: 'Even so faith, if it hath not works, is dead.'"

Jorunn felt a sting of irritation at Valdis' attitude. She had obviously proven an apt pupil to Berit's religious instruction. There was something unnatural about the child, yet in some way familiar. Her speech, perhaps. No longer the high and light singsong of her childhood, her voice had deepened into one more vibrant. The soft sounds of the valley were honed to the clear and distinct sounds of Christiania. Her speech had new precision and a resonance somehow familiar to Jorunn. Valdis turned her face toward Berit for her approval and Jorunn felt her stomach knot. In profile the girl was like Astrid. In her expression she reflected the pietism Jorunn associated with her mother. Swallowing hard she carefully laid her knife and fork across the plate. A sudden constriction in her throat would make eating an impossibility, she knew.

After a moment Berit took note of Jorunn's position. "You are unwell? You have no appetite. Should I send for the physician?"

Jorunn shook her head. "I'm only sick with longing for Halvor. I haven't seen him since I woke. He was out all afternoon, and the girl who cares for him was bathing him when I last asked for him."

"I am sure he will be sleeping now," Berit replied. "Yet if you like I shall have someone show you to his room. You may be excused," she said dismissively, grasping in her slender fingers the silver bell resting beside her plate. As Jorunn left the room she failed to notice the smooth white hand that moved to cover Valdis' smaller one. Berit squeezed the cold fingers in her clasp in gentle approval.

In silence Jorunn followed the straight, black-clad figure of the girl instructed to show her to Halvor's room. They climbed the stairs and traversed the length of the hallway. Gesturing to a closed door, the girl passed on and disappeared down a back stairwell Jorunn had not noticed before. Jorunn quietly turned the crystal knob to let herself in.

The room was in darkness, lit only by a fire that burned on the hearth at the far end of the vast space. In the shadows she discerned a small figure curled in a short bed. She crossed to him, noting the rocking horse that stood ready in the corner for when the child awoke. On top of the nearest dresser a line of small lead soldiers stood at attention, waiting for their leader to quit his slumber and command them. In the midst of it all slept her fair child. Her son lay on his back, his arms lifted above him in surrender to sleep. She sank down on her knees and rested beside him, drinking in the sight of his features. He seemed to belong here. It was as if this room had lain in wait for his arrival. She stood quickly, suddenly disconcerted. An unaccountable feeling of dread washed over her. She fought the urge to take her sleeping child and leave this place. 'There's nowhere else to go,' reason reminded her.

"This place is only safe haven until Stridheim is rebuilt, *gutten min*," she whispered, leaning over to stroke the child's fair hair. "When the time's right we'll go back where we belong. Together, you and I, we'll return to our land. It calls to us. You have to learn to listen for the call and heed it. It'll keep you straight on your course in life."

Gently she stroked his forehead. She sat long into the night with her son, unwilling to leave him, fearing he was in some strange way lost to her already.

Twenty

REDEMPTION

&c Valdis walked down the broad stone steps, alone in the
rush of chattering girls, their natural exuberance exacerbated
by the long hours of confinement they were forced to endure.
They jostled together, giggling unremittingly, enjoying the
camaraderie of youth and high spirits. Some were greeted by
governesses in severe black dresses who waited at the base of
the steps, others were collected by doting mothers fashionably
clad in gowns of silk in muted colors, or rich brocade. Broad-
brimmed hats shaded their eyes from bright sunlight, only their
mouths were visible to Valdis as she peeked up through her
lashes. They were smiling, calling happy greetings to their
daughters. Valdis registered a twinge of envy she knew to be
unchristian, and stifled it immediately. Alone and unnoticed,
she made her way to the carriage that waited for her at the
curb. The driver climbed down to open the door for her and
she stepped up into the gloomy interior to sit opposite her
Aunt Berit.

"Good afternoon, Valdis."

Her aunt's voice was cool, as usual. The small smile she
offered held none of the warmth or excitement so evident in
the other mothers. Valdis felt a flash of disappointment quickly
drowned by guilt. Her aunt was good to her, and must love
her to have taken her in when even her mother would no longer

have her, Valdis reminded herself. She decided she must be a very bad girl to feel anything uncharitable toward her aunt. She dropped her head quickly and squeezed her eyes shut, saying a quick, silent prayer for forgiveness, as her aunt had taught her. She added a small plea for guidance and the grace to be better, for good measure. When she opened her eyes she was rewarded by her aunt's broad smile.

"Have you been good today, Valdis?"

It was her habitual greeting to the girl at the end of each school day. As usual Valdis considered the question carefully before she answered.

"Yes, I believe so, Aunt Berit," she answered earnestly.

"I can ask only that you do your best," her aunt replied.

It was the customary response. It seemed to Valdis to signify that even her best effort was unsatisfactory; she made up her mind to try harder. She must be very good in order to insure that her aunt never send her away.

The carriage continued on its usual course, jostling over cobbled streets, until they came to the part of town where the way was no longer paved. The wheels of the carriage moved smoothly over the dirt road that led to Gronland, where the poor of the city gathered. When the carriage rolled to a stop Valdis braced herself for the smells that would soon assail her. In only a few seconds the driver was there, throwing open the door. The bright sunlight, together with the smell of urine and decay that hung over the area like a fog, struck Valdis' senses and left her stunned. She followed her aunt slowly, dazed and shrinking from the what lay ahead. In her mind she repeated a litany of sorts. *'Even so faith, if it hath not works, is dead, being alone.'* The words gave her little strength or conviction, yet they served as a distraction and made what she knew she must do more bearable. She hated the visits to the poor house. She knew she was a bad girl not to do her Christian duty with a glad heart, yet she cringed each time she stepped through the door of the dark, dank dwelling where those who had no family to care for them in infirmity and old age gathered.

Valdis stepped over the rotting threshold behind her aunt, having to stoop to enter the low doorway. She paused for a moment, letting her eyes become accustomed to the dimness, steeling herself not to flinch when the crones approached. One came toward her, an old woman virtually petrified with age. Her sallow face was blurred beneath layers of grime, her gray hair hung in greasy wisps about her. She stretched out one knotted hand to snatch loaves from the basket Valdis carried. Clutching to her as many as she could carry she stumbled away, back into the darkness, and from it another old woman appeared. She was rail thin, her skin stretched so tight across her face she seemed a caricature of death. One skinny arm snaked forward to snatch a loaf, while with the other gnarled, bony hand she reached up to stroke Valdis' white hair, long tendrils of which fell forward, over her shoulders. Valdis bit the soft flesh inside her cheek until she tasted metallic blood seeping from the wound she created to focus upon, to keep herself from cringing. "Pretty," the old hag mumbled through sunken lips and toothless gums. "Jus' lak an angel."

With enormous effort Valdis succeeded in schooling her face into smooth repose, stifling her urge to run from the fetid smells and dark interior where the hideousness of poverty was tangible. When the basket was empty Valdis turned blindly and stumbled over the threshold to the light outside, where the stench was marginally diminished. Gratefully she found her way inside the haven of the carriage. She sank against the leather upholstery, weak with the effort the visit had cost her. Relief washed over her at the thought her good deed for the day was behind her. She opened her eyes and sat up straight, suddenly horrified at her own weakness. She knew very well that a good deed done with a grudging heart did not count. Aunt Berit had lectured her several times that she must do God's work with a glad heart or it would not please Him. On the contrary, any act of kindness done begrudgingly was a sin against the memory of Christ, and would anger God, His Father. Valdis shivered and dropped her head in frantic prayer for forgiveness, then added a prayer of thanks for the strength He had given her to do what must be done.

She opened her eyes to find her aunt studying her, a smile of approval on her small mouth. For a moment her black eyes glittered in what Valdis imagined could be affection, and she was suddenly happy. She had pleased her aunt, if not God, for her aunt could no longer read the emotions behind her carefully schooled expression. For now, unless God chose to punish her, she was safe in the protection of her Aunt Berit.

Twenty-one

PASSAGE

Jorunn awoke slowly, after fitful sleep, filled with restlessness, her constant companion of late. She rose and crossed to the window, pulling back the drapes to judge the time. The sun was rising over the crest of buildings that lined the street on the far side of the park. They stretched in a long row of chiseled stone facades, their starkness broken by broad bands of relief carved between each floor and etched around each tall window. It made a grand impression and inspired in Jorunn awe of her new surroundings. On the sidewalk below pedestrians hurried along the cobbled street, intent on their errands. So early there was no one in the park. It looked stark, desolate, where it lay naked of soft green. 'It'll be beautiful when spring comes,' she reflected. Immediately she suffered a stab of disappointment at knowing she would still be here many months from now. Egil had returned to the city intent on rebuilding Stridheim according to a plan devised by a modern architect, a man making a reputation for himself in this time of busy growth in Norway. Hans Christian Krogh had been educated in Hamburg, Egil had related, and was one of the first to think in terms of rationality and practicality in farm dwellings. Egil was unwilling to simply rebuild the outbuildings on Stridheim in their original places, where they had sprung up over time and according to need. He was intent on making the farm a model of modern rationalism, efficiency the ultimate aim. To silence Jorunn's protests he reiterated his often-voiced opinion that only those farmers willing to change would survive this new industrial age. While the expansion of railways and growth in shipping had opened new markets for farmers, the protective tariffs they relied on had been abolished. Egil stood firm in his conviction that only expansion and investment in modern machinery would save Stridheim, and Jorunn's joy at Stridheim's reconstruction was dimmed by knowing the way of life she had treasured there was gone forever. Reluctantly she stifled her irritation at Egil's enthusiasm for the changes he welcomed. She had learned to trust his instincts in regard to Stridheim; she did not doubt he would ensure the survival of their place. She pressed her eyes closed and recalled a vision of her land, finding comfort in the memory, reassurance in the conviction that though change was a painful necessity, her land would endure.

"The house will be grand," Egil had said proudly when he shared his plans with her. He pointed with enthusiasm to drawings he sat in his library studying. Jorunn had studied the plans spread before them reluctantly, surprised the changes to her place would be so comprehensive.

"Something of this nature, with a high roof and scrollwork to adorn it," Egil was saying. She glanced at the drawings, yet she was more intent on his expression. His face was alive with an excitement she had never before seen him exhibit. As Egil was reshaping Stridheim he was branding it as his own, leaving his indelible mark on the land. Another look at the house told her it was far larger than necessity dictated, more ornate than she would have like. A broad facade stretched before her, double doors were positioned perfectly in center, symmetrical windows spanned away from both sides. The house would range high above the other buildings, boasting two stories and an ample loft. The first floor would comprise separate rooms for dining and relaxing, and even one designated specifically for spinning, weaving, knitting.

"The library is here, just opposite the sewing room," Egil pointed out, "and stretching along the rear of the house will be new kitchens and pantries."

"I don't need so large an area for simple cooking," Jorunn protested, amazed at the vast room that spanned the rear of the house. The light in his eyes dimmed and she regretted her words. "Although the idea of having all my stores in the house is appealing," she admitted, the thought springing to mind that it would eliminate trips through deep snow and icy wind to visit the creamery, the smokehouse, the loft where flat bread had been stored.

She felt excitement stir. The second floor was divided into five ample bedrooms, one by far the largest, and flanked on either end by smaller dressing rooms. She leaned closer, re-evaluating the merits of the drawings, and let herself be swept along in his vision of the new yard.

For the next several weeks the two of them spent hours closeted in the library, going over every detail of the property, examining every nuance of life on Stridheim and what would make it more rational. At last they had a model of what would be required. It remained only to share their ideas with Hans Christian Krogh so he might implement them.

"It would be best if you met with him,' Egil said one morning. They sat together in the library, as was their custom, sharing coffee in front of the fire. Jorunn watched as the light from the fire played over Egil's features. She found, to her surprise, that she could admire his good looks quite dispassionately. Here, in Berit's house and distant from the life they shared at Stridheim, she felt him to be removed from her. The time they spent together was passed in easy camaraderie. The dream they shared was of Stridheim, something greater than the rest of what was between them. Jorunn turned her mind resolutely toward accomplishing their goal. She balanced her cup on its saucer and placed them on the table beside her.

"I'd like that. It will give me something to fill my time here. The days are long," she replied, her expression wistful.

Valdis was busy with school in the mornings, and spent her afternoons on errands with Berit. Twice Jorunn had strolled down Carl Johans Street, turning on Queen's Street and continuing to Nissen's School for Girls on Custom House Street. When the girls were dismissed Jorunn had taken Valdis to Hansen's Bakery on the corner and ordered shilling buns and hot cocoa. But the conversation Jorunn introduced was left to lie flat. Valdis bid her time patiently, erecting a wall of silence between them, apparently longing to be off on her errands with Berit. Jorunn abandoned her trips to Valdis' school. In defeat she conceded the loss of her daughter, at the same time resolving that Halvor would never slip from her. Resolutely she searched each day for moments when Halvor's nanny deemed it suitable for a visit. It pained her that as the weeks passed his smile for her was less bright, his welcome less enthusiastic. The room he occupied at the far end of the corri-

dor was stocked to the overflowing with toys that arrived almost daily from Egil's mercantile. Her protestations were ignored when she approached Egil in his library and pointed
out it was not healthy for a little boy to be so spoiled.

"It is only for a little while I have him," Egil had soothed.
"Surely no lasting harm can come from a few short months of
indulgence."

The wistful air he unconsciously wore silenced her. She
felt his pain at the thought of losing Halvor all the more in-
tensely because her each and every day was shadowed by the
same fear. Her face creased in lines of agitation at the mere
thought of Halvor slipping from her, lost to the allure of toys and
a doting nanny with nothing to attend but Halvor's every need.

Misreading her expression of discontent Egil said, "You
pine for Stridheim, and your life there," concern evident in
his voice. "But these things take time. You must occupy yourself here meanwhile, for I do not anticipate the house will be
ready before late fall, in time for the harvest at the earliest."

"I'm not complaining," she countered quickly. "But your
point is well taken. 'Time spent in earnest endeavor passes
quickly'. I'm sure you have plenty to occupy you at the mercantile. It'll serve us both well if I oversee the work at
Stridheim."

"The matter is settled then. But if you hope to return to
Stridheim in the fall you must not delay your visit to *Herr*
Krogh. Fetch your things and I shall walk with you to his office. It is only a short distance from the mercantile, and my
work there waits for me.

Jorunn hurried from the room, a new light in her eyes,
new purpose in her step. She pulled on a dark blue coat
trimmed in braid the same deep red as the gown she wore.
'The color of strawberries ripe under a June sun,' she reflected
absently, while tying the ribbons of her bonnet beneath her
chin. She retrieved her gloves from a bureau drawer and
smoothed the fine, soft leather over her hands, humming to
herself, her thoughts busy with pictures she sketched in her
mind of Stridheim restored.

They walked up Carl Johans Street toward the main square.
Rows of windows screened in filmy lace soon gave way to broad
shop windows displaying a dazzling array of goods. Ladies'
shoes and purses of the finest leathers, some shimmering with
beads and satin trim, drew her attention. In the next window,
beneath a milliner's sign, lengths of fine fabric in every imag-

inable color were displayed. Jorunn stared with wide eyes into each window they passed, enthralled at the bevy of beautiful wares offered for sale.

Egil watched her, his face shining with delight at her excitement.

"It's like another world," she breathed. Then her face clouded. "Not better than my own, of course, only different," she asserted with a proud lift of her chin.

Egil laughed out loud. "I'll not consider you disloyal to Stridheim for having done a bit of window shopping," he teased. "As long as you are confined to the city you might as well make the best of it. Anything you take a fancy to is yours. Give my name at the counter, bid the merchant send his bill."

Jorunn made no reply, her attention called already to new sights. Ahead of them lay Stortorget, the main square. Stalls lined the cobbled area, a busy trade being conducted between farmers and tradesmen, and wives looking for bargains. The noise of voices haggling competed with the sound of church bells that rang from the cathedral. Jorunn looked toward it as they turned on High Church Street. Its steeple stretched heavenward toward a bleak, gray, winter's sky, its proportions immense. Jorunn felt suddenly small, dwarfed by the grandeur of the buildings, overwhelmed by the sights and sounds and smells that assaulted her senses. Egil led her along, his hand firm beneath her elbow, unaware of the tumult within her. She experienced a sense of devastating isolation in the midst of this city bustling with people. Never had she felt so alone on Stridheim, not even when snowed in during the winter, when months passed and she saw no other person. A longing for her place washed over her quite unexpectedly.

At the corner Egil stopped. "You shall find *Herr* Krogh's office just through that door and up one flight of stairs. Afterward you might like to stroll through the Bazaar, just there," he said, pointing toward the cathedral, putting his arm around her shoulders to turn her in the right direction. Jorunn stared ahead, not registering the rows of small shops to which he was referring. Her eyes were drawn instead to the window of a carriage that passed. She stared into Berit's dark eyes for an instant before the woman turned away to look forward again.

Jorunn's cheeks burned. 'I'm doing nothing wrong,' she reasoned. Yet she felt uneasy.

Unaware, Egil took his leave and Jorunn wandered up the steps to Hans Christian Krogh's office, distracted, distressed that Berit should have seen her and Egil together. 'Ridiculous,' she reminded herself with a mental shake. 'There's nothing between us now, and Berit has no reason to suspect that anything happened before.'

She was interrupted in her thoughts by a tall man, handsomely dressed in a suit of fine dark wool. He stepped from an adjoining office to greet her.

"You must be *Frue* Halvorsson," he said, extending his hand to her. "It's not often I have the pleasure of a lady's visit to my office," he grinned. "I understand from your husband you are unusually interested in the house and yard to be reconstructed."

She flushed under the misconception she was married to Egil.

"Please, call me Jorunn. I'm not *Frue* Halvorsson." She saw confusion reflected clearly in his face. A look of understanding dawned and he reddened.

"Wait, you misunderstand! I am the widow of *Herr* Halvorsson's brother, and I have a right to the name. But I'm from country people, from the farm we are to reconstruct. I'm more comfortable with the old ways, and am known as Jorunn Sigurdsdatter. The title of *Frue* Halvorsson belongs, in my mind, to my brother-in-law's wife."

Hans Christian Krogh's eyes crinkled as he lifted his head and laughed out loud. "Such confusion," he said still smiling. "I only hope our cooperation on this project will be more successful than our inauspicious beginning."

She studied him, ranging tall above her. His black hair was combed back from a wide brow; his deep blue eyes sparkled with infectious humor. His face was clean-shaven, his mouth wide, tilting at one corner as if in perpetual readiness to smile. She like him at once. Taking the hand he extended she shook it firmly and replied, "I don't doubt it. Let's get started, then. I've already made plans to return home before next harvest. There's no time to waste."

Twenty-two

TRIAL

᠅ The weeks until Yuletide passed quickly for Jorunn. The first snowfall brought the realization that winter was upon them. In the streets of Christiania wagons gave way to sleighs; bright red ribbons wrapped the posts of the gas lamps lining the city streets. On the water in Pipervika below Akershus Castle it seemed all the city's residents fell for the temptation to strap on skates and while Saturdays away sliding over the ice. Egil insisted Valdis and Halvor accompany him on a weekly expedition there; at times Jorunn followed to stand watching from the bank as they skated.

It was after Yule, at the beginning of the new year, that Hans Christian Krogh sent her written invitation to accompany him to a ball being hosted by *Herr* Peter Petersen. She opened the letter as soon as it was delivered, while standing in the front hall. A flush stained her cheeks crimson. She realized for the first time that Hans Christian was aware of her in another capacity than that of a client.

Berit was coming in from her weekly errand to Gronland. Observing Jorunn's heightened color she asked, "What news is it that brings such a flush to your countenance?" An edge in her voice belied the smoothness of her face.

"Nothing," Jorunn replied, folding the note to replace it in its envelope.

Berit's quick eyes caught sight of her husband as he crossed the hall. "Egil, do come! Jorunn has news, something exciting, it would seem. She must share it with us, do you not think?"

Egil followed Berit's bidding. As he approached Jorunn replied with an edge of exasperation, "It's nothing, really. Only an invitation to the ball at Petersen's. I won't be attending."

She turned to leave, but was stopped by Berit, who reached to detain her. The hand that lay on her forearm was as small as a child's, and appeared as delicate, yet Jorunn felt in the clutch of the slender fingers a strength that would not be denied.

"Oh, but you must!" Berit cried, her eyebrows arched in surprise. "Tell her she must, Egil," she insisted, turning to enlist his aid. "Egil and I shall be there, so you need not fear being alone. And I suspect *Herr* Krogh would be very disappointed if you refuse him."

Jorunn avoided Berit's coy glance. "I really would rather not. I have nothing suitable to wear, and I am not comfortable in large gatherings," she said.

"How can you know if you enjoy such parties when you have never been?" Berit asked sweetly, her usually smooth voice false, and high. "As for something to wear, that is easily remedied. We shall call at the mercantile tomorrow. I am certain my dressmaker will alter on short notice whatever you might wish for such an important occasion."

The tension between the two women was palpable. Jorunn looked to Egil in silent plea. He watched their exchange without comment, his face inscrutable. She waited for assistance, and when none came anger began to burn. Lifting her chin she said to him, "In that case, if it doesn't trouble you Egil, I'll do as Berit suggests."

"You must do as you see fit," he answered before turning and disappearing in the direction of his library. The door closed with a sharp click. Jorunn turned back to Berit just in time to see a smile of satisfaction steal across her countenance.

'She resembles a cat,' Jorunn reflected in angry surprise. 'A stealthy black cat who enjoys playing games with its prey.'

Fury at her own helplessness in the face of Berit's manipulation rose up to overshadow her anger at Egil's indifference. Her mouth thinned, her face set in lines of determination. '*Vel*, I'll be her mouse no longer,' she resolved. Without a word she turned and walked from the hall, leaving Berit staring after her.

❧ ❧ ❧

Birgitte had just finished pinning the last lock of Jorunn's hair in place when there was a gentle rap on the door. "*Kom inn*," Jorunn called.

She watched in the looking glass as Berit entered, elfin in a gown of watered silk the color of the forest at midsummer.

"You look well, the gown suits you," Berit addressed Jorunn. Jorunn glanced down at the pale blue silk of her dress pooled in her lap. She had learned to be wary of Berit, and thought it best to make no reply.

"I thought these would complete the ensemble, if you would borrow them for the evening."

Jorunn took the velvet box Berit offered, searching her face for some clue as to her real purpose. Lifting the lid she caught her breath in surprise. "They're beautiful!" she exclaimed.

In the box a necklace and earrings of topaz glittered, blue ice against black velvet. "I can't. They're too precious," she answered, closing the lid and proffering the box to Berit.

"Please, I would be honored. I have no use for them this evening," she said, touching the circlet of emeralds that draped around the delicate skin of her neck. "Everyone at the ball will be wearing their finest jewels; it is only appropriate you should as well. It is important you look your very best for your *Herr* Krogh."

Watching her closely, Jorunn could discern no hint of anything other than kindness in her gesture. Her voice, while unusually insistent, was smooth and cool. 'Perhaps I've misjudged Berit,' she reflected. 'It might well be my own black conscience that goads me when she speaks.' She stifled the urge to refute Berit's referral to Hans Christian as 'hers', making up her mind to give Berit the benefit of doubt.

With a careful smile she opened the box once again and turned back to the glass. Her eyes met Berit's in the reflection and she said, "In that case, I'm honored. Thank you."

Berit stood watching over Jorunn's shoulder as Birgitte carefully clasped the necklace around Jorunn's throat. "You may go now, thank you," Jorunn dismissed the girl, clipping the earrings in place herself. With a final look in the glass she rose and turned to face Berit.

"You are so changed, one would hardly recognize you," Berit remarked as she studied Jorunn's tall figure swathed in ice blue silk. Her golden hair was twisted into a mass of curls hanging heavy at the back of her neck; her face had lost the color the sun had imbued in it during the summer months at Stridheim and was returned to smooth alabaster. Her long neck sloped to smooth shoulders; her soft bosom swelled above the top of the gown. The perfection of her creamy skin was marred only by a small dark mark above her right breast, yet somehow this served to enhance the beauty of her, calling attention to the ripe swell just below it. "It is plain to see why *Herr* Krogh is so taken with you."

Her face guarded, Jorunn replied, "I don't think he's very much taken with me. He's simply a kind man who thought I might enjoy an evening of dancing. I'm afraid I'll be a disappointment. The only dances I know are the ones we dance around the bonfire at midsummer. I expect most of my evening will be spent watching you dance with Egil."

Berit's face flushed a delicate pink, suddenly she seemed curiously animated. "I am looking forward to this evening very much," she admitted.

Jorunn stared at her in surprise, watching as the color suffusing Berit's face softened her countenance. In that instant Jorunn wondered if Berit's interest in Egil was more than merely proprietary. The possibility she guarded him so jealously out of love presented itself, and Jorunn let her blue gaze meet Berit's dark eyes. In an unguarded moment Jorunn stared into the other woman's soul and saw that she burned with an emotional intensity that was frightening, yet in the depths of Berit's gaze there was no love. Jorunn winced and stepped away, lifting one hand unconsciously to finger the circlet of precious stones and metal that wrapped around her neck.

"Come, we should leave now, or we shall be late. This is an opportunity not to be missed," Berit said.

Jorunn stared at her, suspicion dawning.

"I meant an occasion not to be missed, of course," Berit corrected herself with a small smile. Her dark eyes glittered, but not with mirth. Numb with surprise Jorunn let Berit take her arm and lead her downstairs.

Egil and Hans Christian waited in the great hall. "You are exceptionally lovely this evening, Jorunn," Hans Christian greeted her, taking her hand as she approached. Jorunn had a brief impression of Egil's raised eyebrows at the man's use of her first name. She let Hans Christian place her new cloak of black velvet around her shoulders, enjoying the sensuous caress of the midnight blue satin that lined it. She was aware Egil was watching, and was pleased at the frown of irritation he wore. Egil had offered her no refuge from Berit's manipulation of this evening. It pleased her that he, too, felt the awkwardness of the situation. When Hans Christian Krogh offered her his arm she took it gladly, lifting her face to smile at him, to laugh at the witty inanities he entertained her with. She felt Egil's gaze at her back as he followed, reveled in the silence that cloaked him and Berit as they followed the few blocks to Peter Petersen's new residence.

"It is .ndeed a grand building," Berit remarked as they stopped to admire Palladian windows that spilled light onto the sidewalk, bathing them gold.

"Stately," Egil asserted.

"Palatial, reflecting Italian influence," Hans Christian commented. "Speaking as an architect I can assure you it represents the finest in modern improvements," he added. "*Herr* Petersen combined practicality with convenience at every turn. His offices are on the main floor, his warehouse above. The third and fourth floors are reserved as his residence and afford him every comfort. There is a central heating apparatus, an elevator, and," he said, lowering his voice conspiratorially, "he even had several water closets installed."

Jorunn was rendered speechless at the idea of things unimaginable to her only months ago. It was as if life in the valley stood still, while in Christiania the world was accelerating at a pace that took her breath away. A longing for her place, a way of life she understood, was with her everywhere she went, a burden that weighted her more with each passing day. She sensed Egil's gaze on her, knew he watched with happy anticipation her reaction to these modern wonders. "I can't imagine," she murmured lamely, and saw he was disappointed.

"Shall we see for ourselves, then?" Hans Christian interrupted her thoughts, leading them forward, into music spilling through open doors.

Jorunn entered the ballroom clutching Hans Christian's arm for support. 'It's like another world,' she said bemusedly, mentally comparing the golden glow of gas lamps, the rich velvet drapes, the shining hardwood floors, to the house at Stridheim. Her home. She had thought it so fine when Erland had finished it. Simple pine walls and plank floors. No curtains softened the small paned windows. She remembered her desolation at the loss of it a short while ago, and Egil's determination to rebuild something better. Her frame of reference shifted and she understood Egil must view Stridheim through different eyes. Looking up at Hans Christian she thought of the house they had designed together. It would be large, modern, efficient. Those things he would see to. With a surge of

old strength that had lain dormant these past months she resolved to make it beautiful as well.

The evening passed in a haze of people and impressions.
Women floated by in shimmering gowns. Hans Christian was
always at her side, introducing her to so many different people
that at last their faces swam before her. 'No matter,' she comforted herself. 'I won't be here much longer. Soon I'll be
home again, on Stridheim, and these people will be only a
memory.'

She would not dance, unsure of the steps, unwilling to
enter into the whirl of people spinning around the floor. They
wandered through the vast dining hall, the array of roasted
meats, elaborate fruit and vegetable displays, and rich desserts
overwhelming to Jorunn. She was amazed to find that in the
face of such abundance she had no appetite. Without pressing her Hans Christian led her on a tour of elaborate salons
where guests gathered for conversation of varying sorts. In
the library Jorunn spied Egil in the midst of a heated political
discussion centered around Johan Sverdrup. His oratorical
skill unchecked in the face of social constraint, Sverdrup's voice
rang out, clearly audible over conversation and music.

"The time has come to claim for Norway the equality her
due, and if it takes a change in the constitution to accomplish
that, then so be it. With all due respect to the great men who
outlined our government in 1814, times have changed, and
Norway's situation with it. The Swedes have no place in our
government. The power to rule our country should rest in the
Storting, with the government under Parliamentarian control.
It's the only way to ensure a government that represents the
common man. And every man must have the right to vote...."

Hans Christian led her away, saying, "Your brother-in-law's
passion for politics seems unchecked even at such a gala event.
Does he never take time for pure enjoyment?"

Jorunn was suddenly protective, unexpectedly defensive.
"His concern for his land, and that of his fellow farmers, takes
precedence over every other thing. I admire that he works
tirelessly for what he believes in," she replied.

Hans Christian looked at her carefully, one dark brow
raised in sardonic amusement. "It was not my intention to
imply anything other than the greatest respect for *Herr*
Halvorsson. He is a man driven by his cause. And as you say,
his concern is truly for the future of agriculture. He is not
ambitious for himself in government."

"Egil is content to let Ueland and Sverdrup waltz around the political arena, for as long as they represent his cause he supports theirs. His calling is another. His land, Stridheim."

Hans Christian studied her carefully, she felt his eyes probe hers. "You share his calling, I've come to understand. Forgive my impudence, but I must ask. Is there more you share, or am I free to hope you might grant me the privilege of your company when your duties as Mistress of Stridheim do not require your attention?"

Jorunn felt a flush rise from the swell of her breasts to stain her cheeks pink. "I'd like very much to spend my free time with you, *Herr* Krogh," she surprised herself in answering. She knew the smile she flashed was inexplicably coquettish, and her flush deepened.

"Then shall we go up to the roof? It is Petersson's garden of sorts, the entire surface surrounded by wrought iron fencing. If you're willing to brave the cold?" he asked, his face bright, his eyes sparkling. She let him lead her there, suddenly giddy with inexplicable emotion, curious to see what new marvels this place encompassed.

The night air was frigid, but it was clean, the evening clear. Beneath layers of silk and corsets, and hoops draped with frothy petticoats Jorunn relished the fresh air, letting it cool her after the clammy heat of too many candles and people in the rooms below. Yet she let Hans Christian pull her closer, ostensibly for warmth. They wandered along graveled paths, admiring the view of the city below. Gas lamps lit Carl Johans Street, still busy even in late evening. On the other side was the less trafficked King Street; nearby the steeple of the cathedral stretched toward a blue velvet sky. A few stars, small and far away, glittered overhead. Jorunn drew in a deep breath and released it, watching ephemeral white clouds escape her and disappear.

"Ah, listen, Edward Grieg!" Hans Christian exclaimed. "My favorite composer, his music is a breath of spring even on such a cold night."

Jorunn turned to him, listening to strains of music clearly audible from below. "Dance with me," he bid simply. Watching his face in the moonlight, she let him take her in his arms and turn her around Petersen's garden, trusting him to guide her steps. He was sure in his movements; she followed him easily. He closed his eyes and pulled her closer. Tilting her face to his she watched, rapt at his expression, knowing he was lost in the music and movement of their bodies together. She let herself melt to him, knowing he felt this liquid surging too. As the last strains of Grieg's waltz died she lifted her face and waited for his kiss. His lips were full and warm, his breath sweet. Her hand traced the firm lines of his jaw, then slid around his neck to touch the hair that curled there.

His hands encircled her waist and held her close against him. Precious moments, she had no idea how long they stood there. When he finally put her away from him she was loathe to return to reality. She wanted only to sink into the abyss of longing they shared, with no thought for the world outside it.

"We must return to the party," he said, his voice gravelly.

She nodded and leaned her forehead to his chin. "Yes," she agreed, but she had no strength to move away from him.

"May I see you tomorrow?" he asked. "Will you dine with me, at my apartment?"

She heard the raw desire in his voice, recognized it instinctively. She was well aware of what he asked. "*Ja, det vil jeg*," she breathed. "Send your carriage at eight o'clock. I'll be ready."

He put one gentle finger beneath her chin to pull her mouth to his again. Long minutes later he pulled away. "We must return, now, while I still have the strength, if not the will."

"There's no return for us," she teased, her face alight in the dark evening. "And even if there was, I would not want to," she laughed, and turned to pull him back toward the light and the music below.

Twenty-three

TESTAMENT

❧ The next months were as a dream for Jorunn. She and
Hans Christian spent afternoons planning the house and buildings on Stridheim, and evenings sheltered behind the drapes
of his bed. She dined with him virtually every evening, either
in the privacy of his apartment, or publicly, often at the Grand
Hotel, sometimes at Engebrets after attending the Christiania
Theater. Henrik Ibsen's new drama, *The Pretenders*, had just
opened, and played to a full house. Both Hans Christian and
Egil were great admirers of the man's work; he was their con-
temporary and shared in their political convictions. Jorunn
suffered through Ibsen's idealism with little grace.

"I appreciate he has talent, but honestly, Hans Christian, I
don't think Henrik Ibsen the genius you propose. I suspect
it's merely that he shares your romantic notion of a Scandinavian union that attracts you to his work. You're both hopelessly naive if you think Norway would benefit from a stronger
alliance with either Denmark or Sweden. The Danes and
Swedes will do as they have always done, look out for their own
interests, and we'll find ourselves outnumbered, without voice
even in our own government."

"I never said he possessed genius," Hans Christian defended, "merely that he holds the promise of it. And though
you may hope that in isolationism Norway will find freedom, it
is clear to me that with each year the world is a smaller place,
and we all depend on one another to survive. Mark my words,

if we refuse to help Denmark defend her southern provinces from Prussia she will lose both Holstein and Schleswig. On the other hand, if we cooperate, and the Russians continue to threaten our border, then we will stand against them united with Denmark. Sound and rational reasons for a Scandinavian union; not romantic fancy, as you imply."

As they argued they made their way out of the theater and into the chill January night. "You're entitled to your own opinion," Jorunn sniffed. "I'm not going to stand in the street and argue politics with you when I'm starved half to death. Let's walk to Engebrets instead of waiting for a carriage. It's not far, and we'll get there before everyone too fashionable to stroll a few blocks."

She tucked her gloved hand into the crook of his arm with careless disregard for the curious looks cast their direction. Hans Christian knew Jorunn was aware their relationship was the source of much gossip and idle speculation in the drawing rooms of Christiania; he understood that she cared not at all. Her refusal to conform to social constraint, or to accept another's opinion as her own, caused him to admire her. Her spirit and determination awoke in him a longing that was new. Already he could hardly remember life before her; he could not bear to contemplate life without her. He pulled her closer, savoring the feel of her hand on his forearm.

"It is unfathomable to me that you are unimpressed with Ibsen's work. I know the man well, and the two of you have much in common. I think you would like him, and I know he would admire you. In any case, differences in philosophy aside, you must admit his prose is elegant, and his poems are clever. He is the master of his craft."

"I may not like the man's message, but I concede his work improves. Still, genius, if he is capable of it, is in his future, not his present."

"I give up," Hans Christian said with a mock sigh of resignation. "Perhaps a meal will soften your opinion of my poor friend," he teased.

Jorunn lifted her chin; her blue eyes flashed as she replied, "I think you might have a better chance of changing my opinion at your apartment. It seems there you can persuade me to almost anything."

Hans Christian's laughter rang out in the clear, crystal night air. He pulled her closer still and lengthened his stride, enjoying the way she matched his gait effortlessly. "Hurry, then.

We'll have a quick supper and continue this discussion at home."

Hans Christian's apartment was in a new and fashionable area of residences behind Castle Park, where grand mansions were being constructed along wide cobbled streets. It was in a stately building, one he had designed himself, commissioned by a businessman who made his fortune in shipping. The imposing limestone structure housed four apartments, two of which were reserved for the man's daughters. Intrepid women, as strong as their father, they chose not to marry and were installed comfortably in their own places.

Each apartment had two large sitting rooms, one formal and the other more personal, and a dining room facing Frogner Street. From small balconies beyond French doors the sisters could watch the bustle of people and carriages that passed outside, or retire to more private quarters on other side of the apartment, where the rooms looked out onto a square courtyard behind the building. The courtyard was an oasis of green during the summer months, the sweet scent of lilac and jasmine imparting fresh fragrance to the drawing room and bedroom that enjoyed a view of the garden. Each room was perfectly proportioned, beautifully symmetrical. Soaring windows flooded the apartments with light, double panes ensured that the rooms were warm in the winter. When Hans Christian was finished designing the building he was so pleased with his effort he promptly arranged for the purchase of the fourth floor to be his own.

It was here he and Jorunn shared one another, body and soul, swept along in a love affair as much mental as physical. Hans Christian opened her mind to new avenues of thought. He talked to her of politics and business, then challenged her to discover if she not only understood the basic concepts he gave her, but could build further on them. He found her an apt pupil, albeit with an exasperating tendency to form opinions contradictory to his own. They explored philosophy and music, and spent long hours sharing the lives they had led before meeting one another.

Hans Christian related stories of his recent travel to America. He shared with her his impressions of a place so new it hummed with barely controlled energy, and passions so raw war had divided its people. Slavery was an institution there, accepted as an economic necessity in the southern part of the country, where vast plantations sprawled to cover miles of rich farmland. Yet in the North the practice was reviled, and dissension had ignited a civil war he feared would cripple the young America.

Jorunn listened, transported by his stories and descriptions to another place, strange and far away. Intrigued, yet horrified at the concept of slavery. Free will was her most precious possession; not even to deity would she surrender that. The idea one man should own another was repulsive to her. So much world beyond her own part of it; all of it different. She let her imagination take her to places far away: Germany, France, Italy. Hans Christian had traveled abroad as a young man, studying architecture and learning of the food and wine and customs of each land in turn. All this he shared with Jorunn now, reveling in the transformation he sensed in her. From a farmer's wife she blossomed into a cosmopolitan woman, in appearance, at least, and perhaps in some part of her person. He was fascinated with her, spellbound in her presence.

They were careless of the future, swept along by passion. But during the spring months, when the poplars skirting the Royal Palace began to shimmer green, Jorunn became aware Hans Christian planned for a future she knew would not be possible. They walked together down Main Street, the spring wind crisp and high. Hans Christian gestured to where Carl Nordbeck's striped circus tent whipped under the force of the wind.

"On Saturday first-coming I would invite both Valdis and Halvor to be my guests at the circus. And if you are good all this week, you might come with us," he teased, the light in his deep blue eyes bright.

Jorunn laughed, enjoying his ready wit. Then her face sobered and she replied, "I don't think so. Valdis is difficult, now. She's very serious. She insists on spending all her free time with her aunt, doing deeds of Christian kindness."

He stopped and turned to her. "I know their relationship distresses you, but you might have worse complaint of a daughter than that she is too serious. I don't think it's uncommon for both boys and girls of Valdis' age to choose some person other than their parents to model themselves after. There are far worse examples than *Frue* Halvorsson for Valdis to imitate."

With a sigh Jorunn walked on. "You're reasonable, as usual, but I feel with a mother's heart more than I can steer with rational thought."

"Then we shall leave Valdis to her own pursuits. Surely Halvor is not so serious at barely three years of age that he would not enjoy the circus?" he asked, his smile ready as always.

"He's a happy child, that one, his disposition light, not a care in the world," she said smiling at the thought of her son. "He's whisked from one activity to the next here, and it suits him. He's restless, always eager for a change." Then her smile faded and she grew solemn. "I miss him," she said simply. "I think, though, that he's better off in the care of Nanny."

They walked in silence, unspoken works heavy in the air between them. At last Hans Christian stopped. "It is time I should meet your children, Jorunn. You know how I feel for you. If we are to take the next step together it is only reasonable I first become acquainted with the rest of your family."

Jorunn's heart sank. She had lived in unconscious dread of this moment these past weeks, sensing its inevitability. "There's time," she stalled, loathe to face this juncture.

"Choose the time," he replied. Stopping in front of City Hall, framed by two great lions carved in stone, he turned to take both her hands in his. "Your choice. Name the date, tell me when you will be my bride."

Jorunn felt a thrill at the words, a surge of happiness that took her breath away. Then reason reasserted itself and she knew this was impossible.

"I can't, Hans Christian. You know my future lies elsewhere. I don't belong here with you. Stridheim is my home. It calls to me; in my heart I know I must heed its call."

"Is there no other call to which your heart hearkens? Has it been deaf to mine all these months? I thought we were as one, our two hearts beating in unison. Have you not felt the same?"

Turning, she walked quickly ahead of him. She could not deny that she had felt the same. Yet the call of the land she loved was stronger. There was only one course open to her.

Stopping, she waited for him. When he stood by her side she said, "If I could have both you and Stridheim, my life would be perfect. But I can't. I have to choose, and for me there's only one choice. Stridheim is such a part of me, I can't survive without it."

"But a smaller part, now, I should think," he protested. "You have changed; you are no longer the same woman who left your place in ruin. Perhaps you are unaware, yet I have watched the metamorphosis that has taken place these months. You could never be content with life on Stridheim again. It is too simple."

"You say that as if it were an insult," Jorunn snapped, suddenly angry at the slight to her place. "You profess to love me, yet you apparently don't understand the woman I am. It's the simplicity of life on Stridheim that keeps me there. On Stridheim there's only one truth: The land will endure. That's what binds me irrevocably to the place. It will always be mine. Everything else may be lost at the whimsy of fickle fate, but the land will keep me safe."

Her voice lost its angry edge but her eyes told him that she was certain in her course. He looked into their implacable blue depths and insisted, "I would keep you safe."

She stared at him, and let fall the veil that hid her past to reveal the ghost that haunted her. Her husband, her first love. And a glimmer of the despair she had known when he was gone.

Hans Christian was defeated. His heart wrenched; the words he would speak lodged painfully in his throat.

They walked on in silence. Turning on Carl Johans Street they continued alongside one another, but already they were separated; by time and circumstance, by all that had gone before and all that would never be. Jorunn stared toward the Royal Palace that loomed before them, yet did not see it. She saw instead an image of herself continuing up a wide path lined with poplars. Alone. She shivered in the chill May air, pulled her coat closer. At the door to Egil's house she left Hans Christian wordlessly. She could find no words to bid him farewell.

Twenty-four

DELIVERANCE

✣ The beauty of the summer months in Christiania was lost
to Jorunn. All around her people frolicked in the parks and
squares, absorbing the warmth of the sun, letting it invigorate
their spirits. Young people walked secretly clasping hands hidden behind full skirts; toddlers were let loose from their carriages to take their first steps on the uneven sidewalks of the
city, yet Jorunn saw only memories of Hans Christian at every
turn. She longed for Stridheim and the peace she would find
there. Every moment of every day she blotted out thoughts of
him with visions of the yard they had planned. Dreams of the
future kept her alive.

Egil made no reference to Hans Christian's disappearance
from Jorunn's life. She wondered if he might, knowing intu-
itively he had resented the man's presence. He was not free to
stake a claim to her, yet he guarded her possessively, and to
herself she admitted she enjoyed his regard. In truth, it was
the sort of relationship she enjoyed best. Circumstances put
her in control of it.

Berit said nothing, yet Jorunn knew the other woman understood her pain. Jorunn riled at the intrusion of Berit's
knowing eyes, her anger causing her dislike of the woman to
verge on hatred at times. Berit watched her every move; she
felt the burn of those black eyes even when the other woman's
gaze was ostensibly averted.

In August a wave of heat washed over the city and settled
to hold its inhabitants in an unrelenting grasp. It would not

last; it was only a fortnight more or less to be endured, yet gradually tempers frayed. The streets and shops were the scene of mounting tension. In a people used to relentless endeavor there was no thought of slowing their pace until autumn brought relief and cooler temperatures. Shopkeepers labored in their stifling rooms; workers toiled under a sun that beat down mercilessly. Families lived behind stone walls that heated through, by late afternoon turning interiors into baking ovens. The close proximity of buildings along narrow streets quelled the cool breeze from the fjord that might have brought relief, and Christiania's people struggled on, waiting with diminishing patience for the relief a change of season would bring.

Jorunn's longing for Stridheim grew feverish. Her usual languor of this season eluded her. Without the scent of crops ripening under the hot sun she was unable to rest and gather strength for the harvest. Her land seemed far away, her desire for it sharp as a razor's edge. It was on the afternoon of the tenth day of heat that Berit first mentioned Hans Christian. She, too, was affected by the heat. Jorunn was aware that in the last week Berit's eyes had burned even brighter than usual, the only outward sign that the heavy atmosphere affected her. Her brow was cool, with no lines of perspiration streaking it. Her upper lip did not bead with perspiration as Jorunn's did, yet Jorunn sensed in the other woman a restlessness that matched her own, and knew to be wary of her. She avoided her whenever possible. Berit and Valdis spent each morning at church, each afternoon on errands of Christian mercy. Valdis returned from their missions frighteningly pale, nearly faint from heat and exhaustion. Jorunn could imagine the stench of Gronland now. On windy days the smell of that part of the city was vaguely apparent even on the west side of town. In the airless heat of late it was not evident, but Jorunn knew it must hover intensified over the area where the poor and destitute gathered in unmitigated filth and poverty. She longed to stop Valdis from accompanying Berit on her visits there. More than the toll these visits so visibly took on her daughter, the fear of disease suddenly erupting there plagued Jorunn. One afternoon Berit returned with a pale and bedraggled Valdis trailing behind her. Jorunn met them in the great hall, her anxiety for her child apparent in her face as she begged, "Please, Valdis, postpone your visits to Gronland until the weather brings relief to us all. You're all but done in; I can't bear to see you like this."

Valdis lifted one white hand wearily to brush back tendrils of hair that matted to her damp forehead. Her fingers shook, her cheeks were deathly pale in spite of the heat. The girl swallowed hard and managed to speak, though her throat was parched.

"I have no choice, Mother. The Scripture is clear: 'That even so faith, if it hath not works, is dead, being alone,' she intoned. Her voice was hollow, she spoke the words by rote.

Berit hovered near, the look of her intent. Jorunn knew she watched for weakness in Valdis, waited for the girl to falter, and it infuriated her. She saw the woman's hand snake out to squeeze Valdis' trembling fingers. Berit murmured approvingly, "You are a good and charitable girl, Valdis. The Bible tells us that 'Pure religion and undefiled before God and the Father is this: To visit the fatherless and their widows in their affliction, and to keep himself unspotted from the world.'"

She spoke ostensibly to the girl, but Jorunn felt the heat of Berit's dark gaze shift to her and resentment flared. "I'm not asking that she abandon her duties, only that she wait with them until this weather breaks," Jorunn defended.

Berit's praise brought a flush to Valdis' pale face, made her forget her fatigue and nausea. It gave her the strength to defend her calling. "Do you imagine that the poor suffer any less during this weather?" Valdis asked her mother, her voice meek, yet her manner insufferably pious. Jorunn's palm itched to slap her daughter, to erase the look she found so hateful from the girl's countenance.

"Valdis, dear, you forget yourself. Apologize at once, my child, for you break God's commandment when you fail to honor your mother," Berit reproved the girl, her voice silky smooth, her eyes triumphant as she looked not at Valdis, but at Jorunn. "The Lord instructs: 'Honor thy father and thy mother: that thy days may be long upon the land which the Lord thy God giveth thee.' And in Ephesians the lesson is clear. 'Children, obey your parents in the Lord, for this is right.'"

Jorunn watched quick tears well in her daughter's eyes at the reproof. She longed to reach forward, comfort the girl, but she stood frozen in a moment despicable to her, watching her child choke back tears from the wound of the words of this woman she had come to hate and despise. This woman her daughter loved and admired.

"Forgive me, Mother," Valdis mouthed obediently, her eyes obscured by heavy lashes as she stared down at the tips of boots filthy with the dust of the slum.

Jorunn stood silent, choked by her rage at their predicament. She and her daughter were captive pawns in this game Berit played. There was no way to escape woman's manipulation.

"Very well, you are excused," Berit soothed Valdis. "Go upstairs; I shall instruct Hilde to bring you a cool bath. Then you may rest until dinner," she comforted.

Valdis lifted her eyes to Berit, gave her a small smile. Leaning close she brushed her lips softly against Berit's smooth cheek. "You are too good to me, Aunt Berit. I fear I do not do you justice."

"I only ask that you do your best," came Berit's usual reply. Valdis turned to do her bidding without a look in Jorunn's direction.

Jorunn waited until Valdis disappeared from view at the top of the wide staircase before she turned to Berit and lashed out. "She's my daughter; I'll decide what's in her best interests. It's apparent you would gladly sacrifice her on the alter of Christian duty. I tell you now, and I'll tell her later, that she is forbidden to venture into Gronland until the heat lifts. It's dangerous to her health, and I won't have it!"

Berit studied her dispassionately, a small smile twitching at the corner of her mouth, alerting Jorunn that she derived amusement from her distress.

"You may tell her anything you like, for as you say, she is your daughter. Yet you are a fool if you think you might come between Valdis and God's will. Your child is the child of the Father, first and foremost. She listens to His voice even above your own."

"She doesn't hear God! She listens to you, and the will you claim to divine as His. I entrusted my daughter to your care, but I'm still her mother and my will takes precedence over yours. I forbid you to take my child with you to that place again, is that clear?"

Suddenly the light in Berit's onyx eyes flared and the pent-up emotion she guarded so carefully welled to consume her. "You will forbid me nothing, for you are not my mistress, not my superior in any way. I do not consider you even my equal, and would ask nor take no opinion from you. You are a fool," Berit laughed. "You think your opinion matters to me, or even to your daughter? She looks to me now for guidance, and no matter what you forbid she will follow me wherever I go."

Jorunn stood in silence, watching the facade of careful control Berit usually wore disintegrate to reveal what lay beneath. Her fascination at the sudden revelation of Berit's self drowned even her anger. Berit's opinion of her mattered not at all to Jorunn. She dismissed it, hardly listening, concentrating instead on the eyes that burned in Berit's small face, suddenly opening dark doorways into her soul.

"You are too foolish even to salvage from the ruins of your position a decent life for yourself," Berit continued. "Hans Christian Krogh was your last hope, and you turned your back on him. He offered you a respectable station as his wife and you refused him, content to degrade yourself by remaining on Stridheim. You are unworthy of being the child's mother! With so little regard for your own position you have no right to be entrusted with her welfare."

"Is it my position on Stridheim that distresses you Berit?" Jorunn asked coolly, enjoying immensely having the sudden upper hand in her relationship with this woman. "Clearly you covet my position as Mistress of Stridheim! Did you really think I would forfeit that for the mere position of *wife* to any man, simply because society deems the one situation respectable, the other not? I hadn't realized. I thought you were content with your God and your errands of Christian mercy, and your nominal status as Egil's wife. Yet suddenly I understand. You seek everlasting life, that's what keeps you to your faith. In the hope of it you waste your life in the ranks of lowly soldiers for Christ, while I'm Mistress of Stridheim, stewardess of the land. I hold it in keeping for my son after me, I'll live on through him and his children. My life will be everlasting, that's assured. You wager your own afterlife on some hazy concept of a heaven I don't believe exists. Make no mistake, you're the fool, Berit," Jorunn finished, her voice even and full of conviction.

They stood facing one another, their souls revealed for a long moment. Each one assessed the other and found her beneath contempt. They turned away from one another dismissively, the anger drained, and retreated into uneasy tolerance.

Two days later Egil returned and bid Jorunn come. The house was as she had planned, the furniture she ordered was installed, drapes hung in every window. Less than a year after being laid to waste her place was reconstructed. Stridheim lay in wait for her mistress.

Her homecoming took place on a crisp autumn day when the sun was already crossing low on the horizon. As they rode through the valley Jorunn breathed in the cool, clean air, feasted her eyes greedily on red apples that hung in the orchards they passed, reveled in the bounty of wheat that waved in the fields. The earth was ripe and ready. The air of expectancy that always visited when the harvest was near was tangible to her now, her senses enhanced by her absence.

On ascent of the rise on which Stridheim rested she noticed the road was broad and fine, smooth and unrutted. Egil had been conscious of detail in his improvements. As they topped the hill she caught her breath at the first sight of the yard. Her house, the great white timber house she had planned so carefully, ranged high above the other buildings. The outbuildings were painted dull red, fewer and larger than before. Inside each one she knew precisely the dimensions, the equipment she would find. All of it new, modern. Her labor would be cut to less than half that previously her duty, Hans Christian had assured her while they planned. A white fence enclosed the yard in sharp pickets, crisp and clean. The cobbles that paved the yard shone silvery gray in the pale light. As the wagon drew closer she was unaware of the tears that streamed down her cheeks.

"Just as I dreamed," she said softly. Egil stopped the wagon outside the yard and lifted her down. She turned to look at the fields and forest that wrapped around her, stretching bountiful farther than she could see. She listened to the heartbeat of the land she stood on, felt the pulse of it through her. Her own heart beat in unison.

The harvest at Stridheim was unparalleled in abundance that year, and Egil made up his mind to celebrate it. He invited farmers and their wives from miles around and instructed Jorunn to organize a feast. For the people from the valley it would be the first sight of Stridheim since the fire; for Egil it was to be his first meeting with many of the villagers since he left Dal as a young man. Jorunn feared they would be shunned,

Egil's invitation ignored, but on the chosen evening wagons topped the rise and rolled in seemingly ceaseless succession through the gates of Stridheim. Jorunn stood by Egil's side in the wide hall and wished their neighbors welcome, old antagonism suffocated by curiosity. Greedy eyes consumed every detail of the house, and in the weeks to come housewives in the valley whiled away the hours spent washing, baking, knitting, with memories of the grand new house at Stridheim. Visions of heavy damask drapery and fine velvet upholstery gave color to their every day. Images of candles massed in ornate brass candelabra lightened winter's twilight. Over coffee they argued affably over whether they preferred the deep red hue of the great dining hall to the pale wheat gold of the sitting room, or if perhaps the walls of the sewing room, painted the color of smoky heather on the mountain beside Stridheim, were not the nicest of all. About one thing they all agreed: the new home of Egil Halvorsson and Jorunn Sigurdsdatter was the grandest imaginable.

There was no mention of the past in the speeches made at the feast, only faces turned forward to look into the future. Cries of "*Skaal!*" rang loud in the house and yard.

During the toasts Jorunn took note with satisfaction of the faces present. Only her mother and father were absent among those who wished them well. She had had no note in reply when the stable boy had delivered the horse in return to Sigurd Johannesson many months ago. Since that morning there had been no communication. At times, in the darkness just before sleep overtook her, Astrid's voice echoed in Jorunn's memory. "Our daughter is dead," she had said.

It was after the first snowfall Jorunn first had news of her father. She was in the village, supervising the delivery of hothouse vegetables from Stridheim to the greengrocer. Egil's dream of Stridheim had encompassed a great glass house to be erected on the farm. In it they could produce vegetables the year round. The daily running of this new venture was left to Abel Hansen, a young man who had grown up in the village; one Jorunn could clearly remember from earlier days when he wore short pants and spent his days snitching apples from other people's orchards. "You can choose who you like to oversee the actual production of your vegetables," she had told Egil, "but I'll mind the delivery and exchange of funds. I won't entrust our money to the likes of Abel Hansen," she said, in a tone Egil had come to understand marked the final discussion of any topic.

This errand brought her to Dal one day in late November. She overheard Greengrocer Knudsson's wife say loudly to her husband, "It's a shame, sure enough. There's nothin' more to be done for him. I heard Astrid Asbjornsdatter beg the priest to pray for her husband this past Sabbath. I heard her say, "For prayer is all that might help him now." She looked in the direction of Jorunn as she finished, not unkindly, her message clear. If Jorunn was to make peace with her father, she must not waste time.

Abandoning all thought of the vegetables Jorunn mounted and rode at once to Valgaard, the place of her birth. On approach the yard seemed smaller than she remembered, the buildings more ramshackle. 'The yard grows old with its people. It won't survive them by much,' she reflected as she dismounted and crossed the rutted yard. Her rap was answered after a long wait.

Astrid peeked out, her face barely visible in the small opening she allowed. "What do you want?" she demanded. "I admit no strangers into my house."

"I've come to make my peace with my father. You won't keep me from this errand," Jorunn answered simply, her voice firm, the lines of her face hard in determination. Astrid searched her countenance at length before she stepped back and let the door swing open. Jorunn did not hesitate once allowed entry, fearing her mother would change her mind. She brushed past Astrid and walked of old habit to the room where her father slept.

He lay on the narrow bed, his face thin and gray against faintly yellowed linen. His eyes were closed, sunken in his head, his nose too prominent, his cheeks hollowed. Fear and dread warred inside her at the thought she had come too late. Then he gasped for air and she knew him to be still alive. She bent on her knees beside him, taking his cold hand in hers, her voice urgent as she cried, "*Pappa, jeg er her.* I've come to you."

Sigurd Johannesson's frail chest heaved, his breath rattling through it. He opened his eyes to look at her. She waited long seconds, letting her gaze search his. In his cloudy blue eyes, faded to almost gray these last years, she saw the look she longed for. It was one she remembered from her childhood. It was the glance that told her he loved her best of his daughters.

Suddenly the fog in the depths of his eyes lifted and they were clear and bright. "Knew you'd come," he rasped. In a stronger voice he continued, "I've never understood His plan, but I'm resigned to it. I waited, knowin' what He'd have me say."

Jorunn watched her father, confused by his sudden strength. Before she could fathom it he continued, "I let you start out on the wrong path, same way I'd gone. I figured what was good enough for me was fine for you; all in the world I ever wanted was my land. Just like you. The Preacher said, 'What profit hath a man of all his labour which he taketh under the sun? One generation passeth away, and another generation cometh: but the earth abideth forever.' I held on to the Preacher's words, turned 'em to suit my purpose. I figured if only the earth was goin' to last, and my life was spent keepin' part of it, I wouldn't a' lived in vain. My land would be here, long after I was gone, to provide for my people. Made doin' what I wanted easy. But God punished me, gave me no son; now my people are scattered to the wind. You were my last hope; I let you follow down the same road. Wanted to believe that the way I'd gone was right for you. I wanted you to have Stridheim, thinkin' one day our land would merge, be one farm, greater than anythin' in the valley. So proud of you; said to myself, 'She's like me.' And you were. Selfish, determined, willful; my faults plain as day in you, but I wouldn't see 'em, even then."

The old man fell silent, his chest suddenly still. Panic clutched Jorunn, seized the pit of her stomach. She feared him gone. She sensed the importance of what he would say, yet feared his words. When his chest suddenly heaved and with a gasp he continued, she listened well, though with trepidation.

"One day, I walked the land, and I heard Him. A still, small voice inside. The Lord gave me grace, reminded me of Paul's journey to Damascus. Wasn't stricken to the ground or blinded by the light of heaven, but I heard His voice. Just like the Bible says, the scales fell from my eyes and I saw the truth: nothin' a man ever does is worth anythin' 'less it furthers the

gl ᴏry of God, is done in His name. You got to accept the Lord
before He'll show you His way. I knew I was lost. I turned that
day, started on my road to Damascus. Followed Him, called
Him 'Master'. But I found my way too late to save you; my
punishment was in knowin' you were still lost. Your mother
bid me keep still. She'd severed the flesh, said you were dead
to us. For long as I could I hid behind her conviction that a
house divided couldn't stand. But I knew you tol' the truth
when you said my house lay in ruin already, destroyed by the
wrath of an angry God," he wheezed. "From the waste you got
to create another house, strong in faith." He stopped, his face
contorting as he gasped for air.

"*Men Far*, I don't know how!" Jorunn cried, panic threatening to consume her, rob her of control, as she watched his
strength failing. She would promise anything to keep him with
her. "Don't leave me, *Pappa!*" she begged.

"Down the road o' life, to the end now," he whispered, his
voice only a thread. "You got another father to guide you.
Won't let you down like I did. Listen for Him when you walk
His land, His forest. He'll show you the way."

Jorunn nodded, choked by sobs she swallowed, wanting
to soothe him. The light that had burned eerily bright in his
eyes was fading. The look was gone, a sigh escaped his thin
lips. In defeat she lay her head carefully on his chest, feeling
against the softness of her cheek the frail bones beneath which
his heart had ceased to beat.

"You have made your peace, now go." Astrid's voice commanded from just behind her.

Slowly Jorunn rose to face her mother. "He's gone,
Mother."

She watched as her mother's mouth twisted, surprised to
see the wrinkled face of an old woman who had become a
stranger to her. One dry sob escaped Astrid's thin lips, before
she pressed them together in determination. "Then there is
nothing to keep you here," she said, her voice still. Time had
taken its toll, robbed Astrid of her beauty, yet her voice was as
Jorunn remembered. Golden, fluid, powerful. An echo from
the past that caused Jorunn to stare at her, searching for some
sign she might still be welcome in her mother's presence. At
last she conceded and turned to go. Yet as she rode away from
the yard Jorunn was aware she listened for a call, hoped for a
gesture that would never come.

Five days later she saw her mother for the last time. In the churchyard Astrid stood flanked by Ruth and Sylvie, both living within a week's ride of Hedmark County. Ruth, still beautiful, Sylvie a paler, plumper version of the girl Jorunn remembered. Her mother appeared to Jorunn's eyes diminished, unspeakably frail. 'Strangers to me, all of them,' Jorunn reflected.

She studied the gray stone that marked her father's final resting place.

Sigurd Johannesson
August 14, 1780 - November 28, 1864

Poor tribute to his life's endeavor, she and her sisters scant testimony. Her grief swelled to encompass them. She faced them over the grave, a wordless farewell in her eyes. The three women draped in black avoided her gaze; they moved close, marking a bond, when Jorunn hesitated and would make a move toward them. She turned to leave without a backward look.

On the ride home her thoughts were not of them, but of her father. She sensed him near, and marveled at his presence. They had been separate so long it was an unexpected comfort to know he was close. His last hope, he had called her. She remembered his dream, that one day their land should unite, and made up her mind to write to Egil at once, instructing him to settle with her sisters. She would have her father's land, keep it in his name's sake, and when she walked the land she vowed to do as she had promised: listen for the still, small voice she had heard long ago. It had faded with time, as she found her own way, ignoring its soft murmur. She doubted she would hear it again. Yet she had heard it once; she had sensed the power of the Creator in this spirit that ruled the land. Not the voice of her mother intoning God's commandments, or the punishing rhetoric of the village priest, but the whisper she heard in the wind. It had been her solace in moments of distress, her guide in times of confusion. She thought now of striding across the fields of her birthplace in search of her past and found comfort in the idea.

Once, many weeks later, she wondered what had become of her mother. She knew through Egil's inquiries that Valgaard was deserted, yet she had not thought to ask where Astrid had gone to spend her days.

"Excuse me, ma'am," a voice from behind her interrupted. Abel Hansen stood in the open door of her study. In his hands he carried a basket full of ripe tomatoes, their rich red skin glistening in the early morning light streaming through the windows.

"Abel, they're a miracle!" she exclaimed, rising from her desk and crossing to take one of the heavy fruits from him. Outside the snow still lay wrapped around them in a thick white blanket. "If you can grow these, you can grow anything," she said, her voice a rush of excitement. "We have to plan for it. Come, take me to the glass house," she instructed and led him from the room. "I was thinking it was crowded there when last I visited. We'll plan for a new one to be built when the thaw comes," she said aloud as she pulled the heavy woolen cloak snugly about her, her thoughts occupied with her duties as Mistress of Stridheim.

Twenty-five

RESTITUTION

✤ Halvor? Come here this instant, or you'll regret it the rest of today and all of tomorrow; that's a promise, young man!" Jorunn called from the porch that crossed the front of the house.

She listened expectantly, waiting for some sign of life from her son. He had disappeared early that morning, snatching with him two hot buns from the tray Cook was removing from the oven. "Where are you off to, *gutten min?*" Jorunn had asked, looking up from her busy preparations for the evening meal.

"To the village," he replied, mumbling around the huge mouthful he chewed, already making a quick escape from her questioning.

"I'd rather you spent your Saturday with *Herr* Melgaard," she said. "You waste your days free from school in the village, doing I don't know what, but I fear nothing constructive. You'd best start using your time less frivolously. One day it'll fall to you to run Stridheim; there's a lot for you to learn. Melgaard can teach you everything you need to know. He's the best over-seer in all of Hedmark County. His skill is a gift, and one he'd gladly share with you, if only you'd apply yourself, *sønnen min....*"

As she spoke he inched toward the kitchen door, his pock-ets bulging with apples pilfered from the pantry. His hands were full of the buns. He swallowed the mouthful and an-swered, "This afternoon, *Mor.* I'll apply myself then. This morning I promised to meet Rune and Eirik in the square. I'll spend this afternoon with Melgaard, but now I'm late." Having reached the door he turned and disappeared through it.

"Mind you're home in time to greet your uncle! He comes this afternoon, and you should be here waiting for him!" she called after him.

She sighed in resignation. Only time would tell if he would heed her instruction. The boy was growing more difficult to control with each passing year. Of her duties at Stridheim raising Halvor was decidedly the greatest challenge. Most of his time he spent trying to avoid the responsibilities assigned to him. Thus far he had proven inept at every chore she had instructed him to undertake. In summer he was bid help cut hay and hang it to dry, yet most days she discovered him hidden beneath the stacks, lost in slumber, only a short while after he had begun. By mid-afternoon he would have disappeared, slipping away to join his friends in the wood where they entertained one another with stories of dragons and trolls. Such exploits she found exasperating, but easily forgivable in the face of Halvor's disarming, unrepentant grin.

During this past winter, however, she lost all patience with him when she discovered that rather than returning home after school to feed the livestock he dallied in the village with schoolmates.

"Halvor, what you've done is disgraceful, unthinkable even!" she scolded. "To let a dumb beast suffer hunger while you pursue selfish interests is despicable. No farmer worth his salt would consider such a thing," she railed at him.

He had smiled at her, his boyish face assuming its most charming guise. "Surely one of the men could see to the animals, Mother," he began, but she cut him short, for once not placated by his charm.

"It's not their place or their duty! You're the young man who'll be Master of Stridheim one day. If you're to prove equal the task then you'd better start training for it now."

Suddenly his lip curled in disdain. "I'm no farmer, Mother, and I'll never be. I don't want this place. When I'm grown I'll live in the city."

She looked at his surly face and her anger was immediately choked by dread at the idea of losing him. Each holiday he spent in Christiania posed a threat to her. She felt keenly his reluctance to return to the farm. He was drawn to the life of ease and luxury at Berit's house. He thoroughly enjoyed dawdling in the main square with the other boys he found in inexhaustible supply in the city.

In her fear she countered, "You don't mean that, I know. It's only that you're young, and want to have a bit of fun," she soothed. "Accept my apology, and I'll forgive you, *gutten min.* But you have to promise to try harder."

He had kissed her then, and bestowed on her his most beatific smile. She let herself believe that he gave this promise with greater seriousness than those he had given in the past. Yet time passed and Halvor remain unchanged. The area in which he showed greatest perseverance was in pursuit of pleasure.

Midday arrived, and there was no sign of Halvor. Egil's carriage pulled into the yard just as the sun was pausing directly overhead before beginning its descent into afternoon. Jorunn removed her apron and smoothed her hands over the dark blue wool of a new dress. In the hallway she paused to check her reflection in the glass that hung there. Her hair was still smooth in its knot at her neck, her cheeks flushed with the heat of the kitchen. She brushed a smudge of flour from her face with the back of her hand and turned to greet Egil as he entered the hall.

"Nice to have you here," she said, raising her cheek to the light kiss he brushed there.

"It is good to come here. I have missed all of you at Stridheim. The place looks prosperous, as does its mistress," he smiled, stepping back to admire Jorunn.

She felt her color rise as she smiled at him. "You're too kind," she replied. "Come, you must be thirsty. I'll draw you a glass of beer myself."

Settled into the parlor Egil looked about, asking, "Where is the boy? I am eager to see him. Has he grown this past winter? Is he the same?"

Jorunn watched him, his face a mirror of happy anticipation at news of his son. The boy looked so like him. It was frustrating he appeared to share few of his father's more stable qualities.

"He'll probably be home by dinnertime," she said, shifting uncomfortably. "He left early to spend his Saturday morn in the village square with Rune Gunnarsson and Eirik Tomter.

I'm sorry he's not here to greet you. He's difficult to control, and was gone before I could stop him," she said ruefully.

Egil's expression firmed into the one he often wore when discussing his son. "The boy needs a firm hand, Jorunn. You are effective beyond comprehension at everything you do here at Stridheim, yet I believe you allow Halvor too much free rein."

Jorunn bridled. "That's not true. He's a good student, and always polite and respectful of the people in our employ. It's true he enjoys his freedom, and time spent in the company of other young people, but he's only a boy. He'll settle soon. There's plenty of time."

"Halvor has attained ten years of age. He is no longer a child. It is time for him to begin accepting responsibility for certain things. If he is not held accountable soon it will be too late, mark my words. I have given this much thought. I have resolved that the time has come for Halvor to come to Christiania and begin his studies at a school there."

Silence hung heavy between them. Jorunn's face mirrored clearly her distress at the idea. "I won't let him go. He belongs here, on Stridheim. One day it will be his; his learning has to be of this place. It's the only way to prepare him for his future."

"It is reasonable, what you say. Yet we both know he has not even begun to travel the road he must pass in order to one day take responsibility for this farm. Living here has not served to inspire in him the love of the land you feel. It has taught him nothing of the discipline he must have to be master of it. It is time to try another route. I found my way back to the land in a circuitous way, one not easily traversed, yet it made a man of me. The time has come to send my son on a similar journey. Reconcile yourself to this Jorunn, for the sake of our son."

Jorunn's hands grew cold and clammy. She walked to the fireplace to warm them. In the mirror above the mantle she saw her reflection. In her distress her face was mottled red and white. 'I'm old,' she thought, noticing for the first time tiny lines that fanned from the corners of eyes not as blue as they had once been. "Forty-three years gone by so quickly, more than half my life gone. My land, my legacy still at risk."

Watching Egil in the mirror she replied, "For the sake of our son, you say. But he's happy here. I can't pretend to do this for his sake. Still, you're right with regard to his attitude toward Stridheim. He makes no effort to prepare himself; he's uninspired. Maybe it is proximity that breeds contempt for the land."

She paused for a long moment, noticing the fire did not warm her. She was suddenly assailed by the idea that without Halvor to succeed her at Stridheim her life would have been in vain. She banished the thought before it was fully formed. "We'll do as you suggest then," she said with a heavy sigh. When you return in the fall he'll go with you. I'll stay here with the hope that absence will endear this place to him. For the future of Stridheim."

Egil moved to her and took both her hands in his, warming them. "When fall comes you must return to Christiania with us. I have happy news of Valdis. She has chosen her husband-to-be and bids you come for the wedding. It should have been in the summer, but with so much to be done on Stridheim at that time she has agreed to postpone the celebration until after the harvest."

"My Valdis, to be married! I can't think, I can't imagine!" Jorunn exclaimed.

Egil smiled at her surprise. "Berit and I, too, thought she might feel another calling. She has been so devoted in her work for the church. It was, in fact, through her work there she met this man she will take for her own."

"Do you know him? Is it a good match?" Jorunn asked. For an instant her happiness was dimmed by frustration at the idea that Valdis had not mentioned a man in her dutiful, impersonal letters.

"It is a good match, yes, excellent in every respect," Egil informed her. "Berit was thrilled, and Valdis is happy herself. That is the most important aspect."

"Yes, of course," Jorunn agreed readily. "You say the marriage will take place in the fall. She won't come home, to be wed here, at Stridheim?" she asked, hopeful in spite of herself, but Egil's expression relayed the message she was expecting.

"Virtually everyone she knows is in Christiania," he said gently. "She will be married at the cathedral."

'If Erland had lived things might be different,' Jorunn reflected in silent disappointment. 'Maybe the bond they shared would have strengthened in time. From the day I gave her birth my daughter has been an indecipherable element to me. Time and circumstance have only served to widen the gulf that divides us. We're as different to one another as ice to fire. I've got to accept this.'

Yet the bitter bile of disappointment rose up to choke her. Valdis would not lead her wedding procession from the courtyard at Stridheim to the vaulted hall of Dal Church. She would not carry on her brow the bridal crown Jorunn had borne so proudly when she wed Erland. Without asking she understood Valdis would stand before the alter in a white gown in the modern fashion. The *bunad* Jorunn embroidered for her daughter on quiet evenings at Stridheim would not be suitable. There would be no feast in the dining hall, no dance over the cobbles in the dusky light of a summer's eve. Jorunn sighed in resignation. "It's the way things are, the way they had to be."

Twenty-six

VISITATION

The summer was hot and dry, and the crops on Stridheim suffered from it. Egil resolved to spend the months on a plan for irrigation during seasons of drought and left much of the daily operation of the farm to Jorunn and the overseer. Halvor seized the opportunity to run free, spending most of his time in the village. Three times that summer he was escorted home in the clutches of indignant villagers, victims of pranks inspired by a quick mind left uninstructed. By the time the harvest was in Jorunn was resigned to Halvor's leaving. She recognized the irrefutability of Egil's conviction that Halvor must have discipline and a firm hand to guide him. She traveled the road to Christiania torn between her happiness at Valdis' upcoming wedding and her disappointment at having to relinquish Halvor into the care of Egil and Berit. She had lost a daughter to them; she was filled with dread at the idea that she risked losing her son as well.

She found Valdis quite unchanged. She had expected some difference in attitude; a flush on her pale cheeks, an air of excitement at the idea of being a bride and all that would entail in changes to her life. Yet when her daughter greeted her it was with her usual restrained kiss and embrace. Valdis was as cool and steady in her approach to marriage as she was in every other aspect of her life. Jorunn sighed, trying again to resign herself to her daughter as she was, unable to quell the wish that she might be granted some understanding into the workings of the young woman's mind.

Berit did not greet them in the great hall when they arrived. "She is resting," Valdis replied to Jorunn's inquiries. "She looks forward to seeing you at dinner."

Valdis assumed the responsibilities of mistress of the house effortlessly, installing Jorunn in the room she usually occupied on her visits to Berit's house, maintaining with slightly more effort her calm in the face of Halvor's exuberance as he pushed past her on the stairs on his way to his room. He was intent on his errand of unpacking so he would be free to go search in Tullin Close for a game in need of an extra player. On earlier visits he had discovered there were plenty of friends to be found in the surrounding parks. Jorunn felt a nudge of shame for the relief she registered at the thought that for a while Egil would shoulder the responsibility for the impossible. Namely, keeping Halvor on a tight rein.

As they sat to dinner that evening her irritation at Halvor's absence was quelled by the shock of her first sight of Berit. She was greatly reduced. Always delicate, she seemed to have withered in the year since Jorunn had last seen her. Her small hand shook as she lifted her wine glass in a toast to welcome Jorunn and Halvor, her black hair was streaked with gray. Only her eyes burned as bright as Jorunn remembered. The rest of Berit was fading.

Jorunn looked in concern toward Egil, who signaled her silence with a careful shake of his head. The conversation at dinner was centered around Valdis' upcoming wedding.

"The ceremony is to be held at the cathedral, I understand," Jorunn remarked.

"Naturally, for it was there we met. It was our work there that brought us together. It is that which will bind us as man and wife," Valdis answered, her voice cool, like Berit's, yet her aunt's influence had not erased the vibrancy that reminded Jorunn of her own mother. Valdis' voice was like silver bells, ringing clear, and impossible not to attend.

Jorunn watched her daughter carefully. Nothing in her countenance changed at the mention of her future husband. Her curiosity of this man grew. "I'm looking forward to meeting the young man who I hope will be like a son to me," she said, her voice warm. "When will I have the pleasure?"

Valdis and Berit exchanged a glance which puzzled her. She looked toward Egil questioningly. He avoided her gaze.

"Will tomorrow be soon enough?" Valdis asked. "I visit the cathedral early each day. Guthard will surely be there."

"In the morning, then," Jorunn smiled. For an instant she imagined she registered something in her daughter's impassive face that made her uneasy.

⅙ *⅙* *⅙*

That night, long after the rest of the house lay sleeping, Valdis sat in the light of a full moon and stared toward her God in heaven. 'Ask, and it shall be given you; seek, and ye shall find; for every one that asketh receiveth; and he that seeketh findeth; and to him that knocketh it shall be opened,' He had promised. Yet night after night she waited on bent knee, praying for the strength to do His bidding and marry Guthard Myrbraaten, and He withheld this blessing for which she prayed.

"I have spoken to Guthard Myrbraaten on your behalf, Valdis, and he has done you the honor of offering you protection as his wife," her Aunt Berit had explained to her on a cold January morning. Her aunt's words, so casually delivered, had seemed to Valdis to reverberate in the still room. Outside the snow fell to lay in a thick blanket, nearly obscuring her view from the window of the breakfast room. Valdis had felt the walls close in to suffocate her, panic rise to choke her.

"But Aunt Berit, you cannot mean this!" Valdis gasped, whirling to face her aunt. "When you spoke to me of marriage, of the necessity of choosing the right partner, I understood, yet I never imagined *Herr* Myrbraaten as my husband." The idea of the old man occurred to her suddenly and filled her with revulsion.

Noticing the shudder that passed through the girl Berit continued, "We agreed that the most important aspect of choosing your partner in life was that you should share your religious convictions. You must never compromise your faith, Valdis. It is the most important aspect of life. And in marriage your will must be subjugated that of your husband. It is crucial that he, too, recognize God as his master. If you share that view then every other facet of marriage will follow its natural course," she soothed.

Valdis rose from her seat at the breakfast table and walked in her agitation to the window. The translucent curtain of snow obscured her view of the garden, her sight turned inward. In her soul she faced the willful, stubborn nature she was given to bear, and was ashamed. The years of tireless effort her aunt had invested in her had come to little, if the truth were known. She was still the same wicked, selfish girl that had driven her mother to send her away. Outwardly she feigned the humility she had learned was necessary to live in God's good grace and make her acceptable to others, yet beneath the veneer she rebelled at the things required of decent people. While she knew that faith must have works, she detested the stench of the poor and sick; she struggled daily to maintain the air of submission appropriate to one of God's servants. In truth, the things that touched her most in her worship were the beauty of the soaring ceilings of the cathedral, the brilliance of the red runner, the silver cups that shimmered in the candlelight of the alter. The peal of the bells called her to worship far louder than the voice of God. She was moved by the liquid beauty of their resonance, struck dumb with awe as sunlight filtered through the panels of stained glass and washed the walls of the cathedral in rainbows of splendid color. These things made her spirit soar and her heart sing. She seldom heard God's voice. She imagined she divined a whisper of His meaning in some of her prayers, yet the concrete, simple instruction her aunt received eluded her. She had prayed with her aunt often regarding the choice of a husband for herself, since the woman confided she had not long to live and was anxious to see Valdis settled before her death. Day after day Valdis prayed before the alter at the cathedral, night after night she kneeled before the window of her room and begged God for His instruction in the matter, yet He turned a deaf ear to her pleas and gave her no guidance. When she admitted this to her aunt she had seen clearly the woman's disappointment in her. The old fear welled and for an instant she was desperately afraid, terrified at being cast out.

"Please, Aunt Berit," she had begged suddenly. "I believe I understand his answer. God will not tell me His will; He means that you are to guide me in this decision, as in all others. You must pray to Him, for He will settle the matter with you."

Berit smiled a small smile, suddenly pleased with Valdis again, and the girl felt her heart lift with joy. It was right, this message she had divined. She was sure of it; it had made her aunt happy.

Until this moment she had never questioned her decision to place her fate in her aunt's hands. But the prospect of Guthard Myrbraaten as her husband filled her with dread beyond anything she had ever experienced. She had little idea of the realities of marriage. Uncle Egil and Aunt Berit did not share a room, as she supposed was seemly for a couple married so long. Yet she could remember a time when her mother and father had lain together beneath the blankets on their bed each night, sharing warmth and intimacy she could not imagine with Guthard Myrbraaten. As a little girl she had sometimes slept between her parents on nights when even the fire could not keep away the chill of winter, their bodies beside hers a comfort, the pulse of them almost tangible.

She imagined again Guthard Myrbraaten, his look, yet she could not imagine a heart that beat beneath his frail chest, already sunken with age. Nor could she sense any warmth in the clasp of his bony hand when she greeted him at the cathedral.

She turned away from the window and frozen snow outside and faced her aunt, desperation clear in her face, another protest on the tip of her tongue. The look of reproof in her aunt's black eyes silenced her before she uttered a sound. She recognized the shuttered look her aunt wore and felt the chill inside her it always brought.

"Please forgive me, Aunt Berit," Valdis said placatingly. "I am unworthy of the time and consideration you have given this decision. Of course I shall marry *Herr* Myrbraaten. It shall be as you wish."

"It is not my wish," Berit corrected, her look triumphant. "It is the will of God. It fell to me only to divine it. Come, sit and I shall ring for a fresh pot of tea. We have much to plan. Given my illness I thought we should make plans for a spring wedding."

Valdis bit back her cry of protest. 'Please, dear God, spare me this for a while. Give me time to resign myself to Your will....'

It seemed God at last heard her prayer. Her aunt continued, "Yet I feel strong now that the burden of worry for your welfare has been lifted from my shoulders," Berit smiled. "I think the ceremony might wait until autumn. That will give us time to plan for a proper wedding. Your uncle and I shall see to it that you are married in grand style," she smiled at Valdis.

Valdis made no reply, for she was offering a hasty prayer of thanks to God for the reprieve He granted.

Yet these past months He had remained deaf to her prayers, refusing to give her the strength she so desperately needed to face Guthard Myrbraaten at the end of the crimson runner. She had nightmares of him, standing before the alter, his long, wizened face and sunken cheeks cast in shadow by a bright light that shone from above. She awoke from these dreams wet with perspiration, her nightgown clinging to her body, and crawled from her bed to kneel before the window and pray. Yet God let her wait. Only seven nights before she must walk up the aisle on the arm of her uncle. "Please, God," she prayed fervently. "You have shown me the way, please give me the strength to follow it."

❖ ❖ ❖

Jorunn entered the hall leaving the door gaping wide behind her. The door to Egil's library was closed. She crossed to it and opened it without ceremony.

He was alone, studying columns of figures in a book open before him.

"Why didn't you tell me? He's old, Egil, older than you or I! *Herregud*, she can't marry an old man! This is impossible!" she cried.

Egil rose and crossed to close the door behind her. "Calm yourself, Jorunn. No purpose is served by your ranting." He led her to a sofa and set her there, taking his place beside her. "I understand your distress. I, too, was surprised by her choice. Yet the choice is hers. We cannot choose whom she will love."

"She doesn't love him, I'm certain of that," Jorunn interrupted. "I've watched her carefully, and today I saw them together. She may care for him; it's difficult to judge what transpires beneath that cool exterior. But I know deep in my heart that she doesn't love him. There was no connection between them, merely politeness. They can't have anything in common, considering the difference in age and station in life. There's nothing between them on which to base a marriage."

"They share their work, the calling they feel to worship God through deed. They met while raising funds for a housing project designed to give the poor affordable shelter, and they work tirelessly together to better the circumstances of those less fortunate. It is their conviction that binds them together. I believe it will be the basis for their marriage."

"That's not enough, Egil. She is innocent! She has no idea of the reality of marriage. I had no call to discuss those things with her before she left Stridheim, and since she has lived here there have been no grounds for it. I'm certain Berit hasn't explained. She'll be horrified when she learns what is expected of her."

Egil was silenced by what he knew to be true. "Then you must speak with her now," he asserted. "There is still time."

"There is no time! In one week she'll marry that man, a man more than twice her age. The wedding is planned, the guests invited. Valdis will never step away from the commitment she's made. It should never have been allowed. I hold you responsible," she said vehemently.

"It is not Egil's responsibility," came a cool reply from behind them. Turning, Jorunn saw Berit framed in the doorway. She had not heard her approach, or the door open.

"I accept full responsibility for Valdis' decision to marry Guthard Myrbraathen. He is a fine man in every respect, honorable and greatly admired for his dedication to the church. He is a worthy match in every way."

Turning to face Berit, Jorunn shrank from the confrontation. The woman seemed insubstantial, too frail to withstand adversity. "I'm not questioning his character, it's because of his age I find him unacceptable. He's an old man already, his life is behind him. Valdis is only nineteen years of age, a young woman poised on the threshold of life. She deserves a husband who'll share that life with her. If she marries Guthard Myrbraathen she'll be a young widow. I believe Valdis is a woman so strong in her convictions that when she is first wed she will never choose another husband. It's important she choose the right man now. What of the children that will arise from this marriage? They're entitled to both father and mother. Have you considered that?"

"I have," Berit replied, and then continued coolly. "While I cannot pretend to know the burden you have suffered raising your children without a father, I do believe it is entirely possible to do so without the children suffering."

Jorunn's face flamed, her anger at Berit's implications drowning all pity for her. "You know nothing of children, in any case," she flared. "She's my daughter; I entrusted her to you in the belief you would raise her as your own, never dropping your vigilance in guiding her. But it's clear to me that you're not well, and during your illness Valdis has been allowed to follow a course of her own unwise choosing."

"You are wrong," Berit refuted, her eyes burning in her sunken face. "I chose Guthard Myrbraathen for Valdis. I am ill, it is true. It was my duty to see her safely wed before I die. I chose the man I believed to be best suited to care for Valdis and to continue to guide her on the path to righteousness. She will do as I bid. She will marry Guthard Myrbraaten in six days time."

For a moment she leaned in the doorway gloating, before turning to disappear into the hall. Jorunn sat feeling the sting of Berit's words as keenly as if the assault had been a physical one. She sensed Berit had her own reasons for choosing Guthard Myrbraaten to be Valdis' husband. With the canny instinct of another woman Jorunn knew Berit was settling a score with her. In her dark eyes there had burned a message.

'A daughter for a husband.' These many years Jorunn had supposed it was affection that bound Berit and Valdis. In a flash she recognized that Berit had had ulterior motives.

"She's right," Jorunn said woodenly. "The path we chose long ago is well-trodden, there's no turning back now. We simply have to do what must be done, looking forward and not behind."

She left the room, her face pale and set. At the wedding she watched Valdis traverse the carpet that ran like a river of blood from the alter. Her delicate beauty seemed an ephemeral thing as she leaned on Egil's arm. In her profile Jorunn saw again the likeness to Astrid. A chill started at the base of her spine and spread through her, making her limbs frozen, unresponsive. She became aware of hot tears that coursed down her cold cheeks, and lifted a heavy hand to brush them away.

Berit sat only inches to the left of Jorunn. Her tiny frame was withered, the spark of light that usually shone in her dark eyes barely a glimmer. She was aware of the tears Jorunn shed, knew the grief to which they bore testimony. The loss of a child was a grievous injury, no doubt. Berit suppressed a smile at the idea Jorunn's pain. Perhaps Jorunn understood now her own pain, her grief over children never conceived, she mused inwardly. Yet the full extent of her suffering, the torment of living trapped within a barren body, was undoubtedly lost on the brazen whore, Berit reflected with a sigh of regret. The despicable harlot had seduced Egil and taken from her the right to bear her husband's child; she certainly had no sensibilities that would let her feel anything comparable to the emotions that waged constant war within her own tortured heart. Jorunn Sigurdsdatter was nothing more than a heathen philistine, beneath contempt, Berit reassured herself. Yet inexplicably she had never been able to relegate the woman to the ranks of those to be pitied. For this, too, she hated Jorunn. But the passion of her hatred had waned, of late. All her strength gone, nothing left but emptiness inside the glacial hollow of a barren body, consumed by disease. Strangely, she had lived with the idea that in death would come her reward, yet death's call was ringing heavy in her ears, echoing the bells tolling when Valdis turned from the alter and left the church on the arm of her newly wedded husband. Death yawned before Berit as a dark crevice she would not slide into. With a heavy sigh of resignation she rose to follow Valdis from the cathedral. She faced the inevitable, resolute in the awareness there was nowhere else to go.

Twenty-seven

ENLIGHTENMENT

Jorunn returned home in late fall and resumed her work on the farm, but time hung heavy on her hands. Each day seemed monotonous, gray. Her duties as Mistress of Stridheim were greatly reduced in the wake of modern improvements Egil continually made, leaving her a great deal of free time. Her mind tended to drift, to wander backward in time and reflect on that which had gone before. It was a habit quite foreign to her nature, and one she disliked. Time and again the thought sprang to her unbidden that perhaps she had failed her children in some way. Both of them gone from her now. Yet she remained Mistress of Stridheim. That thought always brought satisfaction; she felt new strength surge at the idea. It was for Stridheim she had lived and worked and sacrificed. It was only right that in the end it was Stridheim she should have.

Against her will she began the journey she had promised her father she would take, yet had gratefully postponed. The years had passed in a march of time spent in ceaseless endeavor, filled with plans for Stridheim and the future. Along the way she had collected an assortment of impressions that shaped the present. Shadowy figures haunted her. She sensed once confronted they would reveal not only themselves, but herself as well. She was filled with dread at what she might discover, yet with her father's dying words he had made it clear that this journey of self-discovery was one she must take.

She walked the land of Stridheim, finding she knew the place so well it held no surprises or discoveries for her. She understood the part of her journey she had taken here. It was governed by choice and her own will. It was when she climbed the mountain and looked down on Valgaard she fe' unease stir and had to fight the longing to turn, to flee down the mountain to the safety of the yard at Stridheim. In front of her stretched the acres her father had plowed and worked with sweat and blood until in death the land reclaimed him. Nature encroached quickly. The forest already invaded the western fields. The wheat that had grown there was a memory in her mind, and the memory would die with her. She shivered suddenly.

"...I figure the dirt their bodies were returned to are the only testimony that they ever lived," Erland had said of the men who farmed Stridheim before him. She recognized this truth and faced her own mortality. In death she would return to black earth, only a memory to those who had known her. Like her father she had reasoned her legacy to her children and grandchildren would be the land. It was what she had wanted, what she spent her whole life working for. Pure vanity, she recognized now. Ecclesiastes' words were true. One generation passes away, another survives, the earth survives forever. Yet like her father she had misinterpreted the Preacher and believed her land would sustain her. Like her father, she now realized it did not. Unbidden there sprang to her mind Scripture long forgotten. 'A faithful man shall abound with blessings: but he that maketh haste to be rich shall not be innocent.'

She turned to look again at Stridheim in all its vast greatness, and was filled with a surge of pride that did not quite obliterate the emptiness inside her. Turning back, she faced her past again and knew it was there the void originated. She began her descent of the mountain, into her past, on her road to Damascus.

She walked the fields of Valgaard until the weak winter sun gave quick way to twilight, waiting in vain for something, the light from heaven, a voice. But there was nothing. Not even the still, small voice she remembered from long ago. At nightfall she retreated to her place on the other side of the mountain, frustrated. Her journey begun, she had thought to find answers, had thought that like Saul the scales would fall from her eyes and she would be enlightened, yet she returned to Stridheim filled with questions as yet unnamed and plagued by a sense of urgency. Impatient, yet she resigned herself to the idea her journey must take some time.

Each day she woke early, after fitful rest, and crossed to the other side. For a week she looked to the land for what she sought, and when she came no further in her discovery, she turned reluctantly toward the house.

Henrik's house. It had been fashioned in hope and anticipation of his bride, yet he had died, broken and disillusioned, less than a year later within those four walls. Her mother and father had lived their lives there, together, yet apart. Jorunn's memories of the place were of loneliness, quiet desperation. She was loathe to enter the ramshackle dwelling, yet she sensed it was here she would find what she looked for.

The door creaked loudly, giving way only after a stubborn shove. Inside she found the rudiments of her early life. Three simple rooms with a narrow hallway between. The kitchen was primitive by the standard to which she had become accustomed, the sitting room no larger than Cook's room at Stridheim. Her parents bedroom repelled her. As a child she had not been allowed there; she would not go there now. She shrank from it and turned to the narrow stairway that led from the hall to the room upstairs. The loft was without partition. One large room had housed Sigurd and Astrid's five daughters. She walked through the dusty memories that assailed her, noting the beds seemed lower and smaller than she had remembered. The hay beneath the woven mattress ticking protruded through holes eaten by rodents. A rat scurried across the room behind her, and she turned toward the stairs.

Her boots clattered on the bare steps. She walked quickly, eager to be away. The enlightenment she sought eluded her. There was nothing for her here.

As she neared the base of the stairs the sun broke through the cloud outside to filter through a dusty window pane. Illuminated in its weak rays was the alter at which her mother had spent so much time kneeling. Jorunn stopped, drawn inexplicably to it. Without forethought she kneeled before it; with one hand she traced her father's fine carving. Clean and simple, without the dragons and scrolls her mother despised as heathen and belonging to another time and a pagan religion. The alter was a thing of beauty, the only one Jorunn could remember from her years in this house. Yet she was suddenly aware it was poor substitute for the calling her mother had been forced to abandon. Her father's gift to his bride, meant to assuage the longing she carried within. In front of this alter Astrid was meant to find that which he had taken from her. Jorunn recalled that Egil, long ago, had come to reclaim Stridheim for his own and bid her find a house in the village to call her place. Her anger at him had been in part a reaction to the threat he posed to her security, yet it had also been rage and disbelief that he could imagine any house a substitute for her land. His callous disregard for her perspective had made her hate him in that instant. She saw the alter her father had fashioned in a new light, recognized that the bitterness her mother had harbored had been justified. "It was this that brought me back," she mused aloud. As if she laid down a heavy burden, she felt suddenly light. She bowed her head and prayed, for the first time of her own free will, "The Lord is my shepherd, I shall not want...."

She lifted her face heavenward, inside black lids she imagined a light; first red, then golden, then white and blinding in intensity. She squeezed her eyes tight and it was gone.

She left the house and crossed the yard with the sense of peace that had eluded her all this autumn. She would send for the alter, keep it near her at Stridheim. The still, small voice that had been silent for so long whispered that before it she would find the answers she sought.

Twenty-eight

GRACE

❧ In early December Egil sent word Berit was dead. He asked Jorunn not to come. She was left to wonder if this had been his bidding, or Berit's. She had learned never to underestimate Berit; she did not doubt her ability to reach beyond the grave in a final attempt to orchestrate their lives.

When the snow came it cloaked the world in a bright coat of white, helping to purge Jorunn's mood. She felt her spirit lighten, and resolved to spend the rest of the winter planning a garden that would stretch away from the rear of the house, framing it where it lay in the midst of the fields.

She enlisted the aid of Abel Hansen and together they chose seeds from a catalogue Jorunn acquired. She designed an area of lawn that would be intersected by gravel paths, and planned for beds of flowers in shades of color ranging from deep blue to clear red to bright yellow; a myriad of bright colors to give relief to flat green. She plotted her garden in careful detail, visiting the glass houses daily, urging Abel to try as many varieties as he could find place for. Then they waited, bidding their time impatiently.

The thaw came, and by the time Egil returned for the planting they were well underway. He arrived to find Jorunn behind the house, clad in her oldest dress, a scarf covering her fair hair. Engrossed in giving instruction to the men engaged in leveling the ground, she was unaware of his presence. He stood watching for some while before she turned to find him there, wearing an expression she could not understand.

Crossing to him she took his hands in her own. "Egil, I'm so sorry," she said, looking into his face.

There were new lines there, worn with the grief of the past months. She lifted one hand to gently trace a furrow beside his mouth. He caught it and pressed it to his mouth, closing his eyes for a moment, savoring the feel of her. When he released her hand he was smiling. "It is not from grief alone I age, it is from the worry of our son," he said ruefully. "In these past months I have begun to understand the responsibilities of parenting."

Happy to see him smiling again she replied, "He's like his father." She laughed aloud at his pained expression.

He stared at her, his expression serious. "You look just as you did when first I saw you, fourteen years ago."

She flushed, suddenly aware of her appearance. "That can't possibly be a compliment," she said with a grimace, looking down at the front of her, stained with smears of dirt. "Maybe it's the dress; it's the same one I wore that day."

"I remember," he replied, his voice still, his look intent. She pulled away, leading him to the house.

"I'll change and bid Cook find you refreshment." Her breath was suddenly short, her mind racing at the possibilities that presented themselves. There was something unnerving in his attitude.

She left Egil in the sitting room and went to the kitchen to direct the cook and bid the girl bring her bath water. She took the back stairs to her room, avoiding Egil until she could make sense of their present situation.

When the water was drawn she sank into the tub and rested there. Visions of Egil as he had been that first day assailed her. She retraced in her mind the years she had known him. So much had transpired. This late afternoon she watched the sun set low on the horizon, disappearing behind silver birches only barely beginning to green, and let her mind drift backward, to the beginning. She took careful stock, then let herself slowly look ahead. Always eager for the future, often impatient, now she was reluctant to contemplate what might lie ahead. Hope glimmered and beckoned. She felt suddenly giddy with it. She squeezed her eyes tight and sank beneath the water to drown the laughter that bubbled inside her.

She stood and toweled briskly, then wandered to the wardrobe and flicked quickly through the dresses hanging there. She withdrew a gown the color of cherries ripe in July, and spread it carefully on her bed, fingering the silk, letting it caress her palm sensuously. Drawing a deep breath she dropped the towel and turned to assess her image in the glass of her dressing table. 'The dim light of late afternoon flatters me,' she thought, lifting her hands to caress her full breasts. She slid them to her waist, still small, and across her hips where they flared only slightly greater than she remembered from long ago.

Crossing to her chest she chose her finest shift, a whisper of silk edged in lace. She let it slide over her body, reveling in the softness of the fabric against her bare skin. Returning to her dressing table she picked up a match and struck it, watching the flame flicker, holding it to light the candles on either side of the mirror. The shadows they created served to outline her cheekbones with greater clarity, her jaw was more pronounced. Her face had lost the round softness she remembered from her youth, yet she acknowledged it to be attractive still. Faint brows over blue eyes dark in the candlelight, straight nose, full lips. She touched her mouth with the fingers of her right hand, feeling the softness, watching the light reflect from the gold band she wore. Erland's ring. She had worn his mark for twenty-three years. She slipped the ring from her finger and let it lay on the dressing table. Rising, she crossed to the bed and pulled the dress over her. 'I don't dare look ahead, so I won't," she decided. "This once I'll let the future come to me.'

     ❧ ❧ ❧

The dinner Cook had prepared lay on the table before them, virtually untouched. Jorunn fingered the stem of her wine glass, studying the rich liquid, its color that of ripe currants. She glanced at Egil and he lifted his glass. He paused, searching for words. Finally, in defeat he murmured "*Skaal,*" and waited for her echo.

"To the future," she replied, her gaze fixed firmly to his. She felt his eyes probing, questioning.

He lifted his glass again and ventured, "To us," watching as she raised her glass and drank deeply. He smiled broadly, his eyes alight, as he put his glass to his lips and tilted his head to drain it in one quick gesture.

She stood and held out her hand. Without a word she led him to her room, into her bed, into their future.

Twenty-nine

RENEWAL

❧ What do you mean, he won't come home for the summer? He must! It's not his choice. It can't be," she insisted as she walked with Egil toward the front porch. The last rays of the May sun stretched long fingers of light toward them. Jorunn's hair glittered under its touch, strands of silver streaking the gold.

"I knew you would not be pleased. Yet you must try to understand. He has been invited to travel to France with the family of his closest friend, Pierre Beaumont. It would not be fair of us, or wise, to deny him this opportunity."

"There's opportunity enough here, waiting for him at Stridheim. But he chooses to overlook that. He treats this place with little or no regard!" she cried. To her dismay she felt tears threaten, heard her voice catch.

Egil took her in his arms to comfort her, and for the moment she relented. "Do not upset yourself, it pains me to see you like this," he murmured. "You have not been yourself of late; I do wish you would visit the physician. I could call him to you, if you would rather," he prodded.

Irritated, she pushed him away, a flush rising high on her cheeks. "I don't need a doctor. I'm fine, except for having a son who is hopelessly ungrateful," she retorted. Inwardly she fumed. She needed no physician to tell her what was happening to her body. She had reached the crossroads in life when certain avenues would be closed to her. She had spoken to Helfrid Olafsdatter of the matter and been given herbs from which to draw a tea.

"Got to be expected at this time of life," Helfrid had soothed Jorunn when she had come complaining of fatigue, almost to the point of exhaustion. It was widely accepted in the valley that Helfrid possessed much of the knowledge her mother, her grandmother, her great-grandmother had had in preparing remedies for common ailments. Jorunn had never had cause to approach the woman before, yet in early spring she began suffering from a malaise which caused her to require far more rest than she had time for. Each morning she awoke fighting off the stupor of sleep, longing to turn in her bed and slumber on. All day she wrestled fatigue, and her appetite had increased because of it. She was growing stout from the eating, and she approached Helfrid with the idea that she perhaps needed minerals or herbs added to her diet.

"It's the change," Helfrid had informed her. Jorunn had stared at the old woman, not comprehending. "Has you monthly flow changed?" Helfrid asked, her voice gruff, her manner blunt.

"*Vel*, it hasn't been as usual; lately it's ceased altogether," Jorunn confessed. Helfrid sent her home with a mixture of herbs, and instructions to keep herself occupied and not dwell on her condition. "Jus' nature's way," she reassured.

Inwardly Jorunn fumed with anger. It might seem natural to an old crone like Helfrid Olafsdatter, but she did not consider herself so old. Since Egil had come to her she had blossomed, feeling young again. Her days were spent in happy occupation, in pleasant anticipation of each evening in his company. Their nights were spent in abandon in the great bed they shared. Her life was complete in ways she had never dreamed. Her only strife was that Halvor refused to come home to Stridheim, even while Egil stayed there for longer periods than he had before. According to his own wishes Halvor was left in the care of Egil's manservant, and spent his time out of school with friends. He felt no longing for this place, or for her. He was single-minded in pursuit of his own happiness. His sunny disposition was almost a thing forgotten. He used his smile only when it suited his needs. Jorunn no longer fell victim to his charm. He irked her beyond tolerance, and was the cause for her frequent bouts of change in temper.

"Send for him at once. Tell him he has to come home," she instructed.

"It is too late. I saw him safely aboard the ship before I traveled here," Egil said. "You must resign yourself to this; he will not come here this summer."

With a withering look Jorunn turned and left him, walking in her agitation toward the river. Its ceaseless flow beckoned, the sound of it calling to her as the water rushed high in its banks. She stood at the edge and let the water soothe her.

Egil followed. Approaching from behind he slid his arms around her waist and pulled her to him. "It is better this way," he murmured. "If Halvor were here I could not come to you each night. We would be forced to observe propriety, and I am not of a mind to do so. Will you not change your mind and marry me, so we may throw caution to the wind."

"I've told you, the holy institution of marriage doesn't tempt me. It can be a miserable state of affairs, and simply because most of the world finds themselves trapped in it doesn't mean I'll follow their lead, like a lamb to slaughter. Misery loves company; I suspect that's why the majority insists on including everyone else in their wedded ranks."

Egil laughed. "We are hardly lambs any longer," he teased. Then his voice grew calm. "I have loved you for fourteen years. Since I first saw you, I think. I believe you have felt the same for me. We are not rash young lovers plunging into matrimony without forethought. I waited all these years to be free so I might make you mine, let all the world see you are my wife." Turning her gently in his arms he asked, "Will you marry me, Jorunn?"

Jorunn looked into Egil's blue eyes; in them she saw everything she would ever need. "It's of no significance that our marriage be blessed in a church," she insisted. "In my heart I'm wed to you. The only witnesses I need are here."

He turned from her, the hurt clear in his eyes. "Egil, try to understand. My first marriage was conventional, we were united in a joint venture. Our wedding wasn't a celebration of love, that came after. I don't see the conventions of the church as anything over than a contract. It won't increase the affection we have for one another, so it's unnecessary. If there had been any rational reason for such a contract I'd consider it, but the way things are I won't change what suits us as it is."

He turned back to her. "Why must you be so rational?" he asked with an edge of exasperation. Then he smiled, linking his arm around her shoulders as they retraced their steps to the house. In the hall he pulled her to him and whispered, "I have missed you. Shall we celebrate Halvor's absence?"

Jorunn giggled, a high girlish sound that surprised even her. "*Ja takk,*" she nodded, and turned to race up the broad staircase.

Egil rushed behind her in pursuit. In the bedroom he closed the door and watched as she playfully unbuttoned her bodice, revealing her breasts, round and swollen. "I don't believe you've missed me as much as I've missed you," she teased. "Convince me."

With a low sound deep in his throat he crossed the room and swept her into his arms, carrying her to their bed. He lay her gently there, then stood above her to remove his own jacket and shirt, tossing them carelessly on the carpet. She watched him, her breath quickening. She felt the rush of blood in her veins, spreading intoxicating desire. He lay beside her and kissed her nipples, taking each rosy peak into his mouth and teasing it gently.

She cried out in pain and he stopped abruptly. *"Min kjære,* have I hurt you?" Concern creased his face as he pulled away from her. Not for the first time she noticed that her breasts were sensitive. Another part of the changes her body was going through, she assumed. Pulling him back to her she said, "It's nothing. *Kom,* make love to me...."

Afterward they lay together in the growing twilight, him stroking her lightly, admiringly. "Love suits you," he said. "Your figure is fuller, you are even more beautiful."

"You won't be so pleased with my figure when I turn into a stout old lady," she admonished. "I try to eat less, but I grow fatter all the while. It annoys me," she replied.

"It does not annoy me," he assured her, his hand tracing the fullness of her hip, sliding over the soft mound of her belly and moving upward to cup her full breast. Sliding over her again he looked down to kiss her and she opened readily for him. Against her lips he murmured, "It excites me," and he pressed into her with ardor that abolished any doubt she might harbor.

❀ ❀ ❀

By midsummer, however, she was less willing to allow his reassurance to calm her. She had grown plump, and was miserable because of it. She was unable to control her appetite, and suffered often from indigestion due to the food she craved. In resignation she bid Egil hitch the wagon. "I'll call on Doc Tveter," she informed him. "I can't let this go on. I'll grow as fat as *Frue* Brun."

"Ah, is it that you fear?" he teased. "But *Herr* Brun is a baker, and likes his woman round and soft, so it does not signify that she is so plump she has given up a corset."

"Then you do notice such things, you wretched man!" she accused. "And you promised never to look at another woman," she cried in mock indignation. With a playful tweak of his ear she commanded, "Now go hitch the wagon and drive me to the village. And while I visit Doc Tveter you may confine yourself to the waiting room, keeping far away from the bakery, or you'll answer to me afterward."

✤ ✤ ✤

Jorunn opened the door from the physician's office to find Egil sitting in wait for her. The look on her face alerted him at once to the fact that something was wrong.

"What ails you? What is the matter?" he asked in alarm.

She shook her head, as yet unable to speak the news. "In the wagon, we'll talk there," she replied dazedly and let him help her out into the morning light and air.

She kept her own counsel on the road through the village, forming in her mind the words she would use to tell him. Her thoughts were jumbled, the sight of people and wagons congesting Main Street only adding to her confusion. It was when he stopped the wagon on the rise to Stridheim and turned to her that she finally blurted out: "I'm with child, Egil. The babe will be born around the time of the Yuletide feast, or maybe at the beginning of the new year."

Egil dropped the reins slack so suddenly that the team bolted. He spent precious seconds controlling them, before he could turn to Jorunn. The daze she had been in earlier seemed to have diminished. He read uncertainty in her face, fear in her eyes.

"*Men, kjære deg*, that is wonderful!" he cried. "Yet you are uneasy. Is there something more, some cause for concern?"

"Egil, I'm too old for this!" she wailed. "Valdis is married and will soon be bearing children herself. At forty-four years of age I'm beyond the time in life when I should expect a child. I assumed the changes I noticed meant that my time for childbearing had come to an end."

"Did Dr. Tveter voice concern with regard to your age?" he asked.

Jorunn shook her head. "*Nei*, but he won't have to care for this infant, to raise this child. I don't have the strength for this."

Egil took both her hands in his and looked her full in the face. "This time will be different. This time you shall not raise it alone, for this child will be ours together. I shall be by your side, and a burden shared is a lighter one."

"Don't refer to our child as a burden, Egil!" she cried defensively. He raised one eyebrow and looked at her, relief obvious in his expression. She laughed in spite of herself. "The only hope left is that this babe be born before Valdis sends glad tidings from Christiania. I don't relish the thought of having a grandchild older than my last child."

"Do you mean to say that you intend this child to be our last?" he teased. "In any case, we shall endure," he reassured her. "We shall endure."

⁊ ⁊ ⁊

On a crisp sunny morning one week later Jorunn turned her back to Egil and bid him help her. "The buttons in the middle, Egil. I can't reach."

He fumbled with the tiny fasteners, stretching the pale blue satin of her gown over her thickening waist. "I said we should hasten the ceremony. Another week and you would not have fit into this dress," he teased. He radiated satisfaction, an air of contentment.

"Gloating doesn't become you," she admonished, letting out her breath in attempt to make herself smaller. "Quickly, I want to be done with this," she retorted, yet the happy light in her eyes belied her words.

Turning her he placed one careful finger beneath her chin and lifted her face to his. With a gentle kiss he answered, "I want only to never be done with this."

She pulled away, slipping her arm through his. "Come, we'd best not keep the priest waiting. It's good of him to come to us.

Together they descended the wide staircase and crossed the hall, into the courtyard. The air was cool and clean, the song of birds in the forest their only music. They stood arm in arm to wait. The sound of the priest's approach preceded his arrival as they watched him top the rise and ride into the yard. Dismounting, he came to where they stood framed by red roses. Jorunn turned to Egil. "This doesn't signify. It won't change anything. I'm your wife in my heart; whether or not I'm your wife in the estimation of man means nothing to me."

Egil looked into her blue eyes, saw the determination in her face. "For the child, then, Jorunn."

She nodded, and they turned to face the priest together. United, as one already.

Thirty

PARDON

❧ Valdis lay beneath the smooth silk of the coverlet and waited patiently. She leaned against piles of pillows covered in finely woven damask, rich velvet, cool linen. The light above her cast gentle rays, illuminating her hair in a halo suitable to the rest of her person. Only her hands belied her calm. They clutched the shimmering cover convulsively in spasmodic fits of anxiety.

In her mind she framed yet again the words she would use to tell him. They would be her deliverance, these words. She must choose them carefully. The door to her bedroom opened and Guthard entered, a flush evident on his pale, sunken cheeks. The white lawn of his nightdress was ironed to crisp perfection; his slippers scuffed lightly on the gleaming wood floor until he reached the carpet beneath her bed. She sat up straighter and stretched out a hand unconsciously meant to ward her husband away. She saw the look of him and dropped it to the bed, clutching the covers to her breast tightly with the other.

"Forgive me, Guthard, I am so clumsy. There is something I must tell you, and suddenly I have no words to say it."

The old man stood beside the bed and looked down at his young wife. His eyes were not unkind, but his mouth was firm.

"If there is something you wish to discuss, dear wife, then I prefer you bring it up at breakfast in the morning, or perhaps save it until the dinner hour. This evening I am tired."

He moved to pull back the cover and she cried aloud, "Wait! Guthard, I meant to say there is no need for your visit this evening. Our purpose is accomplished, I am with child," she breathed, her face still anxious, yet hope apparent in her pale blue eyes. She suspected his nightly visits to her bed were as much an obligation to him as they were to her, yet some doubt remained. She feared that even though she was with child he would continue to exercise his marital rights. She prayed he would not. The sight of his gnarled hand clutching the linen of his nightdress brought to mind a mental image of his twisted fingers clutching her breast through the thin fabric of her nightgown and she fought to control the shudder that shook her. 'Please, God, let him be content now. Give me this brief reprieve, spare me these few months, and I will gladly submit to my conjugal duties after the birth of this child.'

God smiled upon her and her prayers were granted. Guthard dropped the hem of his nightdress and stepped quickly away from her bed. His mouth made a round "O" of surprise and for an instant Valdis looked straight into his toothless gums. She averted her gaze quickly, repulsed in spite of herself. She had not realized before they were wed that Guthard's teeth were not his own.

"Praise be to God!" he cried suddenly, and dropped to his knees beside her bed, bowing his head in fervent prayer. Valdis watched him, her glance softening. The light shone on his smooth, bald crown and made him look vulnerable. She released the coverlet she clutched and reached out to stroke his head, press the bones of his thin shoulder. He raised his face and she saw it shone with gratitude and love. She dropped her gaze from his and whispered a quick prayer. Of thanks, then for forgiveness. She was unworthy a man so good. She ended her prayer with a plea that God help her be a better wife.

Thirty-one

RENASCENCE

⁕ Egil, come quickly!" Jorunn called from the front porch.
She clutched a shawl about her shoulders to ward off the chill
of November. In her other hand she held a piece of creamy
parchment.

"What is the matter? Is it time? Shall I ride out to fetch
the physician?" Egil cried as he came running from the barn.

"Nothing so dire," she laughed. "Calm yourself. The babe
isn't due for weeks yet. It'll be a long wait if you don't."

He stood in the yard looking sheepish. She held out the
letter and said, "Glad tidings from Valdis. She's with child,
expecting in the spring."

Smiling, he gestured to her growing belly. "Then you must
hurry with that one or you will indeed have a grandchild older
than one of your own children," he teased.

Scowling at him she retorted, "Do you have to turn a happy
situation into something dreary? I won't speak with you if you
insist on tormenting me." She returned to the house, closing
the door behind her with unnecessary force. Egil's laughter
rang out, echoing in the yard.

Stifling her irritation, Jorunn returned to her preparations
for Yule. Halvor was arriving home for the holidays, and she
looked forward to his visit with great anticipation. More than
a year had passed since he had last been on Stridheim. She
was anxious that everything be perfect for this reunion.

He arrived one week before Christmas Eve, wearing an air
of resignation and looking far older than she remembered him.

At twelve the look of the little boy he had been was diminished; he was becoming a man. His resemblance to his father had faded. She was surprised to see the face of someone she hardly recognized. His fair hair had darkened; his face had grown thin, with a nose too long. His eyes were the same blue, but she had remembered them wider. His happy smile appeared to have become a thing of the past. He wore an air of studied insouciance.

"Copied from his friend, Pierre Beaumont," Egil had informed her when she complained. "It will doubtless fade when his fascination with Pierre ends," he soothed.

Yet after eight days his new expression was wearing her tolerance thin. The gifts she had chosen with such care had elicited scant response, a polite murmur of thanks was all she had for her trouble. Only a third of his visit had elapsed, and already she was using much of her precious energy to stifle the thought that she was looking forward to seeing her son off to school again.

Jorunn lay resting on the sofa, a pillow beneath her aching back, a blanket for which the room was too warm heavy on her lap. In her hands she held knitting long forgotten. She watched Halvor, distracted by his constant movement. He paced from the fire that burned brightly on the hearth, to the window, where he stood morose, watching the snow fall in a heavy curtain.

"Halvor, come and sit with me," she pleaded. "Your constant pacing is driving me to distraction."

"I will not," he replied, his tone short. "I cannot bear to sit. This room is too confining. Might I ski to the village? Perhaps there I would find Eirik, or Rune. Have you no news of them?" His speech was dramatic, each consonant clearly enunciated. Gone were the softly slurred vowels of the valley. Even the sound of his voice irritated Jorunn.

"You may not venture into the village," Egil said abruptly. He laid the paper he read open across his knees. "I have explained that it would be foolish for you to venture into this storm. The snow falls thick and fast; you might lose your way. It has been long since you were here; you are no longer familiar with the way to Dal. In any case, no one with good sense would be out on such a day. Now sit and read, or apply yourself to your lessons. You distress your mother and I will not have it," he commanded.

Jorunn pushed away the blanket to rise, intent on soothing the argument between them. She clambered to her feet, heavy and awkward. Her stomach was grown large and cumbersome. Crossing to the window she placed her arm about Halvor's shoulders, surprised to find he was almost equal to her height. Unconsciously she stroked the babe in her belly, comforted by the thought she would soon have another child to hold.

"Please, Halvor. I understand you miss your friends from school. But surely you can spare their company for a few weeks so we can have time together. I miss you when you're away from Stridheim. If you'd only try I'm sure you'd find peace here. This is your home...."

Pulling from her he said sharply, "This is not my home. My home is in Christiania, and I long to return." His voice rang clear, overtly theatrical in its emphasis.

Jorunn watched him, vaguely repulsed by his manner, wounded at his obvious contempt for this place.

Egil rose from his chair heedless of the paper that fell to the floor. "Apologize to your mother at once!" he ordered. "I will not have you speak to her such. You have been rude and insolent since your arrival. If it is this you learn at school then it is time to find a different place to educate you. Perhaps a tutor would instill in you manners as well as broaden your mind," he threatened.

The arrogance in Halvor's expression was replaced by uncertainty. "Forgive me, Mother," he apologized. "I am not myself today," he began in attempt to appease his uncle. It was a threat Egil had made before, and one he knew instilled fear in the boy. "My school is an excellent one, Uncle Egil. In fact, I have much work due at the end of the holidays. May I be excused to go to my room and work in solitude?"

"Of course," Jorunn said while patting his arm soothingly. "It's difficult to be so confined, I understand that well," she smiled to him, placing an arm across her stomach. "You're forgiven," she said, offering him her cheek. He kissed her dutifully and made a hasty retreat, closing the door behind him.

Egil looked at her in exasperation. "You spoil him, and make excuses for his conduct. The boy must be held accountable for his actions, or he will never make a man."

"I do understand him, Egil. I, too, hate the confinement of this place now. The weather makes it impossible to leave the house, and I'm sick of this room, this sofa in particular. The first thing I'll do after giving birth is have the thing chopped into firewood!"

Egil laughed softly at her fierce expression. "You do not suffer your condition gladly, I know. But your wait is soon over. Dr. Tveter said just after the new year, and that is only days away. Perhaps it would be best to send Halvor back to Christiania. You need rest, and his presence serves only to irritate you, makes you uneasy."

"That's not true," she lied. "But for his own sake maybe that would be best. He misses his friends, and he deserves a holiday. He works hard at his studies."

Egil cast a rueful glance in her direction, resisting the temptation to pursue that topic. They had shared several conversations with regard to Halvor's lack of diligence in pursuit of an education. He resolved not to further incite Jorunn in her condition.

"The house is closed, the servants have free. He will have to stay with Valdis," he replied instead. "Will you write to her?"

"At once," she said, crossing to the desk. "Then I'll share the news with Halvor. At least I'll have done something to give him pleasure this visit." With a sigh she picked up her pen and wrote, inquiring of Valdis' condition at the same time, thinking ahead to the spring when she would be grandmother to a child only months younger than her own. Weeks had passed, yet she was still unaccustomed to the idea. Valdis thought it a happy coincidence, and planned ahead to raising the children together.

"It is fortunate, since I shall never have another, and your child will be company for this one," she had written. Jorunn wondered at the idea that Valdis had no intention of bearing other children, yet refrained from questioning her. As a woman Valdis was as reticent in giving light to her thoughts as she had been as a child. Jorunn despaired of ever having more than a superficial relationship with her daughter. At times she wondered if Berit had shared a closeness with Valdis that eluded her, yet instinctively she knew she had not. Berit and Valdis had shared a bond in their religious fervor, and been united in their work for the church, but Jorunn felt sure no one would ever penetrate the shell of Valdis' reserve. Certainly not Guthard Myrbraaten. Time and acquaintance had proven Jorunn's first estimation of their match correct. She knew Berit had ostensibly chosen Guthard for Valdis based on his devotion to the church and his bearing similar attitudes to her own. She later surmised that Valdis was amenable to the relationship because Guthard was willing to accept her on her own terms. Valdis held herself aloof and unreachable to her husband, and he respected her distance. Jorunn concluded it was this which ensured her daughter's happiness, and accepted that her own relationship with Valdis must be modeled in the same fashion.

Two days later Jorunn awoke to a world bright with cold white snow and pale yellow sunshine. The sky glittered clear blue, unmarred by cloud. She could hear the sounds of Halvor's imminent departure as he instructed the maid in his packing. She grimaced at the tone he used and the words he chose. She reminded herself to instruct him in proper behavior toward the servants later.

'Not today,' she sighed. 'Today I'm too tired with the effort of carrying this child and lack of sleep. And I won't spoil our time together. I'll speak to him in the summer, when he comes home and will be here for a long while.'

She rolled clumsily to her side and pulled herself to her feet. Egil's sheets were cold. He would have been up since dawn, in the greenhouse with Abel Hansen. They were experimenting with a new wheat seed to be tried in spring. She would see little of them if she didn't often wander in the great glass house herself, tending begonias she brought inside to harbor safely through winter.

There was a rap at her door and it flew wide, framing Halvor, his face wreathed in smiles. He fairly glowed in happy anticipation, and she was glad. He vaguely resembled her own little boy again. She was relieved to have made him happy.

"I come to bid you farewell, Mother," he announced, his voice deepening already.

"Safe journey, *gutten min*," she replied, stretching her arms to him. He came to her, let her embrace him quickly, her huge belly between them. He pulled away, embarrassed. She resisted the urge to say, 'I'll miss you.'

"Come back in the summer, then," she said instead.

He turned to leave, replying breezily, "We shall see what the summer brings."

Then he was gone. She stroked her belly, feeling life inside her as the babe turned, taking comfort in its presence.

The next few days she spent in busy preparation for the child's arrival. She felt a surge of new energy, smothering shame at the thought that Halvor's departure had been a relief. She instructed Abel to rearrange the room beside her own, unwilling to have the babe in the nursery yet. All that morning she watched while Abel shifted the furniture to the guest room, a large airy room painted the color of a pale blue sky at twilight. The wide windows looked out over the wood in the direction of Glomma. Now, with the trees thinned, she could almost see it in the distance. Closing her eyes she could imagine it, the water frozen to a winding river of glass. She imagined its rush in the spring when the thaw came and its banks swelled. She would sit here, by this window, and nurse the child while listening to the Glomma's ceaseless, tuneless song, she daydreamed. Jorunn stroked her belly and wondered at the stillness there. For two days there had been little movement. She missed the jabs of elbows and feet to which she had grown accustomed.

As if on cue a jagged pain ripped through her lower back, signaling that the child was intent upon making its appearance. Catching her breath, she sank her teeth into her lower lip and waited for her discomfort to pass. "Egil!"

"What is it you will have this time?" he asked from the hallway where he grunted under the weight of a bureau he helped Abel to move. "Shall we move the piano upstairs in case the child enjoys music?" he complained.

"Egil, now's not the time to indulge your bad temper," she said sharply. Then she doubled over under the force of another pain. He rounded the corner to find her there. Dropping the bureau without ceremony he turned to run downstairs, calling over Abel's swears, "Cook! Send one of the stable boys for the physician; it is time!"

He returned to Jorunn, taking her arm and guiding her firmly toward the bed. "You must lie down," he instructed.

Seeing the determination in his face Jorunn let him lead her to the bed and held her tongue while he fussed over her. Another pain came, low and rumbling, but with a jagged edge. She gasped through it. She looked up at Egil where he leaned over her. Irritation overwhelmed her and she instructed, "It's too important an errand to entrust to a stable boy. Ride for Doc Tveter yourself."

"Of course, you are right. I shall leave at once!" he cried. "You are not to worry. Just lie quiet until our return."

He rushed from the room, calling instructions to the servants on his way down the stairs. She breathed a sigh of relief, then lay back to wait for the next pain, and the next, that would bring this child inexorably from her body.

Thirty-two

ABSOLUTION

ᴥ Jorunn sat quietly in her favorite chair with the babe at her breast. She studied the soft contours of his face. Plump cheeks, tiny nose, blue eyes half-hidden beneath heavy lids. Faint reddish gold brows to match the light dusting of hair on his silken head. She stroked his face gently, felt her heart swell with boundless love. This child was her miracle, the proof she had sought her entire life that there was indeed a God. Faith in Him had eluded her all her life, yet she accepted now this child was His gift, to make her complete. When she cradled him in her arms her love for him crowded out all other thought. No distraction could take her attention from him, nothing else would ever matter as much. She had spent these first months of his life in an aura of wonder, minding the inner voice she too often ignored. The voice of conscience, and wisdom accumulated throughout years, when she had been intent on finding her own way and refused to listen. When she held this child in her arms her world shifted, the broken fragments fell into place. She was whole.

The babe dozed, suckling only ineffectually and intermittently. She pressed his cheek gently to release her breast and stood to lay him from her reluctantly. Downstairs a letter waited for her, and she knew she must attend to it. Valdis had written she was safely delivered of her child. She wrote that all was well with them both, and Guthard was satisfied with the babe, though he had not been blessed with a son. It was a lukewarm

letter, typical of Valdis, and the tepid nature of it did not alarm
Jorunn. It was the news that Valdis had dismissed the nurse
Guthard had hired to care for the babe that alarmed Jorunn.
Valdis had no experience with infants, had to Jorunn's knowledge never been in the sustained presence of one save the afternoons she had spent caring for Halvor when he was a small
child. Jorunn remembered well how overwhelmed she had
been when Harald was born. Astrid had crossed the mountain
and given aid and instruction in the first weeks after his birth,
yet still Jorunn had felt inadequate and unsure. When the
child died she blamed herself, reasoning that with more experience she might have saved him. In twenty-three years the
pain of the loss of her firstborn had hardly diminished; it was
stored away in the dark recesses of her mind. Occasionally it
flared, searing her heart, scorching her soul. She would live
with it the rest of her life. She was afraid for her daughter,
would spare her the knowledge of grief so great and lasting.

Lifting the creamy parchment she scanned the content
yet again and decided to leave the safe haven of Stridheim and
travel to Christiania. She must reassure herself that Valdis was
equal this all-consuming task of motherhood. No matter how
remote the young woman, Jorunn felt keenly that she was her
daughter. She would not abdicate her responsibility as her
mother.

Jorunn traveled in late April, before the road thawed to
become a quagmire of mud. The journey was not usually difficult. The roads were wide and well-traveled; there were inns
and villages along the way at which to rest and take refreshment, yet Jorunn began her journey with a heavy heart,
weighted at the thought of leaving Egil. He was busy in preparation for the spring planting and could not be spared. Yet by
the time the carriage reached Eidsvoll her spirits had lifted
and she looked from the windows with eager curiosity. The
scent of spring wafted through the carriage, making her light
with anticipation. Her favorite time of year, this, and she was
suddenly anxious to see her new granddaughter. Her first
grandchild. She looked down at her son nestled in the crook
of her arm and said to him, "Your niece, *lille venn*, and sure to
be your playmate soon." She sighed, a sound of pure contentment, and settled back against the seat to wait impatiently.

Jorunn's first meeting with her granddaughter came
sooner than expected, for it was late when the carriage finally
stopped beneath the stone portico of Guthard Myrbraaten's

residence. Jorunn climbed wearily down, her legs stiff from sitting, her back aching from being jostled for miles of rutted road. She clutched the babe to her tightly in spite of spasms in her arms and shoulders. He slept soundly, blissfully unaware.

The door opened and Henning, Guthard's butler, stepped out. Behind him a young woman followed, reaching out to relieve Jorunn of the child. Jorunn eyed the slip of a girl, her uniform crisp in spite of the late hour; with some skepticism she delivered the babe to her. "You may hold him for now, but stay close. I'll care for him myself as soon as I have greeted my daughter," she instructed. No housemaid was going to be entrusted to care for her child, on that matter Jorunn was firm.

The great hall was ablaze with light. Valdis came to greet her mother, holding out both hands, accepting Jorunn's kiss on her cool cheek. With effort Jorunn covered her surprise at Valdis' appearance. She was pale, there were deep violet smudges beneath her daughter's blue eyes. Jorunn felt the bones of Valdis' hands when she squeezed them gently and was suddenly afraid for her. She had grown so thin. The soft roundness of her face had given way to hollows beneath her cheekbones, her dimpled chin was too prominent. Jorunn caught her breath. Never had the likeness to her own mother been more apparent.

"How nice to have you visit, Mother," Valdis greeted, and in her voice, too, Jorunn heard the ring of her mother's speech, clear and melodic.

Jorunn concentrated with difficulty on Valdis' words. Behind her another housemaid carried the child she knew to be her granddaughter. The infant wailed incessantly. Scrawny pink legs kicked furiously, freeing themselves from the confines of dress and blankets. Jorunn went to her, drawn to the tiny bundle of fury. She looked into the red, wrinkled face of the babe and was smitten. Her heart turned with love, pure and undiluted, for the little girl. Jorunn reached out to take her from the maid, nestling the infant into the crook of her arm. Almost at once the cries stopped. The babe's features rearranged themselves into soft composure, her lids uncreased and she lifted them to reveal irises of the palest blue. Jorunn stared into those eyes, drowning in a sudden wave of emotion. The child was exquisite. Jorunn turned to Valdis to tell her as much, but the expression on her daughter's face stopped her. Valdis' face was a mirror of incredulity.

"I cannot fathom it," Valdis blurted out. "The child has not stopped wailing since birth, and suddenly she is soothed."

Valdis stared at her mother, disbelief giving way to tears of relief that filled her eyes.

Jorunn went to her daughter and put a careful arm around her fragile shoulders. "*Kjære deg,* you're exhausted. I should've come at once. Go to sleep now, and don't even think of the babe again until you feel stronger. I'll care for her until you are up to it."

Valdis dashed at the tears that streaked her cheeks and opened her lips to protest, but the sight of her mother holding the now docile infant brought on a fresh rush of tears and she turned to stumble up the stairs without further conversation.

Jorunn watched her daughter go with a worried frown. Something in Valdis' expression warned Jorunn that her despair was something greater than mere fatigue. "But she's young,' Jorunn reassured herself. 'And with the resilience of youth she'll be fine in a day or so. Still, I should've come sooner....'

The thought was interrupted by ideas of a more practical nature. "Show me to the child's room," she bid the housemaid. "You come along as well," she instructed the girl who carried her own child. She trailed the housemaid up the stairs and down the long hallway to a room at the far end. Inside gas lamps blazed, turning night into day. "Bring candles," she instructed, "and place them there, on either side of the commode."

She lay Valdis' child on a soft padding of linen atop the commode and sorted through rows of ruffles and layers of blanket to find the tiny person beneath them. In a matter of moments she had the child changed to dry linen and dressed in a double layer of simple undershirts. The little girl was patient during her grandmother's ministrations. She studied Jorunn's face with round eyes as she was tucked into her cradle beneath layers of silk and down. The housemaid returned with the candles and Jorunn bid her light them, then extinguish the gas lamps. The room fell to soft darkness, the only relief the ▯▯n glow from two ornate candelabra Jorunn recognized ▯ to the dining room. With the advent of gas light ▯andoned candles as old-fashioned. Jorunn was ▯used at the idea of these two tiny people becom-med to light reflected from fine, old silver. She smiled at the little girl and watched as her lids drooped and she slept.

Turning to her own child she took him carefully from the maid and bid her go. "It's late, you'll be up again in a few hours. I'll sleep with the children tonight," Jorunn dismissed her.

With the ease of long practice Jorunn changed her babe to fresh linen, settling him into the ornate bed that stood in wait for the time when the young mistress of this room had outgrown her cradle. He never woke, her son. He was an easy babe, a good sleeper. At Stridheim the night maid had already moved from the nursery, for he slept through. Her grandchild, she knew, would not.

That night the little girl woke often, sleeping only fitfully. When she cried Jorunn left her cot and went to her, but would not lift the babe from her cradle. The child screamed furiously at first, then her cries gave way to whimpers. As the pale blush of dawn filtered through the heavy drapes of the room Jorunn took advantage of the dim light to change the babe's wet linen, then tucked her in to sleep again. When the little girl's uncle finally stirred long after daybreak, ready for his breakfast, she slept on. Jorunn settled her own child at her breast and glanced toward her granddaughter, studied her perfect face in utter fascination. A breath of love stirred her heart strings; a surging of emotion welled to close her throat and bring tears to her eyes.

"Silly fool," she murmured, softly mocking. Yet in truth Jorunn reveled in the spectrum of new emotions that colored her every day, made her life bright, knowing that in the birth of her last child she had discovered the meaning of life. The years before were desolate by comparison, wasted in futile attempt to possess the land. Yet she looked back on them without regret. She recognized that while the greater part of her life had been spent on an arduous journey of discovery, her reward was in final understanding. To give new life, foster hope for the future, was the reason for being, she realized at last.

With the birth of her last child Jorunn had come to the crossroads of life and her way had become clear. Never given to reflection, always forging ahead, yet now Jorunn understood that her past had determined her present course, and dared to look back. Her every thought had been for Stridheim. Her land: she had thought it would fulfill her, make her stron and keep her safe. But even the abundance Stridheim

duced could not fill the void inside her. Then God had given her the gift of this last child, and the wound of her emptiness was miraculously healed. The babe's presence in her life gave her new direction, and the still, small voice inside her whispered it was the right one.

She recognized the waste inherent to her earlier years; it was with great effort she stifled the remorse that plagued her when she thought of Valdis, and of Halvor. She had failed them. God's gift of understanding was a dual-edged sword, and razor sharp. She flinched at the prick of knowing she had wounded the flesh of her flesh. Neither of them whole, both casualties of her ambition and greed.

Yet God had granted her a precious new start.

For the next days the three of them lived together in the nursery, interrupted only by Valdis' visits to nurse her child, and the necessary errands of housemaids. On the fourth night they all three slept soundly throughout, waking only when the bright light of early morn shifted to fall across Jorunn's face. She awoke with a light heart and smiled. She had forged a bond with her new granddaughter that would last a lifetime. She set about changing the children enveloped in an aura of complete satisfaction.

Thirty-three

LEGACY

✤✍ Late in May, when the cherry trees blossomed, Jorunn traveled to Stridheim accompanied by Valdis and her newly baptized granddaughter, Christina Myrbraaten. Valdis and Guthard abandoned tradition and gave the child her father's last name. Jorunn was resigned to the fact that Valdis felt no tie to the old ways, had left those behind when she left Stridheim. The name Christina, too, was modern, and foreign in origin. Valdis preferred it to the old-fashioned 'Kristin,' yet insisted her child be called after her Lord and Savior. Jorunn bit her lip to cover her smile at the choice. A less Christian temperament than the one the child possessed would be difficult to imagine. Even as an infant of two months she was demanding and stubborn. Though she had at length accepted that night was for slumber and quit terrorizing the household with her wails of protest at being forced to bed each evening, she still refused to adjust to a schedule for nursing. Valdis spent each day at her daughter's beck and call. The little girl nursed fitfully and ineffectually, turning from her mother's breast to explore with pale blue eyes the world around her. A slight sound, even the whisper of a maid's rustling skirt, was enough to distract the child from the task at hand, yet Valdis refused Jorunn's advice to put the child from her still hungry and make her wait until the next mealtime. Valdis' adamance came as a surprise. Jorunn had thought her daughter would prove as remote in mothering as in every other relationship, expecting a wet nurse would soon be installed to relieve Valdis the necessarily intimate contact of feeding the infant. That her daughter proved to be a mother devoted to her child's every need filled Jorunn with wonder. She was left to contemplate yet again why the relationship to Valdis she hungered for eluded her. Even after so many years Jorunn secretly harbored hope that with Berit dead and no longer between them the shared experience of motherhood might bring her and Valdis closer, bridge the gap that yawned between them. She sensed Valdis' gratitude for the aid and advice she offered, yet she recognized it was tempered by something else. Reserve, perhaps, but more complex. Resentment, pale cold anger.

'What have I done to deserve that?' Jorunn wondered in silence. And her silence was returned. The chasm that separated mother and daughter was a hollow void in both their lives. Not even their shared love for the little girl could fill the years of emptiness.

With Christina sleeping at night Valdis was regaining her strength. The soft contours of her lovely face were restored, her beauty blossomed to breathtaking once again. She looked well, yet Jorunn insisted Valdis travel with her to Stridheim. Her duties as mistress called her back, but she would not abandon her gentle daughter to the little tyrant she had given birth just yet. And Guthard, too, was demanding. He sulked when Valdis turned to the babe and ignored him. It was unpleasant to see a man of his age indulging in such childish attempts at garnering attention for himself, and Jorunn longed to be free of his company. The idea her daughter must share his every day and night revolted her. She quite understood Valdis' conviction there would be no other children.

"I could never love another as I love Christina," Valdis declared, cradling the child to her breast.

Guthard turned with obvious distaste from the picture of his wife nursing their daughter, his expression petulant. "Certainly not, for there are only twenty-four hours in every day, and you spend all of them with her," he complained.

Guilt erased the contentment from Valdis' lovely face; the wound of her husband's words was quick, and deep. The role of perfect wife, perfect mother, eluded her; she was instantly filled with remorse. 'Not good enough, I must try harder," she thought in reflex.

"It's only natural that a woman spend the first months after birthing caring solely for her child, Guthard," Jorunn interceded quickly, exercising for her daughter's sake uncustomary patience. "Every infant demands that much attention, and their needs are impossible to ignore. But I fully understand how difficult the situation for a husband. His whole world is suddenly turned upside down, with mealtimes interrupted and his wife too busy and too tired to attend his needs. It's the chaos typical of every household when a babe is born. Still, it's difficult to bear. It would be more comfortable for you if I took Valdis and Christina with me to Stridheim until the babe has adjusted to a schedule. You'll be spared the interruption of your routine; the house will be calm again. And when your girls return to you they'll be equally well-behaved, I hope," Jorunn suggested with a strained smile.

Guthard hesitated only an instant before agreeing. "Perhaps that would be best," he admitted. "It has been difficult since the child arrived. I have worried for you, my dearest," he said to Valdis. "Though you are much improved, restored almost to your old self, a visit in the country would do you well. I am sure of it."

"We shall come for the summer, then," Valdis exclaimed, suddenly and inexplicably happy at the idea. "Stridheim is beautiful then, and we will escape the dust and heat of the city." Unbidden the thought occurred that on Stridheim she would not be quite so alone in caring for Christina, but she stifled it immediately. Yet it was impossible to quell the guilt she suffered at allowing the idea to surface at all.

The next days were spent in hurried preparation for the journey. The unease Valdis harbored at leaving Guthard alone was abolished by his obvious relief to see them off. They left him in the vast hall of the house clearly aware he would savor silence in their wake.

Life on Stridheim reverted at once to the perpetual rhythm nature dictated. Jorunn's mornings were occupied in giving instruction to the maids and cook, but she turned most of her chores over to young women hired for the summer so she might spend her time with the children. Keeping Christina to a routine was a constant battle, yet she was a precocious infant, and Jorunn was drawn to her irresistibly. While her son lay lost in intermittent slumber, or entertained himself with little pushups in preparation for crawling, Christina fretted, and fussed to be carried and played with. Undeniably demanding, yet her charm cast a spell over everyone who came near her. It was an easy thing to indulge such a beautiful babe, and Christina spent the summer passed from one pair of arms to another, in constant company. When coddled she was all smiles, her pale blue eyes sparkling with good humor, but the instant she was ignored the little girl wailed in protest until a willing pair of arms collected her and held her close. Only her grandmother was capable of putting the babe to bed and ensuring she slept the night through. Christina's will was strong, yet Jorunn's was stronger; at some level the infant understood and accepted this, and of all the adoring faces that were a part of her day she preferred her grandmother's. Even when in the warm haven of her mother's arms the little girl's quick eyes roamed constantly. When she spied her grandmother she squealed with delight, kicking her plump legs, stretching out her softly dimpled arms. Jorunn found her irresistible then, and would abandon necessary errand to come to the babe. While her more placid uncle whiled away afternoons in the nursery, Christina was strapped to her grandmother's chest and jostled to sleep as Jorunn walked the yard, inspecting fruit trees and berry bushes.

The scent of ripe wheat and new apples heralded the close of summer; the harvest drew near. Autumn's crisp chill marked the time when Valdis and Christina must return to Christiania. Valdis rested on a chaise before the open windows of her room, watching the play of light through lace, contemplating the journey. She looked forward to a reunion with Guthard with neither regret nor pleasure. She need no longer dread the responsibilities of marriage, for Guthard agreed that one child was more than sufficient, and she understood his nightly visits would cease. She enjoyed his company as much as any other, and thought it would be pleasant to return to their familiar routine of dinner and conversation each evening.

A gentle breeze lifted the gauzy veil of lace drape, parting it to reveal Jorunn and Christina crossing the cobbled yard. The little girl was strapped to her grandmother's back; from her high perch she peered over Jorunn's shoulder. Berry stains turned the child's lips dark; smears of crimson bled to full cheeks and dimpled chin. Christina's pale blue eyes danced with delight at the afternoon's adventures, her joy in her grandmother's company unadulterated. As Valdis watched them the bitter gall of resentment rose in her throat. She was choking, drowning in her own anger. In silent fury she railed at God, for His persistence in punishing her. To give her a daughter, tempt her with the idea of someone to love, wholly and unconditionally, then deprive her of the return of affection seemed a cruel punishment. Surely her sins against Him were not so great, Valdis reasoned. After so many years devotion she dared to think she might be worthy of some return. She was instantly remorseful. With these very thoughts she proved otherwise. Her character was flawed, her basic nature greedy. Years of prayer had not changed that. God had given her a beautiful child, and still she longed for more. No wonder He withheld the final reward, for it was priceless, and only those truly deserving were entitled. For love she would have to wait, Valdis realized, and resolved again to resign herself to this.

It was only that she had so much emotion pent up, her insides were ravaged with it. Without an outlet it consumed her. She longed for release, to open the guarded gates of her heart and let everything locked inside flow forward, wash over her daughter; yet she feared the flood of such emotion. With a mother's intuition Valdis knew Christina would drown in the tide of such love, for in her daughter Valdis recognized the reserve that separated her from her own mother. The wall of their reserve was a dam constructed to control the dangerous rush of the deep water of uninhibited emotion.

Yet it was more than that, Valdis understood, for she, too, had learned to stem the tide of emotion. But while she longed for someone to break through her own fragile reserve, both her mother and her daughter guarded their walls jealously. They were complete within themselves, the two of them utterly self-sufficient. She sensed neither of them would ever need anyone, and Valdis wanted desperately to be needed. She longed for it with burning intensity. She cloaked that, with the rest of desire, beneath a cool facade.

They must never know of her need, for it was weakness, and with canny instinct she understood both Jorunn and Christina would find such weakness despicable. Valdis had observed that the very strong often despise weakness. She recognized that a very few of the naturally strong nurture and protect the weak, but Valdis considered her mother's early rejection of her, in sending her away, proof she was not one of them. She knew her father had been one of those rare people who shared the inner strength God had granted him. It was her experience that such truly good people were granted a shorter stay on earth. As if God would have them back. Leave her with no one. Alone, always alone.

Nei, that was not true, her conscience reminded. In her father's stead God had given her Aunt Berit, who had shown her the way to Him. Her Aunt Berit had been strong. In sudden revelation Valdis realized the unscrupulous strong exploit the weak. Yet that had nothing to do with Aunt Berit strange it should occur to her now. Her treacherous heart was leading her weak mind down strange and frightening new avenues. She moved quickly from the chaise and settled on her knees to pray. For strength, and the grace to be better. Disheartened, with faint hope after all these years of His refusal.

❧ ❧ ❧

Valdis arrived home to find Guthard full of excitement over a surprise he planned. He had purchased land on the west side of Christiania, where there were still forests and streams, and nature was preserved. Construction had already begun on a new residence he had commissioned. It would be a magnificent place, built from great blocks of pure white limestone, the architecture ornate, in the gothic style, with countless spires jutting upward from a steeply pitched roof. Windows of heavy leaded glass, many of them stained with color, would depict Valdis' favorite scripture. The mansion would be crowned with a dome comprised of eight panels of colored glass, making it the most unusual building in all the city. By the time Valdis returned with Christina work had already begun, Guthard's preoccupation with its progress serving to mask the guilt he suffered for dreading the return of his daughter. He loved her, of course. He reasoned he must, for that was natural, and to be expected. Yet her strident nature churned the atmosphere around her, making chaos of his orderly existence. The shame he felt at knowing he did not enjoy his daughter's company was mitigated by the fact that he was, admittedly, an old man, and age must be granted concession. With that in mind he relegated Christina to the third floor nursery and asked Valdis to indulge him by confining child-rearing and its disorder to the area of the house reserved for it.

"Of course, Guthard, your request is not unreasonable. Easily accommodated, actually," Valdis replied. To her horror her voice broke; she said no more. She turned from him to hide tears that welled in her tired eyes. He wandered away, satisfied he had managed to reestablish order in his household.

The routine Jorunn had established for Christina disintegrated within weeks of their return to Christiania. Valdis' sleepless nights left her exhausted, and unable to cope with Christina's demands for constant attention during the day. After two months Guthard made yet another attempt to restore peace to his environment. He took the decision to hire a nanny upon himself, engaging an older woman with excellent references. English by birth, Mrs. Hartford had first come to Christiania as a scullery maid, but had quickly scaled the ranks of domesticity. She had been serving as nanny to wealthy families of the city for thirty-five years. Her methods were the tried and true ones of traditional child-rearing; she tolerated no interference from the hovering Valdis. During the first month of her employment she managed to undermine the little confidence Valdis had in her ability to care for her daughter. By the time they traveled to Stridheim for the feast at Yule, Valdis was withdrawn, her composure a brittle shell that scarcely cloaked her misery.

Jorunn stared at her daughter in dismay when she stepped from the carriage, biting her tongue to stop the flood of concerned inquiries. They were pointless, in any case. In only a matter of days Jorunn discerned the reason for her daughter's decline, and in the new year Mrs. Hartford enjoyed a new position.

At Jorunn's urging Valdis chose Christina's next nanny. She engaged a much younger woman, one more modern in her methods, more amenable to Valdis' presence in her child's life. Together the two women managed to cope with the little girl's infinite demands until the child's third year, when her will, always strong, took on a new dimension. A temper emerged, and the house quaked, day and night, with the tantrums of a small tyrant. Nanny Bodil left in April, reduced to a quivering shadow of her former self. Valdis traveled to Stridheim with Christina in May, without Guthard, who suffered from the constant turmoil of his house and declared himself unable to undertake a journey which necessitated being confined in a carriage with their daughter. Valdis stared at her husband. It was true; he was old. Her wide blue eyes filled with tears of exhaustion and creeping desperation. She felt woefully inadequate in dealing with Christina, and Guthard was beyond the time in life when he might have shared the burden of rearing their willful daughter. Valdis arrived at Stridheim pale and harassed, nerves already strained vibrating near the breaking point after hours of cajoling Christina to sit quietly and watch the sights through the window. The little girl was not the sort content to let life pass by without partaking of its pleasure. She insisted on riding with the driver, high above the world, looking down on everything in their way. It was unseemly, and dangerous, Valdis knew. In her mind she pictured the horses bolting or a wheel breaking and Christina being flung from her perch to the road. She shuddered at the thought, but remained where she was, slumped against the leather seat. Only four hours remained of what should have been an easy journey on a beautiful spring day. She closed her eyes and relaxed the jaw she was clenching, trying to ignore the throbbing in her temples. Soon she would be at Stridheim, and her mother would deal with Christina. Her mother, who tackled the impossible little girl effortlessly. When summer was over and it was time for harvest Valdis knew she would travel back to Christiania with a different child. Her mother would establish a routine for Christina; the little girl would accept the limits Jorunn defined. For Christina's will, they all understood, was second only to Jorunn's.

Empty of reserves depleted by the cold and darkness of winter, exhausted from coping with Christina, Valdis arrived at Stridheim and gratefully delivered her daughter to her mother's care. In it Christina settled. That summer set the pattern for the years to come. Jorunn kept the child close, fascinated in spite of herself at her granddaughter's antics. The little girl copied her every move, was her shadow every moment Jorunn permitted. Jorunn taught Christina to bake and knit and milk and spin.

"Far more useful than embroidery," she pointed out when Valdis protested.

"For a farm girl, perhaps, Mother, but Christina's life will be different. She should be raised to be a lady," Valdis insisted.

Jorunn look at her daughter with raised eyebrows and Valdis fell silent. "Then pray to God for a miracle, Valdis, because making a lady out of Christina is beyond even me."

Valdis bit her lip in frustration, admitting to herself the irrefutability of what her mother said. Christina was not the stuff of which dutiful young ladies were made. In her mind she heard her daughter's voice pipe, 'When I grow up I shall be just as you, Grandmother.' Valdis suspected that assertion to be prophesy. It was inevitable, she sensed, and while the prospect filled her with a hopelessness beyond despair, she was resigned to fate. Her mother was not. Always Jorunn's reply to the child was the same. "That can never be, *lille venn.* You were born to live another life; Stridheim isn't your lot. It will fall to your uncle; he'll be master here."

Christina accepted this in silence, her discontent evidenced only in the thrust of her still soft, baby-round jaw as she clenched her small teeth. Jorunn eyed the little girl warily, ever watchful for signs of the rebellion she sensed brewing. In the summer of Christina's fifth year the little girl answered, "Then my uncle shall be master, but I shall be mistress. In any case, it is the Mistress of Stridheim who runs the place."

Jorunn turned to her granddaughter, surprised though she knew she should not have been. The child had always been precocious. One look at Christina's determined expression convinced her that the child was serious, yet Jorunn could not contain the laugh that escaped her. Instantly Christina's face suffused with color; her blue eyes swam with tears, but her voice was firm with resolve when she stated baldly: "*Jeg skal.* I shall be Mistress of Stridheim, *Mormor,* and no one shall stop me."

Jorunn was instantly sober. Foreboding gripped her; fear clutched at the pit of her stomach. "That can never be, Christina," she said, her expression serious. "You weren't born to it. You have to follow the path in life meant for you."

Christina raised her chin and stared into her grandmother's face, her expression openly defiant. Jorunn saw clearly the beauty that would be the little girl's. Unspeakably delicate, ephemeral. Eerily like that of the woman in a sketch Astrid had kept to mark her place in the Holy Scripture. Jorunn's grandmother, Sylvie. Rumored to have been the daughter of a witch, her beauty had been unearthly, and she had not lingered long in this world. She died giving life to Astrid, her only legacy the little girl, and this incandescent beauty that was passed on to her great-great-granddaughter. Her mark, a dark smudge above her right breast, followed the line of women who came after her as well. It was on the swell of Jorunn's right breast, smaller and more clearly defined than the blemish her father had borne, and it was pressed in the flesh covering Christina's thin chest. "The mark of the devil," Astrid had insisted.

"Old fool," Jorunn said irritably. But her memories were interrupted by the little girl, who ignored her grandmother's muttering and announced: "I shall choose my own way in life."

Simple words, an echo through time. Jorunn made no reply, for there was none.

Thirty-four

RECKONING

≽ It was a good choice of name. He is like him," Valdis said.
Jorunn turned in surprise. "I think so, too. And Egil talks
of it often. It makes us very happy." She met Valdis' gaze,
enjoying the fragile bond between them. They sat in the warm
summer sun in Jorunn's garden, watching the children play
on the green expanse of lawn that stretched to the wood. A
wide border of red begonias, blue delphinium, yellow mari-
gold bloomed in riotous color, framing a fountain that crowned
the center of the garden. In the middle of this paradise two
children frolicked, until the little girl with hair that shimmered
like white gold suddenly pushed Erland to the ground and fell
on top of him. He lay still, not protesting the blows she rained
upon him.

Valdis sprang to his rescue, calling as she went, "I only
wish my daughter more resembled her namesake. She is not,
I'm afraid, very Christ-like." As she hurried to pull the child
off the little boy who lay passively beneath her Valdis instructed,
"Christina Myrbraaten, rise up at once and apologize to your
uncle. Your behavior is abominable, and will not be tolerated."

Christina lay still on top of Erland and stared into his blue
eyes with her own paler gaze, her expression triumphant. She
rolled slowly off him and stood to face her mother. She blinked
hard twice, squeezing the lids of her wide eyes hard together,
until two fat tears rolled down her cheeks. She caught her
breath in a sob, then let forth an ear-shattering wail.

Valdis scooped her child into her arms, stroking her feverishly. "Hush, darling. Do not distress yourself. Erland knows
how sorry you are, there is no call for tears," she comforted.
Christina's cries stopped and she buried her face against Valdis,
hiccuping softly. Valdis rose to lead Christina to the house.
Erland watched their retreating figures from where he lay in-
ert in the grass. It was with great effort Jorunn restrained her
urge to intercede in the exchange between mother and daughter. Valdis was no match for Christina; Jorunn had always known
as much. Yet she realized Valdis was possessed by a need as
great as life's force to be close to her child, central to the little
girl's existence. When Valdis watched Christina there was a
hunger in her blue gaze that caused Jorunn to shiver. Afraid
suddenly, for her own daughter. Valdis' need made her vulnerable to Christina, and Jorunn sensed danger in that.

'Ridiculous,' Jorunn mentally chided herself. 'Christina's
just a little girl, though a very clever one, and determined to
have her own way. Reared with a firm hand she'll turn out
fine." But her doubt in Valdis' ability to set and keep the limits Christina needed abolished any comfort the thought offered. With a sigh Jorunn went to her son and lifted him,
brushing grass from his clothing.

"It is perfectly acceptable for you to defend yourself against
Christina," she told him as she brushed at a stain on his knee.
"She takes advantage of your goodness, Erland."

She stared into his round face, seeing his wide brow over
bright blue eyes, his full mouth. She felt a tug at her heart at
his likeness to her own Erland.

"Doesn't matter," he assured her, his face unpeturbed.
"She can't hurt me," he reassured his mother, his voice full of
little boy bravado. Already there was a hint of the man he
would one day be in his calm assurance, and it brought back
bittersweet memories.

Jorunn struggled for something to say, some way to explain her unease over Christina's behavior. With a sigh she let
the matter drop. Perhaps Valdis was right and time would serve
to soften Christina, lend her a sense of fairness, and instill in
her goodness. Yet Jorunn felt no conviction at the thought.
She understood the child instinctively. Without a doubt she
loved her, yet there was something in Christina she found unnerving. The child was more than simply naughty. At seven
years of age she had a knowing air, bore in her countenance
the look of someone much older. When Jorunn stared into

Christina's pale blue eyes she felt her heart skip, something unpleasant curl in the pit of her stomach. Always she brushed such feelings aside, chiding herself for being fanciful. Christina was a beautiful little girl, fairer even than Valdis had been. A true copy of her great-great-grandmother, Sylvie. It was impossible for Jorunn not to admire her. She let her affection for the child well, let it drown her unease.

Offering her hand she felt Erland's soft, sturdy one grasp her fingers. They crossed the lawn together, listening to the sound of the river in the stillness of twilight. The smell of roasting lamb wafted toward them in the summer air, tantalizing the senses. As she neared the steps she heard voices in the hall and turned to Erland. "Run up the kitchen stairs and wash for dinner. Pappa arrives soon."

She continued through to the hall, where she found Halvor and Valdis.

"I am relieved he is better. I did not like to leave him, yet he insisted," Valdis said.

"There is no cause for concern, I am sure. He rests most of the day, going out only on errand to the cathedral. He sends instruction to you that you should enjoy your holiday, and bids me relate that he looks forward to seeing you in a fortnight." Halvor's words were drawled slowly and distinctly, his tone as usual insouciant, tinged with boredom. Halvor habitually wore the haughty expression he had copied long ago from his closest friend, Pierre Beaumont. It seemed to Jorunn that in these past years the two young men had in some strange way begun to resemble one another. As she approached she noted Halvor's perfectly groomed exterior, his dandified manner, and struggled to recall the little boy who had roamed the fields of Stridheim with her long ago. There was nothing about this foppish young man to remind her of him. She crossed the hall and called with false enthusiasm, "Halvor, *min sønn*, it's good to see you!"

Jorunn offered her cheek and Halvor kissed it dutifully. She detected the scent of spirits, and was annoyed in spite of herself. "I'm happy to hear Guthard is well. But where is Egil? Weren't you traveling together?"

"He is detained until tomorrow," Halvor drawled in bored preoccupation. "As we were to leave word was sent from the mercantile and Uncle Egil felt he must return to see to the matter. It is nothing that can't be dealt with quickly, I believe, for he assured me he will ride out in the early morning." As

Halvor spoke he lifted one hand to study his manicured nails, then adjusted an elaborate cufflink that glittered against the crisp, white linen of his shirt.

Jorunn stifled her disappointment at having to wait yet another night before she could be with Egil. Since the general elections in '82 political unrest had claimed far more of Egil's attention than she liked. When his interest in government had been to further the cause of farmers and protect their rights as landowners Jorunn had grudgingly accepted that the time Egil's political engagement took from Stridheim was in further service of the place. Yet increasingly Egil was involved in shaping Liberal Party policy, whose primary aim these past years had focused on restructuring the division of power in government. Party Leader Johan Sverdrup was determined Cabinet members should take a more active part in government, and insisted the king forfeit his right to veto legislation. Many within the party had thought such lofty ambition impossible, yet Sverdrup had garnered much respect and many powerful allies during his career in the Storting, and recently he had succeeded in his fight to have the cabinet dismissed. King Oscar requested him to form a Liberal cabinet, and Sverdrup had called on those he trusted most to aid him during this revolutionary time in governing Norway. Egil had, of late, spent a far greater share of his time in the capitol than he had on Stridheim, and Jorunn's patience with his political involvement was wearing thin.

"Johan Sverdrup has been a good friend to us, and to Stridheim," Egil defended against Jorunn's complaints. "Without his support our own causes would never have been so well represented."

"I understand your loyalty, Egil. I admire it even. But you promised that after the general elections you would withdraw and spend more time on Stridheim. Two years later I've hardly seen you."

"It is true, I have been in the city more than I would prefer. Yet none of us foresaw the success Johan has had in restructuring the government. King Oscar has bowed to public pressure; that is unprecedented. At long last we shall have a cabinet that represents the people. It is imperative we band together to further our cause. This is a lifetime of dreams come to fruition, Jorunn. Try to understand. Be patient, my darling," he cajoled. "As soon as the party is better organized I shall withdraw from politics completely. You know there is no place I would rather be than here, on Stridheim, with you and Erland."

Jorunn stifled doubt at his assertion. She knew he preferred their company to any other, yet the allure of politics was deeply rooted in Egil. She took consolation in that Egil had refused the position he was offered in the new Liberal cabinet, though after twenty years of watching the political machinations of those involved in governing Norway Jorunn had come to the opinion that the state of turmoil the government existed in was never-ending. She had begun to suspect there would always be a cause that demanded Egil's attention. That, combined with his work at the mercantile, required far more of his time than Jorunn deemed acceptable. It was his role as Master of Stridheim she considered ultimately most important; she resented anything that usurped his attention, took him from this place. Of late she had pressured Egil to insist Halvor take responsibility for running the mercantile in order that he might at least be relieved of his duties there. The thought occurred that Halvor might have stayed and seen to the matter that detained Egil now, and she quelled her irritation with difficulty.

"Never mind," she said, summoning conviction. "We'll have dinner and you can catch us up on news from the city."

"Uncle Halvor!" Christina's voice rang out from the top of the stairs. She descended, her pink dress floating around her. Her silvery hair was pulled back in shiny ringlets; her pale cheeks were flushed in excitement. She presented a lovely image. Watching her carefully, Jorunn knew she was well aware of it.

Several steps from the bottom the child paused and stretched her arms to Halvor, bidding him. He stepped forward quickly and she glided into his embrace, raising her face to his so he might kiss her pink mouth. There was something new in her way this summer, something seductive. Jorunn felt distaste rise like bile in her throat. She turned from the sight of them and looked to Valdis. This strange new attitude of Christina's was one Jorunn barely recognized, little understood. There was a new depth to the girl that made her oddly unfamiliar. Jorunn's love of the child was accompanied by an awakening sense of unease. Valdis stood watching, an indulgent smile tugging the corners of her mouth. "They are so close, Christina loves her uncle dearly," Valdis remarked. "He spoils her, I fear, yet it is difficult not to."

"Obviously," Jorunn answered dryly, averting her face as Valdis turned toward her questioningly. "Come, dinner should be served."

The conversation at the table revolved around life on Stridheim that summer. The children shared with Halvor their adventures in the barn, where a cat had delivered kittens, and at the river, where they spent their afternoons playing and bathing.

"I have learned to swim, Uncle Halvor," Christina related. "Tomorrow you must come and watch me."

"Of course I shall," Halvor replied, smiling indulgently.

Jorunn was reminded of the picture Christina presented, her pale naked body plunging into the cool blue water of Glomma, and felt uncomfortable. The girl was a child still, and she knew it unreasonable to be disturbed by her nudity. Yet all summer she had wrestled with the urge to send message to Egil at the mercantile and order a bathing costume for her. Watching Halvor now, his face flushed with red wine, his voice thick from too much of it already, she made up her mind to relay a message at once, when dinner was finished. She would bid Egil bring with him costumes for both the children.

"Are you settling into your position at the mercantile, Halvor?" Jorunn asked. "You've been there for some months. Does it meet your expectations."

"It does, unfortunately," Halvor drawled, his smile too wide. He noted her frown and defended himself saying, "It *is* a far cry from Paris and Rome. I *cannot* be blamed for preferring the company in those *fabulous* cities to that which is available in Christiania." He lifted his shoulders in a delicate shrug, twitched the corners of his mouth in a bland and insincere smile.

"You seemed to find Christiania amusing enough before your jaunt through Europe with Pierre Beaumont," Jorunn replied, unable to keep the edge from her voice.

"Yes, well, be it ever so humble, it *is* home," Halvor replied, chortling at his own wit.

Jorunn turned from him in agitation. He was drunk. Again. She stifled her irritation over his behavior with the thought of Erland. It was clear Halvor would never run Stridheim. She was surprised the contempt he had always displayed for the farm had now bled over onto Christiania. It was worrisome as well, since she was relying on Halvor to relieve Egil of his business responsibilities in the city. She watched as Halvor tipped his glass and drained it. Her son was weak. All his life she had made excuses for him, but of late she had faced the truth and accepted him as he was, sensual and self-indulgent. Occasionally the thought came to her unbidden that perhaps if she had coddled him less, resisted his charm, she might have changed his basic nature. Yet the years had passed so quickly, and her time had of necessity been divided between her land and her son. She took solace in the thought that though her son had proven a disappointment, Stridheim was flourishing.

Halvor gestured toward the girl to refill his glass and Jorunn rose quickly to indicate dinner was over. "We'll have coffee in the sitting room," she instructed the girl. "Erland, Christina, time for bed. It's late, and tomorrow's another busy day."

The children made dutiful rounds to kiss proffered cheeks before retiring. On the stairs Jorunn watched as Christina slipped her hand into Erland's. He held it for a moment, before pulling away. Christina reached out and gave him a push before rushing ahead of him, the pink flounces of her dress flying about her in her agitation. Jorunn bit her lip to cover her smile, avoiding Valdis' look as she led the way to the sitting room.

❧ ❧ ❧

"Grandfather, you must watch me! Look, Uncle Halvor! I have learned to swim," Christina called from where she stood in the shallows. The pale blue bathing costume Egil had brought with him framed her slim figure to perfection. She looked enchanting, her long pale hair lifting in glistening strands in the warm breeze, her eyes borrowing color from the deep blue river behind her. 'It would be impossible not to look at you, child,' Jorunn reflected silently.

They watched as she waded into the depths of the water, then bobbed under, resurfacing farther away, her blonde head as smooth as a seal. Erland followed, his little boy's body thin and wiry in the striped costume he wore. He dove into the water and swam with strong and sure strokes toward the bank on the opposite side.

"They are clever," Egil said, his face alight with pride.

"Abel Hansen has taken them under his wing this summer. He's determined to make country children of them," Jorunn laughed.

"He shall have no trouble with our son," Egil replied. "He was born to this land, and loves it. Like my brother before him," he said, his voice heavy with emotion. They spoke of it often, Erland's likeness to his namesake. He possessed the same depth of character that had characterized his uncle. His heart, too, seemed to beat in unison with Stridheim.

Erland met Christina in the middle of the river and passed her, stretching his thin arms in long strokes. Christina dove again, resurfacing not far behind, swimming after in pursuit. They reached the opposite bank and turned, Christina calling, "Race!" as they swam toward the group who stood watching.

"It was never my ambition for my daughter to be a country girl," Valdis said coolly. All winter Christina drove her mother to distraction with her constant yearning for Stridheim. It was the only place the child seemed content, and it annoyed Valdis that her daughter's preference was so obviously for this place. They watched as Erland pulled slightly ahead in the water. "I must be more attentive and restrict any influence Abel Hansen might exert," Valdis continued, to no one in particular.

Christina pulled alongside Erland, arms and legs thrashing, water churning as they swam. Suddenly she stopped still in the water and cried out in pain. Erland swam on unaware, until her screams penetrated the splashing and he turned back toward her. Before anyone on the bank could react he was there, reaching for her, pulling her up as she went under.

She surfaced, gasping. Her arms reached out greedily, grasping. With surprising strength she took hold of Erland and pushed him under, frantic in her own attempts to stay afloat.

Jorunn watched in horror as Erland disappeared beneath the water. His head resurfaced, and in an instant Christina clambered on top of him. Jorunn felt a scream build in her throat as she ran to the river, intent on rescuing her child.

Egil was there before her. She became aware of him only after she stood waist deep in Glomma, feeling the current swirl about her legs, the weight of her skirts dragging her with the stream. She stopped and watched as he gripped both children and pulled them under his arms. Christina flailed wildly; Erland hung limply, water streaming from his mouth. Egil dumped Christina unceremoniously into Jorunn's arms as he strode quickly to the bank carrying his son. Jorunn concentrated on holding the thrashing child, struggling to see what was taking place on land. Egil crouched over where Erland lay, his back to her. She could hear nothing over Christina's wails. She shook the child hard, commanding, "Be still now, or I'll slap you."

The girl's cries were silenced instantly. Jorunn's voice grated in the still air, and Valdis turned from where Erland lay to look in concern in the direction where Jorunn waded ashore with Christina. Valdis hurried to her child, her arms outstretched, murmuring words of comfort as the girl collapsed into her mother's arms, sobbing once again.

Jorunn neared where her son lay. Her heart pounded; the rush of her blood was loud in her ears. She heard Egil pray, "Please, God, don't take my son." His voice broke, and the raw pain in his cry served to remind her of the prayer she had whispered for Harald long ago, when God had turned a deaf ear to her plea. A breath of air fanned the flames of old anger and it began to burn. She looked up at the blue sky over her and felt Him close. In the forest, in the water swirling between the banks of Glomma she sensed His presence. It terrified her. He wielded the power of life and death. He chose to listen, or not, at will. In a flash of clarity she understood. He had surely heard her call, yet He had taken her son anyway. Lifting her face heavenward she cried, "Why? Why did You refuse my prayer?"

Her voice echoed in the wood, then was lost in the rush of river water. In its ceaseless flow she sensed His answer. She heard the whisper of that still, small voice. Like Glomma, life followed its own course, sometimes full, rushing high against the banks, sometimes slow and meandering. One will was powerless to alter its ebb and flow.

Erland choked and gasped where he lay, water pouring from his mouth and nose. She fell on her knees beside her child and bowed her head, giving silent voice to thankfulness that overwhelmed her.

*   *   *

"Merry Christmas! Come in out of the weather, do," Valdis beckoned them. She stood framed in the doorway of her home. It was grand, Jorunn conceded, looking up to the cupola framed in a white swirl of snow. Bearing more resemblance to a church than a residence, it suited Valdis and Guthard. Guthard had shown great foresight in building on the west side of Christiania in an area that was becoming more popular than the houses around the main square. The city was growing rapidly, and homes on Carl Johan were slowly giving way to businesses. Lately Egil had begun considering the offers he re eived for the house there. He spent as much of his time as possible on Stridheim, and Jorunn was seldom in town. Privately, she disliked the house, which she still considered Berit's, yet it was home to Halvor, and belonged to Egil. She would say nothing to influence his decision. She noticed him look about the area on Josefine's Street as they approached Valdis' home, however, and knew he did so with an eye to acquiring property nearby. The area had been developed by Jacob and Henrik Homan, friends of Egil's who had attempted to convince him in earlier years to settle there. It was now one of the finest developments in Northern Europe, used as a model for new areas in Stockholm and Copenhagen. Great villas, rich in architectural diversity and detail, were surrounded by lush gardens. These new residences offered a tranquil, elegant respite from the busy downtown area. As Egil advanced in years he yearned for a place outside the bustle of the main square to retire to in the evenings. He had postponed his decision in the hope that Halvor would rise to the responsibilities of running the mercantile and allow him to withdraw to Stridheim, but though he would soon celebrate his thirtieth birthday, Halvor had yet to settle. He was still more intent on enjoying the pleasures the city offered than in assuming his position in the business. In any case, political duties kept Egil in the capitol. The Storting of 1890 passed a resolution to encourage general arbitration in settling disputes among nations, with the aim of furthering world peace, and Egil had been chosen one of the delegates to the first Interparliamentary Conference. Such a cause justified even to Jorunn the time Egil was required to spend in the city, and in view of the importance of Norway's role in foreign affairs she had ceased to protest his absence on Stridheim. Reluctantly, Egil resigned himself to carrying on his affairs in Christiania and relinquishing Stridheim to Erland. Nineteen years old in only a few days, and already the boy had grown into a man. He was reliable, as solid as the mountains that surrounded his homestead. His love of the land served him well, leading him instinctively in the right direction with regard to caring for it. Egil approached old age knowing that in this one child his dreams would be fulfilled. It mitigated to some degree his disappointment in Halvor.

"I am so pleased you could come to us this year," Valdis said, watching solicitously as a girl took Jorunn's coat. "Guthard's health is much improved, yet I would not like to risk a relapse. The physician has just been, and has allowed him up for your arrival. He waits for you in his study."

Jorunn and Egil followed Valdis through the great hall, Jorunn lifting her eyes upward to the cupola soaring above them. Great arcs of stained glass lent color to the faint light filtering through, illuminating the white marble of the floor in rays of red, blue, green. She watched the play of light on the white velvet of Valdis' gown and her pale hair. Valdis' beauty, undimmed with age, never failed to impress Jorunn.

In the library a fire roared on the hearth. Guthard rested next to it looking diminished, frail, in the leather chair in which he sat. A blanket covered his lap though Jorunn found the room stiflingly warm.

She approached Guthard, leaned to kiss his shrunken cheek. At close hold he seemed even less substantial. The hand he stretched to her was withered, the skin blotched and veins clearly visible. Jorunn was shocked. Valdis' letters had explained that Guthard was ill and not up to travel, yet she was not prepared for such a diminished state. Turning to her daughter in her surprise, the contrast between Valdis' ageless beauty and the old man beside her struck Jorunn afresh.

Egil stepped forward and greeted Guthard, allowing Jorunn time to recover her composure. Valdis was distracted by Christina, who entered just behind them. Glad of the respite Jorunn watched her granddaughter as she approached. She wore a velvet gown the color of fine claret. It was cut low, the soft flesh of her bosom swelling from black lace trim. The dark mark above her right breast was clearly visible, drawing Jorunn's eyes against her will. Christina's platinum hair shimmered, her face glowed luminous, yet as she approached Jorunn noted her smile did not reach her pale blue eyes. They were cold. Jorunn shivered, suddenly glad of the heat of the room.

"*Mormor*, it has been too long. You are looking well," Christina said, her voice cool and smooth, like her mother's, the pitch only slightly higher. Like silvery bells. Jorunn was captivated in spite of herself.

"These past summers haven't been the same without you at Stridheim," Jorunn replied truthfully, careful to mask the relief her words hid. "But we understand you're busy now. You're growing up," she said smoothly, embracing the girl and then releasing her, holding her at arms length.

"I would judge her to be full grown," Egil corrected. He held out his arms and she allowed his embrace. Jorunn surmised from his expression that he, too, was charmed by her lovely granddaughter.

"Thank you for noticing, *Morfar*," Christina smiled. Where is Erland?" she asked, her pale brow suddenly furrowing. "You did not leave him behind?"

The clarity of her lovely, melodic voice was suddenly shadowed by concern, and Jorunn felt uneasy. She had hoped time, and the society of other young men, would dim the attraction Christina so obviously displayed for Erland. It was because of this Jorunn had been relieved these past two years when social obligations kept Valdis and Christina from their summer holiday on Stridheim. Christina would soon be nineteen, and Jorunn had long hoped to receive message of an engagement. Yet with each letter from Valdis she was disappointed. Christina had not yet given her promise to any of the young men who asked for her hand in marriage. She was proving alarmingly devoted in her attachment to Erland. The look on her face as he entered the room was not to be mistaken. The light that had been missing from her pale eyes flickered instantly and flamed as he crossed the room. She fairly glowed with it when he drew near. She watched him hungrily as he greeted Valdis and Guthard.

"Christina, you're even more beautiful," he said quietly when he turned to her. His deep, steady voice gave the words even greater impact. He leaned to kiss her cheek and she turned her head quickly, catching his lips against her own. Erland stepped back, his color high, a look of surprise on his face. Jorunn watched Christina, saw the look of triumph in her pale face. The sense of foreboding that had plagued her during Christina's last summers on Stridheim sank over her. Time, and Valdis' influence, had served to lend Christina a veneer of restraint that cloaked her temper and indomitable will, yet Jorunn recognized the girl was unchanged. She was determined. Jorunn sensed Christina had not given up her intention of one day taking her place as Mistress of Stridheim. Long ago Christina had decided the place would be hers, and while the girl might not realize it, Jorunn knew instinctively Erland was simply a means to her end.

The rest of the evening Jorunn spent trying not to stare at this mesmerizing woman who was her granddaughter, attempting to withhold judgment of her actions and character. Resolutely she reminded herself that as Erland's mother she would be prejudiced against any young woman who practiced her wiles

on him. At dinner Christina delicately rearranged her food
on the fine, white porcelain, scarcely eating, turning her fair
face to Erland and entertaining him with stories of social life
in Christiania.

Jorunn studied Christina's perfect profile, watched as some
of her animation lent itself to Erland's usually grave countenance. She tried to follow Egil's conversation with Guthard
regarding land available in the area, yet she could not tear her
eyes away from the two young people opposite her. Twice she
caught Valdis staring at her, a look of puzzlement obvious in
her expression. 'Doesn't she suspect? Is it possible she hasn't
noticed?' Jorunn wondered. 'Or is she as blind to this as she is
to all Christina's faults?'

'Surely she can't wish for this match. They're blood rela-
tives, it's wrong,' she reasoned in alarm. 'Even Valdis wouldn't
allow her daughter so much latitude in the choice of her mate.'

Yet there was no conviction in the thought, and Jorunn
dared not mention the matter to Valdis. Christina's upbring-
ing was a subject they in silent, mutual understanding never
discussed. While she could not fathom the reason for it, Jorunn
was aware of resentment that smoldered beneath Valdis' cool
exterior, and had long ago decided she would do nothing to
provoke its angry release. For years Jorunn had watched Christina manipulate with growing dexterity those around her and
managed to refrain from interfering in what Valdis should have
seen to, yet clearly did not.

That evening Jorunn undressed in front of the fire, numb
to its crackling warmth and beauty, weighted by worry. "I don't
like the look of Christina when she speaks with Erland," she
said to Egil. "It's not right."

"She is spirited to be sure, and very lovely." He was quiet
for a moment, lost in thought. "Never have we had any indica-
tion that Erland is the sort whose head is easily turned. They
are merely children, used to one another; Christina is polish-
ing her charms on Erland. You have nothing to fear on that
count, I believe. The man Erland will be would never hold the
interest of a woman like Christina for long," Egil reassured her.

Jorunn let herself be soothed, but as the days of their visit
passed and Christina and Erland spent each day in one
another's company, her unease grew. They disappeared to
Pipervika to skate one day, and went to a matinee at the new
moving picture theater another. In the beginning their out-
ings were in the company of other young people of Christina's

acquaintance, but as time passed the two of them disappeared alone for long walks in the park and along Carl Johans Street. On Christmas Eve Jorunn's unease turned to alarm.

An early dinner was served in deference to Guthard, who retired early. Halvor was in attendance, for once forsaking other pleasures for the company of family. He arrived with two bottles of French champagne, evidently having sampled another bottle himself before he came. The atmosphere at dinner was festive. Halvor at his most charming was a force to be reckoned with, Jorunn conceded, as she watched him lift his glass in toast to Christina.

"To my niece, the toast of all Christiania, and the loveliest girl the length and breadth of the city," he said, his voice slurring only slightly. Christina flushed, glowing with pleasure at the attention. Erland watched her, his face impassive. He lifted his glass and sipped, his expression calm. There had been no change in his attitude toward Christina since their arrival. Watching him, Jorunn sipped from her glass in toast to her granddaughter. Her voice joined in a unanimous murmur of "*Skaal*" that circled the table. She breathed a sigh of relief. The tension that had held her in its grip relaxed. The rest of the evening she enjoyed the company of her family, the gifts they shared.

Valdis excused herself early in order to help Guthard retire. Egil stood and stretched, stifling a yawn. "I, too, will have an early night," he announced. "Will you accompany me?" he asked of Jorunn.

"Soon," she promised. "I'll first see Halvor off," she explained, gesturing to where their son lolled in a chair, his head cushioned against the back of it, his mouth open wide in a snore. The champagne and countless glasses of wine at dinner had taken their toll. He clutched a snifter of brandy loosely. Jorunn went to him and removed the glass from his hand, shaking him awake.

"Send for the carriage," she directed Erland, then focused her attention on rousing Halvor from his stupor.

Christina stood watching her ministrations, her expression one of vague amusement. "Make yourself useful. Fetch coffee from the kitchen!" Jorunn snapped at her, irritated beyond control by Halvor's dissipation and Christina's obvious enjoyment of the situation. She watched an ugly flush stain the girl's cheeks, saw her pink mouth curl in insolence.

"We have servants for such errands," she announced as she swept by. "I shall ring for one of them."

Erland returned to coax the coffee into Halvor. Together they wrestled him to the carriage. "I'd best go with him," Erland said, his expression concerned.

"I expect his manservant is used to dealing with this," Jorunn confided in exasperation. "Still, it might be wise. If you would, Erland." She smiled for him a gentle smile, touched the sleeve of his jacket lovingly. "*Tusen takk.*"

He bent to brush her cheek quickly before he stepped into the carriage. She sighed, watching as they disappeared into sparse traffic. She retraced her steps and climbed the stairs to her room. The evening had taken its toll. She wanted nothing more than a hot bath and sleep.

Egil snored softly by the time she slipped between the sheets beside him. She blew out her candle and lay in the darkness, willing sleep to come, welcoming respite from worry that dogged her footsteps. She was reassured by Erland's attitude toward Christina this evening, yet she knew instinctively her granddaughter would not be deterred in her pursuit of Erland. She was merely biding her time, coaxing him relentlessly. Proximity would ensure Christina success, of that Jorunn felt certain. She resolved to travel to Stridheim with Erland as soon as possible. Egil was intent on staying on in the city in order to procure land for the house he planned. He had an appointment with an architect just after the new year. Yet there was no reason she must be in attendance. She resolved to leave him the responsibility of this new house and take her son back where he belonged, to Stridheim.

With the decision relief washed over her. She felt lighter than she had in days. Now that a way was clear to her she relaxed. She was no longer tired. Leaving the bed carefully she wrapped herself in a robe, stepped into slippers. She went quietly downstairs in search of a glass of wine and a book. Both of those, she knew, she would find in Guthard's study.

In the great hall she passed beneath the cupola, it's colors muted in the darkness. A fire blazed in the corner, and she paused to warm her hands. She heard voices, in the sitting room where Christina often entertained. Turning toward it she listened to the conversation.

"I long for Stridheim. It has been so long since I was last there. To me it will always be home," she heard Christina's voice, silvery and insinuating.

"You're always welcome," Erland replied. "It's your home as long as you care to call it that." The simple directness that was characteristic of Erland's speech weighted his words, seeming to give them greater impact.

"Oh Erland, you have no idea how much it means to me to hear you say that," Christina replied, her voice softer, the sound of it muted. Jorunn heard the rustle of silk and knew the woman approached Erland. Without further pause she stepped into the room, in time to see Christina position herself in front of Erland, leaning close, an air of expectancy clear in the profile exposed to Jorunn.

Erland spied her and stepped quickly away from Christina. "*Mor*, we thought you'd gone to bed," he said. "Come, keep company. Sit a while. We're talking about times together on Stridheim, summers past."

Jorunn noted his smile was genuine, his expression welcoming. With a sigh of relief she replied, "*Ja takk*, I believe I will. Fetch me a glass of port, Erland. It's cozy in here."

Christina looked at her, her pale eyes narrowed. Jorunn turned to her with a smile, determined to give away nothing. "This is your room, isn't it, Christina? Is this where you entertain the many beau your Uncle Halvor mentioned?" She smiled, luring the girl into conversation.

"I do not receive so many as Uncle Halvor implied," Christina retorted. "For a long while my interest has lain in one direction. I hold myself true to that."

"*Ja vel*, but then, you're still young. It's too soon for you to decide on one man," Jorunn replied smoothly. "And you're too pretty to bind yourself. Enjoy your youth, and your freedom. They're precious, and come only once in life."

Erland returned with the port. Raising one eyebrow in Christina's direction he asked, "Mother boring you with one of her lectures?" He smiled to take the sting from his words, and Jorunn returned his smile.

Christina looked at them together on the sofa and her face grew hard. "Grandmother is many things, but never, in my experience, boring," she said in her cool voice. "Yet I confess I am tired. Until the morning, then." She swept from the room, icy in a swath of midnight blue silk.

ᛉᚢ ᛉᚢ ᛉᚢ

The next morning Jorunn shared with Egil her intention of returning to Stridheim as soon as possible.

"You must wait until the new year," he cajoled. "I am meeting with the architect then, and have a surprise for you."

"I'll wait for my surprise at Stridheim," she demurred. "I'm homesick."

Egil stared at her. "You are not homesick, you are suspicious. I have seen you watching Christina and Erland."

She lifted her chin, her mouth thin. "Do you deny I've cause for concern?'

"I admit your suspicions regarding Christina's intentions are not unfounded. She does seem to have set her sights on Erland. Yet surely you notice, and must confess, that Erland behaves without reproach toward his niece? He is not attracted to her beyond what is proper; he merely enjoys the company of a young person his own age. Let him enjoy his time in the city. He feels nothing inappropriate, and it is an insult to him to whisk him from harm's way. He is a steady young man. You should trust him to find his own way in life."

She stared at him stonily, resentment clear in her expression.

"And you, my wife," he continued, "would do well to relax and let life take its course. You must accept that there are things you cannot control. What will be, will be."

She remained silent, resolving to keep her own counsel. Yet the thought came to her unbidden. "Not if I can help it."

Thirty-five

SPHERE

❧ Do we have to have this man to dinner?" Jorunn complained. "It's extra work for Valdis, and she suffers already under the strain of caring for Guthard. Surely you could have planned the residence in the architect's office."

"As I have said, there are architectural aspects of this house I would like to copy. It is simpler for him to see them than for me to explain," Egil replied, his tone patient.

"I hope you don't intend to build a replica of this mausoleum," Jorunn snapped. "It's overdone, far too ornate, and not to my liking. It looks more like a cathedral than a home!"

Egil smiled. "You are merely ill-tempered. This is a beautiful house, impossible not to admire." He glanced around at the bedroom they shared. Ornate plaster molding framed the ceiling, from a crown medallion in the center a crystal chandelier was held aloft. "I plan to have gas lighting, and water closets, certainly," he added. "Every modern convenience."

"You brook no argument on that score. I won't argue with you at all if you'll let me return to Stridheim. You can do whatever you like with this house and I'll consider the whole thing one happy surprise."

"You are a stubborn woman. It is too late for you to balk. He should have arrived by now. Make haste, or we shall be late to receive him."

One hand placed firmly in the center of her back, Egil guided Jorunn from the room. They descended the stairs together, Jorunn's face a mirror of resignation, Egil's eyes alight with anticipation. As they reached the hall there was a rap, and Egil hurried to open before Henning could make his slow and stately way from where he hovered near Guthard's study.

The man who stepped inside was immediately recognizable. Time had not dimmed the light in his dark blue eyes, merely gilded his black hair silvery gray. Hans Christian Krogh stood before her, looking almost exactly as she remembered.

"Egil, how could you? You never let on my surprise was to be Hans Christian!" she gasped, walking toward him with both hands outstretched. He took them in his own, and she blushed as she remembered the touch of him. His eyes were candid. In them she saw affection for an old acquaintance, nothing more. She smiled, her face alight with pure delight, and offered her cheek. He brushed it with warm lips.

"There is someone you should meet," he said, releasing her hands and turning to the girl behind him. "This is my daughter, Benedikte."

Jorunn studied the girl, so like her father. Masses of black curls fell down her back; her blue eyes were dark like Hans Christian's; her forehead was smooth and pale over straight black brows. A generous smile framed perfect white teeth. She was captivating.

"I had no idea you had a daughter, and such a pretty one, too," she said softly to Hans Christian. Her unspoken question was clear only to him.

"My wife died shortly after Benedikte was born," he answered, his voice ragged with remembered pain. "But she gave me Benedikte." Looking at his daughter his eyes lit up with the old fire she remembered. "As her name implies, she is my greatest gift," he said, pulling her forward.

Jorunn watched the girl's cheeks turn apple red, thinking, 'Pretty does not do her justice, she is really quite beautiful.' Aloud she said, "I have another son, Erland. You'll meet him this evening."

"Speaking of me, *Mor*? My ears fairly burn," Erland teased as he entered the hall from the sitting room, closely followed by Christina. He approached to greet their guests, extending one hand to Hans Christian. "Honored to meet you, sir," he said in his spare and steady way. "I understand the yard at Stridheim is product of your genius. You must be a far-thinking man. Twenty years after you built the place it's still modern by any standard."

"Your father tells me you are the young man who will run the farm one day," Hans Christian replied. "I am pleased to have been of service."

Erland opened his mouth in reply, but it was lost as he suddenly caught sight of Benedikte. He mumbled something appropriate, the deep bass of his voice unaccountably gruff. His gaze was riveted to the girl, a vision of clear and pure white skin, flashing blue eyes, shining black curls. She flushed under his stare, and dropped her eyes to the floor.

Jorunn watched with amazement as a stain of red rose from the collar of Erland's shirt to suffuse his face. She looked up at Hans Christian and shared a secret smile, covering with effort her amusement at the reaction of their children. Jorunn shepherded them into the drawing room in a flurry of activity in order to cover their confusion and save them embarrassment. On the way she saw Christina fix her pale, cold stare on Benedikte. The look she intercepted was one of pure hatred. With a glare Jorunn interrupted Christina's attention, her face wearing silent admonishment. Christina raised her chin and sailed past, completely unabashed.

During dinner there reigned an air of festivity. Even Valdis seemed more animated than usual. The talk was of times past, of Stridheim, and how the years had proven their plan. Then of the future, of the house Hans Christian would design for them. Hans Christian lifted his glass in a toast, saying, "To health and prosperity in this new year of 1892. May it be a year filled with gladness, and hope for the century that approaches. And to this year's endeavor; we shall plan this new residence that it should stand the test of time and give shelter to future generations."

Egil raised his glass to the toast, echoes of "*Skaal*," went round the table. Jorunn's gaze circled the gathering, resting on each face in turn. Her past and her present were contained in this room. She had a sudden presentiment they would merge in a happy alliance and take her into the future. She lifted her glass in silent toast, and drank deeply.

☙ ☙ ☙

Jorunn traveled to Stridheim alone in mid-January. She was sick with longing for the place, and could persuade neither Egil nor Erland to abandon their pursuits and escort her.

"There is much to be done if the construction is to be underway at the first sign of thaw," Egil insisted. "Not only must I be on hand to finalize the drawings, but I must oversee the conversion of the house on Carl Johan."

Egil had resolved to keep Berit's house, but renovate it with the intention of letting out the ground level and fashioning an apartment for Halvor from the upper floors. Halvor was agreeable. He had no aim to marry, no use for the entire house. Space on Carl Johans Street was in great demand, and it was becoming a common solution to transform first floor accommodations into shops while the upper floors were maintained as living quarters. Many families who owned houses near the Main Square were seeking refuge from the constant commotion of trade and commerce downtown, withdrawing to a more secluded section of town behind and to the west of the Royal Palace. Egil's old neighbors would, in fact, be his new.

The house Hans Christian designed was according to Egil's specifications. It was reminiscent of a French villa that had made an impression on him years earlier while journeying through Normandy. Carved from white limestone, it's grandeur was in the symmetry and scope of the building rather than in the ornate architecture typical of some of the houses being erected in the area. The entryway was framed by a pillared portico, a circular driveway let carriages enter from Gabels Street and return again without inconvenience. The interior would combine the graciousness of the past with the practicality of modern times. Hans Christian and Egil worked tirelessly on their project, leaving Benedikte and Erland to entertain themselves.

When spring came and thaw neared Erland felt the call to return to Stridheim for the planting. For the first time in his life he was torn. He was loathe to leave Christiania and the proximity it afforded him to Benedikte, yet he felt the pull of the land stronger, even, than his feeling for her. He took his leave one afternoon in Eger Square. They walked hand in hand, keenly aware of the green brush of spring on the trees and shrubs surrounding them.

"I have to go, but I'll come back after the harvest. You'll wait for me?" Erland asked, looking for the promise in her dark blue eyes. The wind blew chill, lifting Benedikte's black curls, tossing them against her pale face, turning her cheeks scarlet.

She nodded. "You know I will. Go now, and return to me quickly. I understand this call you feel. It is like the one that binds my heart to yours."

He lifted one hand to smooth her hair from her soft cheek, in that touch feeling her attraction even stronger. He pressed her gloved hand to his lips; then, hungry for the feel of her skin against his he turned her palm upward and with one thumb pressed back the silk of her sleeve to expose her wrist. He pressed it to his lips, feeling her pulse, the throbbing of it echoing the beat of his own heart. For a moment he imagined himself incapable of ever relinquishing her hand or withdrawing from her presence. But the heartbeat of his land was an echo of his own as well, too familiar and insistent to be denied.

❦ ❦ ❦

At Stridheim Erland expected the feeling he had for Benedikte to fade, perhaps drown in the rush he knew would overwhelm him upon his return. To his surprise it grew stronger. The two merged, his love for Benedikte and his love for the land. In late fall, standing in the light of a full harvest moon, he resolved to bid Benedikte come with him, to share life on Stridheim. She was right for this place, he sensed. She belonged here.

In Christiania, bathed in the silver rays of the same moon, Christina stood wrestling with her longing for Erland, for Stridheim. The two had become indistinguishable over the years. In her memory there was no beginning, no end; she only knew she must have both. Yet her longing for Erland had grown stronger this long summer. During the hot month of July she had dallied with Marius Lovenskiold, letting him first whet her appetite, then attempt to satisfy it with the poor substitute his passion was for Erland's. He was handsome, and witty, and he offered the added allure of being sought after. Yet he was a disappointment to her. Her affair with him had done nothing to quench the fire that burned in her for Erland, it had merely fanned the flames. The night of the harvest moon she spent on the balcony of her room seeking inspiration for how to have Erland for her own.

She knew she must make her move before he returned to Christiania, to Benedikte.

❦ ❦ ❦

"I have a great longing for the place, Mother," Christina fabricated at breakfast the next morning. Valdis sat in the direct light of the morning sun, its rays revealing lines of worry that creased her face. Christina noted her paleness, the air of weariness her mother wore habitually since her father had started his steady decline. Old age, infirmity, death. Christina shivered in disgust, her resolve to get away from this place strengthening. Sensing weakness she pressed on.

"You are so busy caring for Father I scarcely see you. The city bores me," she complained. "I long to be at Stridheim, to visit Grandmother and Grandfather."

Valdis sighed wearily. It was a plaintive wail often voiced through the years. In the city Christina was like a caged animal. Pacing, restless. Her poorly contained agitation kept the household in a state of unrelieved tension. Only on Stridheim did Christina seem content. These past two summers Valdis had guarded her daughter carefully. Her jealousy of Christina's preference for Stridheim was an issue she had explored in the deepest recesses of her conscience. Valdis prayed in earnest repentance for God to endow her with the humility to accept that her daughter's regard for her, though second to her passion for Stridheim, was enough. Yet always she wanted more. Emptiness gnawed at her insides, devouring the heart full of goodness and mercy she worked to maintain. She had prayed for this acceptance for many years, yet God refused her prayers, and she was forced to add a growing faithlessness to the never-ending circle of sin that swirled about her. Never good enough. And she wanted so desperately to be good. Faithful daughter, loving mother, devoted wife, she was none of these things. She was so weary. She tended Guthard in his decline wishing she might simply lie down by his side and die with him. 'Though I walk through the valley of the shadow of death, I shall fear no evil.' It was true, God's promise to Christ's followers. This promise he kept.

'God grant me the strength...' she prayed by rote, of long habit, and wearily returned her focus to Christina. Though tainted by other emotion, instinct warned her it was best to keep her daughter in Christiania. In daily prayer she begged God make her daughter accept that her life was here. Yet it seemed He would not hear her prayers, for Christina continued unabated in her longing for Stridheim.

"Your grandmother and grandfather will scarcely have more time for you than I have these days. The harvest is upon them. It is a hectic time of year on the farm," Valdis asserted with as much strength as she could muster.

"Then I shall be on hand to help," Christina insisted, her face set.

Valdis felt the lack of sleep and the weight of the constant care Guthard required heavy upon her. She was too worn to resist any longer. "Very well, then. I shall write to your grandmother advising her of your visit."

"No!" Christina cried. Her mother looked at her in puzzlement, but she covered her lapse and continued smoothly. "I merely meant there is no time. I plan to travel today. I have already bid Hannah pack my things, and alerted Johan that he is to drive me."

She felt the intensity of her mother's stare and concentrated on smoothing the lines of her face into blandness. "I had hoped to save you the extra care of arranging the details of my travel," she continued. "I am aware how sorely pressed you are these days. Please, give this visit of mine no thought. I am grown now, *Mamma*, and capable of managing very well for myself." Christina fixed on her face her sweetest smile and watched for the desired effect.

"How considerate you are, my dear!" Valdis exclaimed, touched by any display of concern for her own well-being. "It is true, I have much on my mind these days," she sighed. "Your father's condition deteriorates daily. I worry so...."

Christina interrupted impatiently, "*Ja vel*, I am certain in your care he will soon improve." She rose hastily, eager now her end was accomplished to embark upon her journey. She kissed her mother, her lips cool against Valdis' cheek.

"I bid you farewell, *Mor*. Give my regards to Father."

She turned to leave, halted at the door by Valdis' voice. "When can we expect your return, Christina? I wonder at the duration of your visit."

Christina smiled, an image of herself as Erland's wife, the new Mistress of Stridheim, springing suddenly to mind. "I shall send word," she replied, and disappeared through the doorway, leaving Valdis to wonder at the suddenly luminous expression on her daughter's face. She listened as Christina retreated, imagining she sensed a new purpose in her daughter. An inexplicable feeling of unease gnawed at her, plaguing her in the weeks to come.

Thirty-six

REALM OF SIN

❧ Christina rode in the carriage, the windows open to the light and air. Greedily she drew in the scent of freshly cut hay and apples hanging ripe on the tree. As she neared Stridheim the sense of expectancy she had borne with her increased almost beyond her bearing. She felt giddy with the excitement of it. Her blood rushed in her veins, making her tingle. She pressed her knees together and felt a hot current of warmth between her thighs. Her longing for Erland would not be contained much longer, she sensed. She laughed aloud in sheer pleasure at the anticipation she felt for him.

In the courtyard the carriage stopped and Jorunn came to greet her.

"Christina, what brings you? Is all well at home?" she asked, concern creasing her brow.

"Well enough, *Mormor*. Mother sends her regards, and bids me tell you Father is much the same. Not improved, yet not very much worse. She cares for him herself, and is worn with the effort, yet she will not have help," Christina confided. "It is why I come to you now. I am intent on removing myself from home so that Mother might concentrate fully on nursing Father. I worry that she exhausts herself trying to care for me, as well. I hope that in my absence she may find some time each day to tend her own needs," she finished, summoning a look of concern.

Her grandmother's blue gaze was sharp, threatening for a moment to pierce the illusion she strove to create. Then

Jorunn's face relaxed. "You're always welcome, of course. Come, you may have your usual room." Christina followed Jorunn, biting the inside of her cheek to stop the smile of triumph that threatened.

All afternoon she waited. When twilight's murky light sank over her room she felt her restlessness grow beyond restraint and left the house to wander in the direction of the fields. She passed the men who worked there, hardly registering them, ignoring their nods of respect in her direction. She looked ahead in the dim light, straining to find Erland. At last she could contain her curiosity no longer. She turned to one of the men who walked by, taking his arm and demanding, "Egilsson, is he here?"

"*Nei, Frøken.* He left for home at sunset," the man replied.

Without acknowledging his answer she turned and retraced her steps, her agitation evident in her brisk strides. She tried to think how she might have missed him. As she neared the yard she stood for a moment battling irritation. In the distance she heard the rush of the waters of Glomma. She thought of it, cool and deep, heard its voice beckon her. She turned to heed its call, thinking of the calm she would find there.

The wood was dark already. She let her feet take her down a path committed to memory long ago. As she entered the forest her agitation evaporated. The night sounds soothed her. An owl called, another answered. She heard brush break and the sounds of an animal startled, racing away. She came to the clearing and in the gray light she looked toward Glomma, finding there what she had been seeking. Erland stood in the shallows, his back to her. She studied the muscles clearly defined across his shoulders and back, let her gaze fall to his buttocks, smooth and hard. Her eyes traced a line down his long legs and she was suddenly breathless, her knees weak. Instinctively she stepped behind the trunk of a massive pine and watched from her hidden position. He raised both arms and dove into the water, letting the river swallow him.

He swam with long, smooth strokes toward the bank on the other side. When he reached it he dove and resurfaced facing her. She cowered there, her breath coming in gasps. Her heart beat hard beneath her breast. He reached the shallows and stood, the water streaming down his lean frame. She caught her breath and squeezed her eyes closed for an instant, savoring the warm, liquid desire that rushed through her. She watched while he dressed, fearful he might hear the sound of her breathing, the drum of her heart, in the stillness of the night. When he turned to disappear into the wood she exhaled and sank to the ground in relief. It was a long while later she retraced her steps to the yard and joined her grandparents and Erland in the sitting room where they waited for her.

✤ ✤ ✤

The days of the harvest passed slowly for Christina, while around her activity reached a feverish pace. The smell of ripe wheat wafted through her open window as she lay in bed in the early morn, filling her with a heavy feeling of expectancy. She rose each day and wandered the fields and forest of Stridheim, occasionally rewarded with a glimpse of Erland as he rode from one errand to the next. She watched him covertly, her lids heavy, her body aching with desire. Each evening she sat across from him at dinner and tried to eat, aware of her grandmother's sharp eyes following her movements. She carried the conversation halfheartedly, her mind working feverishly to find a way to have Erland. He was unaware of her, it seemed. Each day he returned from the fields glistening with the sweat of a day's labor, his muscles rippling beneath the thin linen of his shirt. She waited in the yard to greet him, walked with him to the river, savoring the smell of him that carried in the evening air when they entered the dark wood. She chattered on, about what she could barely remember, searching for some sign he sensed her in the way she was aware of him. Yet when they reached Glomma he waited patiently for her to leave before he bathed. Each evening she retreated into the wood, just far enough to ensure herself hidden, and watched while he undressed and dove into the cool blue depths. The naked images of him burned in her memory; she took them out in the darkness of night when she lay alone in her bed. She must have him. It was the only thing in her existence of which she was certain.

Often she felt her grandmother watching her, her expression curiously knowing. In the days she had been at Stridheim she had scarcely entered into conversation with the woman, yet Christina sensed her grandmother was as clear regarding Christina's intentions as she was herself. It made her nervous at first, then desire drowned every other consideration. She ceased to notice or care what anyone might think. She let her purpose propel her, knew that the time was close, that opportunity would arise and she would recognize it.

It was at the feast to celebrate the harvest that a way became clear. Erland sat with the men he worked with, side by side. Her grandfather presided over the table; her grandmother reigned at the other end. The length of the table there were great bowls of boiled new potatoes, platters of sliced meat, stacks of flat bread. Egil rose and raised his stein in salute. "In the words of the Preacher, 'There is nothing better for a man than that he should eat and drink, and that he should make his soul enjoy good in his labour.' *Skaal!*"

Foaming steins of beer were lifted in toast after toast to celebrate the richness of the harvest. Christina sat beside her grandfather, directly across from Erland, and watched as he relaxed. The air of determination and purpose he had worn since her arrival dissolved as he emptied his glass of beer, then drank again after the girl refilled it. She watched in fascination as the hard angles of his face softened when he laughed at the stories the men told. She sensed with utter clarity that the time was right. She waited for the end of the evening with barely contained anticipation.

A sliver of silver moon was the only light in her room that night. She undressed slowly, watching the glow in the yard dim as one by one the lights were extinguished in the rooms of the house, leaving it in darkness. When the only sound she heard was the call of night animals she crossed stealthily to the door, opening it carefully, tracing her way down the hall to Erland's room.

Holding her breath she turned the handle, feeling its coolness against her hot palm. She entered the room soundlessly and leaned against the door to press it closed. Pausing in the darkness she listened to the steady sound of his breathing. She crossed to his bed on light feet and looked down at his face, relaxed in sleep. She lifted her nightgown over her head and let it drop, a white pool in the darkness. Then she slipped between the cool linen and lay beside him, savoring the warmth she sensed only inches away.

Shifting to her side, her head propped on one hand, she let the other hand slowly traverse his body. Her fingers slid through the tangle of hair on his chest, down to the flat hardness of his belly. She let them slide lower and cupped him in her hand. He sprang to hardness instantly and she moaned softly at the feel of him. He stirred and turned his face toward her, eyes still closed. She leaned to kiss him, covering his firm mouth with her soft lips, letting her tongue trace the warmth inside him. She heard his groan and felt a ripple of desire pulse in her groin, felt warm wetness coat the inside of her thighs. She moved her body to cover his, letting her legs open, resting her knees on either side of his slim hips. He slipped into her effortlessly and she exhaled in a long hiss of pleasure. She rode him slowly at first, until his eyes opened and he stared into her face. She saw his look of uncertainty drown in excitement as he pushed into her, moving with her. He lifted both hands to touch her full breasts, shimmering white in the silver light of the moon. The calluses on his palms were rough against her nipples. A shiver raced through her and she cried out in pleasure, feeling him push against her, meeting her in a tide of desire that carried them away.

❧ ❧ ❧

Christina awoke the next morning and reached instinctively to find him. Her fingers traced the cold sheet and she sat up to find herself returned to her own room, alone in her bed. Sometime after she had slept he must have carried her here. She lay back against the pillows and pressed the linen to her mouth to stifle her giggle of pleasure at the memory of last night. Erland was hers. His surrender was complete. She savored the thought of night after night in his embrace.

Rising, she crossed the room on light feet and stood in front of the dressing table mirror. She studied her reflection, wondering that it was not altered. She had thought such ecstasy would leave a lasting impression. With a sigh she returned to bed and pulled the bell, waiting for the girl to bring hot water.

The breakfast hour was long past when she came to the dining room. There was no sign of her grandparents, or of Erland. She abandoned the idea of food, feeling no hunger, and went in search of someone who might direct her to Erland. In the courtyard, just outside the barn, she found her grandmother.

"*God morgen*," the older woman called, lifting a hand to shield her eyes from the bright sun. "You've slept long. I wondered at your absence at breakfast."

Christina felt sharp blue eyes rake her face, probing her eyes for some clue. She lifted her face toward her grandmother, daring her to guess her secret. It would soon be clear in any case. "The evening was long," Christina replied, her voice silky, her expression smug. She watched closely as her grandmother's face shifted. Wariness was replaced by grim determination.

"It's a pity, you've missed bidding your uncle farewell."

To Christina's ears the words rang out in defiance. Her own assurance faded as she searched her grandmother's countenance for some hint of weakness. Blue eyes battled paler blue, until Christina looked toward the road.

"Erland has ridden out on errand?" she ventured, hearing uncertainty in her own voice and despising the weakness.

"He rode out this early morn, before breakfast," Jorunn replied. "To Christiania, where he keeps his promise to return as soon as the harvest was over. He wasted no time, wouldn't keep Benedikte waiting," she finished, a smile playing over her lips.

Christina shook her head in mute denial. Finding her voice at last she said, "You are mistaken. It cannot be that errand which takes him away." Her voice faded. Doubt assailed her and she rushed past Jorunn into the barn.

"Jens! Saddle a horse for me, and be quick about it," she demanded, her voice rising in her excitement.

Behind her she sensed Jorunn follow, heard her voice clear and low in the dim interior of the barn. "You're too late. He'll never be yours."

"He is mine! He is mine already!" Christina cried, her voice breaking in hysteria.

The stable boy came forward with a dark mare, full of spirit, the horse Christina favored. Grabbing the reins from the him Christina mounted and leaned close over the neck of the horse, spurring the animal into action.

"Christina, stop!" Jorunn cried out, her voice brittle with sudden fear. She watched as the girl and horse merged in sinewy movement, racing through the gate to the road from Stridheim. One hand lifted to her throat to stifle the scream she felt welling there. She was suddenly dizzy, the world around her shifting and distorted, madly out of her control. She opened her mouth to call out again, but words eluded her, her lips unable to frame the cry. A tingling began in her arm, coursing through her upper body. A jagged pain tore through her torso in its wake. She doubled over under the pressure of it, saw the ground rise up to meet her. Then she was delivered from the agony as consciousness slipped from her grasp.

&ờ &ờ &ờ

Christina sat rigid on the back of the exhausted animal as they entered the stable behind the house on Carl Johan. She

would find him there, she calculated. The new house was not
yet complete, and Erland would not go to her mother's house
this time. She slipped from the animal and walked on stiff
legs toward the back courtyard, leaving the horse carelessly
behind, ignoring the shouts of the stable boy.

The back door opened to her touch and she climbed the
stairs to the second floor, entering through Halvor's kitchen.
A girl stood paring apples, dropping the knife in alarm as
Christina appeared suddenly behind her. Christina strode past
her without comment, crossed through the empty dining room
and turned in the direction of the study. Halvor rested in a
deep chair, a glass of wine beside him, his eyes closed as he
leaned his head against the leather.

"Where is he?" she rasped, her voice gritty in her dry throat.

Halvor opened his eyes and struggled to focus. Upon seeing her there, her gown bedraggled, her hair flying wildly about
her, all haziness was erased from his countenance. He lifted
his head and smiled brightly. "Ah, my niece comes calling. A
nice surprise, if not exactly unexpected," he smirked. "You
must be tired, my dear. You look all done in. Sit down, share
a glass of wine," he drawled in mock graciousness.

He proffered his half-full glass, his face twisting into a
smile. She took it, pressing the rim to her lips and draining it
in one gulp. A slow flush stained her cheeks, relieving her
deathly pallor. She held the empty glass loosely in one fist and
ground out, "Don't play games with me, Halvor. Tell me where
he is, or you'll regret it."

Her fingers clutched the stem of the glass and he sat up
straighter. His smile faded and he replied, "If I tell you where
he is, you'll regret it." The smirk was back, his leer broader
this time.

Swinging around Christina threw the glass with all her
might into the hearth behind her. The crystal exploded into
fragments, spraying the carpet with tiny slivers that sparkled
in the firelight. She dropped her head to her hands and felt
bitter tears sting her eyes.

Behind her Halvor approached, resting his hands carefully on her shoulders. His voice was absent of malice, tinged
with regret as he said, "Do not cry for him, *min lille Christina.*
He is not worthy of you." He stroked the back of her neck
where it was revealed through loose strands of silver hair and
continued softly. "He was never right for you. You made up
your mind to have him when you were just a child, unable to

see him clearly. He is a farmer, Christina, nothing more. A simple man with simple tastes. A woman of your caliber would be wasted on him. All the subtle nuances of your character would be forever lost on my brother, my darling niece. For so long now I have waited for you to recognize that. I have bidden my time. I knew that one day you would see him for what he is. Do not cry for Erland, *min kjære*; you will soon see that he has only gotten exactly what he deserves. She is like water, Christina, while you are as rich and full-bodied as the finest claret." His voice was smooth, as rich and sensuous as silk.

She felt his breath, hot on her neck, his lips moist on her skin. His words soothed her. A tingle began at the base of her spine and worked its way upward to where his lips pressed her flesh. Sighing, she let him stroke her, the warmth of his hands releasing the tension in her shoulders.

"Come, you must rest," he said, turning her carefully toward him. He pressed a kiss on her forehead and took her hand gently to lead her toward the stairs.

"I shall draw you a hot bath myself, tend to you with my own hands. I shall take care of you, *kjære Christina*," he murmured softly as they climbed the stairs together.

She followed without protest, standing meekly while he turned the water nozzles to fill the great tub in the far corner of his vast room. She stood mesmerized, watching the steam rise while he slowly undressed her, as he would a child. When she stood naked before him he took her hand and helped her into the tub, watching as she lay down and let the warm water embrace her.

She closed her eyes and let her mind go blank, focusing on the darkness behind her lids. His hands were smooth on her skin as he washed her, the perfume of the soap hanging heavy in the air between them. Exotic, sultry. She opened her eyes and watched the gas light flicker low in the lamp on the wall. When he held a sheet of linen for her she stepped from the tub and let him wrap her in it, following him willingly as he led her to his bed.

He lay her carefully on the silk cover, smoothing silver strands of hair away from her damp face. He opened the linen and patted her softly dry, murmuring, "So beautiful. You are the treasure I have waited for."

She felt laughter well up inside her, hysteria threatening, and stifled it. It escaped her throat as a strangled sob. His lips were warm against her cheek as he leaned to kiss the tears that coursed from the tilted edges of her pale eyes.

"Hold me," she sobbed, stretching her arms to him. Without hesitation he lay beside her. She felt the bed give under the weight of him, let him turn her gently to cover her with the silk. She fell asleep with her head pressed to his chest, listening to the strange, arrhythmic beating of his heart beneath his velvet jacket.

In her dreams she felt soft hands stroking her. Softly, up and down the length of her body. An undemanding touch, gently soothing, slowly exciting. She lay in half-slumber, unwilling to leave this sweet dream. She drifted, gradually feeling her need rise. She moaned softly, spreading her legs in invitation. Gentle fingers touched her, probing questioningly. She raised her hips insistently and pulled him to her, demanding in her desire. She felt his body cover hers, soft and warm, gratifying. Then he filled her, satisfying a need that burned deep inside, at her very core. She lay passive and let him lead her toward the point of no return. When she neared the edge she cried out, opening herself fully to him, and felt him pour into her. Warm liquid, melting the cold ache inside her. He held her to him until she dozed, unaware when he moved away, feeling only the silk cover caress her as she slipped into a deeper dream.

ॐ ॐ ॐ

Christina opened her eyes and focused on the rich red walls that wrapped around her. Confused, she struggled to remember where she was. Her fingers clutched the silk cover convulsively as memory flooded in return. She sat up straight, pulling the sheet to her, looking in panic at Halvor, who lay beside her snoring softly.

She bolted from the bed, taking the sheet with her, exposing his naked white body to the cold morning air. Her only thought was to escape this room and the memory of what had taken place last night. She sensed him watching while she struggled into her clothing that still lay in a crumpled heap in the floor beside the tub. She fumbled with the buttons, her fingers trembling. She watched as a lazy smile spread over his face and she turned from him, staring in disgust at the tub of cold gray water beside her.

"Why rush away, my darling?" he asked, his voice a seductive drawl. "Come back to me, warm me, for I am cold."

"Stay away from me," she snapped, glancing at him with angry eyes as she struggled with her boots. "Don't you ever come near me again!" she cried, her voice rising on a note of hysteria.

He chuckled, his laughter low and threatening. "Or what? What will you do, my little Christina? Will you tell on me? And what will you tell? You were willing, my darling niece, and far from innocent. Will you tell what a pleasurable experience it was for both of us?" he taunted, his eyes glinting with dark humor at her distress.

"Shut up! she screamed, abandoning her laces, unable to control her trembling fingers. "Just hold your tongue and say nothing," she instructed, her eyes wild. "If you tell anyone what we have done I shall kill you, I swear it!" She looked straight into his eyes as she threatened and had the satisfaction of seeing the light in his eyes die. He reached out and pulled the cover over his nakedness in unconscious defense. With a last look of unbridled hatred she left him, fleeing the house. She walked the distance home, mindless of the horse she left behind, drawing in the cold morning air, welcoming its numbing effect on her mind and body.

❧ ❧ ❧

From the window of her room Christina saw the messenger enter the drive. She clutched her robe tighter around her and shivered at what news he might bring. All day she had cowered behind her locked door, praying no word of the events of these past two days would be whispered in daylight. She burned with humiliation and anger. Halvor, Benedikte, even Erland shared an equal portion of the fury that scorched her soul. She longed to punish them, spent all that day planning her retribution. Her hatred of them buoyed her, kept the sickness rooted in the pit of her stomach at bay. When she heard her mother's voice call her she started, felt the sickness rise and mingle with her fear. Her heart hammered beneath her ribs as the door flew open and she confronted Valdis.

"There is news from Stridheim," Valdis said, her lovely voice stretched thin and high with anxiety, her usually calm exterior shattered. "You grandmother is ill." Her voice shook and she stopped, swallowing hard.

Hope dawned in Christina. "What exactly does the note say? Give it to me," she demanded. She snatched the parchment Valdis clutched, read its brief message in a second. A hiss of relief escaped her. There was no mention of her affair with Erland. She was positive her grandmother knew what had taken place, and the idea that she might speak of it terrified her. No one must know of her humiliation. It was all she could think of now.

"Grandfather says she is ill, but not dying," Christina remarked aloud, thinking privately that it would have been better news if she had been. Dying, taking to her grave the secret Christina would not have shared.

"Yes, the news is not all bad, but I must go to her. She asks for me... there is so much between us," Valdis began, her voice breaking. Christina watched as her mother bowed her head and pressed her handkerchief to her eyes. Suddenly she saw opportunity as cold and clear as the light of early morn.

"Yet your place is here, at Father's side," she said, approaching Valdis and linking an arm comfortingly around her. Her voice was gentle, soothing in its soft, melodic rise and fall. "Grandmother understands he needs you. Let me go to Stridheim, tend to Grandmother in your stead." Christina coaxed.

Her mind rushed feverishly ahead. Her grandmother's illness might ensure her silence for some time. If luck was on her side the old woman would die. If not, she would use this time to find out what her grandmother knew of her affair with Erland. Halvor she would deal with later. His reaction as she left assured her he would hold his tongue for a while. She had seen his fear of her, watched as he wilted under the power of it.

Erland would take their secret to his grave, that was her only absolute certainty. Only Jorunn posed a threat to Christina's secrets.

"I shall ride to her at once," Christina reassured Valdis. "Remain here, I shall send word of Grandmother's condition as soon as I arrive."

"Yet she asked for me," Valdis wavered. She thought of Guthard upstairs, alone. In his illness he would have no other person tend to him. He insisted it was only right and proper that family attend one another in their last time on earth, and he was convinced his time grew near. For months he had sensed the Holy Spirit hovering, been certain he was poised on the very threshold of the gates to heaven. Valdis stayed near him night and day, promising he would not leave this world unattended. She was worn near death herself from the strain of constant care, yet there was no one to relieve her. Valdis felt keenly it was her duty to care for her husband; now she was torn by her loyalty to her mother. Surely it was a daughter's place to care

for her mother. The enormity of the responsibility she bore
weighed heavily. Alone. No one to share the burden of living.
"She is ill, not thinking clearly," Christina's silvery voice
insinuated itself into Valdis' muddled thoughts. "When she is
better she will understand you could not come. Let me do
this for you, for Grandmother," Christina wheedled.

The idea Christina might help, might share the responsibilities that overwhelmed her, sent a surge of hope through
Valdis, mitigating her loneliness, diminishing her sense of in-
adequacy.

"She might even prefer me. I believe we have a better
understanding of each other," Christina said, careful to keep
her voice glossy.

Valdis turned to her daughter, smoothed the silvery hair
from her face. At the suggestion her mother might prefer
another old jealousy flared, but the flame was quenched by
fatigue and worry. "I am glad the two of you are close," she
replied, her voice strained. She hesitated only a moment before she continued, her voice flat with defeat. "I have always
sensed a likeness between you. Go to her then. Send word as
soon as you arrive to let me know of the situation."

Christina nodded, letting her mother kiss her forehead,
cool lips against her hot brow. "There is no cause for concern," she said calmly. "I shall see to everything."

❧ ❧ ❧

"*Mormor*, I have come," Christina whispered softly, bending near Jorunn's pillow, letting her hot breath brush Jorunn's
wrinkled cheek.

Jorunn opened her eyes, focusing on Christina's pale blue
irises. "Valdis," she mouthed, her voice barely a croak in her
parched throat.

"You are thirsty, *Mormor*," Christina said smoothly. "You
shall have something to drink. In a while. And Mother shall
come to you, in a while. When I send for her, then she shall
come. First we must come to an understanding. Only when
we understand one another completely will I allow anyone else
to come to you, to care for you, to nurse you back to health."

Jorunn lay watching Christina's face. As cool and smooth
as alabaster, and as hard. She swallowed with difficulty. Christina picked up the glass from the table beside her and lifted
Jorunn with one arm, letting her sip. Cold water trickle down
the side of her mouth, wetting her gown.

"*Mormor*, you have spilled," Christina murmured. We must change your gown. You must not become chilled. In your weakened condition a chill would be the death of you," she said, her voice silky. She turned and crossed to the bureau, opening several drawers before she located the proper one. Choosing a carefully pressed white gown she returned to where Jorunn lay and drew back the covers, revealing her body, half of it lying limp, appearing shriveled already after only a few days.

"First we must talk, reach an understanding," Christina continued, her lovely voice silvery and insinuating. "I fear you might have been left with the wrong impression when I rode from Stridheim. I voiced my concern for my uncle only because I sensed he was on the verge of making a grave mistake. In the week of my visit he confided to me he intended marrying Benedikte Krogh. I was concerned as soon as he said so, knowing my uncle as well as I do," she smiled, her face a mirror of concern. She watched as Jorunn's exposed flesh rippled with chill bumps, pausing a moment in her story to note the shiver that shook half Jorunn's body.

"No one knows Erland as I do, *vet du*. Since we were children we have been of one mind. It is because of this closeness I felt obliged to warn him Benedikte was not right for him. As soon as you related his errand I rode out at once to save him. But I was too late," she sighed. "Erland had given his word already, and knowing Erland as I do I realized he would never rescind it. I fear we shall have to abandon him for the time being. Had he not been so stubborn...," she mused. "Still, there is nothing to be done about that now. Time will serve our purpose, and when his mistake is clear to him I shall be there. For now I must concentrate on making you well, and leave others to their own fate. It is the only course open to us, *Mormor*," she said.

She leaned over and raised the gown covering Jorunn's body, lifting her easily, stripping her of the last of her covering. As she threaded the new gown over Jorunn she spoke to her, murmuring comfortingly, "You must rest now, and leave everything to me. I serve gladly as Stridheim's mistress in your stead. There is nothing you can do now."

❧ ❧ ❧

Egil entered the dining room to find Christina seated at the foot of the long table. He raised one eyebrow in question.

"Grandmother will not be joining us for some time, I fear," she announced, her melodic voice ringing clear. "She is not regaining her strength as quickly as I would like," she sighed, "yet there is nothing to be done for her that time and patience will not accomplish. Meanwhile, I shall see to everything here at Stridheim."

Egil studied her impassive face in the candlelight. In the depths of her cold eyes he saw something flicker and was uneasy. "You may sit in your grandmother's place in her stead for now, but you shall never take her place, Christina," he said gruffly. "Stridheim shall soon have a new mistress. I have word from Erland this very day he is to wed Benedikte Krogh in the new year. After their honeymoon they shall return here, in time for the planting, and Benedikte will assume the duties your grandmother chooses to relinquish to her."

The light he saw flicker in Christina's eyes blazed, her face flushing hot. "The girl is young, and will need guidance. With Grandmother so reduced it is left to me to provide whatever instruction she might need in carving a place for herself here at Stridheim. She was not born to it, as I was. She has no intuitive understanding of this land, as I have," she bit out, her voice crackling with barely suppressed anger.

Egil sat silent at the head of the table, noting the uncanny resemblance of this girl to the one he had first met on Stridheim over thirty years ago. The same fire in her blue eyes, the same determination in her broad face, the same set to her chin. For a moment he savored the sight of her. Then she smiled and he felt the difference. Something emanated from Christina, something Jorunn had never possessed. His unease returned and he said shortly: "With Erland by her side Benedikte shall manage. He knows this place like no one else. In spite of her youth I sense Benedikte is a young woman capable of addressing any challenge. While no one could ever replace your grandmother, with Erland's guidance I have no doubt Benedikte will prove an apt Mistress of Stridheim. She is a clever young woman, her demeanor bears testimony to constancy. And she clearly loves Erland. These things make her eminently suited to succeeding your grandmother as Stridheim's mistress. Together they shall keep Stridheim strong."

Christina's gaze was riveted to her plate as she held tenaciously to her composure.

"You say they are to be wed in the new year. That is too soon," she protested. "Grandmother would be unable to attend their wedding. She is not yet resigned to her chair, and has come no further in her attempts to walk. She has regained the use of her arm, yet her leg is stubborn and will not heed her instruction."

"Your grandmother has made up her mind to attend, and she will. You have much to learn from your grandmother, Christina. It surprises me, your tendency to underestimate her," Egil said, staring down at her. "I would have thought you, of all people, would have understood instinctively the peril in that."

Christina lifted her chin, returning his gaze evenly. "Perhaps you are right. It is a mistake I shall not make again."

"You would be wise not to. It is a mistake she never makes in regard to you."

Christina smiled, her eyes blazing. "It is true what they say, then. Old age is compensated by wisdom." She laughed out loud, enjoying her own wit. She lifted her glass to her grandfather, and waited long seconds for him to return her toast. He stared at her, then looked down at his plate and picked up his knife and fork. Her smile faded, her face hardened. She tipped back her full glass and emptied it.

Thirty-seven

CROSSROADS

❧ When Benedikte and Erland return from their honeymoon you must leave, Christina," Jorunn said, her voice strong, though her speech was slurred.

"She made a lovely bride," Christina replied, averting her gaze from where it met Jorunn's in the mirror. She brushed Jorunn's white hair with long strokes. "So fragile, so dark against the warm white velvet of her gown. I was quite charmed by her."

"It's easy to see why Erland loves her," Jorunn said, her eyes hard in her reflection. Christina met her look, her own pale gaze darkening in anger.

"I would not say as much," she retorted, letting herself be goaded.

Jorunn smiled, victorious. "You can't be here when she arrives to take her place as Stridheim's new mistress," she insisted. "It's time for you to return to Christiania, take up the reins of your life there."

Christina paused, pressing the silver brush to her midriff. "I have no life there," she ground out, her voice harsh. "My life is here, at Stridheim. I will not leave."

"You must," Jorunn insisted. "There's no place for you here. You have to accept that your lot in life is another."

"I shall not leave!" Christina cried, momentarily letting her cool facade slip. She turned away from the mirror, crossed to the fireplace, then turned back to face her grandmother. "I cannot, even if I wished to. I am with child."

Jorunn felt the tingling begin, felt it in the arm that was still sometimes weighted by numbness. She willed herself to be calm, fought to right the room that swam around her. She gasped for air and the black ceiling that hovered above her lifted. Her mind cleared and she focused on Christina.

"Come here!" she commanded. Christina walked slowly toward her, stopping only inches away. Jorunn reached out to touch the woman's stomach. She smoothed her frail hand quickly over the full skirt of the girl's gown, tracing the hard outline of the bulge beneath Christina's waist. Jorunn felt fear well within her. Her suspicions of what had unfolded the night before Erland proposed to Benedikte crystallized and became certainty.

"You have a plan, I assume?" Jorunn asked, knowing instinctively this woman would have thought through every detail of her situation before making it known to her.

"I had thought to remain here until the child comes. In July, after the birth, I will make a move."

"Will you go back to Christiania then?"

Christina laughed out loud, a sound utterly devoid of humor. "Return to my mother's house with my bastard in tow?" Her voice was harsh. "I think not."

"You have to, it's your place. And your mother needs you...."

"My mother has no need of me," Christina interrupted bitterly. "She has her God."

Jorunn stared at the girl, surprised by the pain and anger in her voice. "Try to understand your mother. She loves you."

Christina smiled derisively and said, "Yet she loves her God better."

Jorunn silenced her with a lift of her hand. "She loves God as well. Her faith is His greatest gift."

"What a hypocrite you are, Grandmother!" Christina exploded. "You do not believe in Him, any more than I do," Christina said, her lip curling derisively.

"You're wrong," Jorunn refuted. "I don't believe in religion, but I do believe in God. I wasn't blessed with your mother's unwavering faith, but I've come to my faith in time, and through great doubt. Through it all His presence was undeniable."

Jorunn was silent, pausing to consider carefully the words she might choose to touch her granddaughter. This young woman, so proud and sure, treading a well-worn path beside the chasm of disbelief. A way Jorunn knew well, her own chosen course for many years. She wondered if there were words to persuade Christina to turn, to listen to the still, small voice and find a new way. Sudden inspiration was granted, and she said calmly, "Stridheim."

Christina watched her warily, a spark of interest suddenly flaring in her pale eyes. Satisfied she had captured the girl's attention, Jorunn continued.

"You profess a unity with this place, you've claimed this land your calling. Then surely you hear its voice, His voice. He's in the furrows of the fields, in the new green that unfolds from the earth each spring, in the harvest each fall. He's in the wind, bitter in January, sweet in July. Only He can grant the miracle of a child; when you feel the babe you carry beneath your heart quicken, it's His touch. The years of doubt are behind me, but my punishment for faithless years had to be endured. Spare yourself, Christina, and search for Him now."

Christina stared at her grandmother, noting that the old woman's speech was oddly clear. Her confidence was shaken by the conviction in her grandmother's voice. "Punishment? What punishment?" she demanded, her voice less sure.

"That's none of your affair. It's my pain, I bear it alone. I speak of it now only in warning, so you might avoid my mistake."

Christina laughed, a harsh sound. "Whatever the punishment, you are Mistress of Stridheim. That position makes it possible to bear any other thing. Waste none of your failing strength worrying for me, *Mormor,* for I know my way in life, and I shall manage very well alone. I shall remain here, though not in this house. I shall move over the mountain, to Valgaard."

"Impossible, the place is a ruin!" Jorunn protested. "No one has lived there since my father died."

"The old buildings can be razed, new ones constructed. It calls to me, that place," Christina insisted. "Mistress of Valgaard, that shall be my lot in life, for I choose it. It is what I will have." Then she added softly, "Nothing shall stop me."

Jorunn watched the young woman carefully. In her mind, in her memory, there was an echo to her words. Drowning that she heard a whisper: 'A faithful man shall abound with blessings, but he that maketh haste to be rich shall not be innocent.' That still, small voice... yet she would not hear it. She turned instead toward the glimmer of hope the idea of Christina as Mistress of Valgaard brought with it. Her voice was light with new excitement when she next spoke. "Yes. If that is truly your calling, then nothing will stop you."

Ignoring Christina's startled expression, deaf to the little voice that hissed at her, she turned from it and resolved to support the plan. The decision brought with it a surge of new energy. Valgaard had lain fallow and untended these many years. Hers, yet she had never made it her own. She had not forgotten her father's dream of their lands merged, but his dream had been relegated to the way of the past when Jorunn had begun her journey on a new road. Now that dream beckoned, ambition flickered and flared and burst into an all-consuming flame. The idea that Christina, flesh of her flesh, would take Valgaard and make it her own filled Jorunn with vigor she had thought long gone. Another crossroads, at a time when Jorunn had thought it was left to her only to let life's ceaseless flow carry her to the end. Death hovered near, her body useless and her spirit broken. Yet suddenly a new way opened, a new direction for her, and Christina. Hope glimmered down that way, and with it came a surge of new strength. Old strength, almost forgotten. Again, in her heart she heard a whisper: 'What profit hath a man of all his labour which he taketh under the sun? One generation passeth away, and another generation cometh: but the earth abideth forever.'

"Hush, Preacher! I will not hear you now!" Jorunn admonished. She turned to Christina, ignoring her granddaughter's amazed face and said abruptly, "Then you shall have Valgaard." The light in Jorunn's face dimmed and she added: "But realize that nothing comes without a price. In return for your place you have to relinquish any claim you imagine to both Erland and Stridheim. Neither of those will ever be yours, Christina. My son and my land belong to one another. That's how it will be. It's the price I demand; God will surely exact another."

Christina studied the old woman before her dispassionately. Withered and decrepit, she posed no threat to her future. Yet it cost her nothing, this promise the old woman demanded. She made it lightly, without regard for its keeping. "As you wish, *Mormor*," she said carelessly, dismissing the idea of God, that she owed him anything. He would not touch her. She would be mistress of a place far greater than even Stridheim; she made up her mind to make it so. She would live life by her own dictates. Her grandmother's ramblings did not worry her. Morbid fancies of an old, sick woman.

"We have to act now," Jorunn declared abruptly. "The old buildings can be leveled quick enough. When the thaw comes you'd best be set to build. Ride to Christiania now, at once. Contact Hans Christian Krogh and bid him plan the place for you. Tell him you ask this favor for me and he'll do it."

Christina studied her grandmother's face carefully, but found nothing there to support sudden suspicion her words aroused. Without question she turned to do her grandmother's bidding.

At the door she was halted by Jorunn's voice. "Christina, you've chosen your way in life. It won't be easy, but you'll have to see it through to the end."

Along the road to Christiania the words echoed in her mind, in time to the beat of the horses hooves.

      ❧   ❧   ❧

Christina watched from her window as the carriage entered the yard at Stridheim. The bright blue of Benedikte's gown lit up in the clear spring sunshine. Smoothing her hands self-consciously over the rounded belly beneath the heavy wool of her dress, Christina went to greet them, descending the stairs in time to see Erland bend and embrace Jorunn in her chair.

He looked up and saw Christina, shock registering clearly on his face. He paled, and she watched him place a protective arm about Benedikte's shoulders.

Benedikte's eyes, too, were on Christina. Her expression was one of surprise, and pleasure. Holding both hands out to her Benedikte cried, "Christina, what a happy surprise! No one told us of the joyous news in their letters."

Christina let herself be embraced, Benedikte's fragile form feeling insubstantial compared with her own bulk. "It was certainly a surprise, and not a happy one to all, I'm afraid, for I have decided this child will be mine alone. I have no wish to marry; I will not let convention dictate how I live my life," Christina rejoined in her cool voice. "In any case, I have no need of a husband. This life gives mine direction."

Benedikte looked into Christina's blue eyes steadily, unflinching at her candor. "New life is God's greatest gift. We are happy for you," she asserted quietly, her conviction obvious in her clear countenance. With an upward glance at Erland Benedikte's face brightened, and Christina had sudden presentiment of news Benedikte was to impart. The facade of

278 ☿ JORUNN'S SAGA ☿

careless assurance she cultivated slipped, her face paled at the girl's next words. "In my body, too, there beats a new heart. We shall raise our children together. They shall be as siblings to one another, so closely they shall be reared."

Benedikte's gaze returned to Erland, adoration was clear in her expression. The look of him caused her to fall silent, a flush stained her pale cheeks.

Utter silence reigned. Erland stood transfixed, his eyes searching Christina's.

"Not so close as that," Jorunn interceded, her voice loud, the slur of her speech never more obvious. "They'll have to cross the mountain to find one another," she demurred, pronouncing each word with painstaking care. "Two carpenters work on new buildings in the yard of Valgaard. When the child comes Christina'll live there, on her own place."

Erland released the breath he had been holding, the sound clearly audible in the hall. Benedikte's look of surprise turned to a frown of consternation. Christina turned from them, retreating to the sitting room to cover her anger at his obvious relief.

"Young Melgaardsson will work for Christina, Erland. I made the choice for her, but it will be her place. Soon she'll be settled there. I confess it's given me a new lease on life, our plans these past months," Jorunn continued, knowing full well Erland was not listening. In vain attempt to distract the girl she turned her attention to Benedikte, while Erland seized the opportunity to escape and follow Christina into the sitting room.

Christina heard him approach. "When'll you birth?" he asked.

"I'm no brood mare, do not speak to me of such things," she flashed in anger. Noting the set of his jaw, his clenched teeth, satisfaction at his distress coursed through her and she stated baldly, "In July."

She watched his eyes narrow as he calculated quickly, saw a muscle beside his mouth twitch in agitation. Glancing over his shoulder to where the others clustered in the hall he whispered, "You should've told me, given me warning."

"It would have changed nothing," she hissed. "In any case, by the time I knew it was too late." She raised her chin and looked him squarely in the eye. "This has nothing to do with you. The child is mine, and mine alone. I will not ask for your help, I expect no offer of it. Do you understand?" she demanded.

The others entered the room, curtailing their conversation. He said softly, "Understand this, the child's mine, and always will be. I won't interfere with your plans so far, since they suit me, but don't make any more plans without askin'. You intend to foster my child you better get used to the idea I'll have a say in you both."

Christina gasped, feeling the color drain from her cheeks. She bit back a sharp reply, well aware of her grandmother's curious glance in their direction. She turned her back to him and crossed to the fire. She watched the flames dance orange and yellow, her dismay giving way to utter fury at Erland's attitude. Grinding her teeth to quell the scream of anger building in her throat, she clenched both hands and drew in short breaths to calm herself.

'He shall have no such influence on either my life or the child's. I shall move to the other side of the mountain as soon as possible and his life shall be separate from ours. And if that is not enough I shall declare the child to be Halvor's.' She smiled at the idea of the trump card she held. The situation that had seemed intolerable suddenly shifted, she felt power return to her. 'Sin, as well as virtue, has its rewards,' she reflected, 'and is far more interesting.'

She turned from the fire with a bright smile and joined the conversation, pretending interest in Benedikte's story of their travel. She felt Erland's look, stared into his dark blue gaze. Her eyes laughed at him in silent taunt. 'He fancies himself Master of Stridheim, and seeks to control everyone on this place,' she mused. 'He has chosen his wife with care; one who will not challenge him.' Her lips twisted in a smile at the thought. 'She shall never be Mistress of Stridheim. It is not her destiny. Sooner or later everyone will recognize Stridheim's true mistress, and Erland shall recognize his as well.'

Thirty-eight

INTERVENTION

✣ In the quiet night Benedikte lay beside Erland and listened to the rhythm of his breathing. While he slept she stared into the cloak of darkness, trying to chase away doubt, and fear. They hovered, evil shapes of her own imagination, threatening the happiness she treasured. She thought with longing of the nights these past months when she had fallen asleep in a cocoon of warmth, her head pillowed on Erland's shoulder, his arm wrapped about her. Tonight he had turned from her and slept at once, leaving her to lie awake and stare at shadows cast by unfamiliar objects in a strange place. Her eyes burned, gritty with fatigue, but she would not close them. Imprinted behind each black lid was an image of Christina, lushly ripe in a gown of scarlet wool, sashaying toward Erland in the great hall, the bulge of her abdomen heralding her condition.

Erland had stiffened; she had registered his shock, yet she had dismissed it, assuming any honorable man would feel the same. There had been no news of nuptials in her mother-in-law's frequent letters as they journeyed through Europe. It was clear Christina would birth this child out of wedlock. Benedikte, too, had been surprised. Christina's affair with Marius Løvenskiold had been a poorly kept secret this past summer, yet both were of fine families, equally matched in every way. Christina would not have been the only young woman from their set to approach the altar in autumn bearing in her womb the fruit of passion. Summer in Christiania was exhilarating, the parks lush and green, evenings long and light. In the warm rays of bright sunshine young love was known blossom. Social convention could not check the tide of human nature, nor stem the flood of passion. Benedikte understood the weakness of the flesh, would not judge others who succumbed. Had the call of duty not required Erland to leave her for his land she may well not have remained chaste until their union was blessed, for in her mind she had given herself completely to Erland soon after they first met. All summer she had waited for his return with growing anticipation of the press of his lips to hers, the feel of his broad chest beneath her palms. Had he not been so honorable she, too, might have succumbed to the pleasures of the flesh. She would not condemn Christina for her lapse, yet she could not understand why Christina chose to further flaunt convention in not wedding Marius now, however belatedly. Benedikte had known Marius Løvenskiold since their nursery days. Though he was vain, and some would say shallow, he was undeniably handsome, and in essence a good man. He would never dishonor his family, nor Christina's, by abdicating the responsibility of a child conceived with a young woman equal his social stature. She wondered at the turn of events that led Christina to bear the child alone, was intrigued by what she felt certain had been Christina's decision. It bothered Benedikte not at all that many would gossip, say the child was conceived in sin. New life was truly God's gift, and she rejoiced in Christina's blessing.

Yet the exchange between Erland and Christina had not gone unnoticed, and Benedikte understood Erland was not merely shocked by Christina's condition, but angered as well. The rest of the day he had simmered with barely controlled fury. It was this reaction she found troubling. Perhaps his rage stemmed from a sense of responsibility for his cousin, she reasoned, yet watching them together she was convinced there was something else between them. Christina had been alight with mischief, goading Erland throughout dinner with frequent referrals to her child and their future. When the evening had drawn to a close and the family gathered in the hall to wish one another a good night, Christina had leaned toward Erland and pressed her full lips to his, holding him captive for telling seconds. Benedikte stood trapped in her father-in-law's gentle embrace, aware, yet powerless. Christina had turned to her, something vile in her pale gaze.

"Good night, sleep tight," she said in her smooth as silk voice before turning to saunter up the stairs, leaving Benedikte

shaken, Erland quaking with rage. Her father-in-law seemed
unaware of the maelstrom that swirled, but the grim line of
her mother-in-law's mouth confirmed she had not imagined
Christina's manipulation of the situation. Benedikte had
glanced up at Erland, seeking reassurance, protection; instead
she had seen his lips glisten, still wet with Christina's kiss.

He was powerless against her. Benedikte recognized this
and knew to be afraid. Never had she known such fear, could
not understand its origin, yet instinct warned her and she knew
to listen. In time she might discern the reason for Christina's
hold over Erland, but for now she must simply heed the warning voice and be wary of the woman. There was danger lurking beneath the exquisite facade; evil sparked in the depths of
her pale eyes.

Shivering, cold in spite of the soft eiderdown comforter,
Benedikte crept closer to Erland and slipped her arm around
his waist, pressed her cheek to the broad expanse of his back.
Suddenly, emphatically, she wished Christina gone, removed
from this place and Erland's presence. Resolve stirred as the
idea occurred, and in the darkness of night Benedikte's smooth
face settled into lines of determination. She made up her mind
to make that happen. She sat upright, buoyed by sudden elation, but the chill of night air soon caused her to settle deeper
beneath the comforter. She lay staring into the darkness, no
longer afraid, her mind searching methodically for a way to
take control of her situation. Long into the night she lay exploring new avenues, until the first rays of early spring sunshine heralded the dawn of a new day. In its pale blush a new
idea took shape.

'Perhaps Marius doesn't know of the child,' she thought
suddenly. 'It would be like Christina to leave the city without
telling him.'

Proud and headstrong as Benedikte knew Christina to be,
it seemed likely she would rather leave, give up her position in
Christiania and make a new place for herself here, than face
the shame of her predicament.

'Perhaps she does not love Marius, and would not wed
him for that reason,' Benedikte mused. 'Yet there is the child
to consider,' she reasoned. 'Christina is selfish. A child should
be raised by both mother and father; it cannot be Christina's
choice.

'Marius is really just a silly boy,' she confessed to herself.
'Foolish enough to abdicate responsibility gladly if Christina

refused to marry him. Yet he is decent, and if made to understand his honor is at stake he might be persuaded to marry Christina.'

Benedikte knew a sudden thrill as a solution to her problem presented itself. Tomorrow she must convince Erland he should confront Marius, tell him of Christina's condition and insist he do the honorable thing. Within the month Christina might be wed and returned to her rightful place in Christiania. Gone from Stridheim. They would be safe from her then, she and Erland and their child. She stroked the gentle mound of her stomach beneath the warm comforter, turned to cradle Erland's sleeping form. With a sigh of relief her body relaxed, sleep hovered near. 'Sov godt, I'll keep you safe,' she thought in hazy promise, as she drifted into slumber.

❧ ❧ ❧

When Benedikte awoke the sun's rays were already casting short shadow. Almost noon, and she had yet to bathe and dress. She hurried from her bed and rang for water, eager to find Erland, to speak to him about Marius, and Christina.

She dressed hurriedly, waving her maid away when she would try again to lace her smaller. "Never mind, Rikke," she scolded. "It will do no good in any case. In my condition I shall grow fatter every day regardless. I am resigned to it."

Rikke faced her lady with both fists planted squarely on ample hips. "I promised *Frue* Sørenson I'd do my best by ya in her stead, and I mean to keep my word," she protested. "I won't have ya paradin' about, flauntin' your condition, the way some folks does. It's not decent, it's not. Besides, men folk don't like to see their ladies like that. You don't want the light o' love to dim in the eyes o' that young husband o' yours, now do ya?" she threatened, her round cheeks rosy with outrage.

Benedikte sighed in irritation at the woman's romantic nonsense, yet she turned obediently to let Rikke wrestle with her corset strings. It was true, Erland despised Christina's flaunting of her shape. Benedikte was well aware of his loathing for the way Christina behaved. She would not risk him looking at her with an expression of such disgust. And Rikke's determination to do Nana Sørenson proud was touching, if annoying. Nana had raised Benedikte since the death of her mother, and had entrusted her charge to the care of another with true regret, and some misgiving.

"If I wasn't so down in my back I'd go with you, *jenta mi*, you know I would," the old woman had insisted when Benedikte kissed her fond farewell upon leaving her childhood home.

"I'm a big girl now, Nana, all grown up," Benedikte had soothed. "Rikke and I will do very well together, I'm sure."

Benedikte had noted the disgruntled look that flashed across the old woman's face and amended quickly, "What I mean to say is that Rikke is a fine lady's maid, and will serve me well. No one could replace you, Nana. You must know that."

Suffering Rikke's ministrations now Benedikte felt a sudden longing for Nana. She would have known what to do about Christina. Nana would have shown her the way out of this predicament. Suddenly it occurred to Benedikte that when concrete instruction in difficult situations failed Nana, she would invariably instruct, "Say your prayers and listen to the Lord, *jenta mi*, He'll keep you right." As Rikke fastened the multitude of buttons that strained across her increasing waistline Benedikte decided she would pray about this matter of Christina and Marius before she mentioned her plan to Erland. In matters affecting so many it would doubtless be wise to seek God's counsel. Nana would have insisted on it. But as Rikke knelt down to fasten Benedikte's shoes the sound of scraping boots drifted through the open window, heralding Erland's return from the fields. She must hurry, or be late for the midday meal. There was no time for prayer in the matter. In her experience the Lord could be slow with His instruction, leaving her to wait on bended knee while He pondered her problem. In a flash of memory Benedikte could hear Nana's voice reminding her of the virtue of patience. Perhaps she should wait in discussing the matter with Erland until this evening. Nana had often accused her of having a stubborn disposition, of being unwilling to consider issues from any aspect other than her own. She would prove Nana's estimation of her character wrong in this instance. She resolved to spend this afternoon in prayer and meditation, giving Christina's predicament careful consideration before taking action. The tinkling chime of the clock on her dressing table reminded her there was no time to give the problem further consideration now.

"Be quick, Rikke. The meal is served promptly on the hour," she urged. "*Svigermor* seems nice enough, but I shouldn't like to fall from grace for arriving tardy for mealtimes."

Rikke sent her lady through the door in a flurry, well aware anyone who crossed the Mistress of Stridheim would come out the worse for it. She might look frail in her chair, but the old lady had a tongue as sharp as a razor's edge. She had promised *Frue* Sørenson to protect the young missus, yet she didn't relish the idea of having to stand between the Mistress of Stridheim and anyone who provoked her.

Benedikte entered the dining room after the others were seated. Erland stood, helping her to sit beside him. Silence cloaked the room, and Benedikte was aware a flush rose to stain her cheeks.

"The lady awakens," Christina drawled, her silvery voice laced with sarcasm. "Surely it is late for breakfast, even by city standards, Benedikte. I fear we shall never succeed in making a country girl of you."

The pink flush coloring her cheeks deepened to crimson, but Benedikte lifted her chin in an attitude of unconscious pride. Pointedly ignoring Christina she turned to Jorunn, saying, "Please excuse my absence at breakfast, *Svigermor*. I am unexpectedly tired of late."

"Think nothing of it," Jorunn replied, the slur in her speech almost unnoticeable. "It's your condition. Seems it will last forever, I know, but not to worry. In a few months you'll be your old self again. Just mind you take care of yourself and my grandson," she admonished with a quick smile that lifted only one side of her mouth.

Benedikte's smile was brilliant, reflecting the surge of happiness she experienced at Jorunn's obvious pleasure at her pregnancy. She turned to Erland, lifted her face to his. His grave countenance lightened when he returned her look; he moved one hand to brush hers where it lay on the pristine cloth, his palm rough against the smoothness of her skin.

"The girl had better hurry and serve before I lose my appetite," Christina murmured, breaking the spell of the moment they shared.

"I may be crippled but I'm not deaf, Christina," Jorunn rejoined from the end of the table. "Keep a civil tongue in your head or excuse yourself; it's up to you."

Christina glanced toward Jorunn, her pale eyes dark. Then she fixed a bland smile on her face and said to Benedikte, "Sorry you're not feeling well, *min tante*. You do look tired, not well at all. Perhaps a nap this afternoon? But there now, I see fresh color in your cheeks. You must be feeling better."

Benedikte clenched her teeth at Christina's goading. In sudden anger she made up her mind she would not suffer Christina's presence one moment longer than necessary. There was no time for prayer; she resolved to take matters into her own hands and rid herself of Christina as quickly as possible. She fixed Christina with a hard stare, then turned to smile in Erland's direction.

"I believe what I need is a breath of fresh air and a bit of exercise. A walk with my husband after lunch would doubtless cure what ails me. Do you have the time, Darling?"

Erland shifted uncomfortably, noting the set of his wife's jaw, the thrust of her chin. This was no casual invitation. Across the table he was aware Christina watched them with one brow raised in sardonic amusement. Briefly he thought of the fences he had spent the morning mending; with any delay he would not be through by nightfall. Yet the challenge in Christina's eyes was clear.

"I'll make time," he answered shortly, and was rewarded by a smile of pure pleasure that lit up his wife's face.

An hour later he was regretting the impulse that had prompted him to promise Benedikte a stroll in his mother's garden. Benedikte stood framed against the bright yellow bloom of forsythia, the sun brilliant on her dark curls, her eyes flashing in anger. "What do you mean, it's none of your business? She is your niece, after all. *Herr* Myrbraaten is too aged and decrepit to protect his daughter's welfare. Why should it not fall to you to guard her reputation."

"Because Christina's reputation isn't worth guardin'. She couldn't care less for it, never has. It's too late to bother with that now anyways."

"Too late for her, maybe, but not for us, Erland. I want her away from here! She torments us; why should we suffer her presence when it is despicable to us both?"

Erland clenched his teeth; Benedikte saw his jaw work and understood the depth of his distress. Yet strangely there was no anger in his blue eyes. In the depth of his gaze she saw only anguish. "I'm not master here yet; it's not my decision. And Mother won't tolerate interference in her plans. Besides, as soon as the babe's born Christina will be gone. Valgaard's on the other side of the mountain, far enough away that you won't see much of her," he tried to soothe.

'Not far enough away for me,' Benedikte thought privately. She ground her teeth in frustration at Erland's unwillingness to pursue her plan, a plan so perfect she felt compelled to try again its promotion. Taking a deep breath she regrouped and tried a new tactic.

"If you feel no responsibility for Christina's situation, then you might at least consider the child's welfare. It deserves both mother and father, as any child does," she insisted.

"That idiot Løvenskiold isn't man enough to be a decent father!" Erland exploded. Benedikte felt the shock of his angry outburst course through her, stretching her already strained nerves to the breaking point.

"Having Marius Løvenskiold for a father is surely better than being born a bastard!" she flashed back, her voice too loud, almost a shriek. She watched in horror the look of surprise, then disgust, that crossed Erland's features. An ugly stain of rust rose from the collar of his shirt to his cheeks, his mouth twisted in loathing of the words she spoke. In an instant Benedikte realized her own ill-chosen course. She was suddenly aware that if she continued down this way Christina would certainly win. If she inspired in Erland a sense of responsibility for Christina's situation, convinced him to protect her, and Marius refused his duty, then she would have gambled and lost. The torment reflected in her husband's face at this moment was of her own making; she searched frantically for a way to erase it.

On impulse she moved toward him, threw herself in his arms. "Please forgive me, Erland," she begged. "I understand your disgust, my behavior is appalling."

His arms encircled her slowly, carefully, yet his body was stiff and unforgiving. Panic rose in Benedikte, threatening to shatter her barely maintained composure. The threat of Christina loomed suddenly larger. She realized she trod the edge of a precipice; she sensed a dark chasm of emotion suddenly between them. She had miscalculated in trying to force Erland to deal with Christina; she understood such error could cost her dearly in this game of manipulation Christina played so brilliantly. A sudden calm settled over Benedikte. She released her clutch on the course fabric of Erland's shirt, moved her open palms to stroke his back, pulled him closer to her. The tension in his body gradually gave way and he tightened his embrace, moving one callused palm up to cup her head as she lifted her face to his hungry kiss. His lips were hard, almost punishing; they awoke in her an overwhelming response. She let herself slide into the dark heat of his passion. When he pulled her toward the house she followed on legs that trembled. In a haze of desire they found their way up the back stairs and tumbled together onto the crisp linen of their bed, joining their bodies in a frantic search for completion.

In the garden Jorunn sat in her chair, unwittingly concealed by the high thrust of forsythia behind her. She tilted her face to the spring sunshine, smiling at the lift of her heart, the memory of the surge of passion almost forgotten. Her daughter-in-law had revealed unexpected facets of her character in the exchange Jorunn had inadvertently overheard. New respect dawned at the memory of Benedikte's determination to be rid of Christina.

'The girl's got good instincts, knows to be afraid of Christina,' Jorunn reflected. 'That should serve her well. Got backbone, too. Maybe more'n Erland. He should've listened, stood up to me and fought to protect his wife.'

A twinge of disappointment stabbed at her, but she dismissed it. 'Carryin' a load of guilt around heavy enough to break any man. Can't see the truth, that it wasn't his doin'. Just a miserable pawn in Christina's game. He's as good a man as they come, a fine master of his land, but Stridheim won't survive without a steady mistress. She'll keep him straight, that one. She's strong, and smart... sees trouble comin' and deals with it. Soon she'll figure out how to get him to do what she wants without lettin' on it was her idea. She loves him too much; that's her weakness. Jealousy near pushed her over the line, but she's no fool. First fight's a fearful thing. She doesn't know young love's too fragile to last. Love's a bond tempered by time and trouble. Plenty of both here on Stridheim. Just have to wait and see.'

She tilted her head, reveling in the warmth of the sun on her face. She had instructed the housemaid to collect her at one o'clock sharp, yet it was obvious from the shadow the fountain cast that it was at least a quarter past. 'I'll be runnin' late in my duties the rest of the day,' she thought, and tried to summon irritation at the idea. Yet the day was crisp, the colors dazzling after winter's gray. She would have to reprimand the silly chit for forgetting her, yet it was difficult to be truly annoyed on such a lovely day. She settled back with a sigh of pleasure and listened to the song of sparrows and finches, the call of a lone nightingale. Sweeter than any symphony, she thought as she dozed.

Thirty-nine

WAGES PAID

❧ Summer settled over the valley, and Stridheim grew heavy and ripe with the harvest. Fields of golden wheat waved under a warm and gentle breeze, the forest was lush and green. Christina carried her child easily, not at all burdened under the weight of it. Each day she climbed the mountain to walk the paths and fields Valgaard, glorying in the rich abundance. Melgaardsson had made a fine beginning. The harvest would be small, but more than sufficient to support her and the child. Jorunn waited in eager anticipation for Christina's daily reports of progress on Valgaard, suddenly rejuvenated. Except for the confinement of her chair she was restored to the woman she had been before her illness. Her mind was sharp; she was clear in her instruction to Christina regarding the running of Valgaard. In only a few months she taught her apt pupil a great deal of what she needed to know to make the place prosperous. Christina absorbed it all readily. The flames of ambition engulfed them.

In the heat of each late afternoon Christina passed through the dark wood and came to the River Glomma. She stripped and bathed, letting the cool water soothe her hot flesh. Standing in its blue depths she let the current swirl around her, tracing the smooth skin stretched taught over her belly. The babe lay still when she was there, the usual tumult of arms and legs twisting inside her ceased. She stroked her belly, letting her own peace envelope the child. She waited for it patiently, willing it to stay within her until she could take herself and the infant inside her over the mountain. To her own place, soon complete. The house stood ready, needing only the furnishings to be installed. The buildings were new and freshly painted, the fence that linked them intact, closing them from outside entry. In a few days she would make her move. Then she would welcome the child. She would birth under her own roof, she had decided. She knew Erland watched her surreptitiously, waiting for a sign the time had come for the child to be delivered. Each day she carried it she had the satisfaction of watching his impatience grow. He went about his tasks distracted. She derived pleasure from his unrest. It was her entertainment while she waited.

She left the cool retreat of the water and walked to the bank, standing to watch the water's ceaseless flow, letting the wind brush her dry. Behind her she heard a noise and turned without fear or shame toward whomever might make an appearance. Erland entered the clearing, only yards away. She faced him, watching in amusement as he flushed dark red, his jaw hardened.

"The wagons from Christiania have topped the rise and are movin' in the direction of your place. Get dressed. I'll hitch the wagon and drive you to supervise."

He turned and disappeared into the forest, her laughter ringing in his ears.

❧ ❧ ❧

Benedikte rested on a woven chaise, cool in the shade of the old oak that graced the middle of the courtyard. Occasional rays of sunlight pierced the shifting canopy of leaves, striking her fair skin, burning in its intensity. She shifted uneasily, restless. A sense of foreboding had plagued her these past days; her nights were filled with dark, shapeless dreams, her days shadowed by persistent anxiety. She was waiting for something, though what she could not fathom. Not the babe, for it rested safe in the haven of her womb, yet restless, too. The tumult inside her seemed ceaseless; she unconsciously stroked her belly in vain attempt to soothe the child.

Looking to the distance she could barely discern the shapes of the men in the fields; closer, she watched two girls collect apples from the grove at the foot of the mountain. A wealth of ripe fruit spilled from the baskets in rich red bounty. From the window of their room she had watched Erland cross the cobbled yard a few minutes earlier, and come to wait for his return. He had ventured into the wood. In search of Christina, she suspected. He watched her, Benedikte knew. Surreptitiously, yet she was aware, as was Christina. Benedikte had seen the sly smile that flitted across Christina's beautiful face when she sensed Erland's steady gaze. Christina swayed her hips provocatively as she walked; she let a hand drift suggestively across her full breasts, fall lower to caress her swollen belly. The stain of rust on Erland's cheek testified to his awareness of Christina, yet his attitude, the unconscious curl of his lip, made it clear he despised her. The frown he wore when speaking to her cried aloud his irritation in her presence; yet she held him captive, and Benedikte had almost despaired of understanding the current flowing between them.

Erland reappeared from the darkness of the forest and Benedikte rose to go to him. He crossed the yard with long strides, his face set, his body tense, and disappeared into the barn. She heard him call gruff instruction to the stable boy, and knew he would not welcome her. Whatever the exchange between him and Christina in the wood, it had angered him, as usual.

As if thought could conjure her she appeared, her pale face and silvery hair white in the sunlight, the dark green of her dress melting into the forest. An apparition, a wood nymph. Benedikte resolutely quashed her fancy and made her way toward the woman.

"Surely it is unwise for you to venture alone into the forest in your condition," Benedikte began. "You worry us all," she added pointedly.

Christina smiled, a cold twist of her lips. "I wasn't alone, you need not worry about me. Your husband, however..." She paused for effect, choosing her words carefully, "He seems... distraught."

Christina's laughter rang out across the courtyard, clear as silver bells. Benedikte felt herself flush, hot with anger. The anxiety of these past days crystallized to hatred, pure and undiluted. In utter fury she flashed, "Stay away from my husband, Christina...."

The rest of what she would say was drowned in Erland's voice as he bellowed from the barn door, "Get in the wagon, now, Christina!"

Benedikte saw shock, and fury at the tone he used flicker across Christina's usually impassive face. She watched her sink her small white teeth into the soft fullness of her bottom lip to stifle the reply she would make to Erland, saw the struggle and what it cost her to heed his bidding. Christina carefully schooled her face into blandness and moved toward the wagon. She stopped, turned back to Benedikte, and let the facade drop for an instant. Her lips twisted into a sneer. "It seems your husband will have me. I find it *impossible* to resist a man so determined to have his own way," she drawled.

Words to wound, she flashed a brilliant smile to twist the knife. Benedikte ground her teeth in frustration at the impossibility of her situation. Months of maneuvering in this game Christina played had convinced her the woman was capable of destroying everything she held most precious. Against Erland's will Christina had the power to captured his interest; she held him prisoner. She was stealthy and conniving, tormenting Erland, her wary prey. She played without rules, and to Benedikte even her objective was unclear, for if it was Erland's affections Christina hoped to win, then surely she must understand her game was lost. When Erland's gaze rested on her his blue eyes were chips of ice, his face frozen in an attitude of revulsion. Surely Christina could not imagine she would ever kindle warmth in his regard. Yet the cold voice of reason reminded Benedikte there was heat in anger, and Christina's taunts made Erland furious. The mere mention of the child she carried threatened to erupt the ire that boiled beneath his carefully controlled surface. The source of his anger mystified Benedikte. She knew Erland well, and understood he did not care that Christina violated moral standards in bearing her child alone, nor was he concerned with public opinion. He gave no thought to the shame she brought on their family, for social censure meant nothing to him. After months of reasoning Benedikte had found no logical thought to explain his attitude, and still she was an unwilling participant in this unfathomable game. She clenched her teeth and thrust her chin forward in an unconscious attitude of challenge. Watching them drive from the yard her soft mouth set in a grim line of determination and she resolved to find a way to beat Christina at her own game.

❧ ❧ ❧

Hours later Benedikte lay wearily down, letting the soft mattress pillow her aching body. Her earlier resolve had crumbled during an evening made interminable by uncertainty, and waiting. Irritably she pulled the linen to cover her swollen belly, aghast at its size, still unused to her bulk. Full of resentment, she marveled at the way Christina carried her far greater burden, seemingly unaffected by the heavy swell of her abdomen. She moved easily, graceful still, while Benedikte imagined she waddled like the geese in her mother-in-law's yard. And Christina would soon be quit her condition, while she had months to endure as yet. Bitter gall rose up to choke her, her stomach churned. The indigestion that had plagued her since conceiving this child seemed tangible reminder of her predicament.

The babe turned once, then again. She reached down to stroke her stomach, soothe the child. Again it moved, suddenly shifting to press the air from her lungs, making her gasp. Clumsily she rolled to her side, her belly shifting to let the child lay beside her. Grateful for the relief her new position afforded her, she drew a deep breath, then stretched out one arm and traced the cold sheet where Erland should have lain. He had not returned from his errand with Christina. As she had watched them drive from the yard she had vowed she would win this struggle the three of them endured, yet now, lying alone in the darkness, fear assailed her. All evening she had waited, finally excusing herself from dinner, unable to feign an appetite. The satisfaction of knowing Christina's place was finished and she would soon be gone was erased by new anxiety. The furniture had been delivered mid-afternoon; she could think of no reasonable excuse for Erland's absence from dinner this evening. Anxiety held her in its unrelenting grasp. Resolutely she squeezed her lids together and waited for sleep to deliver her from this agony of distrust. A gentle wind blew, lifting the lace that veiled the window, swirling about the room and carrying with it the murmur of voices from the dining room below. She strained to listen, hoping to hear Erland's voice, deep and steady, mingle with the conversation of her mother and father-in-law, but she waited in vain. The talk was of Valgaard and its restoration, as it had incessantly been these past weeks. She pictured Erland and Christina, alone in her new place, and was sickened by the images her mind conjured. Christina, ripe and lushly seductive, her swollen breasts near tumbling from the low front of her gown. Erland reaching out to touch Christina the way he sometimes touched her, stroking the child she carried, reveling in the swell of her belly and in the softness of her curves. Though he had been remote of late, there were times when he embraced her gently, tracing the roundness of her, his face alight with pride and anticipation. His touch excited her, caused her to long for the release he had taught her was possible. Heat would rise quickly, her swollen breasts would harden to stiff peaks, the new sensitivity of her nipples exquisite, excruciating. Yet these past weeks when she lifted her face, seeking the warm, wet intimacy of his mouth, his lips touched hers in a chaste kiss, with none of the passion she longed for returned. She wanted Erland with physical desire that made her weak; its denial left her forlorn. Yet she had not dared let him see this, would not let him know she was not as pure as he imagined. She feared the look of loathing she often intercepted as he watched Christina sway past, the look of her so sensual it charged the air around her. Alone in the darkness, against her will she was fascinated by the aura of sensuality that enveloped Christina, in awe of her flawless beauty, entranced by her voice. She wondered now if Erland, too, had fallen prey to Christina's seductive way.

Suspicion snaked its way forward in her mind, poisoning her with distrust. In desperation she fought treacherous doubt, refused to give way to jealousy. Benedikte turned toward the window and lay watching moonlight filter through the lace in hazy rays, bidding elusive sleep come. She turned to lie on her back, hating the rise of her stomach beneath the linen, a reminder that the intimacy she longed for was impossible. Erland's touch. She lay waiting, misery a hard lump in her throat, constricted by silent weeping.

❧ ❧ ❧

When the last piece of furniture had been placed according to her directions Christina turned to survey her domain. The house was large, though not as grand as the one at Stridheim. It was to her liking, suited to her taste. She had designed it carefully, and she viewed it now with satisfaction. Everything was as she had envisioned.

Erland watched her, his face impassive. She wondered idly of his opinion, but did not care enough to ask. With a sigh of contentment she crossed to the sofa and rested, smoothing the damask with her open palm. Silky, sensuous, the color of a pale blue summer sky. She traced the pattern with one fingertip and felt another low murmur in her groin, noticed her stomach hardening in steely bands. Not uncomfortable, these things brought the welcome news that her child would soon join her here.

"Everything's ready, then," Erland interrupted her. "Let's get back to the house. It's late, almost dinnertime."

She shook her head. "I'll not be leaving this place. It is my home now. Bid one of the girls pack my things and have them delivered to me."

He looked at her, irritation obvious in his every gesture. "Don't be a fool. You can't stay here alone until after the babe's born. How'll you send word when your time comes? And how'll you care for it? You got no help here, and you know nothin' about babes. Until the child's born and you learn to care for it you live under my roof."

"Under your supervision," she said, raising one eyebrow in skepticism. "And what do you know of infants?" she asked scathingly.

"Nothin', I don't pretend to. But Mother's no stranger to babes, and one of the girls got to have experience with younger brothers and sisters."

Christina laughed out loud. "Grandmother is an old woman, too feeble to care for herself, let alone an infant. And what could a silly chit of a girl teach me about caring for my own child? I shall understand what should be done. What I need to know is already within me; everything will be clear when the child is in my arms."

Erland grew agitated, his anger overcoming his control. "At least there you won't be alone! Quit wastin' time and get in the wagon, before I carry you there myself!"

He took one step toward her, and her smile faded. She acknowledged he was prepared to follow through his threat and stopped him saying, "Please, Erland. Let me do this my way. I will not give birth in your wife's home. Go now, ride for the physician; I feel my time draws near."

He stopped at her words, his determination undermined by the pleading look of her. "Are you in pain? You sure it's time?"

She nodded mutely, unwilling to provoke him further and risk being forced back to his house, filing away the memory of his lack of resistance to her pleas. He hesitated, then said, "I'll ride to the village and fetch Doc Tveter. Is there someone at the house you want to wait with you?"

"Only you," she answered simply, schooling her expression to one of innocent yearning. With hidden amusement she watched as his face mirrored his struggle. On it there was clearly displayed a tableau of pity, guilt, remorse, then resolution. "I'll be back quick as I can," he promised, turning to leave without another word.

In the growing twilight she sat to wait, a victorious smile playing on her lips. Everything was arranged to perfection, everything she hoped for within her grasp. To have it she need only wait. Everything she deserved would come to her, in time. Of that she was certain.

❧ ❧ ❧

Erland returned as twilight was giving way to murky dusk. The windows across the front of the house were black; no candle within relieved their darkness. He dismounted and heard Doc Tveter follow, almost forgetting him in his concern.

In the hallway the smell of new timber was fresh and clean. He stood just inside, letting his eyes grow accustomed to the dimness. From somewhere above he heard a moan begin, then a stifled scream. The hair on his arms rose; fear slithered and curled in the pit of his stomach. The old man pushed past him and climbed the stairs, letting the sounds guide him. Erland took a deep breath to calm himself and followed.

Light shone from an open door. Inside he found the physician leaning over Christina. From Erland's perspective her face was hidden from his view by the swell of her belly. She writhed on the bed, the linen and blankets twisted beneath her. Erland pressed his eyes shut as the old man lifted the hem of Christina's dress unceremoniously, revealing her long slim legs, devoid already of stockings. He probed her vast belly gently. Another moan started deep in Christina's throat. Erland turned from the sight and sound of her as he heard her scream build, pressing his hands to his ears to muffle it. Stumbling in the darkness he made his way downstairs, feeling the walls of the hall that would lead him outside, deliver him into the cool clean air.

In the dim light of a summer night he paced the courtyard, stepping on cobbles that shone pale silver. Christina's screams echoed in the yard, their frequency increasing as time passed. He walked back and forth, fighting the urge to flee, not daring return to that softly lit room where Christina lay twisted on the rumpled bed.

The screams built to a terrible crescendo, ceaseless, causing him to press both hands to his ears in a futile attempt to smother them. He lifted his pale face to the weak moon, wishing for words to a prayer, searching for some connection to the greater spirit he felt here on this land, appealing wordlessly to it for Christina's deliverance.

At last her screams stopped. For a long moment silence fell in a thick, dark blanket over the yard. He heard the wail of an infant. The child's cry split the night and Erland breathed a sigh of relief. Turning, he approached the house. He entered the dark hall and felt his way toward the stairs. Climbing them quickly he felt hope lighten his way.

Doctor Tveter met him at the door to the room. The old man's face was gray in the dim light. He handed Erland a bundle wrapped in white linen. He took the child, clasped it to his breast carefully. Looking down he saw a tiny face, wrinkled in protest, mewling its discontent. Gently he soothed the babe, pressing it to his heart, smiling in wonder as the cries ceased. He shifted the small weight he cradled to study the child's face. Blue eyes opened, tiny slits in a swollen face. Erland started instinctively toward the light in the room, looking to explore this new person he held.

Doctor Tveter moved to stand in his way, blocking his entry. Looking up in surprise he stared over the man's shoulder to where a bulky form lay covered on the bed. A great stain of red spilled from the bed and down its side. For the first time he noticed the deathly silence that reigned in the room.

He faced Doctor Tveter, saw for the first time how aged and frail he had become. "Nothin' I could do for her," the old man said.

Convulsively Erland clutched the infant. It wailed in protest as Erland squeezed, and he relaxed his grip.

"It's a boy, somebody's son," the physician said. He looked at Erland for a long moment, searching. "Nothin' more I can do here. You'd best find someone to help you care for him." He brushed past Erland and disappeared down the dark stairs.

Erland turned toward the bed, mesmerized by the mound there. He walked toward it slowly, drew back the sheet without conscious thought. Christina stared up at him, her pale blue eyes glassy. Her silver hair, dark with sweat, lay spread about her pale face. Her lips had lost their rose blush, turned dark violet. Beside her lay another form. He cringed at the sight of the lifeless infant. Unable to turn away, his gaze was drawn to its tiny face. The features perfect, very like those of the babe he cradled. Reaching out he touched it, feeling the coolness of its skin, in contrast to the warm bundle he held. He clutched the child convulsively and gave vent to the sob that built in his throat. The infant cried out in the night, their voices joined in a cacophony of grief.

A long while later Erland left the room, the stairs already light. He made his way through the courtyard and turned east toward the early sun, climbing the mountain with its rays blinding him. He found his way with difficulty, stumbling, clutching the child in panic to protect it. At last he reached the top and looked down on Stridheim. The buildings clustered there, in the middle of vast acres of timber and wheat, brought comfort to him. In the face of death he reveled in the eternal life of the land.

"This place'll be yours, *sønnen min*. I swear it," he promised the tiny bundle he cradled. The image of Christina, dead and growing cold, filled him with unbearable remorse. Guilt that he should have caused such suffering rested heavy on his shoulders, an impossible burden to bear. He decided he must right the wrong he had done Christina; in that he hoped to find deliverance. He looked into the face of her child and silently vowed to protect him, to rear him as his son, in his rightful place as the young Master of Stridheim. Erland descended the mountain and entered the yard at Stridheim, holding the sleeping child close, pressed to his heart.

Erland's step was heavy over the threshold. The door closed behind him and he paused in the dim light in the hall, trying to think what to do with the child.

"Erland? That you?" A voice from the sitting room startled him. In surprise he turned to his mother, who sat close to the fire. He stood frozen, too weary to search for words to tell her what he must.

She wheeled toward him in her chair, stretching out eager arms for the babe. "My great-grandchild!" she cried, her voice full of wonder. He delivered the child into her keeping, averting his eyes from her shining face. These past months she had been so vital, her zest for living restored. He cringed at the thought of taking that from her.

He watched as his mother expertly shifted the blanket to explore the child. "A son, Christina has a son!" she exclaimed. "Exactly what she needs to help her make Valgaard great. One day these two places will merge, Erland, and together they'll be the greatest farm in all of Norway."

She looked up at him, her eyes gleaming with anticipation of future greatness, pride making her voice thick. The look of sorrow on Erland's face pierced the haze of her dream and she was gripped by sudden fear. "What is it, what aren't you telling me?" She cried out, reaching forward to grip his arm. Erland abandoned his search for the right words and blurted, "Christina's dead, *Mor.* She's died birthin' my son!" His voice broke, his face was suddenly wet with tears of anguish and guilt.

Jorunn felt the tingling begin, watched in horrified fascination as the room began to rock and sway and dance about her confused gaze. She opened her mouth to call for help, suddenly fearful for the infant she cradled. She saw Erland move toward her, felt him relieve her of the great burden the tiny babe had suddenly become. She slumped forward, the carpet rushing toward her in a kaleidoscope of color and light as she relinquished consciousness.

Voices. Near, then far away. Floating, dancing like light on water, the River Glomma. She struggled to open her eyes and found Erland's countenance close. So dear, how she longed to touch his cheek one last time. Yet she must not. She must save her strength for what was important.

"*Sønnen min,*" she began, surprised to hear her strong voice diminished to a thin reed.

"Hush, *Mor,*" Erland soothed. "Doc Tveter's been sent for."

"Can't wait," she croaked, "'Dying.'"

"*Nei!*" Erland cried, but Jorunn silenced him with a look, an impatient gesture she could only imagine, for her body lay lifeless already.

Jorunn watched tears course down her son's face in a steady stream, and would comfort him, but there was no time. The message she must leave him must take precedence, she knew. It burned within her; it was for this she lived these final moments.

"It's true, what the priest says; the sins of the father are visited upon the son. That's all I believe of the man's message. Religion stood between me and God too long. He gave me free will, and the priest would take it away. His greatest gift. My belief in God is hard won; He's proven Himself to me over and over. I wouldn't believe, wouldn't relinquish control and follow the path He showed me. I found my own way in life, and paid a price for it."

Her voice broke, her throat suddenly constricted. Her vision blurred, and she knew it was from a well of tears, yet she felt nothing as they washed down her cheeks. "Christina, too," she rasped in a sob of remorse. "We sowed the wind and reaped the whirlwind. We were greedy and determined. We planted the seed of our own destruction."

Dry sobs wracked her withered frame, leaving her gasping. She heaved for breath and heard it rattle in her chest. Urgently, for she knew her time drew near, she continued. "Death will settle the score for us, but I'm afraid for you. Jealous God, He promised to visit the sins of the fathers on the children. My fault you haven't been raised to listen to His voice, now you got to learn. Time's come for you to begin on the road to Damascus. Keep the faith, and you'll know the way. I'm leavin' you Stridheim, but without Him it means nothing. We only steward the land, it can never belong to us."

She fell silent, the strength it cost her to utter those words taking a visible toll. Erland watched as the light in her faded eyes dimmed. "This place is His, we only keep it a while. When that time's over a new journey begins. Listen for His voice, Erland; that still, small voice. You'll hear it in the land. You're my son."

Relieved of her burden, Jorunn let her body relax in him arms, reveling in the warmth and strength of his embrace. It was comfortable, a place she longed to stay, but another voice beckoned her. Erland called, but she would not hear him. He was promising to keep the land for his son. A sudden worry clouded her peace. The child was not his.

'Ridiculous,' she chided herself. 'Bemused old woman. Dying, no sense in anything you think.'

Yet there was another voice, one she remembered from long ago, far away, stronger now than her son's. And the conviction that Christina's child was not Erland's grew. Suddenly curious, instantly light, she moved toward the voice, let it envelope her. Never thinking there was no return.

Even after she was gone Erland held her in his arms, surprised at how light she was. Her frail body weighed less than a child's. He had never imagined her to be so insubstantial.

"Don't go, *Mor!*" he pleaded, his deep voice raw with pain.

He held on for as long as he could, until they took her from him.

Benedikte's soft hands soothed him, led him to their room. From far away he heard her speak, heard her gentle voice remind him, "'To everything there is a season,' Erland. 'A time to be born, and a time to die.' Your mother's time has come, Christina's too."

Benedikte paused, her throat suddenly constricted. All night she had lain awake, burning with hatred for Christina. She had passed the hours from black night to hazy morn plotting to be rid the woman, and risen to find her wish granted. Christina lay dead, alone and grown cold. The specter of torturous childbirth sprang to mind and fear seized Benedikte. Dark emotion warred; guilt, shame, trepidation, and in their grip panic threatened. In desperation she clung to composure. 'No time for weakness,' she reminded herself. 'Christina is dead, nothing can change that. I must be strong for Erland.'

Her guilt was a heavy burden, one she must shoulder alone. Erland could bear no more. His blue eyes were swollen, tears of grief pooled to overflowing and coursed into the shadowed hollow beneath each high cheekbone. His agonized expression mirrored her own guilt. Even in death Christina's presence held them in its icy clutch.

'You will not defeat me, Christina,' Benedikte vowed in silent resolution. Summoning strength from a reserve within her she had not known existed, Benedikte clasped her arms around Erland and pulled him close.

"You must accept this was God's will, Erland," she urged, yet her voice was high, and false. She fell silent to cover her distress.

Erland leaned against her soft body, felt the swell of it beneath him. The movement of the child in her belly was obvious as he pressed his face to her swollen abdomen.

'God's will,' he reflected in silent despair. All his life he had lived in peace with God, had accepted His presence on Stridheim without thought or question. Suddenly the idea of the power He wielded terrified Erland. Life and death, sin and punishment. An omnipotent God, an angry God, it seemed to Erland He meted out cruel punishment and exacted retribution far greater than was fair or equitable. Anger stirred in his heart, mitigating in some part his unbearable pain. He thought of the lifeless babe that lay next to Christina's ravaged body. Fury at the injustice, the death of innocence, coursed through his veins. He lifted his face heavenward, his cheeks dry, his eyes glittering cold and dark blue. In silence he vowed never again to be lulled to complacency by the presence he sensed when walking the fields of Stridheim. The benevolent God he had trusted in was suddenly a threat to him and those he loved. Erland rose and pulled Benedikte in'o his arms. In his heart he banished God from his life, his people, his place.

&bo &bo &bo

They walked through the wood, cool and damp. Egil led them, his way sure, his feet moving more easily than in a long while. Erland followed, carrying the child. Halvor walked behind Benedikte, weaving slightly, stumbling occasionally over a root. Valdis watched him, her mouth curling in disgust. Halvor caught the look and drawled, "Have you no mercy for me in your cold heart, Saint Valdis?" His lips twisted in contempt, self-mockery. "Pity her poor bastard, Sister. Pray for my salvation; it's your Christian duty."

Valdis stopped, feeling his verbal assault as keenly as a physical blow. "I will not do this! I won't leave her here!" she cried. Her voice broke, tears blinded her. Tomorrow she must lay her child to rest in a cold stone vault, leave her there to wait for her father, who would undoubtedly join her soon. The blow of Christina's death had severed Guthard's fragile tether to life, Valdis feared he lay dying even now. Alone, as she had promised he would not. She had failed him, as she had failed Christina. Never good enough. Even the strength to pray for God's grace and guidance eluded her now.

The others stopped and turned to her of one accord.

"She should lie in the garden of Stridheim, with the priest's blessing," Valdis cried, her voice echoing through the wood, like bells tolling.

"It is not your choice," Egil replied calmly, his voice strong and deep. "This is what she believed in, what she would have wanted." He walked on, his movements resolute.

'It was always about what she believed in, what she wanted,' Valdis reflected in silent despair. 'Nothing and no one mattered as much.'

Her grief was compounded by so many emotions it was impossible to divine where one began and the other ended. Guilt, remorse, anger. And in her heart she railed at God for taking everyone she loved, leaving her alone. She was sliding into a black abyss of faithlessness, losing her way, with no ray of hope as a beacon to guide her. The others walked on, lost from her view as they traversed the winding trail through the wood. Utterly alone.

Overhead, a great wind blew, causing the trees to groan as it pushed and pulled at upper branches, yet deep in the forest the wind was a soft breeze that stroked Valdis' wet cheek. A passage occurred to her suddenly, inexplicably. 'And behold, the Lord passed by, and a great and strong wind rent the mountains, and brake in pieces the rocks before the Lord; but the Lord was not in the wind: And after the wind an earthquake: but the Lord was not in the earthquake: And after the earthquake a fire; but the Lord was not in the fire; and after the fire a still, small voice.'

A whisper of solace in the gentle breeze, in it she divined His presence. Never closer, never greater. For a long moment she stood in the wood and reveled in the grace of His presence, so long sought. When she finally moved to join the others, she was at peace for the first time, at peace with herself, and her God.

They gathered on the banks of Glomma, Erland reciting calmly, 'And he showed me a pure river of water of life, clear as crystal, and in the midst of it was the tree of life....'

He remembered Jorunn floating in the depths of this river, her skin white in the light of a harvest moon. That night Halvor had been conceived. Egil imagined her voice speaking to him. The water rushed high and white, the sound of it all but drowning his words as he prayed. "The Lord is my shepherd, I shall not want. He maketh me to lie down in green pastures, He leadeth me beside still waters."

The child Erland clutched commenced to wail, his high thin cries mingling with the rush of the water, drowning Egil's voice. Benedikte watched Erland shift the infant, clumsy in his attempts to soothe it. She stifled her irritation at the sight of him cradling the babe, ashamed she should have no pity in her heart for the helpless child. Erland insisted they should raise the boy as their own; unwillingly, she had agreed. She had not dared voice her reluctance. Since the death of his mother Erland was changed. Cold, resolute. She understood he perceived it his duty to foster the child, and would not be swayed. Yet when Benedikte looked into the tiny face and saw the likeness to Christina, loathing replaced the tenderness she tried to summon. Agonized with guilt, determined Erland should not discover the depth of her inequity, she took the infant and cradled it to her breast, resting it against the swell of her abdomen. She stroked the babe gently, soothing him.

"*Hysj, lille venn,* there's no need to fret. I'll care for you as my own," she whispered.

As if in understanding the child's cries ceased. Creased lids parted to reveal pale blue irises. His unwavering gaze held

Benedikte's; she caught her breath, shivered involuntarily. In sudden alarm she looked toward Erland. He was lost in thought, staring at the river water rushing past. She glanced fearfully back down at the babe; he lay in peaceful slumber.

'Silly fool, your condition is making you fanciful,' Benedikte mentally chided herself.

Through the fog of her own confusion she heard Egil's voice intone: "Yea though I walk through the valley of the shadow of death, I shall fear no evil, for Thou art with me."

He opened the box he carried and dipped his hand into the ashes. Lifting it he released curled fingers and let the ashes fly in the wind, fall into the waters of Glomma. They watched as he emptied the box, reciting: "Thy rod and thy staff, they comfort me. Thou preparest a table before me in the presence of mine enemies: Thou annointest my head with oil; my cup runneth over. Surely goodness and mercy shall follow me all the days of my life, and I will dwell in the house of the Lord forever."

There was only the sound of the forest, the rush of the river. Then the wail of the infant shattered the stillness, merging with the sounds of Stridheim.

Kimberly Nygaard lived in Norway for ten years. She studied the language, literature and history of Norway at the University of Oslo and speaks Norwegian fluently. She worked as a translator and language consultant and has published fiction and nonfiction both in the United States and in Norway. She currently lives in North Carolina with her husband and two children.